Murder Under
the Tuscan Sun

Rachel Rhys is the pseudonym of psychological thriller writer Tammy Cohen. Her debut, *Dangerous Crossing*, was a Richard and Judy Book Club pick and was followed by *A Fatal Inheritance* and *Island of Secrets*. Rachel's historical fiction focuses on exotic locations and dark mysteries, but her protagonists travel emotionally as well as geographically, pushing to expand the limited horizons available to women of their era and, in the process, discovering who they really are.

She lives in North London, with her three (allegedly) grown-up children and her neurotic rescue dog.

Visit www.tammycohen.co.uk to find out more, or find her on Facebook or Twitter as @MsTamarCohen, or on Instagram as @tammycohenwriter.

Also by Rachel Rhys

Dangerous Crossing
A Fatal Inheritance
Island of Secrets

Murder Under the Tuscan Sun

Rachel Rhys

PENGUIN BOOKS

TRANSWORLD PUBLISHERS
Penguin Random House, One Embassy Gardens,
8 Viaduct Gardens, London SW11 7BW
www.penguin.co.uk

Transworld is part of the Penguin Random House group of companies
whose addresses can be found at global.penguinrandomhouse.com

Penguin
Random House
UK

First published in Great Britain in 2023 by Penguin Books
an imprint of Transworld Publishers

A CIP catalogue record for this book
is available from the British Library.

ISBN
9781529176575

Typeset in 11.52/14.41pt Adobe Garamond by Jouve (UK), Milton Keynes.
Printed and bound in Great Britain by Clays Ltd, Elcograf S.p.A.

The authorized representative in the EEA is Penguin Random House Ireland,
Morrison Chambers, 32 Nassau Street, Dublin D02 YH68.

Penguin Random House is committed to a sustainable
future for our business, our readers and our planet. This book
is made from Forest Stewardship Council® certified paper.

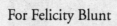

For Felicity Blunt

Prologue

Florence, spring 1946

WE HAVE TO walk the last part of the hill. The departing Germans booby-trapped the road so now there's a small crater surrounded by rubble that we have to pick our way across. One of the stone dragons that used to guard the castle's towering iron gates has been lost to the explosion. The other was beheaded and now its stone stump points towards the space where its missing mate stood.

I was warned, of course, about the damage, but nothing really prepares you for the wanton desecration of war.

Inside the great hallway there is a smell of damp and neglect. One of the panes of glass in the doors that lead out to the courtyard is cracked and I shiver when I spot rat droppings on the stone flags.

In the *salone* I stop still with my hand over my mouth at the sight of the bare whitewashed walls where once every inch was taken up with paintings. But now, on closer look, I see the walls are not quite bare. In places there is writing – the running scores of a game of some sort, what looks to be a poem or a song in German and, at the far end, over the fireplace, a portrait badly done in pen and finished off with a crudely drawn frame.

The leather sofa on which Roberto liked to sprawl is pocked with cigarette burns through which the stuffing emerges in tufts, while the low table at which Evelyn would pour tea has been replaced by an upturned crate.

Only the view is unchanged. I turn my back on the devastated room and gaze across the forecourt and the sloping hillside pitted with olive groves and cypresses, with rough-hewn farmhouses and the occasional terracotta roof, to where the molten city lies bathed in a soft sunlight that hides the damage from enemy bombs, the far-off Duomo lit up like a cauldron of fire.

And now the memories come.

In my mind the pre-dusk hour rings with the low hum of crickets and the irritable chatter of Cecily's cockatoo in its cage in the back garden and the pealing of church bells from the village of Settignano down below and the bigger town of Fiesole high up on a neighbouring hill. Somewhere in the distance a boy calls to his oxen. Wild herbs scent the air – thyme and lavender and sweet bay – while from the kitchen fireplace wafts the smell of olive wood burning in the grate where Renata is roasting a chicken on the mechanical spit.

As long as I don't turn around, I can imagine that the castle is once again peopled with all the ghosts of my life. William, Evelyn, Roberto, James, Alina. Nora with her terrible, beloved one-eyed doll, Matilda. Even Millie, who never saw Italy but would have loved it so.

I close my eyes now because memories can be sharp as

glass and I have been cut too often. But still I hear them whispering behind me in the ruined room. *Where have you been?* And over the top the question that now snaps my eyes back open. Wide.

What did you do?

1

Pinner, March 1927

*Invalid's companion sought for English
household near Florence, Italy. Must have patience
and a tolerable reading voice. Would suit mature
lady with an adventurous spirit. Knowledge of
Italian an advantage.*

THE ADVERTISEMENT, YELLOWING now and crumpled, lay between us on the ugly mahogany side table with the twisted legs that Walter's aunt, who never liked him, had given us as a wedding present.

'But you can't be serious.'

James would be surprised, I thought, if he knew just how many sentences he began with the word 'but'. He would also be surprised to learn that when he was exercised about something a vein popped up on his forehead like a small worm and he looked exactly like his father. His late father.

'I never expected to get it, you see. I answered the advertisement almost on a whim. I was flicking through *The Lady* and there it was in the Classified section. *Italy*, of all places!'

It was true I'd had no thought of actually procuring the position. Here was a pretty daydream to give a warm glow to the cold, dull February days. Moreover, after I'd posted my letter of enquiry, I'd felt the stirrings of something I hadn't immediately been able to place but finally had identified as agency. This was something I'd done without consulting another person. The novelty of it had quickened my blood.

'When the letter arrived this morning saying I had the job, you could have knocked me down with a feather.'

I reached for my bag to show it to him but thought better of it, remembering the violet ink and uneven hand.

'But Mother, this is completely preposterous,' James said. 'This is grief talking, nothing more.'

'James, darling, your father has been dead nearly a year now, so I don't think . . .'

'Exactly! Not even a year a widow. No wonder your thinking is muddled. You don't need to look for paid work. Father left you quite well provided for, and then there's the money I bring home, which is not inconsiderable. As long as you're careful, you can live out the remainder of your life without ever needing to move from this house.'

We were sitting in the chilly, damp-smelling sitting room in Pinner that Walter had insisted on papering in a dark green print so that one felt pressed in on all sides by giant walls of moss. Across from us the fireplace yawned black and cold. The week before, I'd asked Mrs Hancock if she might think about laying a fire to warm things up, but her raised eyebrows and incredulous 'In the middle of the day?' meant I hadn't asked again. A carpet in shades of brown lay on the floor, while an oil portrait of Walter's grandfather glared down in silent fury. There was a musty smell – a mixture of the polish Mrs Hancock used on the heavy brass candle-sticks on the mantelpiece and the stale air caught between the folds of the wine-red velvet drapes.

'But don't you see, James, it isn't to do with money. What they're offering is very little, really. I *want* to do something. I'm only forty-nine years old.'

'Exactly! Nearly fifty!'

'Darling, I know that might seem ancient to you, but I haven't yet got one foot in the grave and I would like to feel useful again. And the Norths are a very well-regarded family. William North is clearly a frail old man now, but he was a very highly respected art connoisseur before his misfortune. And his late wife was a Chisholm.'

'The railway Chisholms?'

'Exactly! And his niece, Evelyn Manetti, Chisholm as was – she's the one who posted the advertisement – lives in the house with her husband and daughter, so it's all perfectly respectable.'

I was aware of talking too much and too fast, as I did when I was nervous or excited. It's at this point where Walter would have fixed on a point over my shoulder with his fierce grey eyes and said something like: 'I'm just looking out for the other runners, my dear. I assume it's some sort of race that has you rushing like this.' Strange to think it was his sense of humour that had drawn me to him during the three months we were courting. It was only once we married that I realized he had but the one joke. And that joke was me.

'But what will people think?'

'About what, dear?'

'About my mother taking up paid employment?'

'Well, it's not—'

'I'll tell you what they'll think. They'll think Father left you destitute and I'm an abject failure of a son who lets his mother take in laundry and scrub kitchen floors.'

'Oh, really, James, now you're being silly. Who are these people, anyway, whose opinion matters so much?'

'It doesn't matter who the people are, Mother. What matters is what they think.'

I shouldn't have laughed. James was so easily hurt. Even as a child he hadn't been able to bear being teased, or being put on the spot or challenged. Had he always taken himself so seriously? I found more and more I struggled to remember the Before James, the little quirks that made me love him so. His softness towards anything smaller or weaker, his capacity to find beauty in small things – the vibrant red of a leaf in autumn, the moment of stillness before the crashing notes of a piano concerto – the giggles that would escape him at the most unexpected times. It was the war that stopped that, or rather the guilt that came with the war that ended five days before he turned eighteen, so many of his schoolmates already lost. It was the guilt that squished down all those extra bits of who he was until he fitted into a mould of his father. Or rather it was the guilt that began that process, and it was losing Millie that completed it.

My late daughter.

Time, people say, is a great healer. However, my experience was that the pain was just as great five years on as on the first day, I'd only learned to hide it better. I suspect we were all the same, my generation of grieving women. When we passed each other in the street or the park or smiled at one another in the post office queue, we took it for granted that we were each enduring our own individual tragedies.

'Mother, please tell me this is some sort of joke.'

James looked so young, sitting there in his Fair Isle jumper and flannel trousers, like the schoolboy he'd been not so very long ago, that I couldn't help but jump up and cross over to him. But when I made to throw my arms around him, he shrank back.

'Darling boy, please try to see things from my point of view. The last few years have been so dreadfully sad – first Millie, then your father. I feel I should so love to grab a little bit of life before it passes me by.'

I watched as James's fears wrote themselves across the planes of his soft, pale face. *Have some faith*, I wanted to tell him. *Trust that most people are good.* But it was 1927, not even a decade after the end of the war, and we both remembered only too well what people were capable of.

'I shouldn't think it'll be for long,' I said. 'When she offered me the position, Mrs Manetti – that's Evelyn Chisholm as was, Cecily North's niece – told me that her uncle suffered his apoplectic attack just over a month ago but has been recovering inordinately well. Oh, and darling, guess what?'

James's expression reminded me that he'd never liked this kind of game, had always been nervous of surprises.

'The Norths live in a *castle*! An actual real-life castle. Can you imagine?'

I knew instantly it was the wrong thing to say. The fantastical detail of the address to which I'd sent my letter of application – Castello di Roccia Nera – only made the entire business seem more outlandish, more suspect.

'You do know, don't you, Mother, that they are under

fascist rule, the Italians? Is that what you want? A load of black-shirted dictators ordering you around?'

'Of course not, but—'

'Why can't you be content with what you have? Why can't you be content here? With me? Oh, I know I'm not Millie. I know *that.*'

The bitterness in his voice shocked me.

'No, James, my darling. You mustn't think that. You're you. You're perfectly enough.'

This was the point at which I would normally give in, had always given in when it was Walter sitting there, determined as I was to shy away from confrontation.

I pressed my nails into the palms of my hand. The silence stretched on until I felt as if it would snap.

2

AFTER ALL MY enthusing to James over the past weeks, my spirits strained from having to be always pointing out the positives, I felt – as the train pulled out of Victoria Station and James's pinched face grew smaller – a distinct sagging. This inner slump was made all the more curious for being accompanied by a simultaneous twisting and knotting of my nerves, as if being tightly wound around a pair of crochet hooks.

Throughout the journey to Dover and the fraught ferry crossing to Calais, during which the sky never raised itself above a pewter grey and the waves were as turbulent as my thoughts, I tried to recapture that excitement I'd felt when the companion position had been merely a thrilling but abstract notion, nothing more.

But now, with thirty-six hours of travelling ahead of me, I couldn't avoid reflecting on how little I knew about the post I had so impulsively applied for or the family with whom I would be living.

Mrs Manetti – I imagined her a quiet, devoted type, sacrificing her own independence to care for her infirm relative – had said 'light duties', stressing that any 'heavy lifting' could be managed by the servants. I'd thought that an odd phrase, as if her ailing uncle were a lump of rock or a pianoforte to be hauled and shifted and shuffled around. I wondered if I'd oversold myself. I'd told Evelyn Manetti that I'd assisted in hospitals during the war, and that was true, but only in the most basic capacity, emptying bedpans, changing dressings, holding the hands of boys and men who could have been my son or my husband as they writhed in pain or called out for their mothers. Even that much had had to be fought for, the amateur nursing positions with the Voluntary Aid Detachment limited to single women only. Us married women – *Comforteers*, they called us, for goodness' sake – were expected to sit at home knitting socks and scarves with only the occasional trip out to visit the wounded on the wards. I'd had to expand my remit by stealth, staying longer, taking on more responsibility, but still it fell well short of being properly trained.

By the time I arrived in Calais, where a porter in a blue overall and battered cap transferred my cases from the steamer to the waiting train without once disturbing the cigarette that hung from his lower lip, I had half convinced myself James was right and I'd made a terrible mistake. All through the journey to Paris and my wait at Gare de Lyon for the Rome Express, my mind turned on me in a way it hadn't done since Millie died.

Then I'd been pierced with regret for all the evenings I hadn't let her stay up late to see me dressed up for a party or a particularly splendid yellow moon, for fear she would get over-tired, and all the iced buns I said she couldn't eat in case the sugar went to her head. What harm would it have done in the end for my dear, darling girl to have gone to bed at ten or midnight or two in the morning or have eaten all the buns she desired? If I'd known she wouldn't even see her twentieth birthday I should have given her the world and not bothered if Walter said it would spoil her. She should have had those pale, buttery-yellow leather gloves she admired, even if they were bound to be ruined after a few wears. She should have gone dancing with the Jameson boy, even if his brother had been court-martialled for desertion. Sometimes you were so busy fretting about the small things you forgot to consider the big things until it was too late.

My spirits were improved by the excellent dinner we were served when we'd scarce pulled out of the station in Paris. Food has always lifted my mood. I make no apology for that. From my narrow berth in the sleeper compartment that smelled like old leather and black tobacco and freshly laundered sheets, I could see my travelling clothes laid out over my cases – my new tweed skirt and simple blouse. I'd had half an idea to have the dressmaker run me up one of the tennis-style outfits the younger women were all wearing, a knee-length sleeveless jersey dress with a loose dropped waist in a pretty colour – apple green or rose pink. But the girls I saw wearing the kind of dresses I yearned for had neat figures that ran straight up and down. I'd looked down at the rounded shelf of my bosom, the curve of my stomach, and heard Walter's voice in my ear – *Do you really think that's suitable, Constance?* – and gone for the tweed. Seeing the stylish women getting on the train earlier at Paris in their fur wrap coats and their ankle-strap shoes, their slim calves showcased in sheer silk stockings, I regretted those uncommissioned dresses.

In the morning, when voices awoke me to the fact we

were in a station, I rushed to the little window and pulled up the blind to find myself greeted by the most wonderful sight – the rose-gold residue of the sunrise reflecting off snow-dusted mountain peaks. A steward, bringing an early-morning pot of tea, confirmed that we were in Modane, on the Italian border. Italy. I rolled the word around on my tongue.

I'd never travelled beyond France. And France only once, when Walter and I honeymooned in Nice, both of us realizing with a heavy, sinking feeling that the person we thought we'd married wasn't the person sitting opposite us across the hotel breakfast table. I was still reeling from a broken heart courtesy of a friend of my brother with whom I fell whole-heartedly, foolishly, joyously in love, only for him to become engaged to someone else just days after we'd made love for the first and only time. I'd plunged into marriage with Walter because, love having let me down so badly, I'd decided the absence of it might provide a sturdier foundation for a relationship. Walter's own motivation was less easy to fathom. 'I thought we nicely complemented one another,' he'd said, the one time I'd pushed him on it. And I'd imagined us then as a set of leather suitcases or a sturdy wool hat and matching gloves.

The train continued to Turin and then the Apennines, where the hillsides were carpeted with grass and trees and veined by tiny streams tumbling down from the mountains, and from there the steady descent towards the ocean and the bustling port of Genoa.

I gazed out of the window at the people disembarking and embarking, kissing and waving, carrying cases and hat boxes, and one black-clad lady with a tiny dog in a basket hooked over her arm. *This is real*, I told myself. *This is happening.*

Off we went again, clinging to the coast with the train periodically plunging into the black tunnels that ran under the cliffs only to burst out into a world made blinding by the preceding darkness. As I became accustomed to the dazzle, I caught snatches of colour – pink-blossomed Judas trees reaching into an azure sky, ripe oranges peeping through shiny green leaves. Lilac wisteria. When finally the train headed inland at Viareggio my mouth became dry, my heart beating so fast that were it not for the steward pointing through the opposite window as we drew into Pisa I should have entirely missed seeing the famous tower listing perilously to the side or the magnificent cathedral.

At Pisa, the cars travelling on to Florence detached from the rest of the train and it was now that the crochet hooks that held my nerves tightly wound began to pull and twist in earnest. A young man with one leg of his trousers pinned up behind him progressed down the platform, the remaining leg swinging on a crutch; another wore a patch over his eye. I was used to such sights back home, but somehow I hadn't expected it here, though of course Italy suffered terribly during that war, so I ought not to have been surprised. Several passengers joined my carriage, among them a man of around my own age, short and stocky with oiled black hair and plump lips beneath a luxuriant moustache, who sat in the seat almost facing me.

He took out a newspaper, but I could sense him darting glances at me over the top. Initially I worried that I had broken some unspoken rule. Sitting in the wrong place, heading the wrong direction. The more he looked, the more flustered I became. I patted my hair to see if it had come loose – it was much longer than the younger women were wearing theirs and tended to wildness. Under the cover of a yawn, I checked my teeth to see if something from my breakfast had become stuck there.

It gradually dawned on me that the looks he was giving me were not of disapproval but, on the contrary, of appreciation. It had been so long since a man had looked at me that way that at first I was rigid with embarrassment, staring out of the window, not daring to turn my head. But slowly a warmth crept over me from my toes up through my knees and thighs and abdomen, waking up the various parts of me as it went, until my whole body burned with life. I snatched a glance and the man smiled; it wasn't a lewd smile but seemed rather to be a collusion. *Here we are, two strangers on a train on this beautiful day, enjoying each other.* And though he was by no means a handsome fellow, his eyes were lively and kind and, to my amazement, I felt deep within me, like the plucking of cello strings, the long-dormant stirrings of sexual desire.

A stylish Italian woman who had joined my carriage at Viareggio began talking to me in heavily accented English. Was it my first time in Italy? When she discovered it was, she grew excitable, listing the places I would need to visit in Florence. 'It is the jewel in all of Italy,' she told me solemnly. 'No, not Italy,' she contradicted herself angrily, 'the jewel in all of Europe.'

Everything in Florence was simply the best, it turned out. The food, the climate, the architecture. The artworks, it went without saying were unparalleled anywhere in the world.

Only when she found out where I would be staying did my new friend's hyperbole desert her. 'Castello di Roccia Nera. Yes, I know of it.' She looked over at me and – did I imagine that her smile was slightly less wide, her tone slightly less friendly?

'I'm to be a companion for the old gentleman.'

'The old gentleman?'

'*Si*,' I tried hesitantly. 'William North.'

My companion blinked.

'Have you been there?' I asked, changing tack. 'To the castle?'

She shook her head vigorously and I was fascinated by the way her plum-coloured beret remained affixed to her luxuriant dark hair.

'No. But––'

Whatever she was about to say was lost in a screaming of brakes, and a commotion in the corridors alerted us to the fact that we had arrived.

The woman jumped up to leave, while I anxiously gathered together my things. My new cloche hat, my good wool coat, both far too warm for the climate, I could already tell. The man with the moustache and oiled hair tucked his newspaper under his arm and raised a hand in farewell.

'Firenze!' called the steward.

I adjusted my hat and stepped out on to the narrow ladder staircase and into the rest of my life.

3

I DON'T KNOW WHAT I'd expected from my arrival at the station in Florence. A grand carriage sent from the castle emblazoned with a shiny coat of arms, perhaps. A liveried servant. What I hadn't expected was a rake-thin young woman in a loose printed blouse and grubby skirt that hung just below her knees and had five smear marks down each side where she must have habitually wiped her hands. Her legs were bare and on her feet was a pair of men's leather boots from which her bony calves rose up like two saplings planted in a sea of soil.

'I am Alina,' she said in a musical Italian accent, approaching where I stood sweltering in my too-warm coat, surrounded by bags. Close up, I saw she was striking. Her face too gaunt to be considered pretty, her nose too dominant. Her fine brown eyes large and expressive, but a fraction too close together over the narrow bridge of her nose. Yet there was such sparkiness about her, such a keen light of animation in her eyes.

For a few long seconds we stared at each other, then something of my exhaustion and trepidation must have shown in my face and she smiled, instantly transforming her angular face into something softer.

It was clear from the woman's dress that she must be some sort of servant, so I was shocked when she led me to a dusty motor car instead of the fly I'd expected. And judging by the expressions of passers-by, the idea of this poorly dressed young woman taking the wheel of this large motor car seemed equally unfeasible to Italians too.

'Are you really going to drive this thing?'

I knew a couple of women back in England who drove, both much younger than me, but the idea of a maid or a housekeeper behind a steering wheel seemed preposterous.

She laughed, a startling sound that seemed to rip straight from her throat.

'Don't worry. I'm quite good. Rupert taught me. That's Mr North's son.'

She was smiling, but there was a tightness to her words, as if they were threaded through with wire.

'And did Rupert North also teach you English?'

'He didn't need to. We learned it together. My mother was housekeeper at the castle so I grew up speaking as much English as Italian.'

'Well, I look forward to telling Mr Rupert North that he did a very excellent job as a driving instructor.'

A shadow passed over the woman's face. 'Sadly, that won't be possible. He died in 1922. He had an injury to his lung in the war and he never completely recovered.'

'I'm so sorry. And Mrs North?'

It was an automatic response now, whenever I learned of a young person's death, for my thoughts to pass directly to the mother.

'She died four months after of a broken heart.'

I was quiet then. Before Millie died, I would have said

such a thing was impossible, but now I knew better. There had been nights I too thought I might die from sorrow, when I wished I could detach my heart from my body and shut it away in a drawer so I couldn't feel any more.

I gazed through the open window. Ours was one of only a few cars on the roads. Otherwise, the traffic consisted of bicycles, trams and small, nippy flies that darted around the more sedate carts pulled by solid, lumbering horses. Through the side streets I caught a glimpse of buildings bathed in the late-afternoon light so that they appeared pink and terra-cotta and apricot and peach, and the famous dome glowing orange in the sun.

Flags hung from windows, flashes of red, white and green with a small square in the middle, red with a white cross. We passed a building where the word 'DUCE' had been daubed on the wall in towering white letters and I stiffened, remembering James's diatribe about the fascist leader, Mussolini.

At a crossroads, a group of black-shirted men stood around smoking, their baggy trousers tucked into black knee-high boots. As the car passed they broke off from their chatter and turned to stare. Alina muttered something under her breath, and her knuckles grew white against the dark brown leather of the steering wheel.

Leaving the city behind, a hillside rose up ahead, cool and green. As we climbed, the road narrowed, banked by high stone walls on one side and trees on the other. The houses here were larger, set back from the road on the slope either side behind tall metal or wooden gates. The motor car did not seem to like what was being asked of it. And neither did its driver, who was grumbling to herself as the engine coughed and spluttered up the ever-steepening incline.

'Since Mr North has been ill, the car is forgotten.'

By this time anxiety had formed a ball in my stomach that bounced uncomfortably every time we went over a bump in the road or a stone, or around one of the alarming hairpin bends. We were passing through woodland now, tall, bushy trees growing up on each side of the narrow road, their branches forming a canopy overhead. Later, I would learn that these were ilex trees, but at the time I mistook them for English oak. To my right, at the bottom of a gully, I caught sight of a deep green pool, surrounded by rocks and reeds and low-hanging leaves, formed at a bend of a gentle stream. A stately heron stood motionless on the far bank, as if keeping guard.

I was a very long way from Pinner.

The protesting motor car was still ascending, zigging and zagging, and Alina's muttering grew louder and more elaborate. Every now and then she would shout out a place name – *Settignano! Fiesole!* – and gesture to the left or to the right, but my attention was solely on the car, willing it forwards. Just when I thought the engine could not possibly withstand a second more of such punishment, we rounded a bend.

'Il Castello,' Alina said needlessly, for there was no mistaking the imposing stone building with the central turret and the arched entrance guarded by tall cypresses that dominated the skyline at the peak of the hill.

The sun was now behind us and the dense foliage over our heads ensured we remained plunged into shadow. From this vantage point side on, the castle appeared black against the deepening sky and I experienced a sensation akin to a blade of frosty grass brushing down the back of my neck. Then the car turned another bend and we emerged into the light and the castle was revealed to be grey, not black at all, with a patina of amber from the reflection of the just-setting sun.

'It's beautiful,' I said, taking in the castellated wall at the top and the formally laid-out gardens to the sides below which the land fell away in terraces down to the valley and a second wooded peak, hidden at first, rising up darkly behind the castle.

'Yes, it's very beautiful,' Alina agreed, unsmiling.

The last part of the road was a straight, narrow avenue stretching almost vertically, and flanked on both sides by a row of cypress trees, culminating in the most enormous iron gates I'd ever seen, the gate posts topped by stone dragons, tongues reaching towards each other across the open gateway.

By now the car was groaning non-stop so it was a relief when we passed through the gates and the land levelled out into a gravel forecourt.

'We are here,' said Alina, as we came to a halt in front of the central turret. Close up, the imposing arched entrance was revealed to be framing a pair of colossal wooden doors.

Fear knotted inside me. What if the Norths were expecting someone younger or more educated or more qualified?

As I climbed out of the car and brushed down my coat, my legs felt wobbly. *You have survived the very worst*, I reminded myself. *Nothing again will ever come close.*

Still, as I glanced up to where the tower loomed against the deepening sky and found myself staring into the hideous face of a stone gargoyle shaped like a screaming monkey protruding from the upper wall, I wondered what in heaven's name I'd done.

4

THE DOORS OPENED on to a vast flagstoned hallway housing a stone staircase that cut through the centre and rose to the upper level. Intricate wrought-iron railings topped by balustrades of polished wood lent it a touch of elegance, while access was guarded by a pair of monstrous carved stone lions sitting sentry on the newel posts at either side of the bottom step. On the far wall, behind the staircase, was another arched doorway, mirroring the entrance, although its doors were made of clear glass, through which I could see what looked to be a large courtyard garden, studded with fruit trees and boasting a lawned area in the middle and around it an overgrown path, its terracotta bricks padded out with herbs and wildflowers.

Now I could see what I'd missed before, that the castle was actually a quadrangle with four sides – completely equal, with the exception of the turret in which I stood – surrounding an enclosed central courtyard.

I followed Alina to the right, through yet another double set of tall wooden doors, which gave out into the most beautiful room I had ever seen. Double aspect, with enormous windows that looked out from the side towards the neighbouring hills, draped in blankets of lush greenery, while at the front, the gravel forecourt dropped away into a sky that was now tinged with amber and rose gold, the lights of Florence just visible at the bottom.

The ceilings soared high overhead, made of carved wood in the deepest mahogany brown, while a pair of immense stone fireplaces, each taller than a man's head and carved with a coat of arms, monopolized either end of the room. The floor was polished grey flagstones, scattered with luxurious oriental-style rugs, while an eclectic mix of velvet-upholstered sofas and chaises longues and leather armchairs were clustered here and there about the place, seemingly without any order whatsoever.

But it was the walls which drew my attention, hung as they were with multitudes of paintings of different sizes, different styles, some oils, some watercolours, some in small black wooden frames, others in ornate gilt ones decorated with cherubs and leaves and flowers of gold, until there was hardly an inch of painted wall visible. There were even a couple of artfully shot photographs hanging slightly separate from the rest of the collection, one of a woman with a wide-brimmed hat pulled down so that her face was completely in shadow, the other of a gnarled olive tree silhouetted against a dramatic sky – both extravagantly framed but jarring in the context of the rest of the art.

'Mrs Manetti and her husband are visiting friends, but I think they will be home very soon,' said Alina. 'I will bring you tea.'

She disappeared through a set of lofty doors at the far end of the great room and I was left alone. Awkwardly, I started examining the paintings on the wall in that self-conscious way of someone whose mind is on the things around them rather than the thing right in front of their eyes.

One in particular drew my attention and, as I stepped in front of it, I found myself suddenly cold, the fine hairs on my arms and the back of my neck standing to attention as if I were in a draught, even though the windows were closed. I stepped to the side and was instantly warm again. Then back. Cold.

It was a portrait in oils, medium-sized, around three feet high and two wide. The subject was a man in early middle age, wearing clothing that placed him firmly back in the annals of history, a dark cloak over a jerkin, a white collar above which a pale, bearded moon of a face appeared to be floating. The man's long, narrow nose overhung a small mouth, the fleshy lower lip almost obscuring the upper, but it was the expression in his intense brown eyes that stopped me in my tracks. He was staring rigidly into the middle distance, at some point past the artist's left shoulder, as if he could see something alarming, something that made him fearful.

I turned my head slowly, as if I might see there what the man in the painting had been looking at all those centuries ago.

'Foolish woman,' I muttered under my breath, seeing only empty air.

There came a sound of a car engine roaring up the hillside at the front, the progress far smoother than my own arrival. Through the front window I watched as first a shiny chrome grille topped by a chrome mascot in the shape of an angel and then a forest-green bonnet appeared through the gates.

A young man jumped out of the driver's seat, holding a boxy black camera in one hand. He was wearing a loose shirt that showed off his broad shoulders and his head was bare, revealing a shock of black, curly hair that he flicked impatiently out of his eyes. As he did so, he must have caught sight of me in the window, and he stopped still, shading his eyes to stare into the house. Feeling like an interloper standing there on my own in their living room, I raised my hand weakly and he broke into a smile, waving his free arm vigorously.

He turned to say something, and now the passenger door opened and out stepped the most glamorous woman I'd ever seen outside of a cinema. Petite, with blonde hair cut into a shingled bob, she was wearing a powder-blue jersey dress that stopped at the knee with a matching cardigan thrown loosely over her shoulders and high Cuban-heeled shoes. She looked directly over to the window and, as soon as she saw me, she practically skipped with excitement, as if I was quite the most welcome sight.

'Oh, my dear Mrs Bowen, I feel just dreadful not being here when you arrived. Please forgive me.'

She'd flown into the room like a tiny blue bird and was holding one of my hands – which suddenly felt big as shovels – captive in both of her own. Up close her eyes were the blue of those first winter irises that bloom vibrant and defiant against the February frost and she wore a scent of vanilla mixed with lemon.

'I am Evelyn Chisholm. Oh, bother, that's a fat lie, isn't it? I'm Evelyn Manetti, as I must keep reminding myself. Look!'

She held up her doll-like left hand to show me the gleaming wedding band that sat on her fourth finger.

'Congratulations,' I said weakly.

'Aren't you sweet? And thank you. He's just the most divine man who ever lived.'

Her husband burst through the doorway, throwing his camera down on to a low table so that he could shake my hand.

'Roberto, my love, I was just telling dear Mrs Bowen that you're the most divine man who ever lived.'

Her claim was not without some merit. Roberto Manetti had one of those faces that really ought to have been carved out of marble and exhibited in a gallery. Classical features – a strong nose and jaw, high cheekbones that stretched his olive skin taut. A surprisingly full mouth and thick black lashes any woman would have been proud of. He wore a tiny golden key around his neck on a delicate chain that glinted in the smooth hollow at the top of his open-necked shirt.

His voice, though, came as a shock.

'Delighted to meet you, Mrs Bowen.' The accent was pure American drawl, in contrast to his exotic looks and surname.

'Oh. Excuse me. I was expecting you to be Italian.'

'I am devastated to disappoint you so early in our acquaintance. My father was Italian, but my mother is American. I attended school in New York, though I came back to Florence the very minute I finished. I am a mongrel, as you English would say.'

'Don't listen to him, Mrs Bowen. His real home is here, and everyone in Florence knows his family. The Manettis are practically royalty. And now we're married, I am too. Isn't it wonderful when things just work out like that?'

At this point, the doors at the far end opened and Alina came in bearing a tray of tea.

'Ah, you are back,' she said, barely glancing at the new arrivals as she moved Roberto's camera aside to set down the tray and began decanting the teapot and china cup and saucer and a small plate of bread served with white butter and a little pot of apricot jam.

'I thought perhaps you're hungry,' she said to me.

'Such a marvellous idea. Please bring extra cups and plates, Alina. I could eat a cow.'

Evelyn might just as well have saved herself the effort of smiling so winsomely, as Alina didn't so much as glance in her direction.

'Alina is our housekeeper, chauffeur, errand runner. We'd be quite lost without her,' said Evelyn once Alina had left the room, and I nodded, though privately I thought the Italian woman had been a little offhand.

The bread was yellow with a thick crust dusted with flour. 'Made from maize,' Evelyn explained chattily when we were installed on facing sofas with the table in between us. 'You should see the size of the loaves they bake. I could just about climb inside one.'

I didn't doubt it. Such a waif of a thing she was, with those big eyes and neat little arms and legs. She apologized again for not meeting me in person. They'd been called to tea at a neighbouring villa. Evelyn rolled her eyes. 'Such a bore. We didn't want to go, did we, Roberto, darling, but you have to be neighbourly in a place like this.'

'Where's your daughter?' I asked, looking from one to the other. 'Didn't she go with you on your outing?'

There was a surprised silence.

'Nora?'

Evelyn Manetti had a laugh like a dainty silver teaspoon clinking against a bone-china cup.

'Oh, it wouldn't be Nora's thing at all. Besides, the Campbells, whom we were visiting, can't abide children, even their own. And just so you know, Nora is my daughter by my first husband, Miles.'

'Exactly. Nothing to do with me,' said Roberto cheerfully. His eyes when they met mine were a mixture of hazel and green, and I felt an agreeable jolt. I was used to men's eyes sliding over me as if I didn't properly exist but was as much a part of the inanimate scenery as the plump leather armchair in the corner or the peacock feathers that had been artfully arranged in a slim white vase. Now, twice in the same day, I'd had the sensation of being not only looked at by a strange man but *seen*.

'I'm sorry,' I said, turning back to my hostess. 'About your first husband.'

Again that questioning look. And another peal of laughter:

'Oh, heavens, don't be. He's not dead or anything ghastly like that. We're divorced.'

'Right. Yes. Of course.'

I'd never met anyone divorced before. The kind of people Walter and I knew wouldn't even have that word in their vocabulary. I tried to imagine a world in which a person could just discard her husband.

Evelyn asked me then whether Alina had taken me on a tour of the castle and, when I said no, she jumped up with alacrity.

'Roberto and I will take you.'

'I only wish I could, my sweet, but I'm afraid I have to go into town.'

'Oh, what a bore! My husband is a big cheese in local politics, Constance – can I call you Constance? Do you mind? He is always going off to have meetings. If you ask me, it's just an excuse to get away from me.'

'Never.' To my surprise, Roberto pulled his wife to him and kissed her full on the lips, running both his hands down over her hips. I looked abruptly away.

We started off through the doorway Alina had used, entering a substantial library smelling of leather and furniture polish. Through the window I could see the hedged garden that ran along the outside of the castle. In the fading light I could just about make out beds planted with lavender and crocuses and pastel-coloured snapdragons. The main part of the library was shelved with books. Only the far end was arranged differently, with the wall to the left housing endless index files in leather boxes that could be pulled out from the shelves like drawers. Some were labelled alphabetically, others bore long Italian names. A row of filing cabinets lined the far wall, while a large wooden desk with ornately carved legs sat in front of the window.

'Uncle Bill's precious archives,' said Evelyn, gesturing vaguely around and wrinkling her nose.

'Archives?'

'For all those stuffy old painters he loves so much. There are thousands of photographs and notes in those files. You wouldn't believe how dull. Details about what brushstrokes so-and-so used and how yellow his yellows were. It's what makes him an expert, you see. Uncle Bill, I mean. So he can look at a painting and know instantly who painted it, whether it's by one of the famous ones or some unknown, real or forgery, just by how thick the paint is. It's made him very rich but, tell me honestly, Mrs Bowen, have you ever seen an uglier room?'

Past the library was a closed door against which Evelyn threw herself dramatically, spreading out her arms as if to prevent me entering. 'You must never come into this room on pain of death,' she whispered, her eyes wide, eyebrows arched so that they appeared as birds migrating up her forehead.

Then she laughed. 'Oh, Constance. Your face! Don't worry, this isn't where we keep the dead bodies. It's Roberto's darkroom, and we are all forbidden to go in there, since I ruined almost all the photographs he took of our honeymoon by bursting in and letting in the light.'

'Are those his photographs hanging in the *salone*?'

'Yes. You are clever, Constance. I just knew you would be from your letter. Uncle Bill was frightfully snooty about me putting them up, he said it spoiled the aesthetic of his collection. But I think they're marvellous, don't you? Such a welcome change from all those grisly crucifixions and ugly old men.'

The castle's expansive kitchen ran across the back wing of the quadrangle. 'Usually, the kitchens are upstairs in these kind of places so the cooking smells don't infiltrate the *salone*, but Aunt Cecily said she didn't want the cooking smells infiltrating her bedroom either, thank you very much.' There was an enormous range with a tank for hot water and a hooded chimney with an open fire underneath, in front of which a roasting spit was suspended between a complicated system of cogs and wheels. The kitchen table was a huge slab of wood, and at one end a sturdy woman with a scarf tied around her head, whom Evelyn introduced as 'Renata, simply the best cook in Tuscany', stood grinding up fresh herbs in a pestle and mortar.

We continued around, past a back staircase leading up to the rear bedrooms, and now we were in the third wing, making our way through a bare, unloved little room with a desk and a map on the wall. 'Nora's schoolroom,' Evelyn said. She surveyed it with her head cocked to the side, frowning. 'I'd forgotten how grim it is in here. I really ought to get around to hiring a new governess.'

'How long has it been since the last one left?'

'Do you know, I can't remember. A couple of months? Maybe longer. Children grow so fast, don't they?'

'How old is Nora?'

'Eight. Certainly no more than nine. Matters of time are so boring, don't you find, Constance? All those years trip-trapping past. *Pttt, pttt, pttt.*'

I think that's when I looked at her more closely and realized she was older than I'd first thought. In her mid or even late thirties, while her handsome husband was certainly some years younger. We walked now towards the front of the castle, where a cavernous space housed a formal dining room. Despite the windows to the front and side, through which I could see the rolling green hills bathed in a rosy pink haze, this room had a chilly, uncomfortable feel. Suits of armour stood guard on either side of the doors and candelabras studded the table. The windows were hung with heavy drapes that I doubted were ever pulled. One wall was dominated by a huge oil painting in which a crowd of robed figures, some clutching on to pillars for a better vantage point, clustered ghoulishly around a man lying naked and seemingly dead on the ground. Evelyn grimaced. 'It's pretty ghastly, isn't it? Give me a bunch of flowers in a vase any day.'

It was a relief to leave that room behind and return to the corridor. There was one room we hadn't entered yet, though we'd passed it going between the schoolroom and the dining room. Now we stopped outside its closed door.

'This is my uncle's sitting room,' Evelyn whispered.

I became painfully aware then of my bedraggled travelling clothes, the new blouse now creased and damp under the arms, my legs sticky under the tweed skirt and stockings, my hair escaping from its pins and springing up around my face. I patted my cheeks, which were warm to my touch.

Evelyn must have sensed some of my discomfort because she held out her right hand in front of her face and slapped it tartly with the left. 'I am an inconsiderate beast, and I'm sure you must despise me. You'll want to freshen up after your journey. I'll show you your room.'

As I gratefully turned to follow her, I saw a dark shadow move across the strip of light under the door of the sitting room and heard a noise like someone breathing heavily through the solid wood.

'Is your uncle able to get up and about?'

She laughed her tinkling silver teaspoon laugh. 'Heavens, no. If he was, why ever would we be in need of you?'

5

M Y ROOM WAS on the upper floor above the schoolroom, towards the back of the castle. Evelyn had told
me that Mr North's bedroom and dressing room were also at
the rear, while her little family had the rooms on the other
side of the quadrangle to mine. I was relieved to find that
my bedroom was quite modest in size compared to the vast,
draughty spaces downstairs. I had a comfortable bed with a
pale green counterpane and two shuttered windows which
opened on to a view of the terraced hillside falling away
towards the river at the bottom of the valley. There was a
farmhouse on one of the lower terraces with a cheerful
orange-tiled roof and immediately beneath my window was
another formally laid-out garden bordered by neat box
hedges, its corners marked with lemon trees in enormous
terracotta pots, and a wooden bench in the middle on which
one could sit and gaze out across the valley to the distant
mountains.

On the floor of my room, hexagonal terracotta tiles slot-
ted together in a tessellated pattern and a small stone
fireplace faced the bed, overhung by a rather charming
painting of two peasant women washing clothes in a stream.

There was a washbasin in the corner, also pale green, while a ceiling light with three individual yellow silk shades gave a muted soft glow. I had a chest of drawers and a wardrobe in rich brown walnut and a sweet rug in shades of green and beige and brown. There was a large bathroom right next door boasting an enormous and frightening-looking iron bath with its own cylindrical woodchip-fuelled water heater attached at the tap end and fed by a complicated system of pipes that clanged and groaned alarmingly.

I looked at my reflection in the vanity mirror and sighed. My long, heavy hair was beyond help, wispy tendrils curling out all around my face like a brown straw halo. My normally clear chestnut eyes, which I knew to be my finest feature, were pink-tinged with exhaustion. As I changed into a loose cotton dress with a dropped waist that failed to conceal the curves of my hips and stomach, I thought about teeny-tiny Evelyn Manetti in her powder-blue frock that hung just right over her petite frame and sighed.

Faced with the task of making my own way downstairs to meet my new charge, my nerve wavered. The truth was, I wasn't a natural nursemaid. I hadn't been patient with Walter in those last weeks when the tumours on his neck that had seemed to come out of nowhere caused him to bellow and rage in pain and outraged disbelief. We'd grown entirely separate by that stage. Sometimes differences can attract, but that hadn't proved the case with us. In the early years, we'd tried to adapt to one another, or at least show one another respect, but then had come the arguments. Firstly, over my oldest friend, Caroline, who Walter believed to be a malign influence over me. Then the suffrage marches – Caroline and I so full of hope and pride as we matched our strides together on the Sunday Procession in 1908. 'Do you have any idea how humiliating it is for me?' Walter had asked me, finally threatening to take the children away if I continued to take part in the public protests. But it was Millie's death that had torn us irrevocably apart. Not the fact of it, but the manner of it. 'Don't let him do it,' my girl had begged me when the physician came with the leeches, and I should have fought, I should have. But he and Walter were so insistent that it was the right thing, the thing that could save her, and at the last my conviction failed. Even now I could weep to think of the indignities my girl faced in her final days. Later, when Walter himself lay dying, I couldn't shake free the shadow of those earlier scenes.

I hadn't been kind.

We hadn't been kind to each other.

At the bottom of the stairs I hesitated between the two stone lions, unsure whether to go back into the *salone* in search of Evelyn or straight to Mr North's sitting room to introduce myself.

As I dithered I had that feeling, a burning sensation in my back, as if someone was watching me, and I whirled around.

Halfway down the grand staircase stood a scrawny girl wearing a pinafore dress that must have been smart when new but now appeared too small, reaching as it did barely to her grubby knees, and staring at me solemnly. I'm ashamed to admit I felt a twinge of disappointment. I was of that generation that grew up being told women and girls ought to be decorative first and foremost, and this child was unambiguously plain with a high forehead and a pale, pinched face cut in two by a long nose that bent at a strange angle into a misshapen end. Her hair was the shade of brown that brought to mind dusty church pews and ha'pennies left too long in old ladies' musty leather purses. She was clutching a doll that had lost an eye so that it stared out blindly from one side of its cracked porcelain face.

I couldn't help comparing her to Millie at the same age – robust and lively, with pink cheeks and a dimple that appeared when she laughed, which was most of the time.

'You must be Leonora,' I said, smiling. 'I'm Constance Bowen, your great-uncle's new companion.'

If I'd been hoping for a smile in return, I was to be disappointed. If anything, her frown deepened.

'I've just arrived from London.' I was trying to raise a conversation. Could the child even speak English? 'The journey was rather long. I've never travelled so far before!'

Finally, she spoke.

'I've been to England lots of times, actually. I should much prefer to live there. The sun here is so strong. Last summer my skin came up in hundreds – no, millions – of red bumps, and when you squeezed them really hard watery stuff came out.'

Her voice was as thin as she was, and my heart went out to her. Childhood was so hard for girls who didn't shine, who were shy or plain or, like me, too much led by emotion, their feelings too big for a world in which young girls were not supposed to take up much space and young girls who were not pretty less space still.

'I should introduce myself to your great-uncle, Mr North. Do you think you could take me to him?'

The suggestion seemed to bring on a flicker of anxiety and I saw her glance at the closed *salone* doors. I was just about to tell her not to worry when she appeared to come to a decision.

'I'll take you. Though I should warn you, Great-uncle Bill gets very cross sometimes.'

'I should imagine it can't be much fun being an invalid. What does your uncle do when he's cross?'

'He bangs the floor like this.' She stamped her little foot on the stone step, hardly making a sound. 'Except he does it with his stick.'

I remembered that shadow moving under the door, the sound of breathing through the wood, and my chest felt tight.

Nora's first knock at the door was as light as if she'd merely brushed it with her fingers. Even so, I sensed a movement inside the room, a new alertness in the air.

'I can't knock louder because of Solomon,' she whispered.

Before I had a chance to question her she had noiselessly turned the handle of the door and was inching it open. Then she stepped back nervously, almost stepping on my foot and leaving me with little choice but to press on into the room.

'Hello? Mr North, I'm . . . *Oh!*'

My greeting tailed off into a strangulated gasp as I found myself confronted by an enormous dog, as tall as my chest and broad across the shoulders with a huge, meaty head from which its black velvet skin hung in folds. As the creature gazed at me, two ribbons of saliva formed at either side of its mouth.

'Well? Am I to be kept in suspense?'

The voice was thick, as if the speaker had a wad of tissue paper in his mouth, and it took a few seconds of adjustment before my brain translated the sounds, but it was also surprisingly deep for an elderly man. I turned – keeping the terrifying dog in my sight – until I could see, sitting in a straight-backed leather armchair, a person who, in spite of the cane in his hand and the shaking of his fingers, was quite clearly not more than five or six years older than me.

I had only time to form an impression of fierce blue eyes before there was a commotion behind me and a waft of vanilla and citrus, and then Evelyn Manetti burst in.

'Forgive me, Constance. How very rude you must think me. I have been in Italy far too long; my manners are hanging in shreds. I'm practically heathen. This is my uncle, William North. Uncle Bill, this is the lady I've been telling you about, Mrs Walter Bowen.'

The words grated, and I wished then I had omitted Walter's name from my application letter and used only my own. Ridiculous after so many years married to be bothered by such a thing, but I had the sense of having missed an opportunity to start afresh.

I turned to Mr North with half a mind to make some mention of it, but my words dried up in my throat at my first proper look at him. It was shock, I suppose, at finding he bore so little resemblance to the invalid of my imagination. As I've said, he was a lot younger than I'd thought. Fifty-five at the most. Though one could see, if one were searching for it, signs of ill health – the cane, a hollowness of the face, dark semicircles under his eyes and a yellow tinge beneath the suntanned skin – nevertheless he gave an impression of vitality. His blue eyes, which glared at me intently, were the colour of summer skies back home and surrounded by fine lines, pale against the brown of his face, as if he laughed a lot, although at this moment, with his stern expression, I could not imagine it. His sandy hair was thick and liberally streaked with grey. Someone had oiled it back from his face, but whatever had been applied to it was no match for its determined curl. His beard, unfashionable now in England, was darker than the hair on his head, although, paradoxically, the grey, where it came through, was lighter, glinting silver amid the brown.

He was undeniably handsome.

'I'm very pleased to meet you, Mr North.'

I felt those keen eyes appraise me and struggled to fix my smile in place. On closer inspection I noticed a slight slackening of the skin on the left side of his face. He said something to me then in that thick voice that I knew to be a result of the cerebral haemorrhage, and I stopped myself from asking him to repeat himself, deliberately holding the unfamiliar sounds in my mind until they arranged themselves into words I could recognize:

'I don't know why you're here.'

Evelyn laughed.

'Now Uncle Bill, don't be cantankerous. We've been through this. Mrs Bowen is going to be wonderful company for you. She can help you stay on top of all your correspondence and read you your beloved newspaper until your eyesight gets better, and she can also play chess.' Here, her eyes flashed to me, as if urging me not to contradict her, although actually chess was one of the few games Walter and I had played together, back in the early days of our marriage. 'I just know the two of you are going to be great fr—*Get away, you great brute!*

She'd broken off to hit out at Solomon, who had come close enough to leave a snail trail of slobber over the skirt of her dress.

'Sometimes I think Uncle Bill only keeps Solomon here to annoy the rest of us.'

We lingered a few moments longer, before Evelyn decided that her uncle should rest and ushered me out of the door to join her husband in the *salone* for a pre-dinner drink. As we were leaving, William North summoned her back, leaving me standing awkwardly in the vast hallway. I glanced towards the *salone* but didn't want to risk disturbing Mr Manetti. Instead I hung back to talk to Nora, who was sitting on the bottom step.

'I think your doll's dress could do with a wash,' I said, examining the horrible thing, which had hinged joints so that the china arms and legs could move independently, and matted wool hair.

Through the ajar door of Mr North's sitting room I heard the low rumble of his voice, followed by Evelyn's reply: 'I've already explained all this, Uncle Bill. I simply can't be here all the time. I have engagements. Responsibilities. I'm a married woman now.'

I feigned an interest in the doll, which Nora informed me was called Matilda, turning it over in my hand while behind the door William North painstakingly formulated his response. Again there was a delay of some seconds before my brain caught up with his speech, but when it did I wished it had not.

'Did you deliberately find someone old and fat so I wouldn't get excited and bring on another apoplexy?'

The doll stared up at me with its one eye while the stone flags echoed with the teaspoon tinkle of Evelyn Manetti's laughter.

6

THE TWO DAYS after my arrival at the castle passed in a sensory blur. The contrast between my life before – the winter months in the moss-walled sitting room in Pinner, sticking to the one room so as not to waste money on unnecessary coal and gas, watching time pass through the window when the weather was too bad to go outside – and life here in Italy was as great as if someone had flicked on an electric light, flooding the world with colour.

April in Tuscany thrummed with promise, flowers of every conceivable hue shyly budding and blossoming like young girls shrugging off their coats to reveal their party dresses. In the central courtyard garden I found red nasturtiums blending in with orange marigolds, and blue and purple irises, their honey scent ripening as the day warmed up. The wisteria vines that wound around doorways and windows sagged with heavy lilac flowers and the smell of wild thyme and lavender hung in the air.

I felt as if I had woken up inside a fever dream where figs and olives and peaches grew on trees and saffron-coloured lichen made the grey castle walls appear as if they, too, were in bloom. If I followed the terrace around the side of the castle, underneath my window, to the back there was a kitchen garden that Alina assured me would soon boast every different type of vegetable. Beans and leeks, onions, artichokes, asparagus, courgettes. There was a glasshouse behind that in which a jungle of vegetation grew greedily up towards the sun – tomatoes and capsicums on one side, and on the other exotic orchids such as I'd never seen before – violet and rose-pink, lemon-white and pale orange. And behind the glasshouse, another surprise, a bird garden with huge cages housing not only chickens and quail, but also pheasants and exotic birds – a pair of flamboyantly feathered parrots and even a white cockatoo – all shaded by cypress trees and umbrella pines.

On the third day I walked down the hillside to the side of the castle in search of the stream I could see from the wooden bench under my bedroom window. The ground was steeper than I'd imagined and the path was overgrown in places – the forest of ilexes meant the sun-deprived soil was wet and slippery.

Reaching the bottom, I was rewarded by the sight of a cool green river pool, flanked by the bluish-grey rock. Down here, the canopy of trees that had shaded my descent opened out, allowing the mild April sun to pool on the surface of the water. I sat down on a rock which felt pleasantly warm and raised my face to the sky. The hours since my arrival had passed in such a blur of new impressions and information that I had scarcely had time to take it all in. Just how far I'd come from the grey streets of home, from the endless procession of houses with their neat front lawns and solid front doors behind which life ticked slowly by to the rhythm of the grandfather clock in the hall. From silent meals sitting across the table from James, neither of us quite meeting the other's eyes, and everywhere the small, bittersweet reminders of Millie – the clumsily stitched embroidered sampler she'd laboured over in the evenings, finally abandoning it before it was finished after James pretended to mistake the little pointy-faced dog for an elephant with its trunk, the china figurine of a ballet dancer she'd fallen in love with in a shop window one summer in Jersey.

Here, I woke up every morning to a peal of bells from the church tower of Fiesole, just out of sight on a neighbouring hill. For breakfast there'd be thick slices of the maize bread I'd had when I first arrived, and apricot jam or wild honey.

Because of its position at the top of the hill, the castle was flooded with light and, despite its size and grandeur, there was a sense of activity about these mornings that made the place feel alive. A good deal of that vitality could be attributed to Evelyn Manetti, who flitted about in her glorious outfits – a silk wrap in shades of rose and apricot, an emerald-green blouse that changed to turquoise in the light, the interchangeable embroidered silk pouches in a range of rainbow colours that she wore on a delicate chain over her shoulder to carry her cigarettes and the lipstick she was forever touching up – like a beautiful butterfly.

I'd never met anyone like her. She had almost instantly assumed a familiarity with me of a type I'd previously shared only with Caroline in the days when the two of us were still close. Strolling around the courtyard garden, she'd loop her arm through mine, and her conversation, too, brought to mind a butterfly flitting from subject to subject with the merest hint of a flutter of gossamer wings. From pointing out a patch of golden freesias and exhorting me to bury my face in the velvet petals to inhale the delicate scent, to chattering about an English writer called Duncan Fletcher and his 'frightful' German wife, Klara, who had rented a house a few miles away – 'an utter hovel' – in which he was writing a book rumoured to be 'total filth', to declaring I had the most divine eyes she'd ever seen, to talk to her was to feel as if one were a leaf floating on a breeze, powerless to steer a course, able only to give in to the sensation of being tossed aimlessly but pleasurably about.

I admit I was enthralled by her, and this went some way towards making up for her uncle treating me as if I were an ugly piece of furniture that had been delivered to his home that he had neither asked for nor wanted but must now put up with. On the first day, I asked if he'd like me to read from a copy of *Bleak House* I'd found on the library shelves. 'Don't you think I've suffered enough?' he asked. I settled for reading to him from a copy of *The Times* newspaper which was already four days out of date, while he sat in his chair, eyes shut, giving not one iota of response beyond holding up his hand every so often in a signal that he required me to fetch Alina's husband, Massimo, the estate's gardener, to escort him to the lavatory or that he wished to be left alone to rest.

The cerebral haemorrhage, which had weakened the left side of his body, had also given him blurred vision, a fact that incensed him.

'Pearson must do something about this,' he told me crossly, as if his physician's failure to fix his eyesight were somehow my responsibility.

I never mentioned what I'd overheard through the sitting-room door on that first day, but the words 'old and fat' often came into my head, and my voice as I read about revolution in Shanghai or the change of leadership in Japan would grow frostier. Even so, I found myself against my will snatching glances at him over the top of the paper. Even in his debilitated state, his presence was commanding.

In the mornings I read his correspondence to him, of which there was always a great deal. Back home in Pinner, letters were a rare pleasure, but here at the castle the post arrived every day, delivered by bicycle up that merciless hill, a stack of enquiries from people wishing to buy paintings, invitations to exhibitions, requests for valuations and authentications. There were begging letters from artists desperate for just a few square inches of wall space in one of William's galleries, and from wealthy American collectors wanting to get their hands on *the* thing – a newly discovered Fra Angelico panel section from the altar of a rustic Tuscan church, a pair of drawings by Luca Signorelli as part of his preparation for his famous frescoes for the Duomo at Orvieto. There was an American heiress insisting he retract his declaration that her recently purchased del Sarto was actually the work of a far lesser known painter, and a British earl wishing to know the value of the statues in the gardens of the country pile he'd just inherited and whether William knew anyone who would take them off his hands.

I would take down William's reply in rough as he always made changes as he went along – growing agitated as he searched for the right word, the right phrase. 'You were misled. No, not misled. Take that out and write, "You fell victim to a charlatan." In fact, make that "willing victim".' Later, I would write the letters out in longhand. There was a typewriter at the castle, but William said the sound of the keys clattering, even in a separate room, drove him to distraction, which was a relief, as I'd never learned to type.

Occasionally, William would struggle to find the word he wanted to say, which infuriated him. He blamed it on the apoplexy, or sometimes the medication Dr Pearson gave him for the apoplexy. At those times I'd offer suggestions, and I soon found myself looking forward to those moments where William would indicate approval with a gruff 'That'll do.' He was less forthcoming on the rare times I questioned whether he meant to sound quite so bullish or downright rude. 'I managed to conduct my business quite well before you arrived,' he said more than once. But I noticed he usually went along with my suggested changes in the end.

Nora hung about the place, shrouded in loneliness. I had no idea what the girl did with her days. Her mother would make small attempts to amuse her – fetching a book from the library she remembered from her own school days, only to realize after a page or two that she had found it deathly dull even then, or suggesting an activity such as sketching, sitting as a model until her attention was taken by a telephone call or a funny little beetle or an invitation she'd forgotten to respond to. Other than that, the child was left to her own devices, and I often glimpsed her from my bedroom window wandering aimlessly along the strip of terrace that ran the length of the house, always in the company of her grubby doll. 'If you need help finding a governess . . .' I began once, only to have Evelyn stop me with a groan. 'Oh, I know I should, but they are almost invariably such silly girls, claiming to be all about education when really they're *obsessed* with romance.'

Roberto Manetti came and went, taking his charm and

his energy with him. I must confess my spirits lifted whenever I spotted the chrome angel on his beast of a car edging through the gate. When I heard the front door shut behind him in the mornings and the crunch of his boots on the gravel the day always felt just that little bit duller. He *noticed* things. 'Such a lovely brooch,' he'd say, or just last night, 'You always have such a refreshing view on things, Constance.'

Together, he and Evelyn were like a couple from a film or a story book, and their otherworldliness was only exacerbated by the intense energy that charged between the two of them when they were together.

When no one was around I was more than happy to be left alone to roam the castle and grounds and absorb the extraordinary, almost inconceivable fact of my being here in Italy amid such beauty. Several times throughout each day I would stop what I was doing to marvel at a particular quality of golden late-afternoon light or a patch of wild violets bursting up through the forest floor or, like now, the sun dancing on the surface of the river.

I took off my stockings to dip my feet in the water, smiling when I imagined James's face if he could see me and gasping when it turned out to be so much colder than I'd imagined.

I withdrew my feet, red raw with cold, and waited while they warmed up in the sun. This evening I had been invited to join the family for dinner. Mealtimes so far had been a strange hodgepodge of gatherings. Mr North often needed help to eat – which he fiercely resented – so I would sit with him while he took his meals in his sitting room before joining Evelyn and Roberto, if they were around, which mostly they weren't, so it would just be Nora and me. The girl would start off shy and silent but, as before, with some cajoling she would become more talkative, though her chatter was a curious mix of fact and fantasy involving imaginary characters with whom she'd peopled the castle and its grounds.

But this evening the Manettis had invited their closest neighbours to dine – a couple called the Wheelers, who owned the villa halfway down the next hillside, its yellow walls partly obscured by towering cypresses and its facade fronted by a formal garden planted in the form of an English country-house maze. I had learned that most of the grand houses in the Florentine hills were owned by wealthy Britons or, at a stretch, Americans, part of a thriving Anglo-Florentine community that had sprung up towards the end of the last century.

'The rich Italians used to adore us,' Evelyn told me. 'We took all these crumbling piles off their hands when they ran out of money and couldn't afford to hang on to both the palazzo in the city and the place in the countryside.' And now? I asked her. 'Now they're sore about it. They think the reason we can afford to buy these lovely houses is because Britain and France creamed off all the money from the Germans after the war and they got nothing. Boo hoo. Honestly, I'm so utterly bored of hearing about the war, aren't you?'

I dressed for dinner with care in a blue chiffon gown that finished a few inches below the knee worn with a blue silk-velvet jacket that was loosely wrapped so that it billowed at the top and fastened over the hips. I was pleased to see that my afternoon walk had robbed my skin of its grey winter pallor and my thick, unruly hair was for once behaving itself.

'How lovely you look, Constance,' declared Evelyn when I walked nervously into the *salone*. 'That blue is divine with your eyes and your hair. You must meet our dear, dear friends Philip and Emily Wheeler.' She lowered her voice. 'They had a falling-out with Uncle Bill so they only come when he isn't around, but I know you will all adore each other.'

The Wheelers were an odd-looking couple in their forties – she was tall and noble-featured, with an aquiline nose and long arms, he a whole head shorter and portly, his round face shiny and pink above his neat beard, in contrast to his eyes, which were flat and dull. From Evelyn I'd learned that he'd inherited the house on the next hill from an eccentric cousin and that he himself had a most unusual interest.

'That's right. Ants,' he confirmed to me, his flat eyes studying my face as if in anticipation of a reaction. 'I'm a myrmecologist, and a damn good one. You know, Mrs Bowen, a person can learn everything they need to know about life from studying ant colonies.'

'Bo-ring,' intoned his wife.

I pretended I hadn't heard her.

'Evelyn mentioned beetles as well.'

Philip Wheeler appeared pleased; his chest visibly puffed up.

'That's correct. I wouldn't like to say I'm the world's leading coleopterist, Mrs Bowen, but I'm certainly up there in the top three.'

'He keeps *discovering* new species of beetles and trying to name them after himself or his sainted mother,' said his wife. 'But then they turn out not to be new after all, just a tiny variation on a species that's been around since forever.'

To my surprise, Nora was also here, almost unrecognizable in a plum-coloured velvet dress that accentuated her sallow skin.

'She did beg me so, and I didn't have the heart to say no,' said Evelyn. 'Roberto thoroughly disapproves of children being present at dinner, don't you, darling?' She planted a kiss on her handsome husband's cheek.

'Just as well I am powerless to resist you, my angel.'

They made such an arresting pair, the two of them. Evelyn was wearing a dusty-pink sleeveless gown that skimmed her hips and plunged low in the back, revealing the perfect 'S' of her spine. Her eyes were ringed in kohl so that they appeared even bluer by contrast to the black line surrounding them, and she wore a pink lipstick that matched her dress. Meanwhile, Roberto's youth and vigour were made more noticeable by proximity to Philip Wheeler's middle-aged girth. As I'd witnessed on that first day, the Manettis were forever touching each other, Evelyn always with a hand on her husband's arm or chest, as if checking to make sure he was real, and Roberto running a finger up his wife's spine or hip. Now his hand rested on the small of her back, but as I watched it slipped down so that it briefly cupped her buttock. I looked quickly away.

'I expect you're finding Florentine life impossibly provincial after London,' said Emily Wheeler, in the sort of tone that implied the opposite to be true. When she leaned forwards, the light caught on her heavy gold necklace, inset with rubies. 'We would love to return for a visit ourselves. See our friends. Go to the theatre. But alas, finances don't permit.'

A curious atmosphere descended then, the air itself feeling tight and still. Evelyn had already told me the Wheelers were hard up, owing to some foolish investments. Perhaps it was embarrassment making the room feel suddenly so stuffy.

When I confessed I had yet to venture into Florence itself, Mrs Wheeler declared herself scandalized and began listing the treasures I was missing out on through this delay, intoning and assessing them in her deep, booming voice. 'Don't bother with the Botticelli – over-rated and over-sentimental, but the Michelangelo sculpture is worth a look.'

On and on she went. Florence had a lot of treasures.

The food, served by Renata, the cook, was unlike any I'd tasted. To start, halved capsicums stuffed with wild mushrooms and herbs – 'Those green leaves are nettles!' Evelyn told me. 'Isn't that wild?' Then fresh fish brought by train that morning from the port at Viareggio and served with a sauce made from anchovies and chopped parsley. And delicious chilled white wine to accompany it.

'Renata is a magician,' I said to Emily Wheeler, biting into a perfectly roasted potato with a crust of rosemary and garlic. Instantly I was aware of having said the wrong thing.

'Well, yes, I should think so. I trained her up myself. She worked for us for years, practically one of the family, until we couldn't afford to keep her on any longer.'

'Uncle Bill offered Renata a fortune to poach her from Emily and Philip,' said Evelyn, laughing. 'They've never forgiven him.'

The table was lit by two candelabras, one at either end, with three candles apiece, so that our faces glowed orange in the semi-darkness. The talk grew louder and more raucous as the wine bottles came and went.

'Have you told Mrs Bowen about your extra houseguest?' Philip Wheeler asked Evelyn, after the plates had been taken away, the eyes of the dead fish staring out from their disembodied heads.

'What on earth are you talking about?'

To my immense surprise, Mr Wheeler then raised his arms and began to play an imaginary violin, his several chins squashed down on to one shoulder as he drew his bow back and forth.

Clearly this meant something to Evelyn, because she entreated him to stop through her giggles.

'We don't want to scare Constance away when she's only just arrived!'

'The poor woman deserves to know what kind of place you've brought her to,' Philip Wheeler insisted.

'The fact is the castle is haunted!' his wife broke in, as if to beat him to the punchline.

Philip Wheeler glowered at her before continuing. 'A little girl lived here in the fifteenth century. Apparently, she was precociously gifted and her father became so scared that he'd brought a witch into the world he had her bricked up inside the castle wall.'

'*Alive!*' his wife interjected. 'With only her violin for company.'

I heard a soft intake of breath and glanced up the table to where Nora was sitting away from the glow of the nearest candelabra, her little face paler than ever, her dark eyes wide.

'Her father is one of the portraits in William's famous collection.'

I knew immediately that it would be the bearded man whose picture I'd stood in front of the day I arrived.

'Local legend has it that previous residents of the castle have woken up in the night to hear the sound of a child crying or a ghostly violin,' Philip said with relish.

In the flickering candlelight, with his round, pink face,

he gave the strange, discomfiting impression of a giant baby wearing the knowing expression of an adult.

After pudding – a strange concoction of halved peaches soaked in wine – we repaired to the *salone* for coffee, once again brought by Renata.

'Is it Alina's night off?' I asked as I settled down on the sofa close to Nora. The girl still looked pale and shaken and I worried what kind of effect the story she'd just heard might have on her.

'Alina and Massimo don't live here in the castle, Constance,' said Evelyn, surprised. 'They live with their children and Massimo's parents in a sweet little farmhouse further down the valley.'

'Children?'

'Yes, two cherubic little boys. At least, I think it's two, though come to think of it, there might be a third.'

I was still curious about the conversation I'd had with Alina in the car on the day I arrived – her voice when she'd spoken of William North's dead son, Rupert – so I asked Evelyn how Alina had come here.

'She grew up here, really, in the castle. Her mother was housekeeper to Aunt Cecily, Uncle Bill's wife. Aunt Cecily was excessively fond of her and paid for her to be educated. There were even' – she lowered her voice and leaned across the table – 'rumours of some sort of *liaison* with my cousin Rupert. Imagine! But then Rupert and Cecily died and Alina married Massimo and moved down to the farm, which really suits her much better than being here with all of us, never really feeling like she belongs. And actually, it works out beautifully with Massimo's mother looking after the children during the day and—'

She was interrupted by her husband,

'I'll never understand how Massimo allows it.'

'Allows what, darling?'

'Allows his wife to go out to work. It's embarrassing.'

Disappointment tugged at my ribs. Of course, many people held the same opinion. Most, even. Yet somehow I had expected more from the engaging Roberto.

Emily Wheeler made a noise like a horse's snort.

'Really Roberto, you need to drag yourself out of the Dark Ages.'

'Exactly,' agreed Evelyn. 'It's not as if Alina is one of those ridiculous English bluestockings from before the war, chaining themselves to railings and throwing themselves under horses.'

Roberto turned to face me, smiling and throwing up his hands in appeal.

'Where do you stand on all this, Constance? You're always so considered and thoughtful about things.'

I found myself growing flushed and flustered under his direct, thick-lashed gaze.

'You can't ask her,' said Emily Wheeler, 'when she is literally here in your house to work.'

'Being a companion is a vocation, not a job,' said Roberto.

'Well, I didn't chain myself to anything or jump in front of a horse,' I began before stopping, ashamed, remembering Caroline's rasping voice when she came out of prison the last time, her throat scraped raw from the feeding tube they'd used after she refused to eat. The distance that grew up between us afterwards that I'd never managed to breach. *I would have marched with you, but* . . . 'But I am grateful to them – those ridiculous English bluestockings, as you call them – for what they did for us. I do think that having brought up a family and run a household since the death of my husband means I have just as much of an idea of what our country needs as a twenty-one-year-old boy, still wet behind the ears, who has never drawn up a weekly budget in his life.'

Emily Wheeler clapped her hands. 'Hear, hear.'

'I think we have a revolutionary in the house,' said her husband, leaning back in his chair to study me with his curiously flat eyes, as if I were one of his precious ants or beetles.

7

I BECAME ATTUNED TO the castle's rhythms and noises, the way the walls whispered when there was a breeze and the pipes groaned in the early morning when the household was waking up.

Every day I discovered new corners that I hadn't yet explored – an alcove in the wall of the upstairs landing that housed a marble bust of an elderly man with a sharply recessed chin, a gentle painting of a vase of flowers caught in a slant of sunlight that hung in the *salone* and had somehow passed me by. I was starting to understand how much fine work hung there on the castle walls, far more than in many of the galleries I'd dutifully trailed around back home, and the fact that I was the sole audience made it doubly enthralling, allowing me to form a personal relationship with the art. The paintings were mostly centuries old, many with a religious theme, although there were more modern pieces here and there, a painting of the French countryside by Pissarro, all muted greens and a wide mauve sky, and even a couple of abstracts by Italian artists I'd never heard of, their bold colours and geometric shapes at first jarring and yet, strangely, growing less so the more one looked. There were sketches in pencil or charcoal, the curved line of a woman's hip, the dip of her back. Taken separately, they seemed to have little in common but, with the exception of Roberto's starker photographs, they shared a subtle beauty and I found myself wondering about the man who'd collected and curated them, what sensitivity might be lurking under William North's surly impatience.

I tried to avoid the portrait of the bearded man with the haunted eyes, that space in front of it where the air grew suddenly cold.

Towards the end of my first week in Italy, Alina offered to take me on a walk exploring the hillside directly behind the castle. I jumped at the chance of spending some time getting to know the young woman who'd met me at the station, but as we unlatched a gate in the back of the walled terrace that surrounded the castle, light footsteps sounded behind us.

'Can I come? Please?' As usual, Nora had her revolting doll under her arm and she was wearing the too-small pinafore dress again, her legs emerging like pipe cleaners.

She was such a funny-looking thing with that long nose that bent at the end so that it was half an inch off centre, I felt myself softening towards her, in spite of her awkwardness, her non-Millieness. How lonely she must be here without any other children for company. And though I'd relished the thought of spending time alone with Alina, I nodded in agreement.

The back hill of the castle was far wilder and more overgrown than the front and descended only a relatively short distance before rising steeply again into the next hillside. The woods here were thicker, the undergrowth more tangled. Although the morning we left behind had been clear and mild, the temperature in here was at least ten degrees cooler, the leaves of the trees running with damp. Alina, wearing only a thin cotton dress, hugged her arms around her chest.

'I always forget how cold it is here.'

The soil under our feet was spongy and slimy, latticed with roots and stems that grew so close to the ground we had to keep our eyes downward to avoid tripping. When I did look up, it was into a dense canopy of trees, through which the daylight appeared only as occasional pinpricks of white. We were climbing at such an angle the backs of my calves felt clenched and tight and I was growing breathless, cursing the extra weight I had allowed to creep on over the last years. I'd always been just that little bit bigger than all the other girls, the tallest in my class, the strongest. Walter had always made it clear he had formed an attachment to me *despite* my size, which other men, he told me in a pained voice – *lesser* men, he meant – might find off-putting. Only Millie had embraced every inch of me, declaring me, when she was younger, to be like a comfortable bed that she could sink into and be wrapped up in and, when she was older, 'statuesque'.

'Do you wish to go back, Mrs Bowen? It is too much for you?'

'Please, call me Constance. No, not too much at all. It's very beautiful.'

This was true, but it was a strange kind of beauty, everything muffled and deathly still, even the birds seemingly either exiled or silent. I had the strangest feeling that we were intruding somewhere we shouldn't. Seemingly Alina agreed, for she said:

'I look at it from the kitchen window of the castle and it

looks so cool and so quiet here, the sort of place where no one will ask things of you. But when I arrive, I remember that it is like this.'

'Like what?'

'Like it is holding its breath.'

'I can hold my breath,' said Nora, who had been trailing behind, muttering to her doll, but had now caught up. 'Look.'

She took a huge gulp of air then pressed her lips together, her gaunt cheeks gradually inflating.

'I do that when I'm hiding and I don't want anyone to find me.'

'Why would you be hiding? From whom?'

But Nora looked away and didn't answer. By now I was struggling, with the terrain and the incline and the damp that was like cold hands pressing on my skin. I was beginning to wonder if there was an end to this hillside, or would we just keep climbing on and on for ever in this unwelcoming place.

But then the air seemed to grow warmer, and the trees thinned out, allowing the light to filter through, and we arrived in a small clearing at what was thankfully the summit of the hill.

'Oh,' I gasped, standing stock still at the strange sight that greeted me. 'I had no idea!'

In the middle of the clearing, a monumental rock grew up out of the earth, flattened on one side, the surface smooth and slippery, reaching up towards the thick, white, overcast sky. The underside, meanwhile, its rough crags padded with green moss, dug down into the undergrowth beneath. The towering rock was hewn of the deepest charcoal-grey sandstone, stark against the low cloud.

'*La roccia nera*,' said Alina. 'The black rock. Normally in this region the stone is lighter grey; *pietra serena*, it is called. No one knows how this came to be here.'

I can't explain the feeling that came over me, looking at that colossal mound of matter that had stood here for millions of years, before the castle to which it gave its name was built, and would no doubt stand here for millions of years after I and Alina and little Nora had turned to dust. Awe, but also desolation. How little we mattered, in the end.

I became aware of Nora, jumping from foot to foot, plucking at my sleeve.

'Come, I want to show you something, something secret.'

The child was more animated than I'd seen her before and I let her lead me behind the towering rock to where a crude structure had been built out of stone, topped by a simple weathered wooden cross.

'This is where witches are buried,' whispered Nora, her dark eyes wide.

'Not *more* witches,' I said, feigning terror.

'Nora, don't scare our visitor when she has only just arrived.' Alina laughed. Turning to me, she explained, 'There is a story that in the sixteenth century there was a long period of terrible weather when all the crops failed. It was during the time when Italy believed in witchcraft. The starving people thought a curse had been put on them and they brought three young, local women up here who they accused of being witches. Then they killed them as an offering to God, asking him to release the curse.'

'They *burned* them,' said Nora, thrilled. 'And then laid their bones out there on the rock.'

'Goodness,' I said, smiling at the girl's theatricality. Still, when I glanced up at that immense slope of flat grey rock, I shivered.

On the way back down, while Nora skipped ahead, pausing occasionally to balance her doll on a branch or help her 'walk' on the spongy earth, I tried to find out a bit more about Alina.

'I hadn't realized you had children. How old are they?'

'Bruno is four and Lorenzo three, and my little Pia is eighteen months.'

There was pride in Alina's voice, but also a note of weariness. How hard it would be, I thought, to work all day for the Manettis and go home to three excitable children who hadn't seen their mama all day.

'How lucky your mother-in-law is around to look after them,' I said.

Alina nodded, her mouth set into a tight line.

'I do envy you,' I pressed on. 'Living in this glorious place, walking to work every day with your husband and then home to your big family in the evening. You have everything you need right here.'

Alina didn't answer and, as I said it, I was aware of an echo in my memory, something hovering in the shadows of my mind. It was only after we'd got back to the castle that it came to me that I'd just said to Alina almost exactly what James had said to me back in Pinner. *You can live out the remainder of your life without ever needing to move from this house.*

Later that afternoon, I sat with William North in his sitting room, Solomon, as ever, lying in attendance by his feet. Though I'd known him less than a week, I could already see a marked progress in William's recovery. Every day he regained more movement down his left side and his speech was a little clearer, though he still struggled with his vision. By this stage, we had established an uneasy accommodation with one another. I would read him *The Times*, starting at the front pages and working my way through. I'd begun by offering some commentary after each story, an agreement or disagreement or an anecdote that related to whatever we'd just read. I considered it a way of giving him some insight into my life so that we might forge some sort of connection.

But William had soon shut that down. 'Can't you just read?' he'd asked in that thick voice. So now I kept my comments to myself, trying not to pay attention to the awkward gaps between stories where the only sound was the low grumbling of Solomon's snores and the ticking of a mantle clock. So I was surprised, this particular afternoon, when William himself volunteered a remark.

'Can you really play chess, or was that something you made up to get the job?'

'I know how to play,' I replied stiffly. Once, I would have qualified that remark or apologized in advance for my performance. It was something most women did. But then I'd noticed Millie doing it too. If she was asked to play the piano, something she did like a dream, she'd preface it with: 'I expect you'll regret you ever asked.' One time when James had a friend staying, she spent the entire weekend apologizing: 'I'm afraid you'll find my conversation jolly dull,' she said when she was seated next to him at dinner. This young man who spoke of nothing except motor cars! It broke my heart that my daughter might consider herself not enough and from that point on I'd made a deliberate effort to curb my own self-deprecation, though it was a hard habit to break.

I fetched the chess set – a heavy marble board with carved marble pieces, each larger than the palm of my hand – and arranged them on the low table within easy reach of William. Then I sank down on to the rug on the far side.

'We do have furniture.' William used his good arm to gesture around the room.

'I'm perfectly comfortable here.'

We began to play, and it felt good to be exercising those underused muscles in my brain. My father had taught me chess when I was a girl, and Walter and I had played regularly when we were first married. But I was the better player and my husband hadn't enjoyed conceding games, with the upshot that either I had to lose on purpose, or he had to admit defeat, so we stopped playing at all, one of many things we tacitly let slide in our marriage. Sex being another, although I think we were both quite relieved about that.

We'd only played two or three moves when Solomon got to his feet suddenly, startling me. His hackles were raised along the ridge of his spine and he was growling softly at the door.

'What's the matter, boy?' asked William.

I went to the door. But when I opened it there was nothing there.

That first match William won fairly decisively. I was still feeling my way back into the game, remembering the different openings, the various mathematical patterns of it all. The second was far more evenly matched. I could tell my opponent was having to make more effort, sitting forward in his chair to better examine the board and assess my intentions. He was using his good hand to move the pieces, but even so it wasn't always steady and there was a moment where he took my bishop with his knight in such triumph that he knocked two other pieces over. I reached out instinctively to stop them rolling and our fingers brushed together.

I snatched back my hand as if from an open fire.

8

'I SN'T THIS FUN, just us girls heading out on the town?'
Evelyn Manetti was speeding down the hill in the motor car in which Alina had first collected me from the station ten days before. In the excitement of my arrival, I had not appreciated before that the top of the vehicle could be folded down, leaving us free to enjoy the sunshine. Or rather, I would have enjoyed it, had I not been clinging on to the door handle as we swung around the hairpin bends with the high wall on one side and a sheer drop on the other.

'I can't tell you how much I've been looking forward to seeing Florence,' I said, when I recovered the ability to speak. 'It's such a pity Nora couldn't come.'

The girl had come flying out of the door when she heard us leaving the castle, begging her mother to take her with an expression of such eagerness on her thin little face that I'd turned to Evelyn to tell her that I didn't mind a bit at exactly the same moment Evelyn said: 'Darling, I'd love to take you, but you'd be bored to tears trailing around the Uffizi for the millionth time and, besides, you really ought to be learning something. Didn't that last governess leave behind some books for you to be getting on with? Latin and such like.'

Nora had turned back then, her little shoulders slumped in such an attitude of resignation I had to look away.

Still, I couldn't pretend I wasn't quietly thrilled at the idea of spending a day with Evelyn. She brought such an energy with her that one felt instantly more alert, full of anticipation for what the day might bring. She looked a picture today in a butter-yellow jersey dress with a matching narrow silk scarf around her neck and her golden hair fluttering in the breeze. Every now and then I would get a waft of her scent – vanilla and lemon, like the flavours of an ice-cream dessert.

'How long did it take you to pass your driving test?' I asked her as we reached a stretch of road that was thankfully straight.

'Oh, I don't bother about that. They're terribly strict in Italy, you know. One is expected to sit an actual exam about combustion engines and all sorts of mechanical business. If anyone asks, I say I learned to drive in England, but they never do. Roberto is quite a big cheese around here. Don't you think he's handsome, by the way? Sometimes I think I could just die from loving him.'

It was such a strange thing to say I could feel myself blushing. No one I knew spoke like that.

We had by now reached the outskirts of the city, tall buildings springing up on either side of us. On the pavements, women's silk parasols jostled for space, while our progress was hampered as we became stuck behind bicycles and horse-drawn traps. With the roof down, I noticed posters for the Partito Nazionale Fascista plastered to lampposts and walls.

'Does it worry you, all of this?' I asked Evelyn, as a column of boys wearing dark shorts and white short-sleeved shirts emblazoned with an insignia I couldn't recognize marched past the car in strict formation under the watchful eye of an athletic man all in black, with a whistle between his lips and hard black eyes.

She shrugged.

'What you have to realize, Constance, is that someone needed to take charge. After the end of the war the Italians were really left high and dry by England and France, and it's led to all sorts of unpleasantness. Poverty and what have you. There were strikes and unions. Some of our friends have had a ghastly time of it with their workers, I can tell you. If it weren't for the Fascisti, there would have been anarchy. Anyway, let's not discuss politics, it's the world's dullest subject. Well, after war.'

The Uffizi was sublime and intimidating in that way grand old buildings are, the weight of history pressing on you as you work your way around, mortality whispering along lofty corridors lined with the work of long-dead artists. There was a crowd craning to see the paintings, all well dressed and doing that thing people do in the presence of renowned masterpieces of peering intelligently at length at the object in question while canvassing the crowd from the corner of one eye to check their appreciation is being observed. Still, I would have gladly lingered in their midst, in front of Botticelli's angelic-faced nymphs or one of Titian's forbidding portraits. However, Evelyn could not seem to settle, flitting from painting to painting, alighting just long enough to sweep her eyes across the glossy surface before moving on once again.

'Can that be enough culture now?' she asked after we'd been in the gallery for less than half an hour. 'Only I do think it's possible to overload oneself with edifying things, don't you?'

After Evelyn showed me the river – the majestic Arno – spanned by the Ponte Vecchio bridge, honey-coloured in the Florentine sunshine and lined with tiny shops selling jewellery and souvenirs, we headed for the Via Tornabuoni, which Evelyn assured me was *the* place to go in Florence. 'I mean, obviously, there are some divine buildings, like the Duomo and whatnot. But I always think you can't really get a feeling for a place until you do what ordinary people do.'

Evelyn's definition of ordinary pursuits turned out to involve two things – shopping and eating. I'd never got the hang of shopping. For me it was something you did out of necessity, a means to an end. Luckily, Millie had been of the same mind. Not so Evelyn. In Parenti, she lingered over some cut-glass wine goblets and walked around picking up silver cutlery and setting it down again. In Gucci, it was leather luggage that caught her eye. There were exquisite handmade shoes to be admired and fur stoles to be stroked.

At one point we passed an English bookshop called Seeber's, but when I asked if we might go inside Evelyn looked at me as if I had taken leave of my senses. 'Why ever would you need to look at more dusty old books when we have a whole library of them at home?'

There were quite a few businesses dotted around the place catering for the British community – a fusty place selling tweeds and jam called the Old England Store, a bank called Haskard's and a chemist's called the Profumeria Inglese – though Evelyn referred to it as Roberts' – which featured a display of elegant soaps and cologne in the window.

'There are thousands of us here in Florence, you see,'

Evelyn explained. 'There's even a British Institute in the Palazzo Antinori with a library full of English books and a rather nice tearoom. And of course there are always balls and parties and things at the British Embassy. You know, one could live here perfectly happily without ever having to speak a word of Italian or eat a single olive.'

For lunch she took me to Doney's, a grand café with four vast pillars holding up the ceiling and white walls decorated with gold friezes. Evelyn was like a child in a toyshop. 'The hot chocolate is to die for here. But what am I thinking? It's after midday. Time for an aperitif. Have you had a Negroni, Constance? Oh, you must. You know it was invented right here in Florence, at the Café Casoni opposite. I suppose I should get used to calling it Café Giacosa now it has changed hands. I do wish the things I love would just stay the same for ever. Don't you? Perhaps we should have gone there. Or to Proccaci's for paninis with truffled anchovies. Don't you hate being given so much choice? No, but Doney's does the best caviar and foie gras, so we are in the right place after all. Hurrah!'

Over our drinks, beautifully cool-looking with a rich orange colour and a slice of orange inside, although rather too bitter for my taste, Evelyn filled me in on what had brought her here to Florence. 'After Miles upped and left me there was an almighty hoo-ha. Turned out he didn't have a bean. We married in a whirlwind just before the war and it was all frightfully romantic. But then he came back from France not quite right in the head, you know, like so many did, and never really worked again, and his family were terribly mean with their money. After he went I had to sell our sweet little house in Kensington and move with Nora back to my parents' place in Sussex. Well, they didn't like that one little bit. The scandal of having a divorced daughter, plus I don't think they much cared for Nora. Well, she's quite an odd little thing, isn't she, with that nose of hers? And my older brother, Douglas, was disapproving. He and his family live with Mummy and Daddy, just waiting for them to pop off so they can inherit the whole thing. Who'd be a daughter?

'Anyhow, Aunt Cecily – that's Uncle Bill's wife – took pity on me and invited me and Nora to come and stay in the castle for a little while. The castle was hers, you know, an inheritance from her first husband, who died when he was very young. Uncle Bill was poor when they met, though he's rich as Croesus now, thanks to all those dreary paintings. Then Rupert got very ill – well, he'd been weak since the war, really – and he died, and then Aunt Cecily died and we couldn't leave Uncle Bill here alone. Besides, I love it here. Especially since I met Roberto.'

I asked her about her husband. Like most women in love, she seemed delighted for the chance to talk about him. Roberto's father's family was very well known in Florence, she told me, but Roberto's father himself had been all but disinherited on account of his gambling. His marriage to an American hadn't helped.

'Poor Roberto feels the stigma very deeply, of not being a pure-blood Italian,' said Evelyn. 'I had to practically beg him to marry me. He didn't want history repeating itself. As I said, the British aren't popular around here at the moment. So now Roberto feels like he has to be more Italian than the Italians, to prove himself, if you know what I mean.'

Then it was my turn to be questioned. 'I want to know all about you.' But Evelyn's powers of concentration were limited. No sooner had I embarked upon an answer to a question about James than she'd be cutting in with a new question about Millie or Walter or the house in Pinner or whether I thought Clara Bow was prettier than Colleen Moore.

And all the time people were coming to our table to say hello, or ask after Evelyn's uncle's health, or invite her to a luncheon or a cocktail party. And I must be introduced and my presence explained. Numerous sets of eyes sized me up and then slid right off me. No matter. I was used to it.

Outside, blinking in the bright sunshine, I realized for the first time just how strong those Negronis must have been. What exactly had been in them?

I had thought we might return straight home, but Evelyn had other plans. More shops where scent had to be sniffed from cut-glass bottles with silk tassels and rubber pump dispensers, and beaded evening bags held up to the light so that they dazzled. We became quite giddy, the two of us, giggling like schoolgirls as we left a shop that sold hats and gloves where the young sales assistant had practically curtseyed to us. How long it had been since I had laughed like this with anyone, I thought to myself. How seriously I took myself these days, since Millie died. In one shop Evelyn bought a pale oyster silk parasol which she presented to me on the way out.

'Oh, I couldn't,' I protested.

'Yes, you jolly well could. I'm only thinking selfishly – you're no good to me or Uncle Bill if you get sunstroke and have to stay holed up in your room with the shutters pulled tight.'

When we set off, Evelyn's arm looped through mine as I

held the parasol over us both, I felt a weight lifting off me. It was something to do with the golden light here in Florence, and the beauty of the buildings, and finding myself here on this adventure after imagining I had left it far too late. I felt like a younger version of myself – far more carefree than I had ever been in my real youth.

Ahead of us was a café where tables spilled out on to the pavement. As we approached, I saw that two of the tables were occupied by Blackshirts drinking coffee and beer, their legs encased in their knee-length leather boots stretched out in front of them in the sunshine. It was the first time I'd come up against the Fascisti in person and I was surprised at how visceral was my reaction, my mouth suddenly dry. They were just boys, really, none older than James, but there was something about the uniform and all the things I'd heard – the people disappearing off the streets, arrested on the vaguest of charges and shipped off to remote prison islands, neighbours informing on neighbours, spies in the cinemas reporting anyone who didn't cheer at the government propaganda films. Evelyn, however, showed no such reticence. In fact, she grew more alert, craning to see before hurrying forward, trailing me on her arm.

She was waving at someone. The jolt of unease that Evelyn was on intimate terms with the Fascisti arrived almost at the same moment as the recognition of just who it was she knew so well.

'Roberto!' Evelyn practically skipped towards the tables of men. 'Roberto, *amore*! Over here!'

9

ROBERTO WAS ALREADY on his feet and coming towards us. As ever, he had a smile on his face, only this time it didn't quite reach his eyes. He seized Evelyn's elbow and steered us both aside.

'Darling, haven't we talked about this? Can't you see I'm working?' His voice was low and tight.

Evelyn pouted. 'You're doing nothing of the sort, you're drinking beer. I can see it.'

A muscle twitched in Roberto's jaw and I saw that his fingers were making soft dents in the skin of Evelyn's arm.

'Princess, you know nothing about my work. How could you, when there is only air between here' – he gently tapped one side of her head – 'and here.' He tapped the other. 'Now, please leave. Everyone is looking.'

It was true that the black-shirted young men grouped around the two tables seemed to be finding the scene most entertaining. One called out something in Italian, and the rest of them guffawed with laughter.

As we turned away, Roberto touched my shoulder. At his neck, under the collar of his black shirt I saw the glint of the gold chain he always wore, with its tiny golden key.

'Mrs Bowen, Constance, please don't think me rude. I know a woman with your knowledge of the world will understand how a man needs to set boundaries around his work.'

I didn't reply, silenced by the uniform he wore. Though I'd caught glimpses of him arriving home at the end of a day, he'd always worn a jacket or his ordinary clothes. It had never occurred to me that the charming, affable young man from the castle might have anything to do with the fascists James had warned me about.

As Evelyn and I hurried past the seated men I could feel their eyes on us. Well, on Evelyn, to be specific, dazzling in her yellow dress and scarf and her yellow hair reflecting back the sun. But if she was conscious of their appraisal, she didn't show it.

'How dare he talk to me like that?' Evelyn had dropped my arm and was striding on ahead, so I couldn't tell if her question was aimed at me or herself.

'I'm sure he didn't mean to—'

'Didn't mean to *what*, Constance?'

'To upset you.'

'And just how would you know that?'

I was reeling as I followed her wraith-like yellow-clad figure to the car. After the confidences of the rest of the day the bad-tempered exchange felt like a physical slap.

But as we drove out of the city and began once again to climb the cool green hillside towards the castle, Evelyn seemed to shake off her ill humour.

'No,' she said, as if continuing a conversation we'd been having all this while. 'I simply refuse to let Roberto spoil our lovely day. You have enjoyed it, haven't you, Constance? Sorry for being such a grouch.'

She turned her big eyes on me just as we approached a

hairpin bend and I hurriedly assured her that of course I had enjoyed it immensely. This seemed to reassure her and she put her tiny hands back on the wheel.

'You should have seen your face, Constance, when you caught Roberto sitting there in his uniform. I thought you would drop dead from shock. But you have to admit, it suits him very well, don't you think? You see, there are really only two choices in Italy at the moment. You can be a fascist, or you can be a communist, and seeing as the communists are the ones getting carted off to prison or getting shot, you'd be pretty silly to choose that option, wouldn't you?'

I hesitated.

'And your uncle? Does he share your husband's politics?'

Evelyn let off a peal of laughter.

'Uncle Bill? Not a chance. There was the most dreadful row when he found out. In fact, I wouldn't be surprised if it wasn't the stress of me marrying Roberto that brought about his apoplexy in the first place. Poor Uncle Bill. I am most awfully fond of him, for all he can be quite scary sometimes.'

'So Mr North's illness coincided with your marriage? Is that why you've remained living at your uncle's house?'

'Good god no. We adore the castle and where else would we go? Roberto doesn't have a bean. And besides, I'm the only family William has now. Even though, really, I suppose I'm Cecily's family, not his.'

'You and Nora.'

'Oh. Yes. Nora. And I suppose Roberto and I will have our own children sooner or later. Roberto is keen to get started. You know, Mussolini has decided that we women should all have hordes of children, to prove our patriotism. Five at a minimum, but there are all sorts of prizes for women who have more – medals and tax cuts. More than a dozen and they practically make you a saint. Roberto can't understand why it's taking so long.'

'How long has it been?'

Evelyn scrunched up her nose as if to concentrate better.

'We got married five months ago. And let me tell you, it isn't through want of trying.'

I felt my cheeks growing warm, and Evelyn laughed.

'Don't look so shocked, Constance!' Then she grew solemn. 'I only hope I'm not too old. Roberto can be beastly about it, but I'm only a few years older than him. Hardly anything, really.'

Her hand went up to her face, almost as if it were an automatic response. In the sharp April sunshine I could see a faint trace of fine lines at the corners of her eyes. To my eyes, it only made her more beautiful, this evidence of a life lived, of laughter.

'You know, one time when we were in the middle of one of our fights, Roberto told me he didn't believe I'd ever given birth. He said I'd tricked him.'

'But Nora—'

'He said there was no chance Nora could have come from me, looking as she does. Isn't that a terrible thing to say? Of course, poor Nora does favour her father's side. Miles's mother was a hideous creature.' She looked guilty then, as she realized what she'd said. 'Not that Nora is hideous, by any means. If it weren't for that nose . . .'

I knew women back home whose children went to boarding school and who developed a curious detachment from them, as if they were only distantly related, but Evelyn's dismissiveness of Nora made me uncomfortable. As if I'd voiced my thoughts out loud, she burst out, 'The truth is, the war made him a monster. Miles, I mean. Nora's father. He cried and screamed all night and had these fits of blind rage where he would lash out.'

'At you?'

'Oh, let's not talk about horrid things any more. Look where we are. In Italy. In the sunshine. We must only talk of nice things from now on. I insist.'

When we arrived back at the castle Nora was sitting outside the enormous front door. I waved, but she turned and fled inside. I felt a warm flood of remorse, remembering how the girl had pleaded to come with us. I wondered how she'd passed the day in those vast, dusty rooms.

'Oops,' said Evelyn. 'I think we're in somebody's bad books.'

I thought then about what Evelyn had said about Nora resembling her father and what she had implied but hadn't said about what happened when her ex-husband 'lashed out' and how that might translate into a reluctance to spend time with her daughter.

Families were complicated.

I wanted to go straight to William North when we got inside. Even though Evelyn had insisted she 'steal' me away for the day, I still felt as if I had abandoned my post. But, more than that, I realized with a surprise that I'd missed sitting with him, reading through his mail – always something new and interesting – concentrating my attention when he talked so as not to have to ask him to repeat, feeling a sly tug of pleasure when he looked at me in a certain way and I knew I'd said something to pique his interest. I'd even missed Solomon's huge, brooding presence – his snuffles and the wide yawns that showed all of his long, pointed yellow teeth.

Evelyn, however, insisted that I have tea with her in the *salone*. I wondered, warily, whether she might want to share more confidences, but instead she chatted about this and that, and produced her purchases from their bags to admire and stroke, and it occurred to me that she merely disliked being alone.

After fifteen minutes of this, there was the sound of a car engine straining up the hill and then the crunch of gravel as Roberto Manetti drove his green motor car through the gates. Though he had on a jacket, my stomach lurched at the knowledge of the black uniform beneath.

Evelyn grew still as she listened to the sound of the great front door opening and I hoped he hadn't come to continue his quarrel with her. Instead, he arrived at the double doors of the *salone* with a bunch of wild poppies he had picked from the roadside on his way home.

'My angel,' he said, opening his arms, and Evelyn flew across the room towards him.

'Constance' – he smiled, while his fingers stroked his wife's ribcage to the underside of her breast, 'I apologize again if I seemed abrupt back there in town. My wife sometimes forgets that I have a serious job to do, but it is no excuse. Can you forgive me?'

'No need for apologies. If you don't mind, I must just go to check on Mr North.'

But William North was in his bedroom resting. Reluctant to intrude on whatever was happening in the *salone*, I went up to my own bedroom to write some postcards, which I'd bought in a little place on the Ponte Vecchio.

I penned a card for our daily, Mrs Hancock, and one for Mrs Sutton, who lived next door with her silent daughter. But what I wanted most was to share my experiences of Italy with someone dear to me. When Millie went to stay with my brother's family in Cornwall during the war, I wrote her long letters every evening detailing my day, how the garden looked now that the spring was here, the way her cat slept all night on her bed as if keeping it warm for her. Now I contemplated writing to my old friend Caroline, but I wondered if it might seem cruel. Caroline had travelled so much while I was rooted to home with children and a husband. But since developing pneumonia in prison, after the feeding tube they crammed down her throat sent liquid to her lungs instead of her stomach, she now grew out of breath just walking to the end of the street.

So instead I poured everything I wished to say to Caroline and Millie into a letter to James. I'd dashed off a card when I first arrived just to tell him I was safe and not taken prisoner and shipped off to South America never to be heard from again. Now I described in detail the castle and the family and Solomon and Tuscany itself – the exact mauve of the far-off mountains in the early mornings, the sharp scent of pine after it rained. It was not how James and I usually talked to one another, but I had no one else to tell.

I was in the middle of relating our trip to Florence – leaving out the shock of Roberto in his uniform – when I heard someone shouting. I followed the loud cries along the corridor and into the turret past the main stairs until I was almost at the point where the Manettis' wing started. There, in a wood-panelled snug area on the far side of the staircase, I stumbled upon Nora, sitting with her doll in an embroidered armchair with fine lace antimacassars across the arms and back.

'Mummy's making her bedroom sounds,' she said matter-of-factly.

'Stop! No, don't stop!' Evelyn screamed.

I turned quickly away, my face blazing. 'Come with me, Nora.'

As I half hauled the poor girl down the stairs, my thoughts were hot and churning. I thought of Roberto's broad shoulders, Evelyn's fragile beauty. His fingers stroking her hip and the underside of her breast. Out in the courtyard garden, still clutching Nora, a white-hot spike of longing skewered me and I stood rooted to the spot. Only when a little voice said, 'Ow, you're hurting my fingers,' did I realize how tightly I was squeezing Nora's hand.

'You weren't here,' said William, when I saw him later that afternoon.

'Yes, Mrs Manetti said—'

'Mrs Manetti is not in charge of this house.'

I bit my lip, waiting for the indignation to pass and reminding myself that William was unwell, that allowances must be made. But still . . . the *rudeness* of the man.

Outrage brought out the competitive streak I'd largely learned to bury over the years. I moved my chess pieces around the board with unnecessary force and focused all my attention on plotting out in my head the repercussions of all the various moves open to me, searching for a strategy that would take him by surprise. Already I was forming an idea of the kind of player William was, his favourite gambits, his weak spots. He was impatient, preferring attack to anticipation.

He did not like to lose.

'This damn medicine Pearson has me on. Makes my mind slow.'

I said nothing.

'Doesn't help I can hardly see straight.'

Still I said nothing.

'I am an excellent chess player.'

Nothing. Even the checkmate was silent.

'No. Really. I must insist we play again.'

'If you're quite sure. Your vision . . . the medication . . . I wouldn't like to take advantage of you.'

I could feel William's keen blue eyes on me and stifled a smile.

We hadn't played long, though William was already down two pawns to my one, when there came the clanging of the front-door bell, followed by a low hum of voices. A few moments later, Evelyn fluttered into the room.

'Uncle Bill, there are some gentlemen here from Cambridge who insist you invited them to view your private collection. I told them that was quite impossible, as you're notoriously mean about your precious art, but they wouldn't have it.'

Two men followed her into the room, both wearing suits without waistcoats and similar eager expressions. They were so sorry to hear of Mr North's illness, and trusted he was getting better. He did remember, they hoped, meeting them at his gallery in London and issuing the invitation if they were ever in Florence . . .?

'We did write to remind you, sir,' said the younger, who had a high, domed forehead and fair hair that was already thinning, although he couldn't have been much past thirty, and who kept one eye nervously on the great dog, who had moved closer to his master and was sitting with his nose twitching in the air, growling softly.

I knew enough of William North's nature to assume he would give the men short shrift, regardless of whether the original invitation had been issued or not. He was not a man to welcome sightseers into his home, particularly when he himself was in this weakened state. So I was surprised to hear him say:

'My niece will show you around. Maybe you'd like to see the castle as well?'

The men struggled to understand his thickened voice, and I realized how quickly I'd grown used to it, so that it no longer sounded strange to me.

Evelyn whistled.

'Well, aren't *you* the honoured guests?' she said, mock bowing to the visitors, who appeared quite as dazzled by her as by the surroundings in which they found themselves.

After the three of them had left, Evelyn waggling her eyebrows comically as she followed them through the door, William lapsed into a dense, brooding silence, making two unforced errors in a row, after which he flung himself backwards in his chair.

'Do you have children, Mrs Bowen?'

It was the first personal question he'd asked me, and I felt heat in my cheeks, as if he'd said something improper.

'My daughter died five years ago, and I have a son who is twenty-six years old.'

'A son. You are lucky. Things are more straightforward with a son. Evelyn . . . isn't always easy.'

'But surely now she has Roberto . . .?'

William made a dismissive noise, blowing air through closed lips.

'The boy is a fool. Have you seen his photographs? Hanging there on the wall as if they are art!'

I remembered the two ostentatiously framed photographs so out of place with the rest of William's collection.

'Surely that is just the confidence of youth. I remember once, when Millie was young, taking her to see the Summer Exhibition at the Royal Academy and her coming straight home and doing a drawing and insisting we go back there to hang it with the others.'

'Roberto is not a child. He is a grown man. A grown *fascist* man.'

'I expect you miss Rupert terribly.'

I meant only to steer the conversation away from Roberto, but as soon as I'd said it I knew it was a mistake. William had opened the door of intimacy just a crack and I'd taken it as an invitation to barge right in. *Why must you be so impulsive, Constance?* Walter used to say.

William North indicated the chessboard. 'Enough now,' he said, leaning back in his chair and closing his eyes.

For the next twenty minutes I read the newspaper, until we were interrupted by Evelyn's laughter, closely followed by her head appearing around the door.

'Tour is over, and our visitors have come to say goodbye.'

'It's a magnificent collection, sir,' said the older of the pair, a sandy-haired man with sandy eyebrows and so many freckles that they formed one large nebulous brown shape across the bridge of his nose. 'That Raphael . . . words fail me.'

'We'll be in touch, sir,' the younger one said as they left, but while he addressed his words to William, it was Evelyn to whom his gaze kept returning.

After Evelyn returned from seeing them out, she put her hands on her hips and stared at William thoughtfully.

'Well, Uncle Bill, I swear you've gone soft in your old age. Inviting randoms to come and traipse all over the castle, pawing your precious things. One of them even brought a notebook so he wouldn't forget anything.'

'They're not *randoms*,' said William. 'They're art historians from Cambridge University. My alma mater,' he added for my benefit.

'I still say it's out of character. If it wasn't for the fact that you met them in London before you became ill, I'd say that brain haemorrhage of yours had turned you soft in the head!'

That night I was awoken by the terrible sound of an animal screaming. I rushed to the window, but when I flung open the shutters I realized the cries were coming from inside the castle rather than out.

Lighting the oil lamp that sat on my bedside table, I hurried along the corridor, holding my shawl closed with one hand. The noise was like someone scraping a fork along my nerves.

In the turret I paused near the section of the upper landing that had been turned into a reading area, where Nora had been sitting earlier in the afternoon. The screaming was coming through the tall doorway where the Manettis' wing started.

I pushed the towering wooden door and it opened with a creak.

'Hello?' I called tentatively, but my voice was lost in the cacophony.

The Manettis' wing was a mirror image of the one in which my own bedroom was housed. Turning the corner into the main corridor, I followed the sound of the screams. Stopping outside a door that was partly ajar, my mouth turned dry and my breath ragged.

I nudged open the door.

Nora lay in bed, her eyes closed, shrieking in her sleep.

Relief flooding through me, I sank weakly on to the bed and put out my hand to wake her.

Her eyes flew open and she stared at me with horror.

'Nora, you're having—'

'No. Get away.' She scrabbled to the end of the bed, where she crouched, shaking. 'You're evil. Wicked. Wicked. Wicked.'

'Nora!'

I was rattled to my very bones. What did she imagine she could see? And where was her mother? Surely Evelyn and Roberto couldn't be sleeping through this?

I tried again, shifting along the mattress to put my arm firmly around her.

'It's all right, lovey. You're quite safe.'

The screams didn't stop instantly, but as I held her by the shoulders they became quieter and further apart.

Evelyn burst in, looking dazed and flustered, pulling a silk kimono around her.

'Oh, Constance, I'm so sorry she woke you. What must you think of me, sleeping through. I was dead to the world.' She sat on the bed next to me and stroked her daughter's trembling arm. 'She has these episodes, I'm afraid. Night terrors, the doctor calls them. Don't you, sweetheart?'

Nora, who had quietened right down and seemed finally to be properly awake, nodded in the crook of my arm.

'I do wonder,' Evelyn went on, 'if she might have inherited them from her father.'

She reached up to smooth down her hair and I bit back an exclamation as her sleeve fell back, revealing an angry red welt that circled her wrist like a cuff.

10

Dr Pearson, whom I met the following day, revealed himself to be resolutely English, right down to the sheen on his pink forehead, which he mopped with a large handkerchief he kept in the top pocket of his stiff dark jacket.

He seemed under the impression I was a trained nurse and launched straight into explaining the complicated system of bodily manipulation I was to learn in order to maintain William's circulation and nerve function. When his meaning became clear, the blood rushed to my chest and throat and I found myself suddenly unable to swallow.

'You want me to . . . massage . . . Mr North?'

'Quite so. Each of the limbs in turn. It's very important in maintaining good circulation and nerve function. But then I'm sure I don't have to tell *you* that.'

'The thing is, I'm not really a nurse.'

'Evelyn couldn't get anyone medically trained,' said William. 'Mrs Bowen here is the best she could do.'

'She advertised for a companion. Not a nurse.' I could hear the outrage quivering in my voice. William laughed.

'She did. But only after the nursing advertisement yielded no takers.'

I was shocked into silence. I had thought I was the best candidate, and now it seemed I was quite possibly the *only* candidate.

Dr Pearson was keen to demonstrate what I had to do. He helped William to the faded olive-green velvet chaise that ran along one side of the room and seized him around the calf, bending his leg at the knee in this direction and that.

'Like this . . . Do you see? Now you do it.'

I took up position next to the black-coated doctor. William lay back on the chaise, so close our breaths mingled in the warm air between us, studying me and my discomfort. I saw a smile flicker around his mouth.

'Grasp his leg, Mrs Bowen. That's right, firm grip. He won't break.'

Under my fingers, William was all flesh and sinew and bone and blood and heat.

'Bring his knee into your chest.'

My cheeks flamed. Even fully clothed as we were, with the doctor looking on, there was something so intimate about what we were doing. That I could sense William's amusement only intensified my awkwardness.

'It's a good thing you're a sturdy sort,' Dr Pearson told me approvingly. 'Not some delicate slip of a thing.'

Now that I'd learned the correct manoeuvre, I was to repeat it daily. And the same on his arm, and I had to give his neck 'a good kneading'. Also I was given a glass bottle containing a tincture Dr Pearson described as a 'pick-me-up', and another containing something to help him sleep. Dr Pearson was at pains to instruct me to keep the two well apart – as if I were a child!

'Can't you do anything about my blasted eyes?' William complained, sitting up on the chaise and rubbing the back of his neck, where the doctor had been particularly vigorous. 'I still can't read a thing. The woman has to do it.'

The woman. Every now and again William North's rudeness took my breath away.

'Patience, William. You've been damned lucky so far. I've a patient in town, nice chap, had the same as you, cerebral haemorrhage. Now he's had the works – pneumonia, then a second apoplectic attack. We've had to resort to bloodletting. Don't look like that, Mrs Bowen. I know it's out of fashion in certain circles, but when there's been a bleed it's imperative to try to reduce the volume of blood.'

An image came to me then of a different doctor, standing with Walter over Millie's bedside. Leeches. *Please don't let him, Mama.*

The memory lodged in my throat sharp as a fish bone.

Dr Pearson's visit seemed to tire William out. Though he usually hated to show any sign of weakness, he asked Massimo to help him upstairs to rest. Wanting to give Evelyn and Roberto privacy, I sat outside on the front steps of the castle, reading with Nora from a copy of *Huckleberry Finn* I'd found in the library, not realizing until Alina told me that its author, Mark Twain, had been a regular visitor to this very region and had even lived for a short while in one of the neighbouring villas.

Nora was a clever little thing, absorbing the book like a sponge, but it was stories about my own children she was most interested in, begging me for anecdotes, which I happily dredged up – the time Millie stuck a bead up her nose or James cut off his own hair – as if they were friends she couldn't hear enough about.

'Did you brush Millie's hair out every night before bed?' she asked me now.

'I certainly did, though she wasn't always very happy about it.'

Nora ran her fingers through her own lanky brown locks.

'Mummy says she doesn't need to brush mine because it is already so straight and fine.' Then her fingers crept to her nose.

'Do you think I might have more friends if my nose was straight?'

'Nora, dear, appearances don't matter, it's what's inside that counts.' But Nora was no fool. I could tell that, despite her years, she'd already worked out that, for women, looks were the only universally recognized currency.

Luckily, I was spared more awkward conversation by the sudden appearance at the gates of an unexpected visitor.

'My name's Jerome Fielding. I was here yesterday evening viewing Mr North's collection?'

'Of course.' I jumped up, brushing the dust from the back of my dress as the younger of the two Cambridge University art historians smiled and tried not to look as if he were shooting eager glances over my shoulder in the hope Evelyn Manetti might manifest there.

'I've come to drop off a letter for Mr North. I could have posted it, of course, but it's such a beautiful afternoon and the Fiesole tram just happened to be passing down below . . .'

When I told him William was resting he couldn't hide his disappointment at not having an excuse to linger.

'I'll make sure he gets it,' I said as he turned away.

I was hurrying to put the letter in William's sitting room, ready for when he came down, when I bumped into Evelyn, coming inside from the courtyard garden.

'I thought I heard voices. What's that in your hand, Connie? Please say I can call you that. I can't stand all this formality.'

When I told her about Jerome Fielding's visit, she grew thoughtful. 'The plot thickens,' she said, snatching the letter and waggling it next to her ear as if she could listen to its contents.

'I'll take this to Uncle Bill.'

'But I'm on my way—'

'I'm heading upstairs, so I'll take it directly to him in his room. And Connie, guess what? I almost forgot, you're invited to the de Havillands' for a garden party on Saturday. They have a villa about twenty minutes' drive from here. Uncle Bill will be making his grand re-entry into society, and you're to be on hand to catch him if he falls – I don't mean literally, of course. Won't that be fun?'

11

LORD AND LADY de Havilland lived in the unimaginatively named Villa de Havilland on a hillside to the east of the city surrounded by a private park planted with cypress trees, pines and ancient cedars and with what was reported to be the finest view of Florence from the first-floor loggia that ran the width of the facade.

As we drew up in Roberto Manetti's shiny green car with the cream leather seats, I felt a tug of apprehension. Evelyn had assured me the whole of Florentine Anglo-Italian-American society would be here. Aristocrats, politicians, actors, artists, poets. What would I find to say to them? I was also worried about William. Although his recovery had continued apace – to the point where I was sure my days in Tuscany must be numbered – he still struggled with his left side, and his speech, while a hundred times clearer than when I arrived, was still not what he would call wireless standard. He was such a proud man. That's why he'd forbidden well-wishers to visit the castle – with the exception of the two men from Cambridge. He was already seething about not being allowed to bring Solomon to the party. 'Alice expressly said, "Don't let your uncle bring that brute of a dog in case it eats the guests,"' Evelyn had told him gleefully.

Evelyn herself was in high spirits, chattering non-stop. 'Watch out that the Black Widow doesn't get her fangs into you,' she admonished her uncle, twisting in her seat to give him a stern look.

For a horrible moment I thought she might be talking about me. Then she laughed at my expression. 'I'm only teasing, Connie. Louise Power is perfectly civilized, but she has seen off three husbands and everyone knows she has her heart set on making Uncle Bill number four.'

In the silence after the car engine had been switched off, I caught William's eye and for once I saw there an uncertainty, as if he were asking me not to let him fail, and something pressed on my heart. Then there was a commotion as a young woman came shrieking to the door dressed like a nymph in a flowing white sheet with a garland of leaves around her aggressively shingled head, whereupon Evelyn, wearing a green dress that shimmered in the light like a dragonfly's wing, leapt from the passenger seat.

'Alice! Oh my, you look a picture. I mean, a literal picture. Like one of Uncle Bill's old oil paintings.'

The nymph did a twirl before grabbing Evelyn's hand and pulling her in the direction of the lawn in the front of the villa, where there was a large canvas tent and from where floated up the sound of an orchestra playing the Gershwin brothers' 'The Man I Love', which reminded me of James, who had played that record over and over a few years before – much to Walter's frustration – nearly wearing out the gramophone.

'Mummy, wait!' Nora all but fell out of the back of the

car in her haste to catch up with her mother, but gave up, trailing disconsolately behind. She was wearing a new peacock-blue velvet dress Evelyn had brought home from Florence the previous day, producing it from its tissue paper with a flourish and insisting Nora try it on there and then. Nora had been so thrilled, and I hoped she hadn't seen how her mother's face had fallen when she saw how it hung from Nora's skinny frame.

Roberto, who had brought his camera with him, carrying it on a leather strap over his shoulder, turned to us.

'I'll help you, Uncle Bill,' he said, practically lifting William off his feet. I saw William's face darken.

'Please don't worry yourself, Mr Manetti,' I said. 'Mr North and I can manage perfectly well.'

So Roberto went on ahead to join Nora, the two of them walking in awkward silence. I felt sorry for them both. Though I'd never seen Roberto be anything other than charming, there was a certain wariness in his dealings with his stepdaughter. Many men struggled around children, I'd found.

The original owner of Villa de Havilland, Gordon de Havilland, was a prominent Whig politician who had retired to Italy after falling in love with both the country itself and an Italian maid. He'd bought the villa and installed his mistress as housekeeper while his wife consoled herself by adopting breeches and cropping her hair and writing apparently execrable verse under the pseudonym of George Havers.

Successive generations of de Havillands had, it seemed, kept up the family flair for unconventionality, the current Lady de Havilland not long home from a lecture tour around

Europe in which she'd extolled the health benefits of heroin and opium and called for their immediate declassification.

'My dear North,' said the current Lord de Havilland, hurrying to shake William's hand the moment we appeared on the lawn. He was a lugubrious-looking man with a long, drooping moustache and matching drooping eyes underscored with livid pink bloodshot crescents.

'This is a wretched affair,' he said, with an expansive gesture that encompassed the beautifully dressed people in their silks and chiffons, the sun playing across the tended gardens, the soft saxophone from the jazz quintet set up on a makeshift stage, the clink of champagne glasses, the smell of roses from the tangle of bushes along one side of the lawn. 'I have been quite envious of you, North, having an excuse to stay home rather than be dragged out to this sort of thing.'

'Apoplexy is an extreme way of escaping a social engagement.'

'What's that? Oh, yes. I see. Quite so. Nevertheless. It's a rotten business having guests crawling all over the place. I've had to lock up my girls for their own safety.'

Lord de Havilland partially withdrew a large iron key from his pocket and showed it slyly to William.

'Who on earth are his girls?' I asked William after the host had sloped off.

'The man collects snuff boxes, thousands of them, which he keeps in the largest room in the house, in damn great glass cabinets that no one else is allowed to look at. Treats them like his babies.'

Now that William had got over his reticence about being out in public again in his diminished state, he seemed almost to be enjoying himself. From Evelyn, I'd learned that, prior to his illness, he had treated social occasions as business opportunities, always alert for new people who, with a single unguarded comment, might set him on the trail of a new find. Then he'd be on the move, dashing around Italy following up reports of newly discovered masters unearthed from dusty attics or country churches, then exhibiting them in his gallery in London to allow interest to build among collectors before hauling them off to New York, where the nouveau riche still regarded old European art as a shortcut to culture and sophistication. Watching him now, I could see how his eyes scanned the crowd, feel the energy pulsing under his skin.

'Watch out, Connie,' whispered Evelyn, who had come up behind us. 'Uncle Bill is one of the most eligible men in Tuscany. The matrons and their unmarried daughters will trample over any woman who comes too close. Even you.'

The *even you* stung.

A chair was fetched, and though William insisted he didn't need it, he sat down, and I thought I detected some relief. Instantly, a crowd formed around him. A woman swooped upon him out of nowhere, beautiful, with glossy black hair in a knot at her nape and creamy skin cushioning her high cheekbones. I had no doubt she was the much-married Mrs Power. 'My dear William,' she said, grasping his hand in hers. 'How we've missed you.' Now the circle of onlookers closed around him, edging me out. I caught William's eye just before my view was obscured entirely by the large-brimmed hat of a woman who had elbowed me aside. He raised his eyebrow at me conspiratorially.

But now I was alone and self-conscious in my tweed skirt and short-sleeved blouse. All around were women dressed in silks and linens and gossamer-fine jersey, some with scalloped hems barely skimming the knees. There were long strings of pearls that swung at narrow waists and silk scarves looped around slender necks. There were a few exaggerated wide-brimmed hats such as the one that had cut off my view of William North, and some sleek cloches resting on hair cut daringly short, but most of the women were bareheaded, their bobbed hair glistening in the sunshine, or else wrapped around with a headband, some embellished with beads or feathers.

A shout went up and the crowd turned towards the house, where there was some activity in the first-floor loggia – the covered terrace with the arched sides and high, vaulted ceiling that ran the length of the facade.

Now the nymph who had greeted Evelyn on our arrival appeared in one of the arches, which were supported on either side by monumental marble pillars. She produced a megaphone of the sort found at racetracks and sporting events and to my surprise began declaiming in Latin. Suddenly in one of the other arches there popped up another nymph, similarly attired and carrying a megaphone through which I was taken aback to hear a very definitely masculine voice booming out. I looked more carefully. This nymph had longer hair than the first and a willowy physique. How peculiar to hear this great, manly voice emerging.

I surmised that these were the two younger de Havillands, Alice and her twin, Edward, who were known, Evelyn informed me, for arranging decadent parties for their wealthy friends, at which they performed lavish amateur productions of experimental works written by their older brother, Harold, featuring themselves in the title roles.

The two now began intoning in English. There was a whole list of Greek gods, and lots of references to intemperate weather – storms and winds – at which the two nymphs swayed this way and that, as if at the mercy of gales blowing simultaneously in entirely opposite directions. Then a mighty rain came and – yes – a great quantity of water was thrown by unseen hands, causing the first nymph, Alice, to shriek. Finally, the villain appeared with a thundering megaphone accompaniment and an alarming explosion of something that released a black plume of smoke into the air and had the two nymphs coughing behind their hands.

I began to wonder how long the entertainment would last, and I wasn't the only one. All around me people were murmuring or trying to catch each other's attention. I looked around for William but could not see through the throng of people surrounding me.

Instead, I decided to go in search of Nora. Though she was happy to be included in the day's outing, I knew she was nervous about the other children. Harold de Havilland had two daughters, one slightly older than Nora and one younger, who were thick as thieves with the children of the Wheelers, the couple I'd met at dinner shortly after I arrived, and from what I could gather there was an uneasy history between them all.

The children did not appear to be anywhere on the lawn. I spotted Emily Wheeler, tall and commanding in a green column dress that showed off the gold-and-ruby necklace she'd been wearing at our first meeting, and a green band around her hair. She was holding a jade cigarette holder and turned on me an expression of the utmost blankness when I asked if she knew where the children were. I was mortified to realize she had no recollection of ever having met me.

'Mrs Bowen. Of course,' she said in that deep voice after I'd reintroduced myself, before suggesting I look for the children in the maze, which was in the villa's internal court-yard. 'Only don't, whatever you do, encourage them to return here. I see quite enough of them at home.'

At the grand entrance to the villa, I hesitated. It was one thing standing in the garden, but another entering the house itself. But I could see other guests inside and glass doors open on the far side of the hallway, which must lead to the courtyard garden.

I intended to hurry straight through, but inside the hall-way I stopped in my tracks, staring around me. Every inch of the soaring space with its grand, dividing staircase was covered in a fresco depicting . . . well, what exactly? Night-marish mythological creatures, half animal, half human, many of them doing things that would fall foul of public decency laws. Monstrous foliage that grew up the walls and spread across the ceiling, vying there for space amid men-acing clouds, and a flock of giant birds, one carrying a child in its beak. The scale of the endeavour was sadly not matched by the talent of the artist. Figures looked either squashed or elongated, with no sense of perspective or realism. Trees were depicted in detail at one end, and then finished off broadly at the other, as if the painter had lost interest half-way through. It was truly one of the least aesthetically pleasing rooms I had ever been in.

'It's quite a sight, isn't it?' Philip Wheeler had come up behind me and was standing at my elbow. After his wife's reaction – or lack of – I was surprised he recognized me. Dressed in a dark green suit in which he was gently perspir-ing, with his round, pink, shiny face, he resembled an overgrown goblin. 'The de Havilland children's handiwork. Harold was about to go off fighting in France and convinced his parents to give him full artistic rein, telling them it might be the last request he ever made of them, then he invited everyone he knew to come and have a go. It turned into a veritable painting *orgy*.'

Philip Wheeler was standing so close to me I could feel the damp heat coming off him, and I shifted away. There was something about the man. The way his skin stretched smooth and shiny over his plump cheeks like the membrane of an egg. The small, flat eyes.

'I'm actually looking for Nora,' I said, and when he looked none the wiser I elaborated. 'Evelyn Manetti's daughter.'

He wrinkled his puggish nose. 'Such a peculiar little creature. But then all children are peculiar in their own ways, aren't they? No structure to them. No discipline. They could learn a lot from the ant kingdom, actually. How to set aside the id. Not always to be thinking of their own gratification.'

A globule of his saliva flew from his mouth as he spoke and lodged on my cheek, and it was all I could do to refrain from rubbing it away.

'All the children are in the courtyard, I think. There was an organized treasure hunt, but I think they abandoned that and have gone feral in the maze.'

I started to move off in the direction of the courtyard when Philip Wheeler put one of his surprisingly small hands on my arm to detain me. His palm felt clammy on my skin. 'A word of advice, my dear Mrs Bowen. Watch yourself around that family.'

'I beg your pardon.'

Philip Wheeler seemed to take this as an invitation to

step closer, so he was all but pressing up against me, his breath hot and yeasty with alcohol.

'They're a ruthless lot. William North married for money so he could launch his own career, his glittering *collection*. And Evelyn Chisholm – pardon, Evelyn *Manetti* – is as bad. Has she told you what happened to the governess?'

'The governess? No. What—'

Philip Wheeler's lips were inches from my face, and I took a very obvious step back. He smiled and held up his dainty hands. 'A story for another time, perhaps.'

My thoughts, as I hurried out through the open glass door to the courtyard, were not kind. I'd come across men like Philip Wheeler before. Bitterness oozing through their pores. He was clearly jealous of William, and I guessed he'd either tried to press his suit to Evelyn and been rebuffed or, more likely, had lacked the courage, desire fermenting into resentment.

I felt sorry for Evelyn. Being beautiful could be as much a curse as a blessing. I wondered what he'd meant about the governess. It had always struck me as odd that Evelyn, who always seemed looking for ways to minimize time spent with her daughter, had not done more to find a replacement for the governess who'd left her post some months before my arrival. I resolved to question Nora.

But when I reached the courtyard I saw no sign of the girl, or of the other children she had been so nervous about meeting, though there was a couple stealing some privacy under a pergola of grape vines and three older women admiring a small garden of cacti in a walled-off area on the far side. I hadn't been there long, however, before I heard a loud shriek coming from the formal box hedge maze in the centre of the courtyard. At first I thought it a shriek of pleasure, particularly when it was followed by a volley of loud, childish laughter. I was glad to think of Nora playing with children her own age for a change and resolved not to intrude. But as I turned to retrace my steps, a boy of about twelve with a defiant shock of white-blond hair dashed out of the exit of the maze, followed by a gaggle of others, boys and girls of different ages, all giggling. I waited to see Nora, already smiling in anticipation, but she didn't emerge from between the hedges. The other children started moving off as a pack.

'Wait!' I called after them. 'Is Nora with you? Nora Manetti?'

The boy who'd come out first exchanged glances with some of the other children and shook his head before bursting out in fresh giggles and running off in the other direction, closely followed by the rest of the pack.

For a moment after they'd gone I stood dithering next to a statue of a naked Greek god. From the twisted vine pergola came the low hum of voices, as the couple I'd noticed earlier conducted an urgent whispered conversation, and for the first time since arriving in Italy I had a keen sense of my own friendless position. I was William North's paid companion, and Evelyn and Roberto's employee. That was all.

The couple emerged from the pergola and headed towards me. The woman – practically a girl, really – was pretty in that way all women are in that fleeting golden moment when the velvet softness of childhood tips into the long-limbed suppleness of adulthood, before the hard edges set in. The man was Roberto Manetti.

'Ah, Mrs Bowen, here you are,' he said, as if he'd been

looking for me, instead of lingering under a canopy of budding green grapes with a woman who was not his wife.

'This is Olivia Averell. She's from New York.'

A stiff smile flickered across Miss Averell's flushed face.

'Roberto brought me out here to see the golden pheasants,' she said in a voice as thin as her accent was broad. 'Only we haven't managed to find one yet.'

After the two had gone back in the house I stayed where I was, feeling disconcerted, though there had been nothing improper about Roberto's behaviour. He was merely being his usual affable self, I told myself.

So preoccupied was I that I didn't at first register the sound that came to me, and when I did I thought it must be a bird, perhaps even the famous golden pheasant that Roberto and Olivia Averell had been seeking. Only after I heard it a second time did it occur to me that it was someone calling. No, not calling, someone crying.

'Help!' It was a pitiful sound, coming from the depths of the high-hedged maze, shrill and tremulous.

'Nora? Is that you?' I was already rushing towards the entrance from which the children had emerged some time earlier. 'Nora, keep talking so I can find where you are.'

But she was crying too hard to speak, the sobs seeming to rebound off the hedges so that the sound was coming from all directions at once.

I plunged down endless narrow passageways and around corners that came to an abrupt dead end. At one such place I found a heap of plush blue fabric on the floor, and even before I'd picked it up I knew it to be the new velvet dress. It had a rip near the shoulder.

'Where are you, Nora?'

'Here.' It was an explosion of sound, reverberating off all the tiny leaves that surrounded me. By now I was panting, as I tried this avenue then doubled back to try another. I came to a junction where two passageways met and saw something there, stuffed into the hedge. I pulled it out and Nora's ugly doll blinked up at me with its blind eye.

'Hurry, please.'

Her voice was near now, and I could hear the little snuffling sobs that punctuated her words. Finally, I rounded a corner and burst into a little clearing at the centre. And, *oh*, there was Nora, huddled in her underclothes, her head buried in her knees so the little nobbles of her bowed spine pushed through the skin like teeth in a baby's gums.

I hurried over and crouched down, putting my arm around her narrow, ridged back.

'Don't fret now, dear. See, I have your lovely dress, and your darling Matilda.'

Nora took the doll from me with a trembling hand and held it against her concave chest while I shook out the velvet dress and brushed off the twigs and leaves that had stuck themselves to it.

'There now. It's not so bad. Only this small tear at the shoulder. That's easily fixed.'

'Mummy will be cross.'

'Not if she knows it wasn't your fault.'

I helped her into the dress, trying not to look at where her bony little shoulder showed white through the rip. Only then did I ask her what had happened.

'At first they were nice to me and asked if I wanted to play a game, and I was so happy. I thought they were trying to be my friends. But then they led me to here and then they weren't nice any more. Why don't they like me? I haven't done anything to them.'

I gave her an awkward hug then, because I couldn't tell her that people are afraid of anything that is different or strange, and Nora, with her crooked nose and her clever watchfulness and her lack of practice in social niceties, was both of those things to them. I couldn't tell her that most children are innately cruel and will seize upon any sign of weakness. Anger rippled through me. Philip Wheeler was right. Insects were far better behaved.

Nora stood stiffly in my embrace, and I tried to comfort her.

'When my daughter, Millicent, was little and someone was mean to her, I used to tell her to imagine how things will be when she's all grown up with a family of her own, surrounded by people who love her, living in her own home, which she keeps just the way she likes it, with her own friends around her and her days free to paint to her heart's content – painting was her passion. These childhood bullies wouldn't even cross her mind, I told her. She wouldn't remember their names or anything about them because her life would be too full of the things that were truly important.

'Sadly, Millie didn't get to be grown up, but she would have done all those things if she had, and you will too, Nora. And believe me, those children today will look at your lovely life and they'll wish they'd been nicer to you.'

Nora turned her pink, blotchy face up to look at me, and I smiled, and hoped with all my heart that some of what I'd said might come true.

We made our way out of the maze. Astonishing how simple it turned out to be when one wasn't in a blind panic.

Really quite a rudimentary layout of hedge-lined passage-ways. As we emerged on to the sun-dappled courtyard there came a commotion by the door to the villa.

'Connie. Is that you? Oh, thank God, you must come quickly.'

Before Evelyn had stopped speaking I was rushing towards her. *William.*

'I don't know what happened. He seemed perfectly fine and then, the next thing, he was on the floor.'

Her voice ran on like a brook as we dashed through that awful ruined hallway and out across the lawn towards the canvas gazebo. An excited knot of people had gathered around something in the middle of the space and, as they stood back reluctantly to let us through, I saw William North, looking pale and bloodless but straight-backed on his chair, his eyes sweeping around the room. When they came to rest on me, there flickered a look of something – relief? Gratitude? – gone before I could work it out.

Evelyn flitted around uselessly, fretting that she couldn't find Roberto anywhere, while Louise Power stood behind William with her hands proprietorially gripping his shoulders and conferring with a thickset woman wearing what seemed to be a large hessian sack, belted in the middle.

'What this man needs is a good strong shot of diamorphine, and he'll be right as rain,' said the stocky woman, who I realized must be Lady de Havilland. 'Marvellous stuff. Completely misunderstood.'

'Not heroin again,' said Louise Power, rolling her eyes. 'You are such a bore about it, Alexandra.'

'Get me away from here,' William hissed at me, under his breath.

Some of the men stepped forward to assist, but I insisted I could manage. I could feel William's humiliation burning through his linen shirt. At least with me there he could project the illusion that we were a couple strolling arm in arm, even if I was in fact propping him up. Not for the first time in my life I was glad of my size and the strength it afforded me.

'I don't understand,' he croaked as we made it to the car. 'I've been feeling so much better.'

'You just overdid it, that's all. It's your body's way of telling you to take things slowly.'

Roberto and Evelyn were quiet on the way home, and I got the feeling they were upset to be torn away from the party, though they were too polite to say so. Nora, her ripped dress overlooked in all the drama, lay back with her eyes shut and her evil-looking doll clutched to her chest. Meanwhile, I sat looking out of the window at the wooded hillside that dropped down to a narrow green ribbon of river and, while my rational thoughts were occupied with William's unexpected relapse, one side of my body burned with the imprint of his.

12

A T BREAKFAST MY head felt thick, as if wadded with cotton wool, and my thoughts were strangely disordered.

'Uh-oh. *Someone* had too much champagne,' said Evelyn, eyeing me over the top of her coffee cup.

'Did you send for Dr Pearson?' I asked her, to change the subject.

'You are an old fusspot, Connie. Do you really think it's necessary? I mean, Uncle Bill had already perked right up by the time we got home and, knowing him, he'll just want to forget all about it.'

'Even so. Mr North had been doing so well up until the party. Don't you think it might be an idea to get him checked over?'

Evelyn remained unconvinced but agreed to make the call.

'It's a lot of nonsense,' William muttered when the physician came edging into the room, one eye on Solomon, who was emitting a low, sustained growl. 'I'm fit as a fiddle.'

Was it my imagination, or did his speech sound more slurred than in previous days?

Dr Pearson declared it was merely a case of over-reaching

himself. 'Your progress has been spectacular thus far, but a cerebral haemorrhage is not to be treated lightly. Respect your own limitations. You're no longer a young man.'

I turned my face away to hide the smile twitching at the corners of my mouth. I could guess how little William would welcome being reminded of his own mortality.

'Perhaps another trip to the baths might be in order,' said the physician. Turning to me, he explained: 'We have an excellent thermal spa up in the mountains at Bagni di Lucca.'

'I haven't got time to wallow around in puddles like a damn elephant,' muttered William.

Evelyn was feeling vindicated when I joined her for tea in the courtyard later that afternoon. 'I knew it would turn out to be nothing more than overdoing things. Uncle Bill will never admit defeat. He is the most stubborn of men.'

It was a beautiful early May afternoon and orange blossom scented the air as we sat at a round wrought-iron table draped with an oil cloth positioned underneath a spreading oleander tree, its leaves studded with pink buds. The sun was warm rather than hot and all around was evidence of life and industry – a gentle buzzing coming from the mass of tangled roses that grew wild over the stone walls, the far-off shouts of the women picking asparagus on a nearby hillside. Every now and then we heard snatches of Renata, the cook, singing to herself through the open back door.

I closed my eyes and let it all wash over me, realizing with a faint feeling of surprise that this was the nearest to a state of complete contentment I'd experienced since Millie's death all those years before.

I had brought my leather writing case outside with me and was composing another letter to James describing the scene. Since that first lengthy letter, I'd sent several more, the words pouring out of me, wanting to paint a picture of my life here – for him or for myself, I couldn't have said. I told him about the orchids in the glasshouse and about the pond in a corner of the courtyard garden in which huge golden fish with double tails made lazy shapes through the water.

Nora came creeping up, doll tucked under her twig-like arm, and sat herself down hopefully next to her mother. I saw Evelyn's nostrils flare silently. An internal sigh. She put an arm around her daughter and ran through a list of questions about her day and the games she'd invented to play with Matilda, and how she was getting on with the book of French verbs she'd left her to read, but I could see she was running out of steam. It upset me to see the gulf between mother and child. Whatever had gone wrong between Evelyn and her first husband, Nora couldn't help looking like her father.

'Why don't you fetch your sketchbook and draw some of the flowers?' I suggested to Nora. 'Then I'll help you label them and later we can press them.'

'Did Millie used to do that?'

When I said yes, she'd enjoyed it very much, Nora ran off happily to the schoolroom in search of her art supplies.

'Nora is such a dear girl,' I said when she was out of earshot. 'When will you get a new governess for her?'

Evelyn picked up a magazine which had been lying face down on the table and began leafing through the pages.

'Soon, I suppose. Only it is such a bothersome process, having to place an advertisement and read all those applications. I've only just recovered from the whole rigmarole of hiring you, Connie. I'm not sure I am quite up to another undertaking quite so soon.'

From my end, the whole enterprise of being employed by Evelyn had been so quick and seamless, almost worryingly so, that I was surprised to hear it had been so taxing from the other, particularly after William had made it clear there were so few applications.

'Besides, Nora's education is not really so important. It's not as if she's a boy.'

Her reply rankled. Remembering the curious thing Philip Wheeler had said the day before, I said, 'What happened to Nora's last governess, if you don't mind me asking?'

Evelyn slammed down her magazine just as Nora appeared, clutching her sketchbook.

'Actually, I *do* mind, Connie. You know, since you arrived, I've tried my very best to welcome you and make you feel at home, but I won't stand for being made to feel like I don't know what's best for my own daughter.'

She got to her feet and stalked inside, not even looking at Nora as she passed her, and I was left sitting alone at the table, my thoughts reeling from the abrupt end to the conversation and the implication that I'd been meddling.

'Was Mummy cross with you?' Nora was matter-of-fact, as if Evelyn being cross wasn't so unusual.

'No, of course not. It was a tiny misunderstanding, that's all.'

Even so, tears burned the backs of my eyes. Alina came out to collect the tea things, and it was on the tip of my tongue to confide in her, but I didn't want Evelyn to overhear and, besides, now I looked at her closely I could see that Alina appeared wan and strained and far from her usual lively self.

Later, I was sitting with William. I'd just read for an hour

111

or so from a fat volume called *Italian Renaissance Painters: A Definitive Guide*, written by a man called George Blandford, a rival art dealer who lived on the other side of Florence. Every paragraph was punctuated by explosions of derision from William and interrupted occasionally for him to explain exactly why everything I'd just read was entirely wrong. By the end I worried he was getting so riled up he would bring on another bleed on the brain so I insisted we stop for tea, after which he nodded off and I practically did the same.

The doorbell sounded, startling me awake, closely followed by a soft knock on the door.

When I stepped out into the corridor, Alina was standing there with Louise Power, the Black Widow, as Evelyn had called her the previous day. The older woman was strikingly dressed in a fitted coral-coloured gown, her long black hair gathered once again at the nape of her neck. The fact that she hadn't cut it short, as so many stylish women had done, indicated a confidence in her looks, as if she knew exactly what suited her. When she saw it was me and not William, her smile slipped down her face like a shop shutter.

'I come bearing gifts from my own vineyard.' She brandished a bottle of wine.

I inched to the right until I was effectively blocking the doorway.

'I'm afraid Mr North is sleeping. He needs to garner his strength after yesterday.'

'Yes, precisely. This is why I am here, to aid his recovery.' She came forward with her arm outstretched, leaving me no choice but to step aside.

'I'll take it from here, Miss—'

'Bowen. Mrs Bowen.'

'Well, Mrs Boland, Mr North and I are old friends so you're leaving him in capable hands. Why don't you go and take a nice walk in the sunshine? I hereby grant you the rest of the day off.'

And then she was inside the room and through the door. I heard William's deep voice, followed by Louise Power's laugh. And then, clear as a bell as I turned to leave, the word 'battleaxe'.

I ran up the stairs with my head bowed.

13

'SLAP ME.'

Evelyn, her blonde head hanging, held out her small, soft hand.

'I insist. I'm insufferable and mean and I deserve to be punished. Hit me as hard as you like, Connie.'

She looked so comical standing there I couldn't help but smile.

'Am I forgiven, then? I'm so pleased. I'm off to the Wheelers' for lunch, and I shouldn't have been able to enjoy one second of it if I thought you were still cross with me.'

'I was never cross with you.'

'Well, you jolly well ought to have been. I'm quite beyond the pale. That's what Daddy always said about me. I don't seem to have that thing that other people are born with that holds you back from doing or saying bad things.'

We were standing at the bottom of the stairs, where our paths had crossed. It was the morning after she'd snapped at me about the governess, and I'd spent a troubled night going over the scene and questioning whether I'd overstepped a line.

'Can I ask you something, Evelyn? Why did the Wheelers fall out with Mr North?'

It was something that had been bothering me as I tried to get the measure of the man I was being paid to take care of.

Evelyn wrinkled her nose. 'A boring business matter. Uncle Bill made tons of enemies, I think, but that's what happens when you get successful, isn't it?'

Over the days since the de Havillands' party, William had shown no signs of a recurrence of whatever malady had overtaken him. However, the rapid progress he'd been making until then seemed to have stalled. He tired more easily than previously. Sometimes I'd look up from the newspaper I'd been reading and catch him nodding off in his chair, his head thrown back. One time, when I'd taken too long deliberating over my next chess move, he fell asleep with his head slumped forward and I was so worried he would fall off his chair that I leapt to my feet to reposition him, only to jump back when he awoke to find his head cradled in my hands.

'Unhand me, woman!' he'd said, and I felt the blood blooming on my chest and neck.

Sometimes I would catch him gazing into the air, as if deep in thought. One such time he interrupted me as I was reading to him from a disturbing novel called *A Passage to India*.

'I am sorry,' he said, and I thought at first I must have misheard him. William North was not the type of man who apologized.

'When you told me about your daughter dying, I should have made some sort of comment.'

'Oh.' I was too taken aback to disagree.

'It made me think of my Rupert, you see.'

'Yes. I quite see. But really, it's I who should apologize for blundering in, asking you about him. My husband – my late husband – always told me I had too little respect for other people's privacy. Only some feelings are too big and burdensome, I think, to keep entirely to oneself, and sometimes it can be a relief to share them.'

For a moment I thought I'd once again gone too far. But then William replied, articulating slowly to make himself understood.

'After Rupert died, if I could, I would have gladly taken out my heart and stamped on it. So that I might feel nothing.'

I was taken by surprise by his remark, which so exactly mirrored my own experience of grief.

'I find it helps to talk to Millie in my head, as if she is still here. I hear her voice clear as a bell.'

'Then you are lucky. I must cut Rupert from my thoughts altogether or I would go mad. My wife, Cecilia, Rupert's mother, died from the loss of him, you know. He was her world.'

Only later did that phrase strike me as peculiar. And I wondered then if William's marriage could have been entirely a happy one if his wife's whole reason for living was wrapped up in their son.

Now that May was underway the weather was growing warmer and I took to getting up early, before anyone else was around, so that I could walk around the castle grounds on my own. I loved that hour just after dawn with the sky's edges still washed pink and the dew beading on the green leaves and in the velvet crevices of the unfurling petals. I loved the sense of the castle easing into life like a wakening beast and the sounds from the valley of the labourers arriving at work. It was as if something had taken seed inside me, a kernel of me that had been buried back in England that was not a wife, not a mother, not a daughter but something else, some essence that existed outside of anyone else and was just mine alone. And with each passing day that seed grew slender tendrils that stretched and reached.

Three days after the garden party I'd finished my early-morning walk and came inside with my thoughts full of the sights and sounds of the Florentine late spring. With ten minutes still remaining before William would be up, I decided to finish the letter I'd begun writing to James the night before, but when I got back to my room I found that my fountain pen, the beautiful Waterman that Millie and James had given me for my fortieth birthday with my name engraved in gold letters along the side, had disappeared. I'd brought my slim, leather-bound writing case with me to Italy, with its individual compartments for envelopes and its pad of thin paper with my English address already imprinted on the top and the leather loop to keep the pen secure. I was sure I'd left it open with the pen lying across the half-written topmost page. I checked the floor underneath the dressing table where I'd been sitting, and under the bed. I even looked out of the window at the flowerbeds beneath in case I'd left it on the sill and it had rolled off. Nothing.

All through the long morning going through correspond-ence with William, tedious communications from accountants and insurers, letters that had to be written again because he'd forgotten something or had second thoughts about how it sounded, I worried about my missing pen. At lunch-time, I hurried back upstairs and found Alina polishing the newel posts on the landing. When she heard about my loss, she insisted on coming with me to my room.

'Is it this one?' she asked, after just a few seconds of searching.

I stared at the pen in her hand.

'Yes. But where—'

'It was right here, between the paper and the case.'

'But I checked . . .'

I stopped, already unsure. I knew I'd looked under the case and riffled through the paper, but had I checked underneath? I thought I had, but my memory was infuriatingly hazy.

'You have it now, Constance, that's what matters.'

Alina was still looking below par, I noticed now, her skin sallow and her eyes ringed with shadows.

'Do you feel unwell, Alina?'

'Not at all. If I seem out of sorts, it's only that there are a few problems in the kitchen. Renata is not happy.'

'Renata?' I couldn't imagine the rotund cook being downcast.

Alina looked around, as if to check we couldn't be overheard. 'Mrs Manetti is coming more and more into the kitchen, checking on Renata's cooking.'

Well, that was a surprise. I hadn't had Evelyn down as hands on when it came to running the domestic life of the castle.

'And you're sure you feel well? I don't know how you manage, with a full-time job and three small children. Your mother-in-law must be a saint.'

Alina laughed, but there was little mirth in it.

'She is a very strong force, my mother-in-law. A force with nowhere to go. It is the tragedy of women in Italy that we can only be strong in our own homes. Outside, we are only wombs that walk.'

14

THOUGH WILLIAM HAD some good spells, taken as a whole, his progress in the week following the garden party was heading backwards rather than forwards. Now when I suggested we play chess, he would more often than not say he felt too tired, and on the occasions when we did start a game his moves were clumsy, his attention sluggish.

Dr Pearson was concerned by his deterioration, although not surprised. 'When it comes to matters of the brain, there exists neither rhyme nor reason,' he said. 'If the deterioration continues, we will have to consider operating.' I took a deep intake of breath. I knew, from my hospital days, what a dangerous procedure this was, how many patients died on the operating table or were left incapacitated. Dr Pearson, however, grew quite energized. 'There's a surgeon at the Santa Nuova Hospital here in Florence who is top of his field. Italian chap, but don't let that put you off.'

'You surely won't consider it?' I asked William after the doctor had left, his handkerchief welded to his glistening bald head, now that the heat was stronger.

'If it's the only option. Or would you prefer it if I died?'

I pretended I hadn't heard and wordlessly began the daily

massage Dr Pearson had shown me. Though the embarrassment was less acute than that first time I performed it in front of the physician's critical gaze, I still found the intimacy almost unbearable and would manipulate William's limbs while gazing fixedly ahead, as if my thoughts were somewhere else entirely. Occasionally, William would complain of feeling like a piece of meat on the butcher's slab or, once, 'a load of wet laundry that must have the water squeezed out'.

Today I was staring off into the middle distance as usual when I grabbed William's thigh as I'd been instructed to do to manipulate his left hip, only I misjudged, positioning my hand much higher than usual. I had a split second of indecision: move my hand and draw attention to the awkwardness of the situation or stay as I was and brazen it out. I decided on the latter and began moving the leg as normal, only to feel an unmistakable stirring against my fingers. I could sense the fire building in my cheeks, but to cut the exercises short would be to acknowledge what was happening, so I stared fixedly through the window, unable to speak or even swallow. When the first muffled noise came, I ignored it, but when it came again, louder, I couldn't resist glancing down, and saw that William was convulsed with laughter.

'For god's sake, woman. I'm a man, not a stone.'

I snatched my hand away and glared at him before turning away to hide. It was natural, of course, I told myself. And not only natural, hopeful. For William, it was evidence that he was still functioning, still *normal*. It wasn't personal. I could have been anyone.

Still it took a long time for my face to feel cool again.

*

As seemed to be the pattern now, this moment of levity was followed by a slump, as if the exchange had drained William of what little strength he had and, that afternoon, unusually for him, he asked Massimo to help him upstairs to rest, leaving me at something of a loose end. I offered to play a game of Snakes and Ladders with Nora, at which she was so disproportionately grateful I felt a splinter of guilt. It took so little to make the girl happy. We settled down in the *salone*, where Evelyn was writing out menus while Roberto lounged on the sofa, leafing through a book on military history from William's library.

From outside came the sound of a motor car labouring up the hill.

'Are we expecting company?' Roberto asked his wife, leaping to his feet, the leather-bound volume crashing to the floor.

'I hope it's someone amusing,' Evelyn replied. 'It's so dull here today.' I'd noticed she often moulded her own moods to fit the shape of his, professing boredom just because he seemed bored, even though I suspected she had been relishing having her husband to herself for once.

The man who emerged from the severe black car did not look as if he promised much in the way of amusement. He was small, certainly a head shorter than me, with a black slit of a moustache and a formal black hat, despite the heat. When Alina showed him into the *salone*, he introduced himself as Mr Webb, from Webb, Fisher and Hewitt, a firm of British lawyers serving the British community here in Florence.

'I have an appointment to see your uncle, Mrs Manetti.'

'I'm so sorry, he is indisposed. Perhaps you can talk to me or my husband?'

Mr Webb, who had removed his hat to reveal neatly oiled black hair, shook his head.

'I'm afraid not. Mr North had some particular business he wanted to discuss with me. We made the arrangement not three weeks ago. Should I wait for him to awake? I'm in no hurry.'

'I'm afraid you would have a wasted afternoon, Mr Webb,' said Roberto. 'The truth is, Uncle Bill's condition has declined quite markedly in recent days. I think you'd be shocked at the state of him.'

I felt obliged to comment. 'Although Mr North is often at his best straight after a rest.'

'Which is precisely why it's so important he conserve his energy.'

After the little lawyer had gone, his car exhaust belching smoke out into the muggy late-afternoon air, Roberto turned to Nora.

'Madame, would you care to dance?'

Nora gazed up, her eyes wide with surprise. As she took his outstretched hand, her little face broke into a smile of such undisguised delight I had to turn away to hide my tears.

Since around the time of the de Havilland party I'd been having trouble sleeping, either lying awake long into the night or else waking up with a jolt in the small hours of the morning with my mind churning. The night of the lawyer's visit I tossed and turned. I kept returning to William and that moment during the massage, and each time I thought about it my body was flooded with a hot mixture of embarrassment and something else, something I hadn't experienced in so long I'd forgotten I was even capable of it: desire.

Shutting down that train of thought abruptly, I focused on Nora instead. She was such an odd but endearing child, stuck here in the castle without friends, her mother too infatuated with her new husband to pay her much attention. I kept remembering how I'd found her all alone in the centre of the maze. The other children's callous laughter.

James, too, had been bullied, at school. He was a sensitive boy and had never learned to tell the difference between insult and light-hearted banter. At home he would climb on to my lap and cry and I would try to explain that if he would only learn to laugh at himself a little and not take everything to heart, the bullies would soon move on to a more satisfying target. Millie used to get so upset on his behalf and vow to take them on herself. Funny, I'd forgotten how close the two of them were. Walter couldn't stand to see James's tear-tracked face. 'You can't show them any weakness or they'll walk all over you,' he'd say. And later, he'd accuse me of mollycoddling. Now I wished I'd stood up for James in front of his father. I resolved to write him yet another letter when I got up.

It must have been two or three in the morning before I finally fell asleep, only for something to waken me again, what seemed to be mere moments later. At first, I thought I must have been dreaming, but just as I closed my eyes I heard it again. The sound of a child crying softly outside my room.

Convinced it must be Nora, sleepwalking in the grip of another night terror, I went to the door to find her, the coolness of the floor tiles coming as a shock against the soles of my bed-warmed feet. But outside, the corridor was empty and eerie in the silvery moonlight that filtered through the windows on to the courtyard. Again I heard it, a plaintive sound, a child's gulping sobs. I hurried along to the end of the corridor, where it turned at a right angle to run along the front of the building, crossing the turret that housed the grand staircase before arriving at the doorway to the opposite wing to mine, where the Manettis had their quarters. This part of the corridor, too, was deserted.

I turned around to retrace my steps, but as I approached my room I heard it again, muffled but desolate. I whirled around, but the corridor behind me was as still as before. It was peculiar, but the noise didn't seem to be coming from anywhere in particular but rather from the walls themselves. But when I pressed my ear to the stone, there was nothing there.

'I thought I heard Nora crying last night,' I said to Evelyn over breakfast the next day.

'I didn't hear a thing, did you, my prince?'

Roberto shook his head. 'I'm a light sleeper. I would have woken up.'

Evelyn peered at me over the slice of toast she had slathered with honey. 'Are you all right, Connie? Only you look a bit pale.'

'I'm fine, Evelyn. Really. My sleep is a bit up the spout, that's all.'

She appeared unconvinced.

'As long as you're sure. I can't have you falling ill. Not now I've come to rely on you so much. I can't think what we ever did without you!'

15

I CONTINUED TO BE concerned about William's lack of progress. In fact, I was starting to suspect he might be
regressing – an infinitesimal increase in the slurring of his
words, a relentless fatigue that had him nodding off in his
chair. Once or twice he had stomach pains that kept him
confined to his bed, but when I suggested recalling Dr Pearson he wouldn't hear of it.

Whenever possible I walked now at lunchtime as well as
in the mornings, sticking to the woods, where it was cool
and where I was unlikely to come across anyone else. Lack
of sleep meant I was unusually jumpy, starting at the slightest unexpected event – walking into an invisible spider's web
in the early-morning mist and wildly clawing the silky web-
bing from my hair, surprising a kingfisher down by the river
which then took off in a flurry of colour and flapping wings.

One lunchtime I came back from a walk down to the
stream and entered in through the back door to hear the
sound of Nora crying echoing down the stone corridors.
The cries were coming from the *salone* and I hurried in,
imagining she was hurt or shut inside. But when I burst in
through the tall double doors I found she was far from

alone. Instead, both Evelyn and Roberto were in attendance, plus Dr Pearson and a tall, thin, silver-haired man
with round spectacles who was fixing an alarming-looking
contraption over Nora's nose – a metal clamp which was
held in place by a metal strap over her skull, like a cage. I let
out a gasp of horror.

'Mrs Bowen, please help me!' Nora shrieked as she caught
sight of me.

'Please try to be brave, Nora,' pleaded Roberto. 'This is
for your own good.'

'You will thank Mr and Mrs Manetti when you're older
and looking for a husband,' Dr Pearson added.

'I don't understand,' I said. 'Is Nora ill?'

'Rhinoplastic corrective surgery,' said the silver-haired
ghoul with a little bow.

'Dr Contarini is one of Italy's leading experts. Nora is
dashed lucky to have him,' said Dr Pearson deferentially.

'Please,' Nora begged. 'Get it off me. Mummy, please, I'll
be good, I promise.'

Evelyn looked as if she was on the verge of tears herself,
and for a moment I thought she was about to be swayed, but
then she glanced at Roberto.

'Darling, you must be brave,' she said. 'It's only for a few
months. Don't you want a lovely straight nose like Mummy?'

'No!' She raised her hands to try to wrest the thing away
from her, but Dr Pearson restrained her.

'The more you do that, the tighter we will have to turn
the screws that grip to your head, so please try not to touch
it. I'm sure that, once you get used to it, you'll forget it's
even there. Now, if you don't mind withdrawing, Mrs
Bowen, I think your presence is upsetting the child.'

'Don't go,' Nora pleaded. 'Don't leave me.'

'Evelyn, don't you think this is' – I wanted to say *cruel* but stopped myself in time – 'unnecessary?'

Evelyn, who looked wretched, refused to meet my eyes.

'It's for her own good,' she repeated.

'Surely it can wait until she's older and can make up her own mind?'

'Quite the opposite!' snapped Dr Pearson. 'Children's bones are far more malleable.'

Roberto put his arm around my shoulders to steer me towards the door. 'I know you think us monsters, Constance, but Nora will thank us one day.'

What could I do but back out of the room, trying to block my ears, but still Nora's cries followed me through the vast stone hallway, all the way to William's sitting room.

'You seem upset,' he said when I sat down, trembling.

I told him about the scene in the *salone*, hoping he would send for Evelyn and persuade her to change her mind. Instead he grew solemn. 'Evelyn is the girl's mother,' he said eventually. 'She must decide what's best for Nora.'

It was the longest sentence he'd managed in a while and I knew it had exhausted him, but I was too unnerved by what I'd just witnessed to let it go.

'Of course. It's only that this thing, this contraption, did seem so *barbaric*.'

'Evelyn is her mother,' William repeated, and this time I knew there was no argument to be made. Though I could see William was fond of his great-niece, there was a distance there that saddened me. Nora was so very much in need of company – and William, too. But it was not my place to interfere, even though every cell in my body was urging me to. *That memory of Millie and the leeches – 'Don't let him, Mama.'* Instead I resumed reading, but the image of Nora's tear-stained face swam in front of the page and I hoped William couldn't hear how my voice wavered.

16

M AY RIPENED AROUND me, purple mists giving way to clear golden mornings. But as the weather grew warmer, so the atmosphere in the castle seemed to curdle. I couldn't hide my disapproval of the terrible contraption Nora had to endure, which essentially held her head in a vice so that the metal clamp attached to her nose remained in place. At night she slept propped up on pillows.

'Please don't think badly of us, Connie,' Evelyn said. 'We are only thinking of Nora. The world isn't kind to undecorative girls.'

Roberto came and went, charming as ever but beholden to no one. Now that the heat was upon us, he'd given up wearing a jacket over his uniform and the sight of his black shirt never failed to induce a shiver. Even when he was home he was often in his darkroom, his own private kingdom. Left to her own devices, Evelyn would seek out my company, insisting I join her for a cocktail in the garden or looping her arm through mine to go for a stroll, which she invariably grew tired of before we'd gone much farther than the castle grounds. Sometimes she even came into William's sitting room and sat watching us play chess and fidgeting before declaring it the dullest game ever invented and insisting we play something different. Occasionally, I'd overhear her begging Roberto not to leave, or catch her standing at the front window, her fingers digging around in the silk pouch she always wore for a cigarette as she watched the back of his car disappear through the gates.

Although there were no repeats of the collapsing episode at the de Havillands' party, William was definitely growing worse. His speech was thick and halting, his eyesight more blurred than ever and he was asleep more than he was awake. Dr Pearson made several more visits, issuing strict instructions to Alina and Renata about what William should and should not be eating and leaving a list of exercises which William declared useless and had to be reminded to do.

Witnessing his deterioration brought back painful memories of Millie, remembering how I'd anxiously monitor her, every morning and evening taking an inventory of symptoms – did she appear paler? Was she coughing more? When you watch someone die very slowly in front of your eyes, you are constantly alert for signs.

Spending so much time together doing very little, our conversations grew more intimate – if one-sided. William found speech tiring so mostly he would ask me terse questions and I would chat to him about my childhood, and how much I'd relished working during the war, that wonderful, unfamiliar feeling of being *useful*. I told him about James and how hard he'd tried to be the kind of son he felt his father expected, suppressing his own personality to fit in with Walter's idea of what a man should be, and how we'd drifted apart in the years since Millie died. I even told him what I'd hardly admitted to myself, that I worried James believed I resented him for being alive instead of her. 'Grief is lonely,' William had said then, pausing between the words. 'We think we can share it, but we can't.'

But while every day I felt closer to William, I felt increasingly distant from my own self, if that's not too fanciful a way of expressing it. Sleeplessness went from an aberration to a habit, and I came to both crave the night and dread it at the same time. Crave it because I spent the days walking around as if I had boulders attached to my feet, my limbs heavy and cumbersome, my mind fogged with exhaustion. But much as I dreamed of being in bed, I dreaded lying awake, my mind churning.

I started to make minor errors. Using the wrong word or starting a sentence and forgetting midway what it was I had intended to say. Once, when Alice de Havilland was over for lunch and Evelyn had invited me to join them, I called Evelyn Millie by mistake and she looked at me with wide eyes flooded with pity. 'Dear Connie,' she said, scooting up her chair so that she could put her arm around my shoulders. 'What a lot you've had to bear. No wonder you sometimes get muddled.'

Outside, the warmer weather was bringing changes to the landscape. The hillsides were ablaze with wild red poppies and clusters of yellow sunflowers dotted the valleys.

Inside, I felt myself growing every day more tense, like a guitar string being wound ever tighter. I could see from the mirror over my washstand that my fatigue was showing in my face. Sometimes in the mornings, my hands shook.

On the second Saturday in May I was even more tired than usual, following another broken night. After a light lunch taken outside sitting under the olive tree, William and

I made the painstaking journey back indoors, where I was in the middle of reading him a letter from a publisher in London interested in commissioning a new book from him on Florentine art, when we heard a commotion by the front door and then Emily Wheeler's rasping voice.

I was surprised when Evelyn brought the Wheelers in to see William. I knew there was no love lost there.

I tried not to meet Philip Wheeler's eyes, remembering how close he'd stood to me on the day of the de Havillands' party. I'd been widowed for a year by now and had learned that there are certain men who see any woman over the age of thirty-five, particularly single women, as an easy touch, believing them so desperate for company as to welcome any kind of attention.

The Wheelers seated themselves on the velvet sofa. They were full of talk of the controversial English writer Duncan Fletcher, who had just been to tea with his wife.

'He's an interesting enough sort, though really quite gaunt and ill-looking,' was Emily's take. 'We took them for a walk in the roof garden and I worried in case a stray gust of wind might blow him clear away. Unlike his wife.'

'It would take more than a gust of wind to blow *that* one away,' Philip Wheeler cut in.

Evelyn clapped her hands together.

'I heard he's writing the filthiest book,' she said, her eyes wide. 'No publisher will touch it with a barge pole, apparently. I cannot *wait* to read it.'

While they were chattering I was preparing William's afternoon medication, adding the drops of Dr Pearson's tonic to a glass of water. I'd begun giving him a couple of drops more than the doctor had prescribed in the hope it might boost his strength. He was just raising the glass to his lips, using his good hand, which had now become merely his less bad hand, when Evelyn shrieked and snatched the water from his hand.

'That's the wrong vial, Constance!' she yelled, pointing to the glass bottle on the sideboard from which I'd just measured out the drops. 'That's the sedative. Are you trying to kill him?'

'No, the sedative is in the bottle with the—' I stopped short. The sedative had a skull and crossbones on the label to differentiate it from the bottle of vitamins, but because I always kept the two bottles well apart, with the sedative on the left and the other on the right, I hadn't even thought to check. In my drowsy state I'd just picked up the bottle from the right and measured it out. The bottle that I now noticed bore a skull and crossbones on the label.

'I'm so sorry – I don't know how it happened. The bottles were in the wrong places. I would never—'

'You must be more careful, Mrs Bowen.' Emily Wheeler frowned at me. 'Medicine is a serious business.'

'It was a mistake, that's all. Anyone could have made it,' said Roberto.

Evelyn softened.

'Of course you're right, dear heart. And poor Constance has been so tired recently.'

'Not sleeping well?' Philip Wheeler enquired, turning his probing eyes to me. 'Guilty secrets keeping you awake?'

'Not at all.' I tried to smile, but humiliation burned like acid through my veins.

That evening I went up to my room earlier than normal, determined to get a proper night's sleep. It was still light outside, and dust motes swirled in the air as I opened the door, but something stopped me in my tracks, a sense of things disturbed. I ran my eyes around the room, taking in the cases stacked up in the corner, the opened book face down on the bedside table. My gaze fell on the dressing table, where there was a small bottle of scent and a slender glass vase with some roses I'd collected from the garden.

And my silver-backed hairbrush.

The hairbrush I always kept in the drawer.

17

OUTSIDE NOW THE sun was hot enough to warm the stone walls of the castle so that they threw out their own heat as I passed on an early-morning stroll. In the courtyard four large lemon trees in terracotta pots yielded yellow fruit the size of a baby's head. The flowerbeds were an explosion of colour – pale pink daphne flowers with their heavy, sweet scent, tubular lilacs with their purple clusters of blossoms – and they were alive with bees from morning to night, emitting a gentle, low-level hum.

The day after the scene in William's sitting room, I came across Alina picking herbs for the day's meals – fat bunches of sweet-smelling basil and sprigs of rosemary and wild thyme. On an impulse I found myself telling her about the hairbrush not being where I left it, surprised to discover it was still weighing on my mind.

'It's not the first time I've thought someone might have been in my room,' I admitted, thinking of the pen that had disappeared and then mysteriously reappeared.

'Has anything been taken?'

'No.'

I felt foolish now and regretted having spoken.

'You know, sometimes, when the children have kept me awake for two or three nights in a row, I find myself imagining all sorts of things and getting in a terrible state,' Alina began. 'One time I came to work and was halfway through the day before I realized I still had on my nightdress under my clothes!'

After I'd helped Alina collect the cut herbs in a wicker basket we sat for a few moments on a low, faded apricot wall that bordered the vegetable garden near the castle's back entrance. Behind us came the squawking of chickens and guineafowl in the bird garden. From here we could see into the kitchen window, where Nora was sitting on the solid oak table chatting to Renata, the metal octopus clamped to her head momentarily forgotten.

'I wish Evelyn would hurry up and find her a governess,' I said softly to Alina. 'It's not right that a child should be so lonely.'

'She probably doesn't want to risk a repeat of the last.'

'The last?'

'Diana Swift. She was a nice girl. A bit silly, but she was very young.'

'Silly?'

'Oh, you know, emotional. She cried a lot over very trivial things – a beautiful sunset, Solomon coming too close. Once she burst into tears because Nora painted her a picture for her birthday. She always had an embroidered handkerchief in her hand to wipe her eyes. Nora adored her.'

'I suspect Nora would adore anyone who paid her some attention.'

Alina murmured in agreement.

'So what happened to Diana?' I asked, recalling how Philip Wheeler had prompted me to find out.

Alina glanced around.

'She caught Mr Manetti's eye. She was awfully pretty, you see. I think she was . . .'

I could tell Alina was fishing for the English word, so I supplied a guess. 'Flattered?'

'Exactly.'

'And Evelyn suspected?'

Alina nodded. 'Mrs Manetti didn't even let her take her things when she left. She had them all packed up and sent after her. Nora was heartbroken. She didn't get a chance to say goodbye.'

After Alina had gone back to work, I remained on the wall, feeling uneasy. Now I understood why Philip Wheeler had told me to ask about the governess. To show me what happened to people who got on the wrong side of Evelyn. I thought it probably amused him, pointing out to me how precarious was my position in this world, at the mercy of other people's whims. Perhaps on some level he thought it would remind me of my place, make me more likely to be grateful for crumbs of friendship from someone like him.

The truth was, I actually felt sorry for Evelyn. I could see how greatly infatuated she was with her handsome young husband and I was old enough to understand what infatuation could do to a person. Working at the hospital during the war I'd developed a crush on one of the surgeons, a married man with two young children. He had a reputation as a ladies' man and made it very clear he wouldn't be averse to taking matters further with me. 'We could have some fun,' he'd said. I'd resisted, but it had taken all my reserves of willpower, and I'd passed the days and nights consumed by thoughts of him, jealous of the smallest attention he bestowed on the other female nurses and voluntary staff. It seemed to me that Evelyn was as much of a force of nature as the breeze itself, and just as incapable of modifying her feelings. If she'd suspected Roberto's head to be turned, she would have acted rashly, impulsively, in the heat of the moment. But I would be all right. Evelyn knew she had nothing to fear from me.

All the walking and the change of diet meant that, for the first time in my life, I was losing weight, the bones beginning to push through my wrists and chest, the sculpture of my face slowly revealing itself, like a Roman mosaic floor painstakingly unearthed under the archaeologist's trowel. But rather than welcoming the changes, as I'd always assumed I would, I suspected my new, gaunter look was unbecoming. Lack of sleep painted shadows on my newly hollowed face while the sun left my hair dry and dull.

The day after my conversation with Alina dawned grey and soupy. I glanced up from my book – the same volume, by William's nemesis, George Blandford, which I rationed out, a few pages at a time, for fear of raising William's blood pressure – to find him gazing over at me intently.

'You are not well.' It was a statement, rather than a question.

'Nonsense, I'm fine.'

'You are growing thinner.'

'Not really. And besides, I had weight to spare.'

William said something now that I couldn't quite hear and had to ask him to repeat, which I knew he hated, because it reminded him of the frailty he was trying to ignore.

'I said you looked fine before!'

'Oh!' A flush crept up my chest and neck. Perhaps it was embarrassment that made me blurt out: 'Not too old and fat, then?'

Instantly, I wished the words unsaid, and it seemed William did, too, for he had a look of shock about him, his mouth falling slightly open, his eyes widened.

'That was a private conversation.'

'Then perhaps you should have spoken more quietly.'

I went back to the book, but I was aware of the unsteadiness of my voice and the hot prick of tears at the back of my eyes.

When, eventually, William nodded off, I didn't stay with him as I normally would but, after making sure he was secure, went outdoors to clear my head.

I avoided the courtyard, where I was bound to bump into Alina or Evelyn or sometimes Renata, sitting on the back-door step cleaning artichokes with her skirts hitched and her legs wide, her face still puce from standing over a steaming pan. Instead, I went out through the front door, heading around the side of the castle, hoping against hope not to find Massimo weeding the banksia roses or the azaleas. Luckily, I had the long side terrace to myself.

Lowering myself on to the wooden bench, I gazed out across the stepped hillside to the distant mountains and allowed the tears to come. *Idiot,* I scolded myself. Why should I mind whether William North thought me fat or whether, conversely, he now thought me too thin? I was here in Italy for one reason only – to keep him company until such time as he no longer needed me. I ought not to let myself get so invested in his opinion, whatever it might be.

The day felt damp and bad-tempered. Over the five

weeks I'd been in Tuscany the landscape had got under my fingernails, until the thought of not waking up every day to see the wooded hills or the mauve mountains in the distance was like imagining myself suddenly blind or lame, deprived of something that made me whole. Sometimes it felt as if the golden light in the mornings and late afternoons was made liquid and flowed through my veins like blood.

But in this day's grainy, grey light, even the majesty of the scenery – the towering cypresses, the umbrella pines like upturned hands – failed to move me. Instead, I tortured myself, thinking of the day I would have to once again pack up my cases and board the train back to England and my life that felt not so much like a life but rather a comfortable waiting room for death. Sometimes when I pictured myself in that cold, green-walled room in Pinner it was like I was preserved in aspic.

Perhaps I could stay? Take some rooms in Florence, a hotel suite, or even an apartment. There were plenty of Englishwomen doing the same. I could let out the house back home, or James could take it over completely and send me a small stipend to live on. Surely it would be cheaper to live here than in England. I wouldn't need much.

But whenever I imagined James's face if I were to put such a proposition to him, my nerve failed me.

I don't know how long I sat out there surveying the hillside with unseeing eyes, but now I began to imagine William's contrition at awaking to find me gone. *Good.* I made my way around to the front of the castle with its bared-teethed gargoyle monkeys, but even before I'd reached the heavy front door, which I'd left ajar, I could hear voices raised in alarm.

Turning left out of the turreted hallway, I hurried towards William's sitting room, where Evelyn was standing in a state of agitation, issuing instructions to Massimo and Alina, who, between them, were trying to raise William from the floor. Solomon paced the floor restlessly, his huge eyes never leaving his master for a second.

'Where have you *been*, Connie?' Evelyn asked, once William was laid safely out on the chaise longue, his eyes open, and already grumbling.

'You know perfectly well you're not to leave Uncle Bill unless you've made completely sure that he can't come to any harm, and what happens? I come along and find him lying on the ground and you nowhere to be seen.'

'I'm sorry,' I said. 'I thought he was secure. I was sure—'

But was I? A memory of positioning his stick next to him was dissipating into the air.

'If it hadn't been for Solomon coming to find me, who knows how long he might have been lying here like this,' Evelyn went on. 'Really, Connie, you must take more care.'

The thick fug of the castle's night-time silence contained myriad different sounds if one only listened carefully enough. Creaking floorboards, the tinny clang of the bathroom pipes, sometimes even the far-off noise of an express train thundering through the distant valley. Some nights I would lie awake, straining for these other sounds. Other nights I would fall asleep straight away, only to be awoken abruptly by something that dissolved into thin air when I tried to identify it.

The night of my argument with William, I awoke to a strange noise that, as usual, stopped as soon as my brain fumbled to make sense of it. Even so, I sat up in bed to listen. There it came again, a high-pitched, plaintive sound. I walked to the door. As I said, I was used by then to the castle's sighs and groans, but this was different, as if the noise had got into my very blood.

I opened the door and listened. Silence. I relaxed. There was nothing there, just a combination of lack of sleep and an overactive imagination. But just as I was pulling the door closed, I heard it again. This time, it was unmistakable. The searing, vibrato sound of a violin.

Impossible. The sky outside the window on the opposite wall, looking out across the courtyard, was oily black. Who would be playing music at this time?

I crept to the end of the corridor, intending to make my way to the turret to listen at the top of the grand staircase to see if the music was coming from the *salone* downstairs, but as I progressed along the icy flags a chill spread from my feet up over my whole body and I found myself frozen to the spot as a single haunting high note reverberated off the stone walls.

It was the gramophone, I told myself. Someone else who couldn't sleep. I forced myself onward, but as I approached the point where the corridor opened out into the turreted hallway the music stopped abruptly. Peering over the bannisters at the top of the stairs, I could see only thick darkness. No movement, no sound.

I padded softly back to my room, closed the door silently and got back into bed, pulling the sheet up over my face until the only sound I could hear was the thump of my own heart.

The following morning, as I stood at the window with

the May sun warming my cheeks and a dove cooing gently from the top branches of a nearby tree, the fears of the night before seemed preposterous. Roberto, finding himself awake and restless, would have been playing a record to help get himself back in a mood for sleep. Or wasn't it possible it was not music at all? Could I have confused it for some other thing – the fighting of wild cats out in the woods? The call of a peacock or the screech of Cecily's white cockatoo?

At breakfast, after Evelyn commented on my yawning, I made a joke of it.

'I had the strangest night. I thought I was being serenaded by a violin playing somewhere in the castle.'

Evelyn and Roberto exchanged a wary glance.

'I worry it's all our fault, these problems you are having in sleeping,' said Evelyn eventually, setting down her fork. Her voice was kind, and I was glad the quarrel of yesterday had passed. 'We should never have let the Wheelers tell you that silly story of the little girl walled up by her father. If we'd have known you had such an active—'

'Oh, no, it's nothing like that. In fact, I'd quite forgotten the girl in the wall.'

This wasn't quite true. In the small, dead hours of the night I had once or twice allowed my thoughts to wander to the portrait of the pale man with the dark beard and the fearful expression. That cold spot on the floor in front of it. But it was unbearable to me, having presented myself as entirely sensible and trustworthy, that the Manettis should think of me as fanciful and overwrought.

'Just as long as you are not overdoing things, Constance,' said Roberto. Normally, he was so busy – off on his own in his darkroom, or else out in town in his black uniform – but when he turned his attention to me completely, as he did now, I felt quite short of breath.

'No, no. Not at all.'

As I made my way to William's sitting room, apprehension fluttered like a trapped moth in my chest. I mustn't give the Manettis any reason to think I was not up to the job for which they had hired me. While the castle was starting to feel oppressive to me at times, the thought of leaving it and Italy and William North and returning to my half-life in Pinner was unendurable.

18

A s May began its slide into June the heat became something tangible that I wore on my skin like an extra chemise, not oppressive yet but noticeably present. By now it had become a habit to sleep only a handful of hours a night and the new thickness of my thoughts was so much a part of me that I no longer registered the extra effort in summoning a memory or formulating a plan, or the way I now scrabbled for words, too often giving up and having to substitute a different word that wasn't quite what I meant.

William and I had never mentioned again the 'old and fat', but it lay between us like something blocking a lovely view.

Though ours was quite a one-sided correspondence, my letters to James had become something of a lifeline, a way for me to process all the different things happening in the house. My old friend Caroline still hadn't replied to my first letter. I didn't blame her. Our experiences had diverged so much by now. With the distance of geography and time I could see how she must have felt let down by me. The plans we had made together, in the early idealistic days when the momentum for women's suffrage seemed unstoppable, the exhilaration of those first marches, feeling sure we were marching into history. But then the stakes were raised and the protests became more volatile. Walter made his ultimatum and I stepped back. Caro always said she understood, but we both knew it was a failure of courage on my part. She had kept her nerve, endured ridicule, hostility, prison, while I had stayed at home. No wonder she didn't reply.

So instead I poured everything out to James – my impressions of the castle, the scenery, the city of dreams, as Florence was so often called. I told him about the Manettis and the Wheelers, the strange noises in the night that kept me awake. It wasn't at all how James and I talked, but by this stage my life in Pinner seemed so distant that I had forgotten how strained my relationship with James had become and remembered only the happier times when Millie was still alive and we were a little team of three.

I was upstairs in my room one golden evening, writing to him about the dinner Evelyn was planning for the Fletchers – the celebrated writer of filth and his 'frightful' wife – when the strangest thing happened. The birds outside, which had been trilling their usual end-of-day song, fell silent, along with the cicadas and the turkeys and chickens in the poultry enclosure at the back of the castle. The whole world stilled until the absence of sound became almost deafening. I had time only to register the peculiarity of this when there came a terrifying rumble that rose up seemingly from deep inside the hillside itself, like some gigantic ancient creature stirring, and then everything started rocking, the pictures on the walls tilting, the bedframe shaking. I looked out of the window and the hillside was moving, but then I realized it was the castle walls themselves that were swaying. And now the painting above the fireplace, with its bucolic scene of women washing clothes in the river, their skirts hitched up their bare legs, went crashing to the floor, the bed sliding to and fro, plaster cracking and groaning beneath the ripping wallpaper. I was too shocked to cry out, able only to watch in awe and disbelief as the earth prepared to burst through its own crust.

And then it stopped. Just as suddenly as it had started.

There followed another silence, while I held my breath. Then all hell broke loose. From somewhere in the back of the castle where William's quarters were came the sound of Solomon barking, while Nora screamed from the top of the stairs. I heard footsteps outside my room and then pummelling on the door. Roberto bursting in. 'Are you hurt?'

'No. Have you checked on Mr North? Please. Hurry.'

My chest pulled tight, breath held. And then the news that William was fine, the back of the castle being less severely affected than the rest. Air being released in a long sigh of relief. In fact, when I went with Evelyn and Roberto to tour the castle, my wing turned out to have taken the brunt of the force of the earthquake, one bedroom two doors down – mercifully unused – with a jagged crack three inches across running the width of the room.

Gathered downstairs with Evelyn and her family, I drank brandy from a dusty bottle that Roberto produced from the cellar. Even Nora had some, diluted heavily with water, though she pronounced it disgusting. Half hysterical with the delayed shock of it all, we replayed our own experiences to one another. 'I was in the darkroom preparing the stop bath . . .' 'I was on the sofa with my feet up, I thought you were playing tricks on me, darling.' 'I was fast asleep and my bed was *shivering.*'

The following morning dawned clear and pure and fresh, as if the night had never happened. Evelyn and Roberto were up unusually early, and together we took a second tour around the castle, checking for damage, which, all in all, appeared to be miraculously minimal. Inside, cracks in the upper walls ran from the door frames to the ceilings, while other cracks forked like lightning along the stone flags. An outside wall was reduced to rubble, a roof collapsed over one of the kitchen storerooms. Heaps of masonry – bricks from fallen chimney stacks and broken tiles ripped from roofs – were piled around the base of the castle walls. Dust and broken glass. Roberto had his camera with him and stopped every few steps to take photographs.

'Why must you photograph such ugly things? Who wants to see pictures of rubble?' Evelyn complained after she'd entreated him, unsuccessfully, to take a picture of her posing in front of the roses.

'You're as bad as your uncle,' he replied, and I could see he was annoyed. 'Art isn't just pretty flowers and the same boring religious scenes, princess. There's beauty in imperfection.'

William joined us, shuffling slowly, supported by Massimo. 'Not as bad as '95. Thank god,' he said, after he'd seen enough. And then, gruffly, with a quick glance at me. 'Glad to see you're still alive.'

When the others all went inside, Nora and I lingered by the front steps. The earthquake was the most exciting thing to have happened to her in a very long time and she was determined to wring every last drop of drama from it. We stood looking up as she pointed out damage the others might have missed, a crack in one of the battlements, the flagpole broken off halfway. 'I'm going to check the dragons,' she said, darting off towards the stone statues on the monumental gateposts. I stood watching her for a few moments, revelling in the sheer relief of being alive, and of seeing Nora for once so full of childish energy. 'Come on, Mrs Bowen,' she called to me.

I stepped towards her just as something whistled past my ear, a blast of wind that sent me stumbling forward while something crashed to the ground behind me on the very spot where I'd been standing just a moment before, the earth shuddering under the impact.

Twisting my head, I saw something moving at the very top of the castle turret, but it had vanished before I could properly make out whether it was a person or a large bird. Heart thumping, I surveyed the wreckage scattered around me on the gravel where I had fallen. Spotting a fragment of stone engraved with bared teeth, I realized it was the remains of one of the two monkeys that kept guard over the castle entrance from their sentry position just under the battlements.

'Connie, are you hurt?' Evelyn came flying down the front steps and flung herself down in the dust next to me, examining my face. She was joined a split second later by Roberto and Alina.

'The quake must have damaged the gargoyles,' said Roberto, craning his neck to look up. 'I'd better go up and secure the other one, though I could do without those damned stone steps.'

'Roberto gets claustrophobic,' Evelyn explained after he'd gone. 'Thank god you are all right, though, Connie.'

Alina, meanwhile, was helping me to my feet, surveying me up and down with her watchful brown eyes.

'You were lucky, Constance,' she said softly.

But as I brushed myself down and tried not to let the others see how my legs were trembling, I didn't feel lucky at all.

19

APART FROM A few minor after-tremors, the earthquake was soon forgotten, but it left cracks in the life of the castle that could not be so easily filled. As we slipped into the sultry heat of June the atmosphere became sticky with tension. Evelyn continued to exert her authority in the kitchen, to the grumbling irritation of Renata, who frequently threatened to go back to the Wheelers, and Alina complained of being forever quizzed on this or that aspect of William's care and progress. 'Since the de Havillands' party it's as if Evelyn doesn't trust anyone.' I was worried that Alina had lost some of her sparkle. Her face was drawn and there was a moment's delay between a thing happening and her reacting to it. She was noticeably subdued. Always slender, now she wafted through the stone corridors like a ghost.

As the heat built outside and we sought shelter within the cool stone castle walls, my logic seemed to desert me and I found myself wondering whether the castle itself might be effecting this change on Alina and on William, who continued his incremental regression back into infirmity from the almost recovered man I'd met two months before. At night when I couldn't sleep, I even wondered if there was something malevolent stalking the corridors, draining the life force from us all. My mind was so often fatigued and sluggish. When I stared at the latticework of fine cracks the earthquake had traced in the plaster of my bedroom walls, sometimes they looked like snakes.

One night, I thought I heard the violin again, and strode out of my bedroom in my nightgown, determined to find the source. Thinking it might be coming from the top of the turret, I went through the little door at the back of the upper landing behind the grand staircase and up the spiral stone steps that led to the tower, eventually emerging on to the roof of the castle itself, above where the single surviving stone monkey, leashed now with rope, mounted its lonely vigil. I had been here only once, when I first arrived and Evelyn took me up to show me the view, but like Roberto I disliked the narrowness of the staircase, with the stone walls pressing in on either side. On this night, the walls themselves seemed to hum along with the violin strings, but as I reached the top, once again, the noise stopped abruptly.

I began to think more and more about the little girl in the wall. In the night heat she became confused with Nora, and I sometimes imagined her with that metal clamp glinting as she played her sorrowful violin. By now I knew the portrait of the father as intimately as if he were a real-life acquaintance. I pictured him with his head in his hands on hot June nights like these, listening as I was to the sound of his daughter's bow or, worse, of her softly crying in the walls.

Occasionally, I'd think also of the black rock that dominated the hillside behind the castle and of the three women burned there as witches by the same townspeople among whom they'd grown up, who they'd called friends and neighbours. I pictured them being led up past the castle and through the woods, following that steep path I'd climbed with Alina in my first week in Italy. The crops had failed. God was angry. A sacrifice needed to be made. When did they realize that the sacrifice would turn out to be them?

So ran my thoughts. On and on in a disordered mess that matched the tangled rose bushes that twisted around each other up the castle walls.

Yet there were still moments when I recaptured some of the blissful happiness of those early days: sunrises that exploded across the sky in a fireball of pink and golden light, causing the breath to catch in my throat, mornings with William where he'd seem almost like his old self and we'd talk about what I'd just read out in the newspaper – the growing unemployment both here and back home, Charles Lindbergh's miraculous solo flight across the Atlantic. The valley on the far side of the castle blazed with yellow sunflowers that always ignited within me a corresponding blaze of optimism, while in the late afternoon my soul was soothed by the pale gold of the wheat fields.

Evelyn was throwing a dinner in honour of the much-discussed Fletchers, who she insisted were as poor as church mice so would be grateful for a decent meal. The Wheelers had been to visit them, arriving unannounced at what Emily described as 'a hovel lit by oil lamps, and decorated with DF's own dreadful paintings'. Roberto seemed to be in two minds about the whole affair, torn between his desire to be seen to be entertaining such a celebrated writer and concern that the Fascisti would consider Fletcher's books degenerate and he might be tarred by association. It was still jarring to me to be reminded of Roberto's political affiliation, for all

Evelyn explained that his membership of the party was merely a matter of pragmatism, you were either with them or against, and any fool could see which way history was heading. Besides, she said, at least the Fascisti were taking a stand against the communists. The Wheelers were having all sorts of trouble with their labourers striking for more autonomy, their crops stalled or ruined. That's what happened when the old order was challenged, she said. Anarchy.

The day of the dinner, she was flitting around the castle, one minute standing over Alina in the dining room overseeing the arranging of the cut flowers, and then off to the kitchen to ensure Renata wasn't scrimping on the more expensive ingredients.

'We're having roast pigeon with wild-mushroom sauce and chicken livers, and shallots and carrots and French beans. Don't you just want to gobble it up right now, Connie? I want all our guests to come away saying they've just eaten the most delicious meal of their lives and I want everyone else to be wild with jealousy. This castle was just made for parties, don't you think? Aunt Cecily lived such a *small* life here, with Uncle Bill away most of the time, but I want the castle to be full of fun and laughter and gaiety. The war was over nearly ten years ago. I think we owe it to all those boys who died to have as jolly a time as we possibly can.'

We were finishing breakfast and she had a glow about her as if she were lit from within. At moments like this Nora sat entranced, following her mother with her eyes as if she could learn her by rote, like the times tables I was trying to teach her.

'Can I be at the dinner, Mummy? Please? I would stay very quiet and well behaved.' Her little face shone with hope between the metal straps of her nasal contraption.

'Oh, darling, I expect you'd find it frightfully dull,' said Evelyn quickly. 'Far more fun to have tea in the kitchen with Renata and your own sweet Matilda.'

She glanced at the misshapen doll in Nora's lap.

Nora nodded, but her entire body sagged.

'Why don't you eat with me and your Great-uncle Bill tonight?' I suggested. 'I'm sure he'd be delighted to have an extra guest for dinner.'

I wasn't sure of any such thing. It was an abiding regret to me that William kept himself at such a great reserve from his great-niece. The girl was so lonely and he himself so cut off from his previous busy life it seemed a natural thing that they might both find some comfort in each other, but William was of that generation of men who had spent too long away from home – thanks to the two-headed dragon of work and war – and the affairs of children were as alien to him as those of the workers in the fields.

'I won't hear of it. I insist you join us, Connie,' said Evelyn. 'It's going to be such fun. I've given it a flight theme in honour of Charles Lindbergh. We're going to eat pigeon and dress in feathers and listen to "The Flight of the Bumblebee" on the gramophone.'

I'd been both surprised and touched by Evelyn's insistence on inviting me to join them whenever she had guests, though in my current weary state I felt sure I must be very dull company indeed.

Sometimes I wished I could be left in peace, but to be a paid companion was, I was discovering, to occupy a nebulous status within the household. Neither servant nor equal, I existed in some middle plane where I didn't comfortably fit anywhere. It was perfectly right and proper for the Manettis to include me in their social engagements but, equally, no one would have been surprised if they did not. The only given was that the choice to invite or not to invite was within the gift of the host. The companion must accept whichever came her way.

'Did you know,' Philip Wheeler had commented once, sitting back in his chair and steepling his hands as if he were about to impart some deep philosophical truth or explain at length why ants and beetles were so much more successful as a species than humans, 'the word "companion" comes from the Latin *cum*, which means "with" and *pan*, which is obviously bread. So, literally, Mrs Bowen, you are here to work for your supper, as it were.'

'Don't listen to him, Connie,' Evelyn had said, slapping him on the arm.

So it was that when Nora came to have tea with William later that afternoon, I was there merely in a supervisory capacity. At first the two of them were stiff together, Nora cowed by her great-uncle's presence. It was the first time William had had a good look at the nose contraption and I could tell from his darting glances that he was shocked.

At first the atmosphere was stiff and uncomfortable and I found myself talking far too much to fill in the silences between the two of them. Whenever I caught William's eye, he glared at me crossly.

As the air grew more constricted, I realized I couldn't leave Nora here when I went upstairs to prepare myself for the dinner I had no appetite for attending. I was on the point of suggesting she accompany me to my room – pretending I needed her advice on how to wear the feather headband I'd had to borrow from Evelyn as a nod to the night's theme, when a most peculiar thing happened. She stood up and crossed the room to where her great-uncle had, unseen by me, dropped the fork with which he was attempting to spear his food and wordlessly replaced it in his hand before returning quietly to her own tea. Something about the dignity with which the young girl performed this small act of kindness brought a lump to my throat. I suspected William himself was not unmoved. 'Thank you,' he muttered.

I excused myself and went in search of Alina, who was coming to sit with William, leaving Nora and her great-uncle eating in a silence that seemed, if not companionable, at least less awkward than before. Upstairs, I put on my blue chiffon dress with Evelyn's borrowed headdress, complete with marabou feathers and a marabou feather bag she'd insisted would complete the look. Rather than carry it around empty, I put in it a silver compact and a small vial of a concoction Renata had made for me to rub into my skin to repel the mosquitoes that feasted on me night after night, made from all sorts of plants from the garden, of which I could recognize only lemon, basil, eucalyptus, lavender and mint.

The Fletchers were a strange pair. He pale and ethereal with faded red hair the colour of a bloodstain after it has been rinsed and rinsed again, she sturdy and enquiring with a disconcertingly direct gaze and a blunt manner of speaking. They had recently returned from the coast, and she recounted amusing anecdotes about the trip in her heavily accented English. Evelyn had told me it was an open secret that both Fletchers had had lovers throughout their marriage and that Klara's current paramour drove Duncan into fits of jealous rage. I found her fascinating. So unashamedly plain, large-boned like me, and yet with this lusty self-confidence. Was that all it took? I found myself wondering. If you considered yourself irresistible, did you automatically become so?

Certainly, her husband seemed terribly uxorious, content to sit back and let his wife take centre stage. He was not well, Evelyn had pre-warned me. Tuberculosis. Just like Millie. I instantly felt protective towards him, this man with his chalky complexion and piercing blue eyes and stubborn Midlands accent.

Also at dinner were the ubiquitous Wheelers and Alice de Havilland and fey little Olivia Averell, who wafted in wearing all white as if straight out of an Impressionist painting, including a diaphanous white cape which was attached at the wrists and gave the effect of angel wings. Evelyn hadn't wanted Olivia to come. 'She adds nothing to the conversation,' she'd complained to her husband when Roberto told her he'd invited *Livvy*, as she was known to her friends. 'She has not a single original thought in her head. What will Fletcher think of us, having such an empty-headed creature around the table?'

'Women are not required to be original, my darling. Just agreeable and easy on the eye.'

Evelyn had slapped him playfully on the arm then said, 'Well, I can't see that she's much use in that department either. She is so *unformed*. One might as well have a jelly sitting at the table.' She let her face sag, her lower jaw hanging loose in imitation.

But when she arrived Olivia seemed actually to be glowing, particularly next to Alice de Havilland, who was attired all in black like a moth, despite the heat that still hung in the air.

We hadn't long sat down when Miss de Havilland, seated opposite, turned her attention to me. She wedged into her eye socket a large, black-framed monocle of a kind I hadn't seen anyone wear since I was a child. The monocle was attached to a long black ribbon which was in turn attached to the bosom of her dress – a strange garment made entirely of ostrich feathers. Her right eye through the monocle was large like a conker, and her entire appearance was quite alarming, her brows painted directly on to her forehead in the shape of a bird – black arches of permanent surprise.

'Have you any talents, Mrs Bowen? You look to me like the sort of woman who might play the harpsichord or perhaps the flute. Do you play the harpsichord or the flute?'

'I'm afraid not, Miss de Havilland.'

'Then perhaps you paint, or write poetry? Although, to be frank, most of the people who claim to write poetry write it very badly, so it is not much of a talent.'

'Neither, I'm afraid.'

'Then how do you intend to entertain us this evening? Please do not tell me you intend to perform an interpretive dance. I simply cannot abide interpretive dance. Unless it is I who am doing it.'

'Entertain you? I don't understand.'

'Tonight's theme. Flying. I intend to recite Keats, "Ode to a Nightingale".' She stood up suddenly, clutching her chest. '*My heart aches, and a drowsy numbness pains my sense, as though of hemlock I had drunk,*' she proclaimed to her fellow diners.

'A little premature, don't you think, Alice?' said Roberto, who had managed to get hold of a pilot's white scarf, and a pair of aviation goggles, which he was wearing on his head.

'I was just explaining the theme to your help here, but she seems not to have a clue what I'm talking about.'

A chill was spreading across my chest and down into my

stomach. The combination of wounded vanity at being referred to as the help and dread as to what this 'entertaining' might entail turned the food to dust in my mouth and I put down my fork.

'You remember, Connie,' said Evelyn, who was dressed all in fluffy yellow feathers like a baby chick. 'I told you this morning that everyone is to do a turn of something flight-related?'

'No, I'm sure you didn't mention it.' But even as I said it, I was doubting myself, going back in time to that conversation over breakfast. I hadn't really been listening. Evelyn chatted so much that sometimes I allowed her voice to trickle over me like a burbling brook.

'Constance, I think the earthquake must have turned you quite deaf,' said Roberto. 'She certainly did tell you. I was right here.'

'Well, it doesn't matter,' said Evelyn. 'It must be jolly hard being away from home and all your normal routines, Connie. You're bound to get confused from time to time. I'd be an utter *wreck*.'

Klara Fletcher was on one side of me, and I saw that she had brought along a token in honour of the evening's theme in the form of a small, intricately carved black-lacquered bird with a tail which, with one flick of her wrist, snapped open to reveal a semicircular fan of the daintiest peacock plumes, one inlaid over the other.

'You have a lovely face,' she said to me, apropos of nothing, and I was glad of the draught of cool air coming from her ornate fan to soothe the sudden heat that flared up from my chest. 'I vould like to paint you. Although, sadly, I am a very bad painter. Vorse even than DF.'

'What are you saying?' Evelyn demanded to know. 'I insist you tell me everything.'

The meal inched along. Olivia Averell, who was on my other side, was one of those young women who keep their eyes averted from the old as if age were an embarrassing affliction and she was doing a kind, tactful thing by pretending not to see it, having as it did nothing whatsoever to do with her. As a result, she gazed at the napkin ring in front of her or the gravy boat to the side while answering my ever more desperate queries in a voice so small it might have been merely a sigh, so I had to crane to hear her. Yes, we were indeed fortunate to live somewhere so beautiful. No, she didn't follow politics. She left that to the men. No, she would not be staying in Florence during the heat of August but would spend five weeks in England, where she already had a full programme of parties and dances to attend. 'That sounds quite exhausting.' I was joking, but when she turned her pale eyes to me they were deathly solemn. 'I eat a great quantity of raw vegetables to keep up my strength.'

Time seemed to pass in slow motion. Philip Wheeler was railing about a rival coleopterist from America who had written a paper denouncing Wheeler's latest research into water beetles as 'bunkum'. Alice de Havilland immediately declared 'bunkum' to be a most satisfactory sort of word, while Evelyn insisted Roberto put on his goggles and imitate a water beetle. People got up, moved around, sat back down. I became aware distantly of Klara Fletcher fidgeting beside me, picking up random objects from the table and replacing them heavily.

'It is gone,' she said now, silencing the table. 'The little peacock fan.'

'Perhaps it flew away,' suggested Evelyn, who by this time had had quite a lot to drink.

'Damnation. It vos my mother's.'

'Really? I thought we'd sold all her things,' said her husband.

And now pudding was served, a jelly in the shape of an aeroplane, which was greeted with whoops of admiration. People got up to do their turns, Roberto and Evelyn together performing a duet from *Madame Butterfly* in hammy operatic style, Duncan Fletcher reading from his new book in flat northern tones. Nothing remotely filthy, to the disappointment of the Manettis, just something about a man lying in bed watching a fly moving on a dirty windowpane.

I found my thoughts drifting back to William, who had been out of sorts by the time I popped into his sitting room on my way into dinner. He'd declined to attend the gathering, I believed through a combination of antagonism towards the Wheelers and not wanting to be seen in public in his current state. But that didn't prevent him being peeved that I was going, and we had quite a tetchy exchange. 'The girl's chatter gave me a headache,' he said when I asked where Nora was. I felt stung with disappointment, even though I could see it was an excuse. Already today he'd had two spasms of stomach pain that he'd tried unsuccessfully to pass off as indigestion.

Oliva Averell put a small, damp hand on my arm. 'Could I have some of that mosquito cream you were using earlier,' she whispered. 'I'm being eaten alive.'

The borrowed marabou feather bag had been hanging by its gold chain on the back of my chair. Now I slid it across the table towards her. 'Of course.'

While Emily Wheeler intoned an incomprehensible

poem she'd written expressly for the occasion on the subject of Lindbergh's Triumphant Dawn, Olivia snapped open the heavy brass clasp and . . .

'Oh!'

It wasn't a particularly loud exclamation but, given that the girl hardly ever spoke above a murmur, it was enough to still the proceedings.

'I'm sorry,' she said. 'But isn't this . . .?'

In plain view, as if it had recently alighted there by itself, was Klara Fletcher's missing peacock fan.

'I don't understand,' I said, feeling as if an invisible corset were being laced up tight around my ribs. 'I didn't put that there.'

There was an awkward pause, and then Klara Fletcher leaned across me and plucked her fan out of my bag. 'I do zis all the time. Put things where they do not belong. In pockets or bags. Without even noticing I am doing it.'

'Although, to be fair, sometimes you do steal things on purpose,' her husband corrected her.

Everyone laughed, but I caught Evelyn looking at me with a worried expression. It was absurd. I couldn't have made such a silly mistake.

Could I?

The sound of the doorbell cut through my unvoiced question. I turned to look through the front window. There had been no sound of a car engine arriving.

A moment later Alina appeared in the doorway.

'There's a visitor at the door, a young man,' she said to Evelyn, who had turned to her with her eyebrows raised.

'What does he want?'

'He wants to speak to Mrs Bowen. He says he's her son.'

20

WHEN MY CHILDREN were little, they seemed to grow and alter the second they were out of my sight, so that at the end of a day's absence I'd notice features I could swear had not been there when I waved them off. And if we were parted for longer – when my mother was ill and I went to Surrey to nurse her, when James went off to school – they often appeared, when next I saw them, to be other creatures entirely to the children whose dear faces were as familiar to me as my own. Angles sharper, curves flattened. When I embraced them they did not fit in the place I was used to them fitting, but instead came to my chest or my shoulder or my neck, and I would have to learn them all over again.

Seeing James come through the doorway of the Castello di Roccia Nera, so utterly and completely out of context, my initial reaction was not that of a mother but of a woman grateful for any distraction from a recent public humiliation observing a pleasant-faced young man who had no connection to her at all. My next reaction as my brain scrambled to catch up was shock at how little he resembled the James of my memory. Had his skin always been so pallid, almost translucent? Had his expression always been so serious?

Surely he had aged two years or more in the two months since I'd left England? Only when, after casting nervously around the room, his eyes came to rest on me, did recognition finally sink in, and I got to my feet. 'Oh, but . . .'

Evelyn was already up and advancing on James.

'You are dear Connie's son? She never said you were so handsome.'

I saw James flush pink from across the room as she took his hand in both of hers.

'James, is everything all right? Is there bad news?' It was the only reason I could think to explain his presence.

I hurried towards him, conscious of all eyes on me, aware that I might not be behaving as a mother should.

'Don't worry, Mother, there is nothing wrong. The house in Pinner has not fallen down.' James's attempt at joviality seemed yet another way of distancing the man who stood here from the solemn son I had left behind.

'I had holiday owing to me, and I thought I might as well take it here. Your letters made it sound like paradise on earth.'

Now I remembered all the pages of feverish description I'd sent him. How in my head he'd taken the place of Caroline and Millie, my lost correspondents. He must have thought I was losing my mind.

'And that's perfectly true.'

Conflicting emotions tied themselves up in a knot in my stomach. I was happy to see James, of course. *My boy!* But also nervous of what he might think. I tried to see the scene through his eyes – the Fletchers, the Wheelers – Emily Wheeler dressed like Lindbergh himself with a leather jacket and a matching hat that sat on her head like a bowl, with long flaps reaching down over her ears, Alice de Havilland in her ostrich-feather dress and old-fashioned black monocle. The marabou bag open on the table.

'You look so different, Mother.'

'Perhaps I've lost a little weight. But I had plenty to lose so I am quite happy about that.'

James nodded, although he didn't look entirely convinced. 'I've taken a room in a *pensione* in the town,' he said, as if in answer to a question no one had thought to ask. 'It's perfectly nice, though there are rather a lot of stairs. I have a view of the river.'

All this time, Evelyn was hovering around him like the little jewelled hummingbird she wore as a brooch. Now she took his hand and pulled him towards the table, ignoring his protests, pressing him down into the empty chair next to hers. I saw the pink flush of his cheeks and the way he glanced from her, glowing like a buttercup in her yellow feathers, to her handsome husband in his goggles, and a chill fluttered over me on moth wings.

'Have you come far?' asked Olivia Averell, whose flagging energies seemed marginally restored by the unexpected arrival of a mysterious young man.

As James explained his journey, I saw him take stock of the young girl across the table next to me. Of course, he would admire someone like Olivia Averell, though I knew he was far too sensible to imagine chances where none existed. However, when I looked back to my son, I saw his gaze had slipped away from the American heiress and back once more to the Manettis' end of the table, drinking in yellow feathers that quivered in the air like dandelion fluff.

After James had been quizzed, and then had to listen to a

recounting of the earthquake, which seemed to leave him quite shaken, the conversation turned to politics.

'It's the ingratitude I can't bear,' Emily Wheeler was saying in her unignorable rasping voice. 'We do everything for them apart from tuck them into bed at night, and this is how they repay us.' She was talking about the workers who lived in the farmhouses on their land, I realized with a sinking feeling.

'The *mezzadria* way of doing things has always worked perfectly well, that's the thing. We give them a place to live and all the equipment, and they supply the work. Anything we sell or grow gets divided down the middle. It couldn't be fairer. And now they're threatening not to work unless we hand over control or pay them. As if we've got the money to do that!'

She said this last very pointedly, and Evelyn shrugged, ruffling her feathers. 'Nothing to do with *me*.'

'Honestly, Roberto,' Mrs Wheeler went on. 'Thank god for your lot. Otherwise everything would be falling apart.'

I'd hardly dared look at James while Emily Wheeler was talking, and a quick glance across now confirmed my fears. He was listening to the conversation with pressed lips, and the fingers clutching his fork were bloodless at the tips.

'What about free will?' he asked when he could stay silent no longer. 'How will these people ever be able to make different choices without being paid for their labour or given autonomy over the things they produce?'

Emily Wheeler looked at him blankly.

'Why would they need to make different choices? They have food. Somewhere to live.'

'Are you really saying there should be no chance for them to better themselves? Or change their lives?'

Roberto cut in. 'Of course no one is saying that. But if it becomes every man for himself, the entire system will collapse. These things must be done in an orderly way. Someone must be in charge.'

'In many ways, it's no different, really, to your mother's situation,' said Philip Wheeler, his round eyes black plugs in the pink sheen of his face. 'She gets her board and meals, and perhaps a little stipend on top, but not enough to – what was your phrase? – make different choices.'

I felt as if I'd been slapped, and James's face darkened.

Klara Fletcher cut in. 'You know, I'd be quite happy to have everything done for me, not one shred of self-determination left. I'd be like a foie gras, doing nothing except opening my mouth for food. Then, ven I'm fat enough, you're all very velcome to eat me.'

21

WHEN I AWOKE the next morning after another fitful night, I felt at first that I must have dreamed James's arrival. Then, once I knew it to be real, came again the knot of conflicting emotions. Happiness that I would get to spend time with him and to introduce him to the beauty I had found in this place. Guilt that he'd come all this way because of letters I'd sent him only because I had no one else – because there was so much in my head and I'd needed to tell *someone*, but not because I needed to tell *him*. Nervousness at what on earth we would find to say to one another during these two weeks he was to spend in Florence. And above and beyond all this, a sense of apprehension that had to do with the changes in me that I'd tried to ignore, only to see written large in my son's expression, and with his disapproval of Roberto.

Not to mention the prospect of introducing him to William.

While I'd written enthusiastically to James in my letters about the castle – the way the branches of the giant camphor tree fanned out around its trunk like a peacock's tail, the lizards that basked in the sunshine on the lichen-covered castle walls – and about Florence itself, I had made only the most cursory mention of my charge, never imagining the two of them would actually meet.

That morning William was well enough to tackle his growing pile of unanswered correspondence and so we went through it slowly, but my mind was all over the place. He'd got into the habit of saying, 'Blah blah blah,' when he wanted me to finish off a letter for him. But this morning I couldn't think of the right words and he tutted in displeasure. Then it was time for the daily massage. After the occasion when I'd misplaced my hands, we'd developed a routine whereby I performed the exercises with military precision, while William closed his eyes and either went to sleep or pretended to.

Today, though, his gaze remained trained on my face.

'You're scared of your son.'

I was so surprised I almost dropped the foot I was holding. I'd told him, of course, about James's unexpected arrival, but hadn't gone into detail, priding myself on my professionalism.

'That's ridiculous. I'm excited. That's all.'

It had been arranged that James would come to the castle later that day so that I could show him around properly in the daylight. As I sat in William's sitting room waiting for him to arrive, I felt as agitated as I had in the first days of my courtship with Walter, all butterflies and knots. When the bell sounded, William insisted I help him get to his feet.

'Here's your son, Constance – Mrs Bowen – all the way from England,' said Alina, showing James in.

As James stared at William, I realized I had never corrected James in his – and my own – initial assumption that the invalid I was tasked with looking after was frail and elderly. Even in his reduced state, William cut a handsome figure, broad and bearded, his keen blue eyes undimmed by all he had been through.

'Delighted to meet you, sir,' said James, recovering himself enough to proffer his hand.

William carefully shifted his weight, leaning on his cane, so he could return the handshake.

'Why don't we all sit?' I said.

There followed ten minutes or so of awkward conversation with William asking James questions with laborious care, while James in turn studied his face, trying to deduce what he was saying from the shapes his mouth was making, a horrible silence following after each one while James's brain processed what he had heard and turned it into words. I found myself saying in my head the same phrase over and over. *Please like each other. Please like each other.*

Alina reappeared in the doorway, offering to sit with William while I showed James around.

'Why don't you walk up to Black Rock?' she suggested. 'It's so lovely and cool in the woods.'

I was in no hurry to revisit the place which had exerted such an unnerving pull over me, but I knew that, unlike the walk down to the stream, which was fairly well used, we would have the hill behind the castle to ourselves.

I led James through to the kitchen, stopping to introduce him to Renata, who paused in the act of skinning a rabbit to look James up and down. Then she nudged me and said something in Italian before roaring with laughter.

Through the back door and out into the blazing heat, where James immediately broke into a sweat, so I hurried him through the back gardens to the cool shade of the trees.

I combed my mind for something to say, firing off a series of questions about his work in the accountancy firm, which he answered sparingly, finally drawing a line under the subject: 'Isn't it enough that I have to devote so many hours of my life to my job, without having to talk about it on holiday too?'

We laboured up the hillside in silence, the heat making the walk more arduous than the last time. I'd hoped that having shed some weight might make the climb easier, but in fact it only made me feel weaker.

By the time we arrived at the clearing at the top the silence had calcified around us into something hard and solid. I saw James blink as he took in the towering rock, bulked against the white heat of the sky. The only shade was under the overhang of the rock, where the temperature never rose and the stone felt cold and damp with lichen.

'What is this place?' asked James, shivering even while the sweat dried on his brow.

I told him about the legend of the failed crops and the local girls burned as witches, trying to keep my voice jolly, as if this were a fairy story and not something that had actually happened here in this very spot where we now stood.

James, his skin pale and clammy in the shade of the rock, listened with a pinched, wary expression that I recognized from when he was an easily scared child being teased by his sister and seeing danger in every dark corner, every creaking pipe or floorboard.

Sensing the need to change the subject, I told him again how glad I was he had come.

'Your letters were so very unlike you. I thought you might be having some kind of mental collapse.'

'Don't be silly. I've always written long letters.'

'You've always written long letters *to Millie*. I'd be lucky to get a recap of the weather and a "wish you were here".'

I remembered the summer Millie went to stay in Scotland with her friend Penelope. The pages I wrote her, with all the little details of the day.

'You told me William North was a doddery old codger.' James plucked a piece of moss from the ground and rubbed it between his fingers.

'I said no such thing.'

'Well, you implied it. Instead, I find he's younger than Father.'

'What are you saying, James?'

James threw the moss to the earth.

'I'm not saying anything. Except these aren't our kind of people, these Manettis and Norths.'

'And just what are our kind of people?'

'You know very well. *Ordinary*.'

'Oh, darling, don't you ever feel you would like to experience something a little *extraordinary*?'

'No! Not if I had to go back to normal life at the end of it. Back to Pinner. Back to putting on a suit and getting on the train every morning and going into that office and watching that clock.'

I was astonished. James rarely talked of his work life. Never talked like this.

Evelyn was waiting for us in the courtyard with the table set for tea. She laughed when she saw the state of us.

'Mr Bowen – can I call you James? Pretty please? You look as if you're on the verge of melting. Come sit here by me in the shade. Renata has made lemonade and I promise it will revive you instantly.'

She wore a white sleeveless top with white wide-legged linen trousers which came high in the waist and emphasized the narrowness of her frame. Such a waif, she seemed light as air.

James, who hadn't addressed a single word to me during the entire descent from Black Rock, perked up as we approached, and I saw him run a hand through his hair.

I watched my son's normally clenched expression open up like a flower as our hostess chattered. *Don't begrudge him this*, I scolded myself. *He is a young man, on holiday in Italy. Let him fall unsuitably in love. Why not?* Still, there was a rock in my stomach.

Unusually, Roberto was also in attendance. I hadn't noticed him at first, as he was crouched down trying to photograph a butterfly that had alighted on a splendid tree peony.

'It's so wonderful of you to lend us your mother in our hour of need, James,' Evelyn said, pouring tea. She was wearing a silver bracelet around her wrist and when she raised her arm it slid down almost to the elbow. 'She has been such a godsend. Not just to my uncle but also to me and my daughter, Nora.'

I looked around then. It was unlike Nora not to have come running out at the sound of voices.

'Should I fetch Nora?' I asked.

'Oh no, I don't think so, Constance. I left her very happily playing upstairs.'

I suspected Evelyn wanted to keep Nora hidden from James, just as she kept her from the visitors who trooped in and out the front door to lunch or dinner. Though she'd gone along willingly enough with the plan to straighten

Nora's nose, I'd noticed she kept her eyes averted from the metal frame, as if she couldn't bear the sight of it.

I knew I ought to make more of a fuss. It was not right for the child to be denied even basic scraps of human contact. But Nora was not my responsibility. There was a shameful part of me that also wanted to keep Nora hidden away, not wanting to see James's reaction, or risk him asking me how I'd allowed such a thing to happen.

'I honestly don't know what we'd have done without darling Connie these last months,' said Evelyn, returning to her theme. 'She's been such a help to William, and to all of us, even the servants. I just hope she hasn't stretched herself too thin. We've had to get quite stern with you, haven't we, Connie, about overdoing things and getting all muddled.'

James turned to me, but before he could ask what she meant Roberto cut in.

'I insist on taking your photograph,' he said to James, smiling. 'You have such a noble sort of face. Will you come and sit for me?'

James reddened and I could see he was torn between wanting to refuse and not wanting to seem rude.

'Oh, do let him,' Evelyn said. 'He's very good. And he's perfectly right. You do have an awfully nice face.'

James allowed himself to be led off to pose stiffly underneath a persimmon tree. He didn't look at Roberto, but rather kept his gaze averted to me, and I could see in his eyes how uncomfortable he was.

As soon as Roberto had pressed the shutter James tried to move off, but Roberto called him back. 'And one against the castle wall back here. The light is so perfect on the roses.'

Reluctantly, James followed, the two of them disappearing behind the tree.

'Your son is not a natural model.'

'No. In that respect he takes after his mother.'

When James emerged, still flushed with embarrassment, Evelyn took pity on him and patted the seat next to her under the pergola.

'Come, I need to know all about you. We lead such sad little lives here in Italy, cut off from everything that's happening in London. I insist you tell me every last detail of the plays you've seen, the parties, the nightclubs.'

James had to break it to her that he went to very few parties and couldn't remember the last time he saw a play.

'Though I should very much like to,' he said, surprising me. 'I did once think I might like to work in the theatre. Not acting, but staging and designing sets. I think I might have been quite good at it.'

It was the first I'd heard of it, and I felt at once both wounded that he was telling Evelyn, practically a stranger, something so personal, and at the same time inexpressibly sad on his behalf that he had nurtured such dreams and now spent his days working for a firm of accountants in a draughty office above a travel agency in Holborn.

Why hadn't he told me? I was overcome with anger at myself. How often over the past years had we sat across the table from one another in the dining room in Pinner and, instead of seeing a young man with secret hopes and ambitions, I'd imagined only a cardboard copy of his father. How had I allowed my son to become such a closed book to me?

And what would it take for us to find a way back to one another?

Evelyn, oblivious to these undertones, suddenly clapped her hands together.

'I've had the most splendid idea. We'll have a fancy-dress ball here at the castle before James goes home to his dreary job.'

'A ball? But surely it would be better to wait until your uncle is a little stronger?' The thought of William being surrounded by noise and disturbance when he was so ill made me outspoken.

Evelyn put her head to one side. 'On the contrary. It will cheer him up. Everything has been far too gloomy since Uncle Bill got ill. As the mistress of the castle, I insist we should all be as gay as possible. And besides, it's a terrible admission that you don't go to many parties, James. Everyone should go to at least one party a month. Roberto, my darling, can't you get your Mr Mussolini to make a law about that?'

In his lap, James's hand curled into a fist.

22

THE PROSPECT OF a ball seemed to give Evelyn renewed life and, over the following days, she darted around the castle corridors like one of the fireflies that gathered outside at dusk these hot summer evenings, dots of lights that swooped and soared and were never still.

I was worried about William and the toll entertaining on such a big scale might take on his health. I knew he would not want to appear weakened in front of his friends and neighbours and would push himself beyond what was healthy in order to see out the evening. But more draining than that were the endless preparations – the succession of tradesmen and musicians and florists and dressmakers. Evelyn had procured the legendary head barman from the Rivoire for the evening to mix cocktails and an English chef was being brought in to oversee the canapés, much to Renata's outrage.

After much discussion the theme had been selected. Jules Vernes's *20,000 Leagues Under the Sea*. Evelyn had only ever flicked through the novel, but that didn't deter her from deciding it would be a broad enough canvas to encompass women wanting to show off their figures as mermaids and sirens and men wishing to grandstand as pirates or mariners or naval officers.

Roberto was at first apathetic about the whole enterprise. I'd noticed he tended to reserve his enthusiasms for ideas that he had originated himself. He was soon won over, however, when Evelyn insisted the cream of Florentine society would be clamouring for an invitation, and declared he would have a water tank constructed in the castle grounds, where revellers could put their aquatic costumes to the test.

Evelyn had had to be dissuaded from having a model built of the *Titanic*, half submerged next to an iceberg.

'Over a thousand people died in that ship. Children, even,' I reminded her.

'Yes, but it was so long ago,' she argued. 'Ancient history, really . . .' She saw my face. 'No, you're quite right, Connie, I'm a monster.'

As Evelyn's planning got underway, I kept a close eye on William. I knew he wasn't happy about the steady stream of visitors, the noise of banging from various sets being built, but he did not have the energy for a fight, although once I heard him raise his voice to Evelyn when the two of them were alone and I was returning from an errand. 'Just who is footing the bill?' I heard him ask, but Evelyn claimed not to understand what he was saying.

Only once did I dare voice my concerns to Evelyn, as I sat opposite her at the table while she leafed through swatches of gauzy green fabric for the costume she was having made.

'Oh, this is divine, isn't it?' she said, holding up a square of sheer material that changed colour in the light.

'Yes, absolutely. Except . . . I worry the excitement might be too much for Mr North. He is so easily tired these days and—'

'Oh, good god, Connie, the man is not dead. Allow him a little fun, for heaven's sake. It will perk him right up. And the beautiful Black Widow herself will be there, which will be better than a thousand tonics. Or perhaps that's what's bothering you?'

She'd narrowed her eyes and was looking at me with her head on one side. The blood rushed to my ears.

'I don't know what you mean.'

'Is the real reason you're against the ball because you worry Louise Power will steal Uncle Bill away from you?'

'What are you talking about, Evelyn? I can assure you I have no—'

But Evelyn had already broken into peals of laughter.

'Oh, Connie, your face is priceless. It's a *joke*, silly. Of course I don't think you're scheming to marry Uncle Bill and get your hands on his fortune. Why do you think I deliberately advertised for an older companion? A man in my uncle's situation could be an easy target for the wrong sort of woman.'

I felt hot suddenly, the air too thick and stuffy to breathe.

Naturally the Manettis would have chosen someone old and plain enough not to be a threat. It made perfect sense.

So why did I feel winded, as if someone had kicked a very heavy leather football into my stomach?

Evelyn offered to drive me down to Florence to meet James the following afternoon. She had errands to run, she told me, which I assumed to mean more shopping or perhaps meeting friends for cocktails. William had complained of a stabbing pain in the morning, and I was loath to leave him, particularly since Alina, who normally sat with him in my stead, was under the weather herself and had had to go home.

'I can look after Great-uncle Bill,' Nora had insisted. 'Oh, please let me.'

My protestations died on my lips at the sight of the child's hopeful face.

In Florence, Evelyn's errands seemed miraculously not so urgent after all, and she insisted on showing James and me the delights of the city. I was secretly relieved to have her company after my unsuccessful outing to Black Rock with James a couple of days before. I had supposed he would wish to go straight to the Uffizi or to the vast marble Cathedral of Santa Maria del Fiore, with its famous red dome, but he seemed quite content to trail around in Evelyn's wake, assuring us that, armed with his trusty Baedeker guidebook, he would cover all the tourist sights while he was on his own. Instead, we had tea in the courtyard of the Palazzo Antinori, where the British Institute occupied the first floor, and then went to Old England Stores to pick up the English newspapers for William. And all the time Evelyn was telling us stories about the places and people we were passing: 'Over there' – she used her rolled-up parasol to point to a tall, thin building where a woman on the top floor was lowering a basket on a rope to collect parcels from a delivery boy in the street – 'is where Alice's brother Harold has an apartment that he keeps only to write in. Can you imagine, that enormous house of theirs, and he says he can't find a single quiet spot to work? And that place' – she indicated a little trattoria tucked away in a cobbled piazza – 'is where Roberto's brother bet him that he couldn't eat every single dessert on the menu. And he jolly well did.'

'I wish you could come to London and give me a tour,' said James. 'I imagine I should see my city in a very different light.'

The only sour point came when we saw a disturbance outside a bread shop, a young man without shoes being dragged roughly away by two blackshirts.

'I suppose there's still awful poverty in Italy,' said James.

'Yes, it's terribly sad,' said Evelyn. 'But really, Mussolini is the man for the job. Strong leadership is the key, Roberto says. Anyway, let's not get all gloomy when it's such a divine day.'

We strolled along the bank of the immense River Arno, past the St Regis Hotel, a former palace now turned into a grand hotel where horse-drawn traps waited alongside motorized taxi cabs to ferry guests around, and Evelyn told us how these riverside streets all had the word 'Lungarno' in their names, 'which is very well suited, because it makes one think of lungs and one can breathe freely, here, don't you agree?' she said, leaning over the stone wall and inhaling deeply.

I saw James take it all in, the beautiful city, the yellow light, the shining woman, and despite the pleasant warmth of the day, a shadow passed over me and I hugged my arms tightly to my chest.

We headed to Ponte Vecchio, where Evelyn wanted to pick up a ring that had belonged to Aunt Cecily that a jeweller in one of the little workshops that lined the bridge was resizing to fit her slender finger.

'Isn't that Mr Wheeler?' I just caught a glimpse of a man's back – squat and square – leaving the jeweller's and hurrying off in the other direction.

Evelyn craned her neck. 'Is it? Bother, we missed him.'

Inside, the tall, grey-complexioned shopkeeper, bald apart from a few remaining long strands of grey hair that fell forwards over his face, was bent over a gold necklace inset with rubies.

'It must have been Philip,' said Evelyn. 'That's Emily's favourite necklace. Her grandmother gave it to her.'

'Ah, Signora Manetti.' The jeweller straightened up and smoothed back his strands of hair with long, straight, yellow-tipped fingers.

Evelyn said something in Italian, which she spoke in a slow, musical way. I heard her mention Signore Wheeler and the jeweller nodded, launching into a long, involved reply.

Evelyn turned to us, eyes wide. 'He just *bought* it from Philip! Emily's necklace!'

She waited until we were outside the shop to say more.

'I knew the Wheelers were broke. But I had no idea it had got this bad.'

'I'm sorry to hear that,' said James, who looked uncomfortable discussing the financial affairs of someone he hardly knew. 'So many people are struggling at the moment.'

'In this case, they've only got themselves to blame, really.'

'You said they'd made some poor investments?' I said. We had come off the bridge now and were walking up one of the cobbled side streets, dodging the gaps in the pavement where the basement doors had been opened up to let air into the sweltering kitchens and workshops. Evelyn sighed.

'The truth is, Philip Wheeler was always jealous of Uncle Bill. He'd inherited his house and a bit of money – god knows you don't get rich grubbing around in the earth looking at ants and beetles – but he saw how Uncle Bill was making a fortune buying paintings and he thought, "I'll have some of that, thank you very much." But he didn't have Uncle Bill's connections, or his expertise. Anyway, he made a couple of misguided impulse buys that lost quite a lot of money. Then, two years ago, one of his murky contacts offered him the chance to buy what he assured him was an early Giotto "liberated" from an obscure monastery somewhere. It cost a packet, but Philip was sure he could sell it on again for twice as much. He didn't tell anyone he was buying it, he was so convinced Uncle Bill would swoop in and snatch it from him.

'But then the collector he tried to sell it on to, an American heiress whose family had got rich making soap powder, of all things, asked Uncle Bill to authenticate it, and Uncle Bill . . .'

'. . . said it was a fake,' James and I chorused. By now we'd stopped in one of the cobbled piazzas, where a group of roving musicians were going table to table singing and playing guitar.

'Exactly! And poor old Philip was left with a painting that was virtually worthless.'

Now it made sense. The strange atmosphere whenever the Wheelers were around William. Philip Wheeler's bitterness.

'There was a terrible scene where Emily came over and virtually threw herself at Uncle Bill's feet, begging him to change his mind. But, you know, Uncle Bill can be quite ruthless. Very ruthless, actually.' A shadow passed across Evelyn's face as she looked directly at me. 'He said business was business and he was only as good as his reputation so he had to give an honest evaluation. But Philip maintains it was sour grapes because the painting didn't come to him first.

'Don't you hate it when people you love fall out? I've told Emily that when the castle eventually comes to me they shall have their pick of the wretched collection.'

*

Later that evening, I sat reading to William from one of the newspapers we had bought in Florence. His sitting room was suffocating, filled with the day's pent-up heat, but he refused to allow me to open a window, insisting he felt cold.

As I read, I glanced at him from time to time over the top of the paper, thinking about what Evelyn said about his falling-out with the Wheelers. It was no secret that William had a reputation for being single-minded in business. You didn't amass the kind of fortune he had by being kind or making exceptions for your friends.

But what else should he have done? If he thought the painting was by another, lesser painter, wouldn't it count against him if he'd said anything different? In many ways, I admired him for having the courage of his convictions. It couldn't have been easy to stand up to the entreaties of his neighbours and his niece. I thought of the times in the past my nerve had given way – when I'd stepped back from the suffrage movement, leaving it to women like Caroline. Braver women. When I'd failed to stand up to Walter and that doctor with the leeches. '*Mama, please don't let him.*'

As I reached the end of an item about the flooding in Mississippi, I looked over at William and saw, with a start, that he was staring at me, his eyes wide with panic.

I threw down the paper and rushed to his side.

'What is it? Are you in pain?'

He shook his head, but I could see he was struggling with something, his face turning first red then purple, as if he were being starved of oxygen. I was about to call for help when he made a gulping sound and then opened his mouth, gasping for air.

'Couldn't swallow,' he said when he'd had a chance to recover. 'Thought I would burst.'

He closed his eyes, and for a few moments neither of us spoke. I presumed him to be asleep until he said softly, without opening his eyes, 'I am scared, Constance.'

There was a swelling in my chest then, and a lump came to my throat. I bit back the urge to pretend I didn't know what he meant. I knew what it would have cost him to make such an admission and he deserved more than platitudes.

Instead, I reached out my hand and laid it momentarily over his own, feeling how long and elegant his fingers were, and how cool his skin under my palm.

'I know,' I said.

23

THE MORNING AFTER the Florence trip, dawn found me wide awake and restless and fretful with apprehension, though I couldn't have said why.

The day was already warming up and I decided to take a walk down to the river before the heat got too much and the rest of the household stirred.

As I descended the hillside under the cool green canopy of the forest, my spirits rose. In contrast to Black Rock Hill, where the overhead foliage was so thick and dense that the air always felt damp, there was something magical about these woods to the south-west of the castle. Dappled sunlight danced on the dry earth, and birdsong rang out from the trees, which were a mishmash of cypresses and elms and oaks and ash, smaller junipers and even olive trees, all brushing shoulders amicably, rather than vying for space.

Down by the river, which was more like a wide stream where a sharp bend had created a deep pool, a green dragonfly hovered. On the far side, the heron I'd glimpsed on my first day in Italy stood one-legged, gazing across to the opposite bank. I sat myself down and removed my shoes and stockings so that I could dangle my bare feet in the cold water. Lying back, I watched as a wash of blue chased the last remnants of pink from the sky, and the air began to hum with the sound of bees and flies and the piercing call of a swift speeding overhead.

Forgetting my earlier unease, I was engulfed by an immense and overwhelming gratitude. To be permitted such beauty, such peace. I think all of us who'd lived through the uncertainty of the war years, not knowing what devastation was being wrought on our soldiers or in our name so far away or what the future would hold for us all, would never again take peace for granted. Even a decade on, it seemed a luxury and a privilege.

I leaned back on my hands and raised my face to the dappled sun, but as I sat and basked, the fine hairs on my arms rose up, as if being brushed by an icy feather, and I became convinced that I was not alone.

I sat up straight and looked around, but though I thought I heard something in the undergrowth off to the side I could see nothing out of the ordinary. It would be a rabbit, I told myself, or even a badger. I remembered Nora telling me with relish about snakes that lived by the river and snatched my feet out of the water.

I tried to return to the quiet joy of a few moments before, but the mood had been broken. A toad grunted from the nearby weeds, a guttural sound that grated in the air, and my feet itched as if reacting to something in the water. I pulled on my stockings and shoes and slithered off the rock. But there! Wasn't that something moving up ahead? The dark shape was gone before it had even taken form. I'd heard there were deer in the forests, though I'd never seen any. Wild boar, too. The prospect of coming up against an angry female boar protecting her young did little to soothe my nerves.

I began the ascent towards the castle, stumbling once over a tree root and another time on a vine. Sweat beaded on my upper lip and trickled down my spine, and I stopped, panting, to lean against the slender trunk of a silver ash. The uncomfortable sensation of being watched returned, and I turned my head this way and that. I pressed on, my heart now thudding in my chest. As I climbed, I heard noises behind me – twigs cracking, heavy breathing to match my own. Twice, I glanced behind and, though the hillside appeared deserted, I was still convinced that at any moment I'd feel a hand on my shoulder wrenching me back.

By the time I burst out into the open air at the top of the hill near the castle gate I was gasping for air and I felt as if my lungs would explode. I hurried towards the castle and stopped for a moment outside the iron gates, standing under one of the stone dragons with my hands on my knees, waiting for my racing pulse to return to normal.

When I was finally recovered enough to go inside, I found, to my great surprise, that James was there, already seated at the breakfast table, chatting to Evelyn, who was dressed only in her satin nightgown, with a satin kimono belted over the top.

James, flushing pink, jumped to his feet.

'I was up early so I thought I'd take the tram to Ponte a Mensola and have a walk up the hillside, but I didn't realize what an uncivilized hour it was until I'd woken everyone up,' he said.

By everyone, he clearly meant Evelyn.

I wondered uneasily how Roberto would react if he came

down and found his wife half dressed like this with a virtual stranger. He gave the impression of being easygoing, but I'd already seen that there was a steelier side to him. I thought about how much attention Roberto paid to Olivia Averell, though he knew Evelyn didn't like it. Could Evelyn be deliberately trying to make her husband jealous, using my son like one of the pieces on William's chessboard?

'Shall we go for a walk before Mr North comes down?' I said, offering my hand to James. 'Why don't I take you up to the castle roof?'

I didn't relish the idea of going up all those narrow turret stairs, after having all but run up the hillside, but I wanted to get James away. I saw him glance over at Evelyn, as if waiting for her to protest.

'I wouldn't like to disturb Mr Manetti,' he began, his face reddening noticeably. But Evelyn only smiled and continued sipping her coffee. In the harsh morning light, she looked her age, but all the more lovely for it.

On the way up to the roof, as the narrow steps wound interminably upwards, I remembered the night I'd run here in my nightdress, chasing the notes of a non-existent violin, and felt a rush of shame. What had I been thinking?

Out on the parapet, James inhaled sharply as he took in the view. Undulating green hills that cradled the sparkling city as if in a bowl, the dome of the cathedral blazing in the sun like a brazier. Below us the terracotta roofs of neighbouring villas and farmhouses dotted the hillside all the way down to the glittering river that snaked through the valley. In the distance the ring of mountains as usual appeared purple against the indigo sky. Only the looming bulk of Black Rock Hill to the back of us was in shadow.

James leaned over the stone battlement.

'You know, Mother, when I was back at home, I couldn't imagine what had possessed you to leave everything behind and come out here, but now I quite envy you. This landscape, that city. The company you have found here.'

I watched his grip tighten on the stone and knew without needing to look that he would be blushing.

'Yes, the family has been very welcoming. William is very—'

'I wasn't talking about Mr North, though it is perfectly plain how much you admire him.' I felt the blood rush to my face.

'I was talking about Evelyn,' he went on. 'She's so strong and brave, in spite of all the obstacles she's faced. Her parents all but disowning her, that brute of a first husband running off and leaving her to raise her little girl all alone. No wonder she jumped into marriage with Roberto.' His voice cracked when he said the last word, and again I felt afraid for him. As far as I knew, he'd never had a sweetheart. He was emotionally vulnerable.

'Is that what she told you?'

'No. Of course not.'

For a moment we stayed side by side in silence, gazing out at the view. James cleared his throat.

'Evelyn told me she's been worried about you.'

'Me? Why?'

'She says you're not sleeping well and you've allowed yourself to become upset by a silly story someone told you.'

'That's ridiculous. Why ever would she say that?'

But even as I protested I was remembering how pale my bare feet had looked in the moonlight when I'd come up here in search of that phantom violin.

Back downstairs, Evelyn was now dressed in a sleeveless dress with a daisy print, a yellow band around her hair. She was going into the town, she told us. Why didn't she give James a lift?

'But your husband—'

'Oh, Roberto won't mind. Anyway, he comes and goes as he likes, so he can hardly object to me doing the same.'

'If you're sure it wouldn't be any trouble,' said James.

There was no reasonable objection I could make, so I remained silent, but that didn't stop unease from tying my nerves into knots as I stood in the hallway watching the two of them make preparations to leave together. They'd just stepped outside when there came a commotion behind me and Nora came flying down the stairs.

'Wait! You said you'd take me the next time. You promised!'

I'm ashamed to say Nora's medieval-looking nose device had become so much a part of her by this time that I scarcely registered it, but James's face drained of colour at the sight, forcing me to see it again through fresh eyes. The sheer barbaric horror of the metal strap clamped over the girl's small head.

'No, Nora. I'm sorry, darling, but it's just not possible.'

Evelyn's tone was brittle, and I could tell that she, too, didn't relish having to confront the reality of her daughter's appearance through the objective gaze of a stranger.

'But Mummy, please. You said.'

'I said no, Nora,' Evelyn snapped. I felt rather than saw how James flinched. 'Now run along.'

'Why don't you come with me to visit Great-uncle Bill?' I offered, watching Evelyn loop her arm through James's.

'Poor Nora,' she was saying as they walked towards the car. 'She has been so brave, but she is at that age where she would like to live in my pocket.'

James turned his head, just once, as he opened the car door for Evelyn to climb inside. Our eyes met, and it was I who turned away first.

24

IT WOULD BE another four days before I saw my son again. William took a turn for the worse, lying on his chaise longue, unable to speak or eat. All I could do was sit near him, reading aloud. Every time I glanced over and saw the pallor of his skin, my heart tore softly. Dr Pearson was called again and questioned me so closely on my administering of the medicines that I almost felt as if I were under investigation. He remained with William for some hours, manipulating him and testing his responses. He'd brought with him a large wooden box that Massimo was summoned to fetch from the car. It was a Galvanic electrotherapy machine, he told me proudly. The latest scientific development. He insisted I leave the room while he applied it, and when I came back inside there were angry red patches on William's forehead. Shortly afterwards I was asked to leave again. I suspected the doctor was administering an enema – such things held little distaste for me after working in a hospital during the war – but when I asked Dr Pearson about it, he seemed appalled, shutting me down with a firm 'These things are between a patient and his physician.' I was light-headed with relief when the doctor finally gave William a dose of something that seemed to revive him sufficiently for him to sit up and manage a spoonful of honey.

'It's a complicated case,' Dr Pearson said, standing in the hallway, mopping at the perspiration that trickled down his forehead. 'When there has been damage to the brain, it is almost impossible to predict how things will go.'

He instructed that from this point on William's food was to be administered only in semi-liquid form, so it must be pulverized or turned into soup by Renata before being served.

'The swallowing difficulty is something we see quite often with cerebral haemorrhages,' he said. 'We must be very careful to avoid choking or infections of the lungs if the food gets into the airway.'

I'd telephoned the *pensione* where James was staying to tell him I was needed at the castle, so it wasn't until the following day – a Sunday – when William was well enough for me to conceive of leaving him with Alina, that I took the bus into town. We'd arranged to meet for lunch so I took him to Procacci's, a jolly sort of place on the Tornabuoni where you could have oblong-shaped bread rolls called paninis filled with salmon or fresh anchovies or slices of cured ham.

James seemed in good spirits, telling me how he'd stood for so long in front of Michelangelo's *David* at the Galleria dell'Accademia the previous day that he had developed cramp in his right calf.

'I hope you weren't too disturbed by Nora's appearance when you were last at the castle,' I began as we enjoyed a coffee. 'I ought to have given you some warning.'

James looked grave. 'It did come as a shock, I can't lie. The thing looks like some kind of medieval torture device.'

'I know. I did try to intervene, but Roberto is very hard to say no to.'

James bent his head and I saw how his mouth was set into a grim line, but when he spoke his voice was gentle.

'It's not your place to intervene. You were in an impossible situation.'

I felt a weight lifting, knowing that he did not blame me, although I still harboured guilt that I hadn't done more.

'Anyway,' I said, changing the subject, 'you must tell me what you would like to see here in Florence before you go home next weekend. Why don't you write out a list? The time will pass before you know it.'

Now it was James's turn to look uncomfortable, determinedly stirring his coffee with a teaspoon that, whenever it struck the china, sounded like Evelyn's laugh.

'Actually, I've decided to stay on, Mother.'

I stared at him, waiting for his words to make sense.

'I telegrammed Mr Tucker at the firm and told him I needed more time here in Italy, and he has allowed me to take a week from next year's holiday allowance, which is very decent of him. So here I am!'

He said the last with a half-hearted flourish, as if he'd been intent on defiance but lost his nerve partway through.

'But why?' I saw his face fall. 'Don't misunderstand me, darling, I'm very glad to have you with me longer, I just don't want you to feel you must rearrange your whole life because of me.'

'Not at all. Obviously, I want to reassure myself you are being treated well here. And I'd rather not rush home straight after the ball in case I can be useful in terms of clearing up or some such thing.'

I gazed at him, open-mouthed. This was James, who grew tongue-tied in gatherings of more than three or four and had repeatedly broken his sister's heart by refusing to join her in dressing up for one or other thespian endeavour. That he had willingly sacrificed his meagre yearly holiday allowance to make the most of his time in Florence, where there were so many treasures it would take a lifetime to see them all, I could just about understand, but to reorder his plans to fit in around a party?

Of course, I knew what lay behind his sudden change of plan. Not what. Who. All at once I was overcome with frustration.

'You do know she's married, don't you? Evelyn Manetti. I don't want to see you make a fool of yourself.'

The words were out before I had a chance to check them. James at first looked shocked, and then angry.

'A fool? Shall we talk about who is the real fool in this family, Mother?'

'I don't know what you mean.'

'William North. I've seen the way you are around him. Fussing about, making any excuse to touch him. I never once saw you look at Father the way you look at that man. Not once. I honestly think you believe he is going to recover and marry you and you'll be mistress of the castle and never have to go back to Pinner again. You think I don't know how much you detest your life there? *Our* life?'

I couldn't speak, shock closing up my throat.

My immediate reaction was fury. How dare he accuse me of something so preposterous? But so close on its heels as to be almost simultaneous came the realization I had been fighting for weeks.

He was right.

Not about the marriage bit; I wasn't completely deluded. But about my feelings for William. The fact that I *had* feelings for him and that these went far beyond what was appropriate.

Hearing James speak the words out loud brought home to me the idiocy of my situation. I knew what kind of man William North was. He might not have married Cecily for her money, but it certainly factored. And if a woman didn't have money, she ought to be beautiful like Louise Power. That 'old and fat' still rang in my ears. We had built up a connection over the weeks, but it was like the connection an inmate builds with his jailer. It was based on dependence – a bitterly resented dependence at that. When fighting fit, William North, the handsome, charmingly ruthless art connoisseur who would bankrupt his own neighbours rather than compromise his reputation, would not have given me the time of day. I was quite sure of it.

But none of this could I admit to James. I could hardly admit it to myself.

'How can you be so unfeeling and cruel?' I burst out eventually. 'William is *dying*. Can you not understand that?'

I felt faint, my hand coming to my mouth, but it was too late. The words were out. I had never admitted, even to myself in the most private, dark hours of the night, that William might not recover, that he was in fact deteriorating each day and would soon reach a point from which there would be no turning back.

I felt myself tremble all over.

'Mother, are you all right? I'm sorry. I shouldn't have said those things.'

James leaned forward, his hand hovering above my own, as if he were afraid to touch me. We did not have this kind of language between us any more, the easy language of intimacy, and now neither knew how to acquire it. Instead, we remained both of us locked into our agonized silences, while the other diners chattered around us and our coffee grew cold.

Sitting in William's sitting room, hours later, reading to him from a two-day-old copy of *The Times*, I remained agitated. I could hardly bring myself to look at my charge. If James had divined my feelings, surely they must be written all over my face? Who else had noticed? Evelyn and Roberto? William himself?

It was late afternoon, but the drapes were still drawn against the relentless sun, which increasingly made William's head hurt. He was sitting in his chair with his eyes closed, propped up by cushions, while I was on the sofa facing him.

I was reading an account of the recent solar eclipse, which hadn't been viewable here in Italy but ought to have been a spectacle in England, except that cloud had all but obscured the view.

Stopping mid-sentence, my eyes filled with tears. As William was asleep, I allowed the tears to fall silently, though I had no idea whether I was crying because at some point in the not-too-far-off future I'd be going home and leaving the clear skies of Tuscany far behind, or because of the things James and I had said to each other – and the things we could never say – or because I'd finally admitted William wasn't getting better.

After a few minutes, I pulled myself together. What had I expected? That this life in the castle would last for ever?

I went to the window and pulled the curtains back, judging that it would be all right now that the white heat of the day had dissolved into something softer and less hostile. Easing the window open, I looked out across the flowerbeds to the edge of the gardens where the hillside fell away into the deepening blue of the late-afternoon sky. The air smelled of honeysuckle.

Back inside the room, William seemed to have slipped into an awkward position. As I gripped him gently by the shoulders to manoeuvre him into place, his eyes suddenly snapped open.

'You were crying.' His voice was weak through lack of use, yet still every word rang clear as a bell.

'No,' I lied.

But even as I said the words the tears were slipping down my cheeks. I tried to turn away, but William grabbed hold of my hand with a grip that was surprisingly strong.

'I'm not blind, woman. Crippled, but not blind.'

I knew how much effort it had cost him to speak, but his sympathy only made things worse. I was horrified by my lack of self-control. The last time I'd wept in company was Millie's funeral, and afterwards I really thought I'd cried a lifetime of tears in one day – that there simply weren't any left. Yet here I was once again awash with them.

'I had a terrible argument with James,' I said between sobs. 'Sometimes I feel like the two of us are total strangers with nothing in common but an accident of birth.' A memory came to me then of James as a small boy, sitting on my lap and searching my face with the most earnest expression. 'When I grow up I shall marry you, Mummy.' The memory only made me cry more.

'I don't mean that,' I said to William. 'I love him. I do. I just disappoint him all the time. And today we were very unkind to each other.'

William's hand had been covering mine. When he moved it I felt bereft, until he placed his palm very softly on my wet cheek. For a long moment, we looked at each other. Then James's words came crashing back into my head: *I honestly think you believe he is going to recover and marry you . . . Who is the real fool in this family, Mother?*

'I'm sorry,' I said, tearing myself away so that William's arm fell heavily back to his side. 'I don't know what's come over me. Ignore me.'

I fled from the room, instructing Nora, who was playing in the hallway, to sit with her great-uncle as I had a headache.

She fixed me solemnly with her brown eyes.

'It must hurt a lot to make you cry so much.'

I couldn't reply, but as I burst into my room and threw myself on my bed, I couldn't help thinking how right she was. Something was tearing inside me, something precious, and it hurt more than I thought possible.

Wrung out by my bout of self-pity, I slept early, only to be once again woken up by the sound of a child crying in the early hours of the morning. For the first time, my reaction was one of fury rather than fear and I was flooded with resolve to find out once and for all what was behind these nocturnal disturbances.

Wrapping my shawl around me, I lit the little oil lamp and stood for a moment in front of my door, waiting.

There. It came again, a soft sob, such as Millie used to

make when she was frightened in the night but didn't want to wake us.

I stepped out into the corridor and looked to the left. Nothing. Then the right. A blur of white, like a girl's nightdress, disappeared around the corner before I could get a proper look. I hurried to the end of the corridor and . . . Yes, there it was again. Only the briefest of glimpses, but it was definitely a young girl in an old-fashioned white lace nightdress, fleeing down the stairs.

'Nora?' I called out. 'Is that you?'

My own blood was deafening in my ears as I chased after the vision. Downstairs in the great hallway, I hesitated by the lion on the newel post. The double doors to the *salone* were closed, but I could hear what sounded like music playing softly and was about to rush in when across the courtyard I glimpsed a flash of white disappearing into a door at the far end of the corridor that led towards the kitchens. I hurried in pursuit, my heart pounding. Was it Nora, in the grip of another night terror?

Reaching the end of the corridor, I threw open the door through which the figure had vanished, realizing only after I'd plunged inside that it was Roberto's darkroom, where I'd been strictly forbidden to go.

I held up my lamp, peering into the black shadows.

'Nora? Are you in here?'

Nothing.

There was a counter running the length of the room on which rested flat trays half filled with liquid. A string passed overhead from one side of the room to the other on which a dozen or so photographic prints had been pegged out to dry. I saw the photograph of James in the pergola, scowling, and one of me, my face looking shockingly lined as I laughed at something someone was saying.

There were two framed photographs on the far wall. The first one was of a political rally and, when I drew closer, I recognized the tiny figure of Mussolini himself, il Duce, dwarfed by the vast flags hanging behind him. The second photograph showed a scene of a group of girls in pinafore dresses arranged on the steps of a building that looked like a schoolhouse, the sunlight reflecting off their long, shiny hair. The girls ranged in age from around five to fifteen or so, but all had the plump, clear complexions of the well-to-do. It was a nice composition, though nothing special, yet as I moved away something snagged in my mind, some loose thread of memory. But before I could explore it my attention was caught by a series of photographs pegged out at the far end of the line, of what, on first glance, I took to be a sea creature in a net.

Only when I came up close did I realize what I was looking at and my hand flew to my mouth.

The photographs were of Evelyn. Naked and trussed up like a piece of meat with bindings criss-crossing her body and her hands tied behind her back, a strip of cloth around her mouth, gagging her, she lay on a sheet covered in a pattern of swirling leaves.

I took a step backwards and as I did something moved behind me, a swoosh of white lace emerging from behind a filing cabinet, flying through the door before my still-reeling thoughts had a chance to catch up.

I shot out after her, desperate now to get away from those shocking images.

The corridor was empty, which meant the apparition

must have gone through the first door, to the library, but when I entered I could already see the double doors at the far end that led into the *salone* swinging shut. The roaring in my ears had risen in a crescendo and I felt a scream building somewhere deep inside me.

Without stopping to think, or to consider the music I'd heard earlier, I followed the figure through the second set of doors and stood blinking.

Impossibly, there was no sign of the girl in the nightdress. Instead, Evelyn and Roberto, dressed as they had been at dinner, were coolly dancing close together to Duke Ellington's orchestra playing on the crackly gramophone.

'Connie! What on earth?'

The two of them had stopped to stare at me, and I had some belated sense of how I might look, wild-eyed and barefoot, with my hair loose and tangled around my face.

'There was a girl,' I panted, addressing myself to Roberto, because I couldn't bring myself to look at Evelyn, with those photographs so fresh in my mind.

Roberto and Evelyn exchanged a blank look.

'She came in here not even a second ago. Wearing a nightdress. You must have seen her. She was crying outside my room. I thought it was Nora.'

Now the blankness was replaced by concern, which was much worse.

'We've been here all evening, and no one has come in,' said Roberto. 'But I'll happily take a tour around the castle with you to put your mind at rest.'

I cast around the room wildly, searching for the elusive child, but I could see nothing but the usual furniture and the paintings gazing from the walls. The energy that had propelled me here drained away, leaving me weak with embarrassment and a bone-deep fatigue.

Perhaps I was wrong and the figure hadn't come in here after all but had somehow managed to hide herself in the library.

Perhaps she was only a figment of your mind, came a voice inside me.

'No,' I told Roberto quietly. 'That's not necessary.'

'You were probably having a nightmare, like one of Nora's night terrors,' suggested Evelyn. 'There was a boy at my brother's prep school who regularly walked around in his sleep, and one night he walked right out of the open window and broke both his arms!'

'Yes,' I said, trying to force my leaden legs to move. 'That's most likely it.'

As I made my way out of the room I saw them glance at each other. Evelyn's eyebrows were arched in alarm. Roberto shrugged in response.

I knew they must be thinking I'd lost my mind.

As I lay in bed while the long hours ticked slowly past and the slits in the wooden shutters brightened from black to grey and then slowly to white, I thought they might well be right.

25

RISING EARLY, I went outside to sit for a while on the bench overlooking the valley while the day ripened around me. Whenever I thought about what had happened in the night, I felt a sharp pain behind my ribs and I had to press my hand to my chest and remind myself to breathe.

I tried instead to concentrate on my surroundings and gradually the beauty of the landscape calmed me. I had had a bad day, that was all. The argument with James followed by the moment when I'd cried so uncontrollably in front of William, all of it had mixed with the heat to create some kind of febrile waking dream. I tried to ignore the fact that I could still taste the adrenaline in the back of my throat as I'd chased the ghostly white figure through the castle and feel the shame hot on my skin when I'd seen the photographs of Evelyn.

Making my way around to the back garden, I saw the kitchen door was open, the smell of onions and peppers and garlic already seeping into the building heat outside. But as I skirted around the vegetable garden, past the courgette plants with their bright yellow flowers, I once again heard the sound of crying. For a terrible moment I thought that my night-time terrors had followed me here into the clear, hopeful light of a new day. But when I followed the sound around to the far side of the vegetable patch I came upon Alina sitting upon a stone step, weeping into the crook of her arm.

'What is it, Alina? Let me help you.'

She glanced up at me, her fine, expressive face blotchy with misery.

'Thank you, Constance, but I'm afraid there is nothing you can do for me.'

I sat down beside her and put my arm around her. Her shoulder blades were sharp.

'Please. There must be something I can do. I am a good listener, if nothing else.'

It was true that during those war years working as a volunteer in the hospital without medical training, I had more often than not felt of most use when sitting on a folding canvas stool next to a soldier's bed while he talked to me, not of the terrible things he had seen, although that did arise from time to time, but of the place and the people he had come from – the smell of his mother's blackberry pie, his little sister's giggle, the back wall that divided his yard from his best pal's. And did I know what had happened to that pal? Albert, his name was. Or Dougie. Or Ned. Could I find out? All the lost, broken boys pouring out their homesick hearts while I held their hands and pretended to be someone they loved.

Alina took a deep breath and seemed to stiffen. *She will not talk to me*, I thought sadly. *She will get up and walk away.* And yet she stayed.

'I am pregnant, Constance,' she said at length, her gaze fixed on the flagstoned path at her feet.

My first reaction was relief. This wasn't such a terrible

thing, another child. It was what happened in a marriage, after all. Then I thought about the three young children Alina already had at home, all of them under five years old. How she arrived in the mornings with her husband and her whole body seemed bent over itself, and only when she entered the castle on her own did her back straighten and her eyes grow clearer and brighter, how sometimes she seemed to linger in the evenings finding new jobs to do, an invoice she'd forgotten to draw up, a clock that needed winding.

'Alina,' I ventured, 'does Massimo treat you badly? Is that why you seem not to want to go home?'

'No, Constance. No. Massimo is a good man. He tries. It is not his fault.'

'So what is it?'

'Massimo's mother. She hates me. Massimo is under her thumb – that's the right expression? Massimo's family, they are not really Fascisti' – here, Alina lowered her voice and looked around, as if nervous of who might be listening, even here in the garden surrounded by insects, humming into life – 'but it is part of her power game, Massimo's mother, to insist that we must be good citizens by producing many children to populate the Italian state. You know families who have at least five children will pay less tax? It's il Duce's latest programme. Battle for Births. Do you think it has a nice sound?'

Alina let out a harsh bark of laughter that twisted up her face.

'She is all the time telling Massimo how he must be a man and a patriot and have more children. But really, it is so they will act as unpaid labour for the farm. And it's a way of keeping me in my place.'

My mind was reeling. Of course, I knew of families back home with seven or eight children, or more, crammed into one or two rooms. You saw them from the windows of the tram, crowded into front yards no bigger than a handkerchief, five-year-olds in charge of babies, toddlers playing untended in the dirt. I knew sentimentality was a luxury that came hand in glove with money. Yet still the cynicism Alina described took my breath away.

'What could she possibly have against you?' I asked.

Alina sighed.

'She is a clever woman who had no choices in her life and that has made her bitter. She resents that I have a working life that gets me out of the house, even though she needs the money that I make. And she also resents . . .'

Alina paused and pressed her lips together as if unsure she should say more.

'She also resents that I have known love.'

In the early-morning hush, I heard the sound of her swallowing.

'But she should be glad her son has a wife he loves and—'

'Not with Massimo.' When Alina was annoyed, her nostrils flared. 'I'm talking about Rupert North. We were in love. As you know, my mother was housekeeper here before me, and so Rupert and I grew up together and we loved each other. We had talked privately about marriage, when he came back from the war. We had such plans, but then he became ill.'

She put her hands to her forehead and I felt once again the sharp points of her shoulder blades against my arm.

'After he died and then Mrs North died, my dreams died with them, you know. Not only dreams of marriage to

Rupert, this man I loved with every part of me, but of what our life would be together. The freedom I might have.'

'But surely Mr North—'

'William North is many things, but he is not sentimental.' I'd noticed before a note of bitterness when Alina spoke about her employer. 'He kept me on here, and as far as he was concerned that was as far as his obligations went. He would never have agreed to Rupert marrying me, but when Mrs North was alive there was the hope that she at least might be on our side.'

'And she left no instructions in her will?'

'She was lost in her grief. Drowning in it. She could not think of anything more.'

I was quiet then. I knew all too well how that felt.

'I also was empty and lost and completely without direction,' Alina went on. 'When Massimo came and declared himself, I thought, "At least here is somewhere I could go. Here is a path in this desert of nothing." And at first, I was grateful to him, and I thought the children would be something I could give to him in return, and something that would give me a purpose. And I do love them. Really, Constance, you must believe this is true. I love them with my whole heart. But, God help me, they are not my whole life. And sometimes when I go home to that house at the end of the day with Massimo's mother saving up all day every bad thing the children have said or done, all the effort she has had to make to feed them and to dress them and to stop them fighting or crying or causing trouble, so that she can release it the minute I walk into the door like she is turning on a tap, and the children themselves pulling at me, each one wanting some attention from their mother, I feel like I am a grenade about to explode. And now this.' She looked down at her lightly rounded stomach. 'Another one, when my body is still not recovered from the last. I am exhausted, Constance. I want to get to know my children, but each time they grow to a point where we can begin to communicate, there arrives another. And another. Tell me, is this my life now? Child after child, like a sow, because Massimo cannot bear his mother's disapproval?

'I was promised a different life. It's terrible to grow up without hope, but it's far worse to be given hope and have it snatched away.'

I wondered if her bitterness was directed at William and Evelyn for not honouring Rupert's promises or at fate in general for its cruelty.

'And what happens when the baby is born? Mr North allowed me to come back to work – I think because he knew it's what Mrs North would have wanted. But now he is ill, Mr and Mrs Manetti are in charge. What if they dismiss me?'

'They wouldn't! Surely?'

'Constance, you must understand life is hard here for many people. Everyone would like a position like mine. Mrs Manetti has told me many times that her husband wants to give my job to his cousin. She says she has to fight for me. What if Mr Manetti uses this as a reason for letting me go?'

'Evelyn would never allow it. I know she is scatty sometimes, but she has a good heart.'

'Mrs Manetti will do anything to please her husband.'

Before I could stop it, an image flashed across my mind of Evelyn, naked and bound. I shut it down fast.

Something occurred to me then. 'Alina, the other day when you were unwell, had you taken something or done something to get rid of the baby?'

'Oh!' Alina clasped her hand to her mouth, her head hanging.

I remembered then what country we were in, and how the suggestion I had just made was the greatest sin of all.

'I am sorry,' I said quickly. 'You don't need to answer that.'

For a few moments, we sat in silence. There was nothing I could say to make her life different so, instead, after a while, I began talking about mine. I told her about the row with James, though I left out his accusations about my feelings for William. I told her about how jumpy I was all the time, how I'd imagined myself followed and the figure I thought I'd seen in the night.

'I worry my mind is becoming . . . unreliable,' I said. Hearing the words spoken out loud gave me a jolt of fear that I tried to disguise with an unconvincing laugh.

'What are you two giggling about? What is happening? Why are you sitting so close?' Evelyn had approached so silently both Alina and I were taken by surprise, the two of us leaping simultaneously to our feet, hurriedly brushing at our clothes.

Evelyn was wearing her silky kimono and her face was scrubbed and bare like a child's.

'Honestly, Evelyn, it was just mindless chitchat because we both happened to be up early. Only now I can see it's time to be getting to work.' I mimed looking at my wrist watch.

Evelyn's gaze flickered between Alina and me. I saw her take in Alina's tear-blotched face.

'If you have time to sit here gossiping, Alina, then we're clearly not keeping you busy enough.'

Evelyn was laughing, but Alina's gaunt cheeks turned

crimson and she hurried away through the kitchen door. I rose to follow her, but Evelyn called me back. She put her head on one side, and I knew what was coming.

'How are you feeling this morning, Connie, after your night wanderings?'

I closed my eyes, my stomach hard and heavy.

'I'm so embarrassed. I've never done anything like that before.'

'Poor old thing. I think we have been expecting too much of you.'

'No. Not at all. I'm very happy here.'

The thought that she might tell me to go home wrapped itself around my throat until I could hardly breathe.

There was a long, still moment where the birds seemed to stop calling and the kitchen fell silent. Then the silence was broken by a loud squawk from Cecily's cockatoo in the aviary and Evelyn smiled.

'Hurrah! I'm so glad. I don't know what I'd do without you, Connie. Now that's out of the way, have you thought about what you'll wear for the ball?'

I blinked, taken aback by the non-sequitur.

'No, and to be honest, Evelyn, I'm still worried Mr North isn't well enough.'

'Uncle Bill is very lucky to have you to worry about him, Connie. But you didn't know him before he got ill. He was all in favour of parties. Not because he liked people particularly, but because he considered them a useful way of making connections. He never knew who might happen to mention a stash of old paintings in a dead grandmother's attic, or a mouldy old church in the middle of nowhere that had a particularly interesting fresco. This ball will buck him up no end, especially if he has the likes of Louise Power fussing over him. He always did go quite gaga over a pretty face.'

Evelyn looped her arm through mine. The scent of yesterday's perfume wafted up from her gown, the vanilla and citrus smelling stale in comparison to the fresh mint and thyme that grew in such abundance around the garden.

'I want you to wear something fabulous for the ball, and I have the best idea. You shall be Amphitrite, Poseidon's wife, goddess of the sea. I've been finding out all about her. Emily Wheeler belongs to the Anglo-American amateur dramatics society in town, and she can dig you out a costume, and I'll find you some of Aunt Cecily's jewels to finish it off. They're big and old-fashioned and perfect for the part. Oh, Connie, I know you think it's frivolous when Uncle Bill is so ill, but I do think we have a duty to keep our spirits up, don't you, when life is so often drab and dreary?'

I found myself nodding, my protests melting, as ever, in the heat of her enthusiasm. Sensing the softening of my resolve, Evelyn squeezed my arm tight.

'And Roberto will so love acting the host and showing off to his friends and family. If it were up to him, he'd make it the law that all these grand old buildings were back in Italian hands. Sometimes I think he only married me so he'd get to live here in the castle.'

'I'm sure that's not so. He adores you.'

'Don't look so worried, Connie. I was only joking. And anyway, it doesn't matter in the slightest. I'm so wild about that man I don't give a fig why he's with me, as long as he is. You know, sometimes I worry love will devour me whole and all that will be left of me is the shoes I stand up in.'

*

Later that afternoon I was sitting reading to William in his sitting room when I became aware of a commotion outside. Seeing that William was dozing, I crept out to find the cause. I was so sleep-deprived and my general state of mind so jumpy that my thoughts leapt directly from the slightest anomaly to catastrophe and I was already thinking the worst. Another earthquake. It might happen.

In the back garden outside the kitchen door, a group had gathered. Renata, Alina, Roberto. Massimo was kneeling on the ground, looking at something laid out on a sheet of newspaper.

I went up to get a closer look – and turned away, my stomach convulsing. But the object on the paper exerted a pull and I found my gaze drawn back to where Cecily North's prize cockatoo lay torn to shreds, its white feathers dyed red with blood, the spaghetti of its intestines protruding from a gaping hole in its side.

Massimo said something in Italian and Alina translated.

'Someone left the door of the cage open. A fox must have come inside.'

'Or Uncle Bill's wretched dog,' muttered Evelyn.

Roberto turned to me, smiling.

'You see, Constance. This is your noise from last night. Not a child crying, but a fox doing battle with a bird.'

On its side, the cockatoo stared at me with its one black vacant eye.

26

I WAS NERVOUS ABOUT seeing James again after our last painful encounter. It mortified me that my feelings for William might be so easily read. The thought of Evelyn and Roberto, or William himself, seeing what was in my foolish heart was unendurable.

Acknowledging that James understood me better than I could have imagined meant having to renegotiate from scratch the arm's length relationship we'd built up. Was he ready for that kind of intimacy? Was I?

He arrived at the castle at cocktail hour two days after our altercation, on Evelyn's invitation. From the window of William's sitting room, where I was reading out the sales lists from the manager of William's gallery in New York, I watched James approach through the gates and was taken aback at how altered he appeared after his ten days in Italy. It was the golden hour, when all the world appeared to be set in amber, like ants caught in the resin of the trees, and James's hair, lightened by the sun, seemed almost aflame. His skin had been lightly bronzed from his days of strolling around Florence's wide squares and gardens and he was wearing a loose white shirt with the sleeves rolled up, tucked into flannel trousers. In one hand he carried a panama hat that I presumed he must have bought here in Italy, as I'd never seen it before. He walked with a looseness I had thought he had left behind in childhood, as if the heat had softened up his joints, and indeed his whole face seemed to have lost the tense lines that made him sometimes appear older than his years.

'James is here,' I remarked to William, who mumbled something I couldn't quite understand. Today had not been a good day and he had grown irritated both with his own inability to form the words and my lack of comprehension, at one point slapping his hand against his forehead in frustration. It was only as I made my way out to the courtyard, summoned by Evelyn, that I wondered if he might have said, 'He'd better not make you cry.'

James and Evelyn were lying side by side on wooden steamer chairs that had been set up on the lawn, now that the ferocity had gone from the day. Once again I felt a splinter of misgiving, seeing their fair heads so close together. Evelyn's legs were bare and her knees bent so the hem of the lemon-yellow dress had slid almost to her thighs. Those shocking photographs came to me and I shut my eyes tight. As I approached, she said something and the two of them erupted into laughter.

'Constance, you didn't tell me you and James had fallen out the last time you saw each other.'

Startled, I swung my gaze to James. Surely he hadn't told her what we'd argued about? For a second I wondered if that's what they had been laughing about, the two of them. My 'crush' on William.

'He refuses to tell me what it was about, even though I've shamelessly begged. You Bowens are so horribly discreet.

But whatever it was, I insist the two of you make it up this instant. I can't have two of my favourite people in the world falling out. Come on, Connie. Kiss and make up.'

Weak with relief that James had kept my secret, I obediently crossed to James and bent to drop a kiss on his cheek, trying not to mind how he stiffened under my touch.

Nora appeared in the doorway that led to the entrance hall, shyly standing with Matilda, as if unsure of her welcome. She'd come to find me early that morning, still distressed about the dead cockatoo. 'I used to talk to him,' she'd told me sadly. 'He was my friend.' In truth I was also missing it. I hadn't realized how much the bird's loud chatter was woven into the very fabric of the castle.

'Come, Nora,' I summoned her, and she skipped over to join us, her face pink with pleasure.

'Ah, here's my darling girl,' said Evelyn.

James sat up in his chair and I thought for a minute he might take his leave. I'd rarely seen him in the company of children and imagined he might find it uncomfortable. Irritating, even. Instead, he held out his hand to Nora.

'May I?'

Nora nodded and tentatively handed over her precious Matilda. I studied James's face, waiting to see him recoil from the grubby object, its hideous one-eyed countenance echoing that of the dead cockatoo. But he merely turned upon the doll a look of utmost solemnity and inspected it, turning it slowly and nodding to himself, like a physician examining a patient.

Nora watched, spellbound, as only a child entirely unused to attention would. Eventually, having lifted the doll to his ear as if listening for a heartbeat, James spoke.

'I'm pleased to tell you the child will live, thanks to your excellent nursing care, Miss Manetti.'

'Oh, Nora isn't a Manetti,' laughed Evelyn, as if the notion were amusing. 'She's an Aston, like her father.'

I saw Nora's face fall.

'Very well, Miss *Aston*, I commend your expertise in looking after this poor child. I prescribe plenty of rest and some hot milk every evening. Understood?'

Nora nodded again, her eyes not leaving James's face.

'She is a very dear little thing, though,' she said eventually. 'She never cries. She's a brave little soldier.'

Evelyn burst out laughing.

'Oh, Nora, you are a scream. Imagine you remembering what Aunt Cecily used to say to you, from all those years ago.'

For a moment, Evelyn looked at her daughter with curiosity, as if seeing her for the very first time, and Nora looked as if she might burst with happiness. But the mood was broken when Alina arrived outside to tell Evelyn she had a telephone call, and when Evelyn returned some minutes later her entire demeanour had altered.

'Whatever is the matter?' I asked.

James had got to his feet. 'I hope it isn't bad news?'

'Terrible news,' confirmed Evelyn, dropping heavily into her chair. 'My ball is just about ruined. Oh, I could cry, I really could. All the work I've put into it. The Fletchers aren't coming. And they were really the key to the whole night. I was going to *force* DF to read from his filthy book, and now they're not even going to be here. It's too much.'

I thought for a moment that she might cry.

'Damn rude of them, if you ask me,' said James. I'd

noticed his way of speaking had changed since he arrived, to mimic the Manettis'. 'What's their excuse?'

Evelyn appeared momentarily sheepish. 'DF has had some sort of relapse. You know the man suffers from tuberculosis. Well, one only has to look at him to see he's that sort, with that blue skin of his. Apparently, he'd been out picking peaches – in the heat of the sun, would you believe? – and then he came back inside and the next thing was Klara heard a sort of gurgling sound from the bedroom and there he was with blood gushing from his mouth. Which is all very sad for them, obviously, but so frustrating for me.'

My eyes met James's and I knew we were both remembering those terrible days with Millie, when she was near the end.

'That poor, poor man,' I said. 'Is he all right?'

A shadow flickered across Evelyn's face.

'As far as I know, he is weak but recovering. There's talk of them going somewhere cooler for the summer. I do hate it when people just up and leave like that.'

'It is not Mr Fletcher's fault, surely?' said James. 'I imagine he didn't practically bleed to death merely to disrupt your plans.'

'No, of course not.' Evelyn took a deep breath. 'You are right, James. I am being selfish and beastly. Please ignore my atrocious manners. Here . . .' Once again she held out one of her hands, as she had done for me before. 'Give me a good whack. I deserve it.'

'I shall do no such thing!'

James laughed, but as Evelyn turned away I saw his face slacken and fall.

*

I spent so much time with William that I sometimes imagined there was one skin covering the two of us. I was attuned to his ever-changing moods, knowing instinctively when to stop reading or talking to let him rest, and whether his grimace was one of annoyance or pain. Unlike the first weeks, when I had felt as if I must fill all the minutes with activity or chatter, we could now spend long stretches of time in silence without awkwardness.

It was only now that I realized how my late husband and I had remained strangers to one another our entire married lives. Only on his deathbed when he was truly afraid did Walter reach for my hand and our eyes met for the first time in years, and I felt a connection finally to this man who'd shared my home and my bed but had never known what I feared or desired, never asked what I dreamed of when I closed my eyes. I'd felt such sorrow then, gripping hold of him, that we had failed each other so profoundly.

Not so with William, whose thoughts and needs I anticipated as if they were my own. Occasionally, it even seemed as if the feeling ran both ways. Sometimes I would think him asleep and stare out of the window lost in my thoughts, only to hear him say, 'Something is bothering you.'

It was obvious when William was having a good day because he would argue with me. It didn't matter what about, it was the principle of the thing, that to agree would be to somehow cede ground, or make me complacent. If I opened the window, he'd ask if I wanted him to be bitten to death. If I closed it, he'd complain of suffocation. If I read the front pages of the newspaper, he'd interject whenever Prime Minister Baldwin's name was mentioned. 'Idiot!' he might say, or 'Preposterous!' But if I read the inside pages, he'd huff and puff as if they were beneath his interest.

On bad days he'd submit to my ministrations without a murmur, allowing me to remove the shoes that I judged too constricting or to adjust the cushions behind him, not raising a 'For god's sake, woman, he's a dog. That's what dogs do' when I used a hankie to wipe up Solomon's slobber.

When there had been two days straight without a single bad-tempered exclamation, I asked Evelyn to summon Dr Pearson. The physician presented himself at William's sitting room with a face the colour of raw liver.

'I shall never get used to this uncivil heat,' he panted, sitting down heavily in an upright chair. 'I cannot see what need there is for it.'

As if the weather had no business being so immoderate.

There was a soft knock at the door and then Nora appeared. I watched her face turn pale as she recognized one of the doctors responsible for fitting the hated brace to her head.

'Ah, Leonora. Come here, child, so that I can see what—'

But Nora had turned and fled before he could get to the end of his sentence. Dr Pearson gazed after her, perplexed.

'One wonders if the child is quite all there,' he said, and I bristled with an anger that took me by surprise. I looked at William, sure he would intercede, and when he failed even to open his mouth, I knew things were bad with him and my fury left just as suddenly as it had arrived.

Dr Pearson asked me to leave while he examined his patient and administered the electrotherapy, and I reluctantly acquiesced. As I neared the door I glanced over at William and his eyes met mine, and there was such a look of fright there that I paused.

'Is the machine really necessary?' I asked, forcing myself to stand my ground while Dr Pearson's little eyes widened in surprise. 'Mr North doesn't like it, and I can't see that it's having—'

'Are you a qualified physician, Mrs Bowen?'

'No, of course—'

'Or perhaps a trained nurse?'

'No, as I told you before, I never—'

'And yet you know better than I with my thirty-three years of experience?'

I shook my head and left the room, pacing the corridor outside, which was at least cooler than the rest of the castle, with its thick stone walls that admitted no sunlight.

From the open *salone* door I heard the sounds of Evelyn and Roberto arguing, their raised voices bouncing off the stone. I hoped Nora wasn't having to listen to it. It was something I'd prided myself on when my own children were younger – that Walter and I had always managed to be civil, that they'd never had to cower in corners trying not to hear their parents yelling at each other.

A few minutes later I heard the sound of heels clicking on stone, and Evelyn came into view. The skin around her eyes was puffy, as if she'd been crying.

'The doctor is here,' I said. 'I hope he will get to the bottom of what is wrong with Mr North.'

'I hope so, too. It's ghastly to see Uncle Bill so helpless. You have no idea what he used to be like, striding around the place, always on the go. He had horses then, which were kept on farmland in the valley, and he'd come thundering down the hillside. He was mostly away, of course, in Paris or New York, but whenever he was around the castle would be full of artists and philosophers and all these clever people, with Uncle Bill popping off here or there, coming back with new paintings, so pleased with himself. When I was a girl I wanted to marry someone exactly like him.'

'And surely you have!'

She looked at me strangely, but then the door of William's sitting room swung open and Dr Pearson appeared. When he saw Evelyn standing there in her sleeveless dress that clung to her body almost as indecently as if she wore no clothes at all, he looked even more flustered than usual and reached at once for his large white hankie.

'Mrs Manetti. I'm glad to catch you. I would like to have a word about your uncle's condition, if I may.'

'Of course. We'll go into the *salone*.'

I stood in the corridor, unsure whether to follow, until Evelyn called over her shoulder. 'Come on, Connie.'

'I'm sure Mrs Bowen is anxious to go back and resume her duties with your uncle,' said Dr Pearson, without looking at me, and I felt a cold feather of fear run up my spine at whatever he wanted to say that required such privacy.

'Constance is the person who has the day-to-day care of my uncle,' Evelyn said. 'Of course, I do what I can with every free moment, but I can't always be here, so it's only right that she hears whatever it is you have to say. I'll call Alina to sit with Uncle Bill.'

When we were seated, Dr Pearson appeared ill at ease, darting looks at me from eyes that were almost buried in the fleshy folds of his face. I could tell he was still smarting about how I'd challenged him over the electrotherapy machine and wondered if that's what he'd wanted to discuss with Evelyn.

'I'm afraid I must confess to having grave concerns,' he

began. 'As you know, Mrs Manetti, your uncle suffered a cerebral haemorrhage some months back and we were initially surprised and delighted at the speed of his recovery. However, that recovery now seems to have not only halted but reversed.

'Sometimes this happens, and we have no idea why. But what is strange about your uncle's case is that his decline does not seem to be following a pattern but is rather stopping and starting, going backwards and forwards.'

'Yes, I've noticed that,' Evelyn said. 'Why do you think that is?'

Dr Pearson hesitated, and again he glanced at me. 'In cases like this we are duty bound to examine the consistency of care that is being given.'

My still-sluggish thoughts took a moment to catch on, then I gasped. 'But I—'

'Constance takes excellent care of my uncle,' Evelyn said, and my eyes swam with tears. 'I couldn't have asked for a more loyal, attentive companion.'

'But, as we've ascertained, Mrs Bowen is not a qualified nurse. It's a great responsibility, administering medicines and performing physical manipulations.'

'No, I assure you, I am always careful.' My voice cracked and Dr Pearson wrinkled his little pug nose.

'Please don't become agitated, Mrs Bowen. No one is accusing you of anything.'

Evelyn covered my shaking hand with her own. 'Dear Constance, I can't bear to see you getting upset. Perhaps you ought to return to Uncle Bill after all. Be assured, I am here fighting your corner.'

When I went back into William's sitting room, the blood

still rushing around my ears, he was wincing, and I could see right away that Dr Pearson had left him sitting in a way which was pressing on his painful left arm, so I helped him get more comfortable. There was a sore-looking red patch on his head where the electrotherapy machine had been attached. He couldn't talk, but he nodded a thank you.

The door opened and Evelyn swept in, followed by Dr Pearson.

'How is my favourite uncle today? You're looking handsomer than ever!' She bent over to kiss William on the cheek, not seeming to notice how she nudged him back into an awkward position. Her gaze fluttered around the room, as it did when she was nervous, and when it fleetingly met mine she gave a smile that was gone just as quickly as it arrived.

Standing stiffly next to William, Dr Pearson cleared his throat.

'I have been discussing matters with Mrs Manetti, and I should advise you, Mrs Bowen, that my own suggestion was that you be relieved of all duties relating to the nursing care and dispensing of medicines in relation to Mr North. It's too great a responsibility for someone of a nervous disposition.'

I watched his mouth move but struggled to absorb his words. All those months and years during the war I'd dragged myself into the hospital to give what support and succour I could to men who had no one else, never once betraying horror at some of the injuries I saw – the holes where other things should rightfully be – noses, hands, faces. 'They ask for you, you know,' the matron had told me, 'the one with the kind face.'

'However,' Dr Pearson went on in his pompous, nasal

voice, 'Mrs Manetti has generously argued your case. She explained that you have been distracted with the arrival of your son, but she assures me you are normally highly competent. So what I would like now is for you to demonstrate how you administer Mr North's medicines so I can be completely certain you know what you're doing.'

I felt my confidence shatter, while at the same time I bristled with anger. I knew myself to be on the edge of something and dared not look at Evelyn in case her sympathy tipped me over.

I stood up and walked over to the sideboard where I kept the medications. But when I tried to measure them out, my hands shook and droplets of the tonic sprayed out over the wooden surface. I heard Dr Pearson tut under his breath. I gave a commentary on what I was doing but, distracted by the force of his disapproval, I misspoke as I opened the cork on the restorative tonic, initially calling it the barbituric acid he'd prescribed as a sedative before instantly correcting my mistake. But it was too much for the physician. 'For heaven's sake, Mrs Bowen, you must be more precise.'

From William came a strangled noise, and I saw him try to flap his hand. I wondered if he was trying to come to my defence, but Dr Pearson took it as confirmation that my patient was as disturbed by my carelessness as he was himself.

'Don't exert yourself, Mr North. I will not leave until I am quite satisfied Mrs Bowen is fit to discharge her duties.'

I couldn't hold back then.

'I assure you, Dr Pearson, I am always diligent looking after Mr North. It is only the situation here, finding myself under such scrutiny, my capability called into question—'

'I'm afraid your unravelling under the slightest pressure does little to assuage my concerns, Mrs Bowen. How will you cope in a crisis if you crumble like this when I am merely exercising my duty of care for my patient? Mr North's welfare is paramount to me, as it should be for you. It is my responsibility to make sure the care he is getting from you is not making him worse rather than—'

Dr Pearson broke off with a loud exclamation as a small figure bowled into the room and, without hesitation, kicked him in the shin.

'Nora!' Evelyn looked amused rather than horrified, though she clapped her hand quickly over her smile.

'Leave Mrs Bowen alone. You're a horrid, horrid man.'

Nora's face was flushed and her little fists were clenched.

I glanced over at William and saw he was looking straight at me, though whether in support or condemnation I couldn't tell. I took hold of Nora's narrow shoulders and steered her from the room, turning my face down towards hers so that no one could witness the rage pulsing at my temple like a drum.

27

WHEN I'D AWOKEN that morning to a sky dense with pewter clouds, I'd been relieved at first to have a respite from the blazing sun, but a few hours later as I waited for James underneath the statue of Neptune in the vast Piazza della Signoria, the damp, hot, overcast sky seemed to be pressing down on me. My white cotton blouse, which had started out crisp and fresh, now stuck to my skin, and my rayon stockings, so modern back in England, now felt as if my legs were encased in bandages.

Across from where I sat at the base of Neptune's fountain were the beautiful, soaring arches of a covered *loggia* between the pillars of which a row of other statues peered out at the gloomy weather.

'Sorry I'm late,' said James, approaching from behind so that I jumped at his tentative hand on my shoulder and he snatched it quickly away.

James had a list of sights he wanted to visit, compiled with the help of a fellow guest at the *pensione* and his trusty Baedeker and written in a notebook in his neat, careful hand. I saw that some of those had already been accounted for and through these he had drawn a line just as straight as if he had done it with a ruler.

We headed towards the Duomo, but it wasn't the cathedral itself that held James's interest so much as the octagonal Baptistery nearby with its colossal, intricately carved bronze doors depicting scenes from the Bible.

'You know, Michelangelo called these the Gates of Paradise,' he said, and though I could see why he was impressed, I couldn't help but feel the heavy weight of history. All the craftsmen who had laboured here, all the years of life lost to a chisel and hammer.

I wanted to go back to the Ponte Vecchio to look again at a bracelet I'd spotted there, feeling a need for a memento of my time in Florence. I was thinking ahead to when I'd be back in England, eking out my activities – a visit to the library, tea with James on a weekend afternoon, the odd matinee visit to the theatre or the cinema as a treat. I was already anticipating how, on long winter afternoons where nothing lay in store beyond a few more pages of my novel or the crackle of the wireless, I could lift my sleeve and see the tiny silver discs each finely engraved with a fleur-de-lis, linked together by a delicate silver chain. Then I would forget any sad times I'd had here and remember only that I'd once lived in a castle and awoken each morning to a hillside steeped in mist and the smell of herbs and lavender and bean fields in flower.

As we returned from the bridge, with the bracelet wrapped in tissue paper in my bag, I felt a lifting of the dark mood that had overtaken me since yesterday's scene with Dr Pearson.

So much so that I told James what had happened as we

walked, fashioning it into what I hoped was a humorous anecdote. The doctor's pomposity. My own clumsiness. But rather than finding it amusing, James stopped, and I saw that his brows were knitted into a frown.

'I don't understand you, Mother. When it comes to looking after others, you're the most competent person I know. What has this place done to you? Why are you letting these people make you doubt yourself?'

I was touched by his words and took James's arm as we strolled along the arcade that flanked the northern bank of the Arno, watching the swollen black clouds kiss the surface of the water to our right.

We hadn't gone far when I became aware of a small man coming towards us who seemed vaguely familiar.

'Do you know that man, Mother? Why is he staring like that?'

I barely had a chance to register the charcoal slash of moustache and the old-fashioned black hat before the man spoke.

'I beg your pardon, Madam, but aren't you Mr North's companion? My name is Mr Webb. We met at the castle. I am Mr North's solicitor.'

Now I remembered how he'd arrived for an appointment after William had grown too unwell to see him.

'How is Mr North? I was very saddened to hear his recovery had been set back.'

'I'm afraid he is quite weak,' I replied. 'His condition has deteriorated further in the weeks since you were last there.'

Mr Webb shook his head. 'I am sorry to hear that. I have acted for Mr North for over twenty years and he is a very fine man. Very fine indeed.' He glared at James as he said the last line, as if James had contradicted him.

I had thought we might walk on after this exchange. The walkway was narrow and we were causing an obstruction, but still Mr Webb blocked our way.

'You see, Mr North wanted to see me on a certain matter. He was most insistent. And now . . .' Mr Webb tailed off. He didn't move, and I formed the definite impression he wanted to say more.

'Have you a message you'd like me to convey to Mr North? He doesn't speak much these days, but he understands everything.'

Mr Webb opened his mouth, only to close it again.

'No. I won't take up any more of your time. Please pass on my best regards and tell him that if he still wishes to see me about the matter we discussed he has only to send word.'

'Well, that was odd,' remarked James as we moved away.

I murmured my agreement. It wasn't so much the lawyer's words as the way he had fixed me with his intense, dark eyes, as if trying to communicate something to me.

By the time we emerged from the other end of the arcade, the sky had darkened further and the air around felt swollen and full, and before we'd gone more than a few steps the heavens opened, releasing torrents of rain that drenched us instantly.

'This way,' said James, taking my elbow, and we ducked down a side street, with me holding my inadequate bag over my head, eventually ending up once again in the Piazza della Signoria, where we took shelter in the covered *loggia*, laughing at each other's bedraggled appearance.

'I wish Father were here to see us. He'd find us comical.'

I gazed at James in surprise.

'How strange that you should see him like that.'

James stood by my side, staring determinedly out at the rain.

'The thing is, Mother, he did have a sense of humour, it just wasn't yours. He was a Victorian at heart and you an Edwardian, but there were ways to get to know him and to find out what he thought amusing, to find common ground.'

I was flabbergasted. I'd spent so much of James's childhood arbitrating between him and his father, and yet now it seemed they had after all found their way back to one another in adulthood. And where had I been? Too busy entrenching myself in one position to allow for the existence of another?

'I was very fond of your father,' I began. 'I nursed him very faithfully for the last year of his life. I don't think he could complain.'

'You have always done your duty, Mother, but you closed him out in other ways, just as you did me.'

'I don't know what you—'

'Millie, Mother. Your all-consuming grief. You were so greedy with it. You didn't allow us any part of it, not me, nor Father.'

'That's not true.'

But as we both gazed out side by side at the water that was coming down now in solid sheets, I trembled, and I couldn't for the life of me tell if it was with righteousness or regret.

In bed that night, I found myself going over in my head the scene between James and me, wondering if I had got it all wrong. Walter and I had not had a marriage of passion, that much had been obvious, but might there have been a way for us to carve out some sort of understanding? We had been polite, and I had always, always, been a dutiful wife. But had I looked hard enough for things to love about him? I thought about what James had said about the period after Millie's death. I knew Walter had been grieving, but hadn't I, in my heart, always felt his grief to be in some way inferior to my own?

I lay with my eyes open, listening to the rain and wishing, for the first time since my husband had died, that we might have the chance to start over.

My thoughts were so fevered that when I heard the faint sound of sobbing, I thought at first it was a manifestation of my disturbed mind, a whispered memory of Millie in those last terrible weeks, crying softly in the night when she thought no one could hear her.

When I ascertained that it was coming from outside, I ignored the jolt of fear that shot through my veins and strode across the room, grabbing my lamp on the way.

As I reached the end of the corridor the crying stopped, and I stopped too, hardly daring to breathe in the sudden stillness.

The crying started up again and I forced myself to carry on. Approaching the top of the great staircase, I saw the outline of a ghostly shape.

'Nora? Is that you? Whatever are you doing here?'

The child was sitting huddled on the top step with her doll in her lap and her head in her hands. As I hurried to sit beside her, the metal on her face glinted in the moonlight.

I put my arm around her shaking shoulders.

'What's the matter, Nora? Come on, you can tell me.'

But that only made her cry harder. I pulled her head on to my shoulder and waited for her sobs to subside.

'I'm bad,' she said finally, between great big gulps.

'What nonsense are you talking? You're not bad, Nora. You're kind and you're good.'

'No, I'm bad, and that's why I must wear this as a punishment, like the man in the iron mask.'

When Nora first asked to read the leather-bound volume of Dumas's classic she'd picked up from William's library I'd warned her that it wasn't suitable for a girl her age. Now I could kick myself for letting her talk me into taking it away.

'My dear, you're not being punished for anything. You're sensitive and brave and I love you very much.'

I felt her quieten and there was a silence in which the very air seemed to breathe.

'Mummy and Roberto were shouting. Roberto said she was like a rock around his neck. A rock with an ugly barnacle. And then Mummy said, "I hope you're not talking about my daughter." Mrs Bowen, what's a barnacle?'

I pressed my lips together and hugged her tight, my body pulsing with anger. I knew people said terrible things to each other in the heat of an argument and I knew also that Roberto would never have said such a thing if he'd known Nora could hear. But still, the cruelty of it.

Nora gradually slumped into me, her head growing heavy on my shoulder, the metal thing digging into my skin as we sat side by side and listened to the rain.

28

THE DAY OF the fancy-dress ball dawned fresh and clear. Only the lush green of the laurel leaves below my window and the citrus tang of the air that sparkled on the back of my tongue like the sherbet lemons I used to slip under Millie's pillow so she'd find them when she got home hinted that the world had been washed clean overnight.

It crossed my mind that the scene with Nora, too, might have been some kind of feverish figment, but I could still make out a faint pink mark on my shoulder where the metal band around her head had pinched my skin. I was up later than usual so I dressed hurriedly and went in to see William.

Since James had levelled at me the accusation of being in love with William, I was acutely aware of my feelings around him and I realized this had become the high point of my day – seeing his face, reading in it the kind of night he'd had, whether he was in the mood for talking, or just being still, his grouchy 'About time' when I walked in, belied by the glint in his eyes. I ran my fingers over the new silver bracelet that would one day have to stand in for everything I was soon to lose.

But William barely looked up when I came into the room. His skin had a greenish tinge. There was no grumpy greeting, no pretend outrage at my invented lateness.

I chattered to him as I went around the room, plumping up cushions and opening that day's stack of correspondence, but he made no response and my heart grew heavy.

My concerns increased when I tried to give him the morning's medicine that I had measured out and checked and checked again. As soon as he saw me approaching, William grunted and turned his head to the side. 'Come on,' I said briskly. 'I'm not trying to kill you.'

I tried again, more firmly this time, to direct the spoon to his mouth, only to find myself sprayed with glutinous liquid when William's arm shot out, knocking the spoon from my hand.

'Oh, for heaven's sake.'

I stood up and began brushing droplets from my arms and clothing. Suddenly I felt furious. If he was so concerned about me making mistakes, so ready to listen to pompous Dr Pearson and ignore all these days and weeks and months I'd sat here, tending to his needs, reading to him, feeding him, divining from a twitch of his eye or a movement or a sigh whether he was in pain, or was bored, or hungry, or frightened at his own mortality, well, let him find someone else then.

'If you're not happy with my company or my competence, I'll tell Evelyn to find someone new,' I said, grabbing a muslin from the pile in the medicine cupboard and dabbing at my clothes.

When I finally turned around, William's face bore a look of such misery that my fury drained away just as quickly as it had arrived, replaced by guilt and deep, abject pity. 'I'm so sorry,' I said, kneeling down on the floor in front of him so that I could look at him properly. William held my gaze and, looking into his eyes, the conviction grew inside me that there was something very, very wrong.

I desperately wanted him to get better and I knew that if I didn't follow Dr Pearson's instructions to the letter he would hold me responsible for William's decline. Yet I felt in my bones that I needed to listen to whatever William was too weak to say. James had been quite right the day before when he accused me of having lost trust in myself. But surely I should at least trust William?

I stood up and put the lid on the medicine.

'I'm sure it won't hurt to miss a dose.'

When I turned back to William he gave me the briefest of nods. I nodded back, quite unable to speak.

The castle was buzzing with people. The stone corridors rang with shouts from the kitchen, where Renata was issuing commands to an army of extra helpers drafted in from the surrounding farms and villages, and with the sounds of hammering and sawing as the props and decorations were put in place. Alina, still looking pinched and haggard, was everywhere at once, overseeing the women charged with polishing the floors and furniture and the men bringing wooden cases of wine and champagne up from the castle's vast cellars, dealing with the problem of filling up the newly installed water tank outside and attaching swathes of sheer turquoise fabric to the ceilings and walls to give the impression of being underwater.

Evelyn was as excited as a child at Christmas, flitting

about in a silk floral dress with billowing sleeves that made her look as if she might take flight at any time. Her friend Alice de Havilland, who rarely looked at me or acknowledged my existence, was staying overnight in the castle so that she and Evelyn could prepare themselves together, and she strode around the place wearing a man's flannel trousers and declaiming aloud extracts from the Jules Verne novel that had inspired the theme of the ball. I knew she was what people referred to as an original, but I found her rude and exhausting to be around.

Everywhere there was evidence of the theme for the night. A giant statue of Neptune to rival the one in the Piazza della Signoria was dragged up the hill by two horses on the back of a cart and stood guard outside the castle doors. Evelyn had contracted local carpenters to build timber stage sets and a pair of giant waves now bisected the courtyard garden while on the right side of the castle a ship's prow protruded from the ground as if from a capsized liner.

On the ground ran rivers of fabrics in shades of blue and green and foamy ivory, some sheer, some studded with sequins, mixed together so that the whole resembled a gushing waterway, and at the far end of the courtyard, not far from the covered pergola, Roberto's tank, slightly less grand than he'd envisaged, was nevertheless up and filled in readiness for the hardy. Evelyn had even had fresh seaweed brought in from the coast on the early-morning train from Livorno so that the area around it smelled briny and brackish. Meanwhile, a fleet of wooden boats bobbed on the surface of the pond, above the enormous, rare goldfish that flicked their double tails disapprovingly in the depths.

James had come over early to 'help', but I couldn't see

much evidence of that. Instead, he trailed after Evelyn like a love-struck puppy, though I noticed he also kept a watchful eye out for Roberto, periodically scanning around him and freezing every time the handsome Italian-American came into view.

I felt pinpricks of worry seeing my son drift around in Evelyn Manetti's wake in his ivory-coloured linen trousers and his white shirt and new straw hat. He was laying himself so wide open, like one of the orange snapdragons Evelyn was now snipping from the bed that bordered the courtyard garden, their spread, violet-tipped petals offering themselves up to her scissors.

Nora had asked me to plead with Evelyn that she be allowed to attend the ball. Her mother had told her it would be full of drunken grown-ups and no place for a child. But before I could approach Evelyn, who had by now roped James into being her flower carrier and was busy adding to the armful of stems that were fast occluding his vision, a heart-stopping boom sounded behind me, followed by a loud cry.

My first thought was of another earthquake, but when I whirled around I saw that Alina, emerging from the kitchen corridor with a tray of cut-crystal glasses, had tripped on a flagstone, sending the entire lot crashing to the ground. She herself was sitting awkwardly surrounded by shattered shards, her face twisted in pain.

I rushed to her aid, but Evelyn arrived before me.

'Oh, for heaven's sake, Alina, do you have to be so clumsy?' she asked, her face dark with anger. 'Those glasses were part of Aunt Cecily's dowry. How could you be so careless?'

I brushed past her and sank down next to the stricken housekeeper. Glancing over at James, I saw he was gazing at Evelyn wide-eyed. When I gestured to him, he roused himself as if from a trance and, throwing his flowers down on to a round garden table, hurried over to help lift Alina to her feet.

Once she was up, supported on either side by James and me, we could see she had several cuts on her legs from which the blood was trickling in rivulets. She was also bleeding quite badly from a deep gash in one of her palms.

The sight of so much blood clearly had a sobering effect on Evelyn – or perhaps it was the fact that James, her erstwhile acolyte, now refused to meet her eye.

'Oh, my dear Alina, I had no idea you'd hurt yourself. I'm sorry for shouting. I was upset because the glasses had sentimental value, but now I feel like a rotten brute. Will you forgive me?'

She'd put on a baby voice and cocked her head to one side so that her bobbed hair swung like a shiny curtain of yellow silk.

'Of course, Mrs Manetti,' said Alina, her head lowered.

'Hurrah! I do hate it when I've been beastly to someone. It's like I'm carrying a boulder around in my heart. How very kind you two Bowens are.'

She was beaming as if all was forgotten, but when I looked at James his face was set hard.

As we made our way inside, I could feel Alina trembling through her thin cotton dress.

'Are you sure you haven't done yourself any damage?' I asked as we limped along the corridor towards the kitchen.

'I don't think so, Constance. Thank you.'

After we'd left Alina in the charge of Renata, who instantly designated one of her helpers as temporary nursemaid, to the young girl's evident dismay, James declared he needed to return to his *pensione* to prepare for the evening ahead. Hovering by the front door, turning the brim of the panama hat in his hands, he said, 'It must be nerve-wracking to organize a party like this, don't you think? Evelyn and Roberto are under a lot of pressure. I mean, I'm not excusing her for shouting at the housekeeper, I'm just saying she might have had her reasons.'

But even as he tried to convince me I formed the strong impression that the person he was really trying to convince was himself.

All day I worried about William's strange behaviour that morning when I tried to give him his medicine. I wished that the ball weren't happening. It seemed to me that William's health was now hanging by a spider's thread. I knew Evelyn was keen for William to be a part of the festivities and, while I was touched by her belief in the healing power of gaiety, I worried about the toll such over-stimulation might take on him.

I was dreading having to dress up in clothes that were not my own to mingle with people who had not the slightest interest in me. I wished Evelyn and Roberto weren't so insistent I attend. And though I knew they meant well, I also wondered if Evelyn thought it might reflect badly on her if I didn't appear, as if she were excluding me.

All that afternoon, Evelyn was a whirl of motion, the scene with Alina seemingly forgotten with all the tasks to be done – the scenery to vet, the cocktail list to oversee, the telephone to answer – directions given, dates, times, hair to wash and style, costumes to take out of the wardrobe for last-minute checks and adjustments.

By the time she came to find me in William's sitting room she was abuzz with excitement, practically levitating in the doorway. Seeing that William was asleep, she gestured me out into the corridor, to the irritation of Solomon, whose great head had to be dislodged from my knee.

'I've laid out your costume on your bed. Oh, Constance, I can't wait to see you in it. You shall be so *imperious*! We will prostrate ourselves at your feet.'

I summoned a smile. 'I think I will be the prostrate one. I am awfully tired.'

Evelyn stuck her fingers in her ears theatrically.

'*La la la*. I won't hear it. This is going to be the party of the year. Of the century. Dusty old scholars will be writing about it in the history books. And you, Constance, are right here in the thick of it.'

The costume came from a production of *A Midsummer Night's Dream* that Emily Wheeler's theatrical company had put on, with extra accessories pilfered from the props box. But the *pièce de résistance* would be a towering golden tiara that the late Cecily North had apparently had specially made for another fancy-dress ball some years before, set with emeralds and sapphires, which Evelyn assured me looked just like the real thing. 'You must fetch it from Aunt Cecily's bedroom. I haven't the time to do it myself.'

I protested that I couldn't possibly go poking around in the late Mrs North's things, but Evelyn shut me down. 'Good grief, Constance. I have found you the costume and laid it out on your bed. Surely you don't need me to dress you as well? Besides, Aunt Cecily left all her jewellery to me, so those are not "Mrs North's things" at all, but my things.'

After she'd given me directions to the room and left, I returned to my customary seat in William's sitting room feeling unaccountably nervous. What on earth was wrong with me? Where was the sense of adventure that had brought me here, to Italy, to this castle?

William moaned gently in his sleep and I crossed over to him and pressed my hand to his forehead, feeling the soft warmth of his skin. His hair, threaded with silver, had not been cut for weeks now, and reached to his collar; I pushed back a strand that had fallen over his brow. I couldn't shake off the sense I'd had earlier of there being something terribly wrong. When William opened his eyes abruptly, I stepped quickly back.

'Everything will be all right,' I told him, knowing he was as apprehensive as I was. 'The party will come and go and then all this racket will stop and you will feel better. Besides, it might do you good to see fresh faces. I'm sure you must be sick of mine. And if you tire of it, Massimo will be on hand to take you back inside.'

I left it as late as possible to get ready, but when I could put it off no longer I made my way upstairs. By now, the sounds were building and the castle vibrated with anticipation. From the courtyard came the sound of an orchestra tuning up, while from the front came the hammering of the labourers who'd been drafted in to transform the castle gates into the entrance to an underwater kingdom.

As promised, the costume had been laid out on my bed. I had a prickling of unease at the thought that Evelyn had been in my room and had to remind myself she had been doing me a favour. And wasn't it practically her house, anyway, so she had every right to go where she pleased.

The costume smelled musty, as if it had been stored in a chest or at the back of a damp cupboard. I shook it out and held it up to me while I stood in front of the full-length mirror. The main part of the dress was teal-coloured velvet, floor length and roughly stitched together. I'd been quietly afraid that it would not fit. Despite my recent weight loss, I was broad-shouldered and large-framed, but the style of the thing was loose and flowing and it went over my head easily enough, and was held in place by a golden belt and a sash that crossed over from shoulder to waist, both decorated with a variety of shells from which emanated a sour, salty smell of decay. The whole thing felt rough and itchy and, though the heat was not as stifling as it had been earlier in the week, still I knew I would find it suffocating after an hour or two.

Over the top of this base garment were lighter, sheerer fabrics fashioned into cloaks and trains that had to be draped and tucked in a complicated fashion according to a photograph that Evelyn had helpfully left showing the actress who had last worn the costume. I stared dolefully at my reflection, seeing, in place of the statuesque Amphitrite, a flustered woman with long, unmannerly hair and skin darkened by the sun. I turned to see the back of me and cried out in pain as something sharp pierced my side.

Fumbling around in the folds of the costume, I found the culprit – a pin, fully two inches long, which had been left inside.

I quickly realized the plain outfit called out for accessories. There was a trident leaning up against the bedroom wall which turned out to be a pitchfork painted gold, but more was needed. Evelyn was right. I needed a crown.

Evelyn had given me directions to Cecily North's bedroom. It may sound strange, but I'd never fully explored the upper floors of the castle outside of my immediate environs. Apart from that one night when I'd gone to console Nora, I hadn't visited the Manettis' wing, or seen William's rooms.

At first it seemed odd that Evelyn had directed me towards her own quarters, but then it occurred to me that William might well have moved rooms after his wife died, whether to make way for his niece and her daughter or just to spare himself painful reminders. Even so, it felt strange to be crossing the turret that housed the great staircase and, tucked in at the back of them, the narrower stairs that led up to the castle roof, and making my way past the reading area with its armchair and wood-panelled walls, and entering in through the double doors that led to the Manettis' apartments.

Evelyn and Roberto's corridor was exactly parallel to my own; in fact, if I peered through one of the long slit windows I could see across the courtyard garden, now a hive of activity, to the corresponding point in my own wing. And yet it felt a hundred miles away. Here, instead of the austere stone walls and floor, there were everywhere drapes of printed fabric and thick rugs in bold colours. There were marble side tables with fresh flowers and startling modern paintings on the wall in the new surreal style that William would have detested. Though the furnishings were more homely, there was an atmosphere here in this part of the castle that set me on edge, a sense of things breathing behind the heavy curtains, and though Evelyn herself had sent me, I felt myself to be trespassing.

Evelyn had directed me to the furthest room along the corridor, and I crept along on softly padded rugs, past the open doorway of Nora's bedroom. Seeing it in daylight, I felt a slide into liquid pity at the sight of her neatly made-up bed, her wooden stool, her bookcase with its leather-bound books lined up in order of height, the absence of life, of laughter, of carelessly strewn toys or favourite pyjamas laid out on the counterpane. It wasn't a horrible room by any means, and yet there was a sense of desolation and a lack of any suggestion of Nora herself. I recalled Millie's childhood bedroom, with the roses on the eiderdown and on the wall-paper and the blot on the carpet where she'd knocked over her ink pot in her enthusiasm for something or other. How her dolls – one with her hair severely cropped after Millie had turned hairdresser for the day – were always lined up on the bed, where she'd be reading to them, as if they were her children, and her shoes lay wherever she'd kicked them off. How I'd loved to step into that room, where the window was always flung open wide so that Millie could try to entice the birds on to her windowsill with tempting seeds.

The memory brought to mind the poor cockatoo whose death Nora had felt most acutely, and I turned heavily away. Further along the corridor another open door gave way on to a huge room decorated in shades of green and purple. After a quick glance behind me I stepped inside. Here the windows were festooned with forest-green silk, and the same material formed a canopy over the four-poster bed, which was itself fitted with a coverlet decorated with a leaf motif in shades of thistle and sage.

I'd seen that coverlet before.

The reminder of the photographs I'd seen in Roberto's

darkroom – Evelyn naked and bound on this very bed – brought a rush of heat to my face, and I hurried away.

The corridor led past a dressing room and a lavish yellow bathroom to the door at the very end where Evelyn had told me I should find Aunt Cecily's things left in her room, practically undisturbed since the day she died.

Outside the door, I hesitated. Only the thought of my costume, unfinished and lacking, kept me from turning around and leaving the way I'd come. Until that moment I'd considered myself a reluctant party guest, but now I realized some of Evelyn's enthusiasm had rubbed off on me after all. If I was going to be Amphitrite, I wanted to be the *best* Amphitrite. I knew Roberto would be there with his camera, and I imagined myself back home in Pinner, taking a photograph down from the mantelpiece and remembering a time when I was, briefly, a goddess.

I nudged the door open. The room was not particularly large, but it was exquisitely decorated, with honey-coloured walls and a counterpane of the same shade on the ornately carved bed. Unlike my own room, with its terracotta tiles, which were so cool underfoot, the floor in here was polished wood and there was a rug with a pattern of ivory and gold.

Evelyn had told me the room had been barely touched since Mrs North's death, but even so I was taken aback by the quantity of personal effects and the way they seemed to have been casually left out, as if the owner had only been temporarily called away, not dead for several years. I felt uncomfortable wondering what it meant that William had left her things so preserved that there were still strands of hair in the silver-backed brush on the dressing table and a book of verse on the bedside table, as if she were expecting to return to it this evening.

I was touched seeing a vase of cut roses on a round table near the window. The flowers were apricot in colour and beautifully matched to the decor and I felt a rush of affection for Evelyn, tending to her beloved aunt's room. She'd told me she'd left the tiara out for me on the writing desk and I was relieved to find it just where she'd said.

I knew Cecily North had had the tiara made for another fancy-dress ball just like this one, and the craftsmanship was impressive. The gold had dulled with time but the gems were sizeable and convincing and the whole thing felt satisfyingly heavy in my hands. When I tried it on, it was quite tight, and I tried not to think about Cecily North's dainty, neat head.

I left the room and retraced my steps along the corridor, glancing through the window and across the courtyard garden, as I had done before. I stopped. Through the narrow window of the opposite castle wall, I saw the door to my room open. Holding my breath, I watched as a figure came out and hurried, head bent, down the corridor.

The size of the window offered only a glimpse, but it was enough to recognize the tall, slender frame, the sweep of dark hair.

Alina.

29

THERE HAD ALWAYS been two halves of me. The half that longed for change, for adventure, for *life*. And then the half that knew how lucky I was to have a family, a home, the time to lose myself in the pages of a book or to sit out in my garden and listen to the blackbirds and the wrens, the chaffinches and the sparrows. The part that was always pushing out the walls, trying to burst free (*'Why must you always be so big, Constance?'*), that had marched so proudly behind the 'Votes for Women' banner in 1908, feeling as if we were walking into history, and the part that wanted to turn my back on the world and enfold those I loved in my arms and keep them safe.

As the hour of the ball approached, those two opposing halves did battle inside me. I was both excited about the night ahead and in dread of it. Dressed up in front of the mirror in my bedroom, I felt like a stranger to myself. A woman capable of behaving in any number of unknown ways. In the flowing robes, with the magisterial tiara nestling in my hair and my hands gripping the trident, I exuded a sense of power and purpose.

I went to find William, who was under the care of

Massimo and Alina, and was relieved to see his face had regained some colour. He even managed a smile at my appearance.

'You see, Mr North, you must do everything Constance tells you,' said Alina. 'See how she is armed?'

Alina herself was still not quite restored to her former self, but she looked for once relaxed. Optimism furled through my blood like smoke. Perhaps we had all weathered whatever it was that had been hanging over us these last weeks and come through the other side.

'Did you come looking for me earlier?' I asked her.

She looked startled.

'No.'

Now it was my turn to be taken aback. I'd seen her clearly. Hadn't I?

'You look . . .' William's voice, weak and laboured, tailed off, and I moved closer to catch what he wanted to say. My heart, stupid and treacherous and flabby with hope, leapt up in my chest.

'. . . like a warrior.'

Oh. What had I expected? That he would tell me I was lovely? Beautiful, even? Why would I even wish for that, when the only men who had called me these things – my brother's friend, who'd been my childhood sweetheart before he married someone else, and the married surgeon in the hospital during the war – turned out not to be trusted?

But chasing on the heels of disappointment came a sliver of something else. Something that creaked and groaned through underuse. Pride. I might not have the fragile, delicate beauty of Evelyn or Olivia Averell, but I was strong and I was resilient. Wasn't I here? A thousand miles from home, holding my ground among people I had never even heard of three months before? Warrior wasn't so bad.

I adjusted the tiara, which was too small and pinched my skull in a way that made me feel a new kind of pity for Nora. Outside the window we could hear the strains of the orchestra already playing in the courtyard, a modern fast-tempo tune, heavy on piano and trumpet and strings. Already there were the sounds of car engines spluttering and horses whinnying down in the valley. I sent up a prayer that those arriving by trap wouldn't attempt the hill.

There was a knock on the door and James appeared, looking self-conscious in his naval captain's get-up. 'Evelyn borrowed it for me from one of her friends. Do I look ridiculous?'

'You look extremely handsome.'

It was true. James had a glow and a vigour here in Italy that was lacking back home. He seemed younger, but at the same time more at ease with himself. We smiled nervously at each other and I wondered if he was thinking, as I was, how we were different people here in Florence. How we would never have stood like this in the front room of the house in Pinner, so conspicuously dressed and full of anticipation for an evening of frivolity.

William was reluctant to leave his sitting room. I knew he was remembering how he'd collapsed at the de Havillands' party and worrying about a repeat. I hadn't forgotten the scene that morning with the medicine. The despair I'd felt coming from him, and my subsequent conviction that in order to protect him I'd need to follow instinct rather than instructions.

I leaned down so that my face was near his. 'You don't

have to do this. No one will blame you for not wanting to be part of it.'

He looked directly at me, and I felt that jolt of being seen as he gave an infinitesimal shake of the head.

From the corner of my eye I saw James look away.

'Put your hands up!'

Nora leapt into the room, brandishing a dagger, her head encased in a gladiator's helmet. To my relief, Evelyn had given in to her entreaties and had allowed her to come to the early part of the evening, providing she cover up the metal straps across her head, 'for her own protection'. The costume, which was completed by a green tabard and green stockings with a leather sheath slung over her shoulder for the dagger, was a fairly broad interpretation of the theme, but Nora was so transparently thrilled with herself, her small body vibrating with excitement, you couldn't help but be swept up in her enthusiasm.

'Don't hurt me,' said James, his hands above his head, quaking in mock fear.

I examined the dagger, which was surprisingly heavy – and worryingly sharp.

'This looks awfully real.'

'That's because it *is* real, silly! Great-uncle Bill gave it to me.'

'*Lent*.' William corrected her, effortfully.

With William supported by Massimo and leaning heavily on his stick, and the rest of us bringing up the rear, we slowly progressed to the courtyard, where the branches of the trees were hung with lanterns and flaming torches guided the way along the paths.

I felt a tug on my arm.

'You were right earlier, Constance,' Alina said in a low

voice, as we hung back from the others. She was standing away from a lantern so that her face was in darkness.

'I did come to your room. I was tired. I have been here at the castle since before five o'clock this morning. There is so much to do. Every time I finish one thing, Mrs Manetti finds me another. And another. I came to your room to have a few minutes' rest, because I knew no one would look for me there. But it felt like an intrusion to be there without you, so I didn't stay.'

'So why did you deny it?'

'I don't want Massimo to worry.'

It made perfect sense. So why did I feel a nagging unease every time I pictured Alina slipping out from my closed bedroom door?

But as we proceeded across the courtyard any lingering doubts were soon lost in the sheer splendour of the scene that greeted us. Everywhere there were astonishing-looking people dressed in swimwear or as underwater creatures. On a raised wooden dais at the back of the courtyard the orchestra was playing a Charleston and already several of the guests were up and dancing, while shrieks wafted over from the swimmers in Roberto's water-filled tank. The night was still and warm and there was a sense of wildness in the scented air, as if anything might happen.

A section of the garden off to the side had been laid out with round tables and chairs like a cabaret club and, as we were making William comfortable, Louise Power swooped in, wearing a floor-length emerald sleeveless gown that seemed sewn to her body and plunged low in the back, revealing her long spine, curved like a butcher's hook. She wore green silk gloves that reached almost to her bare shoulders and a magnificent golden crown sat on her silky black hair.

'Another Amphitrite, I see,' she said, looking me up and down. 'We shall have to form a club.'

I smiled, while the strength and pride that had surged through me a short while before escaped, as if someone had opened up a valve.

I tried to stay close to William, as I'd promised, but there was a never-ending stream of people wanting to tell him how well he looked – *such liars* – and what a fabulous party it was. I watched them as they turned away, their false smiles fading as they exchanged looks of wide-eyed shock at William's altered appearance. Alina and Massimo were lurking nearby, but even they were pushed back by the steadily growing knot that surrounded William's table.

'We're only in the way here. Shall we find the Manettis?' asked James, who had been shifting from foot to foot. He was holding Nora by the hand, the two of them subdued by the spectacle all around them.

There was a crowd of flamboyantly dressed guests right in the centre of the courtyard, where two thrones had been erected, both decorated with long strands of green material arranged to resemble seaweed, and shells bigger than dinner plates. I knew that's where we would find our hosts, so reluctantly I led the way, threading through the throngs of people, some of whom had formed a long line and were dancing along to the jazz band. I winced as I saw them trample the flowerbed underfoot, uprooting clumps of geraniums that lay flattened, their red petals splattered across the stone path.

I caught sight of Olivia Averell standing talking to another young woman, both of them dressed as water nymphs in costumes of diaphanous chiffon showing off their long, lean limbs, and garlands made from green ribbon twisted with coral and smooth fragments of sea glass.

'You remember my son, James,' I said, ignoring the way she shrank back at my approach.

'Of course.' Her voice was as soft and insubstantial as the chiffon she was wearing.

We exchanged awkward pleasantries about the party, and Olivia visibly blushed when Roberto's name came up.

'He's dressed as Poseidon,' she said quietly.

'Undressed, you mean,' squealed her friend.

'There they are!' My chest tightened at the excitement in James's voice as Evelyn's laughter floated over the heads of the crowd like a wind chime in the breeze.

'Mummy!' cried Nora, darting towards the sound. James and I followed, pushing through the throng of people around the throne, coming up short as we broke through to the front. I saw James's mouth fall open.

Evelyn was arranged on the throne, dressed as a mermaid, with a flowing yellow wig and a skirt made from sequined turquoise fabric that clung indecently to her legs, ending in a fishtail that swished on the floor beneath her. Her top half was encased in a tight flesh-coloured garment the same material as a woman's rayon stockings, decorated with sewn-on shells covering her breasts so that from a distance she appeared to be wearing nothing at all.

'No wonder the poor old sailors were always being lured to their horrible deaths on the rocks,' James said, recovering himself.

Evelyn threw back her head and laughed, revealing her white swan-neck.

Sitting next to her on a matching throne was Roberto. I saw instantly why Olivia Averell's friend had been so arrested by his costume. He was wearing only a short sheet arranged around his waist, loincloth-style, like a marble statue of a Greek god, the rest of him being completely naked, apart from a coating of glittering blue paint. In his hand was a trident similar to mine.

'Ah, the Bowens are here,' he said, before leaning over the back of Evelyn's chair to give her a long, lingering kiss. James, suddenly appearing fussy and overdressed in his naval outfit, looked away.

Nora darted forwards to show off her costume to her mother, leaving James to make stiff conversation with Roberto.

I felt a presence by my shoulder. Someone standing far too close. Hot breath on my neck.

'He really ought to take care.' It was Philip Wheeler, dressed as an octopus, with arms made from stockings stuffed with feathers hanging off his jacket.

'Who?'

'Your son.'

'I don't know what you mean.'

I was relieved when Evelyn turned her attention to me. 'Oh, Constance, you look—' She broke off, frowning at me.

There was a commotion behind me as Alice de Havilland appeared, dressed as a giant crustacean in pearlescent pink, with a protruding claw made from tin attached to a mechanism hidden in her sleeve which she could use to snap it open and shut. 'Someone's going to get it,' said Philip Wheeler.

'Evelyn! Roberto!' Alice's voice was so loud I had to check twice to make sure she hadn't brought her loud hailer with her. 'Summon the police this minute. I've been robbed!'

A rumble of interest went around the guests, who had largely fallen silent. Evelyn had a half-smile on her face, as if she didn't know whether this was a joke. But Roberto looked serious, and I remembered all the Florentine bigwigs he'd invited, hoping to impress. 'What are you talking about?' he said.

Alice paused to make sure she had the crowd's attention, though her outlandish costume meant all eyes were anyway on her.

'In case you hadn't guessed, I am Her Royal Highness the Crab Queen,' she declaimed, prompting a group of young men dressed as tropical fish to let out a huge cheer.

'However, I must inform you, the *pièce de résistance* of my costume has been stolen from my room. It belonged to my grandmother, the marchioness, and is *beyond price.*'

Cold needles pressed themselves against the soles of my feet then spread up my legs and arms, as Roberto said, 'You haven't told us what it is that's been stolen.'

'It's a solid gold' – Alice de Havilland's booming voice came to an abrupt halt as her eyes, which had been scanning the crowd, locked on to mine – 'tiara.'

The gorge that had been rising in my throat, even while my sluggish mind refused to acknowledge what was happening, now came rushing up and, for a terrible moment, I thought I might be sick. Everyone was now staring at me, and at the thing that was digging into my skull so that I felt a pressure building up, as if my temples might be crushed at any moment.

'Mother?' James's face swam in front of my vision.

I reached up and touched a tentative hand to the tiara.

'This belonged to the late Mrs North. It's a costume prop, nothing more. Evelyn told me—'

I turned my pleading eyes towards the mermaid on her throne. *Tell them*, I instructed her silently.

But Evelyn was still staring at me, her brow knitted.

'I did tell Constance that she might find something among Aunt Cecily's old dressing-up things, but my aunt's room is the other side of the castle to the guest room where Alice is staying. Surely you must have noticed all Alice's personal belongings, Constance?'

I tried to picture the room. There had been the hairbrush and the novel. But already the scene was clouding over. Had there been other items I'd glossed over? A nightdress laid out on a pillow? A travelling case open on the bureau? Shoes kicked off on the rug? Had I really been so blind?

I snatched the tiara from my head as if it was burning me, feeling the metal scrape my skull, and held it out to Alice de Havilland.

'I'm terribly sorry,' I stuttered. 'It was a mistake. I had no idea. Please. Take it.'

It was James who stepped up to take the golden crown from my trembling hands.

'Here.' He handed it to Alice de Havilland, who held it suspiciously, as if she might catch something from it. 'My mother must have become confused. The castle is so large, with so many rooms, it might have happened to anyone.'

'I wasn't confused,' I said. 'I followed Evelyn's instructions. She sent me to the Manettis' wing—'

'Then you've been in our room as well?' said Roberto,

259

putting his hand to his chest as if struck by worry. 'Perhaps we should check our own valuables.'

There was a loud titter from the tropical-fish group.

'I wouldn't have sent you to *our* corridor, Constance,' said Evelyn kindly. 'You're our employee, not our guest.'

I felt as if she had taken a gun and shot me through the chest, a hole opening up inside me through which all my delusions of the previous weeks were falling – my sense of being needed, my pride in my job, my growing friendship with Evelyn Manetti, all of it disappearing into an immense black lake of shame and humiliation.

'Off with her head!' declared Alice de Havilland, who was now wearing the tiara atop her shell-encrusted pearlescent silk turban.

A huge cheer went up from the crowd.

James, his face purple with embarrassment, put a hand on Roberto's arm.

'Roberto, surely you can't believe that my mother . . .'

Roberto looked down at James's pale fingers on his blue-painted flesh. 'Are you trying to *steal* me?' he asked. And then, addressing the rest of the guests, 'Perhaps it's a family trait.'

As laughter erupted around me, I turned and pushed my way through the crowd.

When I reached the deserted main hall I all but collapsed with relief, but before I could make my way upstairs someone grabbed my sleeve and I found myself being wrestled across the stone floor to the narrow, dark, enclosed space behind the grand staircase where the telephone table was housed. There was that familiar hot, yeasty breath and a feather flew on to my lip as Philip Wheeler pressed the stuffed arms of his costume up against me. Only, this time, there was no one watching.

'I warned you to be careful of Evelyn and Roberto,' he murmured. 'This is a family without principle or scruple. They will eat you up.' Before I knew what was happening, he fixed his wet lips on my neck and sank his teeth into my skin. Then he raised his head so his face was inches from mine. 'And spit you out.'

Then he pressed his mouth over mine, his tongue fat and flabby as a rolled facecloth as he forced my teeth apart, his hands freely roaming over me. I felt myself suffocating and wrested my head away. But he gripped hold of my arms and wouldn't let go. 'Women like you are two a penny,' he said. 'Single. Desperate. *Surplus.* I might be your last chance before it all closes up down there.' He moved his hand between my legs. 'Like a tomb sealing shut.'

Now that he was only gripping my arm with one hand, I summoned all my strength and raised myself to my full height, which was a good few inches more than his, and shoved him as hard as I could. He stumbled backwards, stuffed arms swinging, and I darted past him with my heart hammering and a silent scream building in my throat.

I took the stairs, two at a time, not daring to look behind me. But long after I'd reached the safety of my room and locked the door and scrubbed myself over and over at the washstand in my room, and felt my juddering breath return to something close to normal, I could still feel the imprint of Philip Wheeler's teeth in my neck.

30

SURPRISINGLY, I SLEPT soundly the night of the ball, waking up groggily with a soreness at the temples and the nagging feeling of something having happened, a tugging at the hem of my thoughts. After it came back to me – Philip Wheeler, the tiara – I pulled the sheet over my head as if I could physically block it from my mind.

But when I reached a point where I felt I must surely dissolve in humiliation I felt the faintest pull of something else, some slender thread of the same steel that had seen me show up at Homeleigh Military Hospital day after day during the war in my long blue skirt and white apron to change dressings on boys who'd lost eyes, or arms or legs, or had gaping wounds into which the surgeon had packed little bags of salt that caused them to scream in agony and clutch hold of my hand as if I were the only safe thing left. The same thread that had kept me getting up in the mornings and putting on clothes and brushing my hair after Millie died, when all I wanted was to stay in bed with my face turned to the wall. The thread that had brought me here to Italy, when I ought to have been back home making jam to sell at the Women's Institute fête. All I had to do was find that thread again and follow it back to its source. The source that was me.

It was this vestigial kernel of my old, truest self that gave me the strength to get up and go downstairs, where the army of local people Evelyn had drafted in to tidy up were making themselves busy, some mopping and sweeping the stone floors, others dismantling the props for the party. I watched as five men attached ropes to the statue of Neptune and hauled it into a waiting cart. When I couldn't procrastinate any more, I knocked on the door of William's sitting room and entered without waiting for a reply, setting my shoulders back and my head high. Ignoring his questioning look, I snatched up the newspaper.

'They are about to unveil a new war memorial in Belgium,' I told him, keeping my eyes fixed on the paper. 'I don't know how to pronounce the place – Ypres, is that I-pres or E-pres, do you suppose? Anyhow, it is called Menin Gate and dedicated to all the soldiers of the British Empire whose graves are unknown.'

I was talking too much because I didn't want there to be a hole in the conversation into which William might pour his pity or what little remained of my pride might slide.

'Will they travel there, do you think?' I pressed on. 'The grieving parents, I mean. To a different country so far away, to stand inside a vast stone box and think about their boys?'

From the corner of my eye I saw William raise his hand to get my attention, but that just made me more determined not to stop.

'Don't you suppose they think about them every moment of every day anyway? Isn't that what you and I have learned, that grief is something you carry with you like a permanent passport stitched to the inside of your heart? It isn't something made from stone or brick or—'

'Stop, woman!' William's voice was no less authoritative for being so croaky.

I looked at him, pressing my lips together to prevent myself babbling on into infinity.

'You want me to talk about last night?'

He nodded, as if relieved to be saved the effort of spelling it out.

'I did not steal anything. Have never stolen anything in my life.'

William made an ugly noise, expelling air through his nose, which made Solomon wake from his sleep on the rug next to him and lumber to his feet.

'I know that.'

As soon as the words were out I felt myself growing lighter. He believed me.

'And I'm sure I followed Evelyn's instructions to the letter. I couldn't have made such a silly mistake.'

Even as I said it, I wondered if that was true. The problem was that whenever I tried to go back to that moment out there in the corridor with Evelyn, it was murky, as if I were viewing the scene through a thick London fog. I could see Evelyn's expression as she gave me directions, but her words were muffled.

My thoughts were interrupted by a noise outside the door and Solomon's low growl before Roberto burst inside without bothering to knock.

'Perhaps you could come to the dining room, Constance? We need to clear the air.'

He saw my expression and put his hands on my shoulders.

'Don't look like that. I'm not going to shoot you.'

Evelyn was looking pale and slightly green-tinged, but she was already dressed, which was unusual for this time of the morning. She wore a prim navy frock I hadn't seen before. In the unfamiliar dress and her delicate, post-party state, she reminded me of someone else, but it took a few moments before I realized that, for the first time since I'd met her, I could see the resemblance to Nora.

Alice de Havilland was lying on the floor in a voluminous black kimono with her arms stretched out either side in a crucifixion position. Her eyes were closed, but there was a long cigarette burning between the fingers of one hand.

My stomach crumpled as memories of the night before assailed me, her cry of 'I've been robbed' echoing around my thoughts.

'Ah, here you are, Constance.' Evelyn's tone was bright as polished silver. She didn't jump to her feet, as she normally would have done. 'I thought we ought to set things straight after that *unpleasantness* last night.'

'That's one word for it,' said Alice from the floor. Evelyn continued as if she hadn't heard.

'Roberto and I have discussed it, and we agree it was most likely an innocent mistake. We know you've been in a bit of a state recently, so we've had a long chat with Alice here and filled her in about the lack of sleep and everything and she's very sportingly agreed to let the whole matter drop. So if you just apologize to Alice, we'll all move on and put last night behind us.'

Alice de Havilland propped herself up on her elbows and stared at me as if I were one of the statues in the piazza.

'That tiara is immensely valuable. My grandfather gave it to my grandmother. He used to make her wear it while they had conjugals.'

I felt a rushing in my head. This woman didn't know the first thing about me and yet, here she was, judging me.

'I didn't steal anything.'

Roberto stepped towards me. 'Of course not. Not deliberately.'

'No, you don't understand. Evelyn gave me the wrong directions. She told me to go right out of my room and across the front of the—'

'There!' Evelyn sounded triumphant. 'I said *left* out of your door. Honestly, Constance, it's a wonder you made it all the way here to Italy on your own when you can't even follow the simplest instructions.'

'I *did* follow them!'

I was aware of sounding like a child. 'You said to cross the top of the stairs.'

'Yes. The *back* stairs. After you'd turned left!'

No. Surely that hadn't been what she said? But the memory of our conversation in the corridor outside William's door was taking on the hazy quality of a dream.

'She ought to have some cocaine,' declared Alice, studying me intently while blowing a perfect smoke ring into the air. 'It's very good for sharpening the intellect. Mummy swears by it.'

There was a pounding in my ears, and my legs felt weak.

'If I was in the wrong, I apologize for my mistake,' I said in a rush. 'Now I really must get back to Mr North.'

'Don't take any detours on your way,' Alice de Havilland called as I hurried out of the room. 'My valuables are locked in the safe.'

Evelyn's teaspoon-on-china laugh was like a tiny pickaxe in my brain.

31

'I FEAR I AM losing my mind.'

Once the words were out, I felt a sense of relief, though I couldn't bring myself to look at James. What if he were to agree? What if it had been apparent to everyone else but me? Wasn't that how it happened, senility encroaching so insidiously you didn't notice, like a frog in water slowly being brought to the boil?

'Some of us might suggest you lost it some years back.'

I shot James a sharp look and was rewarded by a wan smile.

We were walking down by the stream. I had telephoned James at lunchtime at his *pensione*, sneaking into the back hallway where I'd had my unpleasant encounter with Philip Wheeler just hours before and whispering into the receiver, hoping no one would overhear.

The conversation had been perfunctory, neither of us wanting to linger, so I had been able to glean little of how he was feeling. He was such a private person, so reluctant to draw attention to himself, that I didn't see how the very public shaming of his mother, followed by the snub from Evelyn, could have caused him anything but abject mortification. Would he be angry, I wondered, or pompous in that way his father was when he felt he hadn't been listened to – *and now see the result!*

But when James had stepped off the tram some minutes earlier, he had seemed neither of those things but rather reflective and determined. His face had lost the eager, relaxed look of earlier days, and the thick shade of the trees robbed his skin of its newly acquired golden glow, rendering his pallor almost grey.

'I haven't slept,' he said now. 'I have been trying to find an explanation for the Manettis' behaviour towards you, but I cannot find one.'

There was a metallic, bitter note in his voice that I didn't like.

'You don't think I'm crazy, then? *Muddled*, as Evelyn would say?'

'It's true you haven't been yourself. But I think it's this place. It does strange things to people. I don't know if I have been quite myself either.' James snapped a dry leaf from the branch of an overhanging linden tree. 'What I know for sure is that you're not a thief. These *Manettis*' – he said the word as if their very name was suspect – 'I'm not sure they're very nice people. Do you know, at breakfast this morning in the café around the corner from the *pensione*, there was a man reading the *Daily Telegraph*, and we got chatting. Turns out he's been living here for three years, working at the Thomas Cook travel agency. He seemed to know all about the castle, and the Norths. You didn't tell me Roberto Manetti is up to his ears in gambling debt?'

'No, that's his father. That's how his father came to be disinherited by his family.'

James shook his head.

'Roberto also apparently owes money all over the place. And yet there they were last night, lording it up with that over-the-top party. I think you should come home with me, Mother. I can't leave you here like this.'

My mind was whirring. Wouldn't it be a relief to do as he said? To go back home, where there was no chance of bumping into Philip Wheeler, no demands on me, no need to worry about getting things wrong or misunderstanding. Where I could sleep uninterrupted in my bed.

But then I came up against the fact of leaving Italy, this stream, these woods, and Nora and Alina and the Manettis, for all their inconsistencies. Even the castle itself, which exerted over me such a curious pull even while it pushed me away with its creaks and its sighs and its soft noises in the night. And when I tried to visualize how it would be to take my leave of William, for all I knew leaving him to die, the thing became impossible.

'I'm afraid—'

'Yes, I thought as much. It's because of him, isn't it? This William North?'

'No!' We were seated now on one of the low, flat rocks by the stream, and I turned my face to the green water in case there was something there that gave me away.

'I have a responsibility, James. A duty. Not just to Mr North, but to Nora too. The child is miserable.'

'Yes, because her mother is in thrall to a much younger man – a *fascist* – who doesn't give a ha'penny about anyone but himself.'

'James!'

The metallic note I'd heard earlier had now taken over completely, twisting his voice until I didn't recognize it.

'Evelyn has been very good to me,' I said. 'You mustn't disrespect her. She is young, that's all, and easily governed by her emotions and her impulses.'

James turned his face to me, and it was dark with outrage.

'She is not young, Mother, no matter what she might have the world think! She's easily over thirty-five, quite old enough to know how to behave, and how to look after her own daughter. And he is worse. Sometimes I wonder at your lack of judgement.'

We walked back up the bank in silence, and I felt further from him than ever.

Before he set off back for the city, I attempted to make things right.

'Bitterness is a dangerous thing, James. It eats you up from the inside if you let it.'

'You're mistaken, Mother. I'm not bitter. I'm just angry with myself for being a dolt and allowing myself to be taken in by the Manettis. And you should be angry too. That friend of theirs made you out as a common thief and they found it amusing. Well, something has to be done. I have five more days here and I intend to spend them digging around to find out just what kind of people you've become mixed up with. Meet me at 6 p.m. tomorrow in the Piazza della Signoria. Think of an excuse to get away. They owe you that much.'

32

'A ND YOU'RE QUITE sure he wants to see us?'
'Yes, I told you, didn't I?'

James and I were shoulder to shoulder inside a wooden lift, narrow as a coffin, that creaked its way jerkily up the belly of the building on Via del Proconsolo, one of several streets running south from the Piazza del Duomo towards the river. We emerged on the third floor, dragging the metal grille across the folding wooden elevator doors to set ourselves free.

Directly in front of us was a wooden door bearing a brass plaque: *Webb, Fisher & Hewitt.* Our appointment was with William's solicitor.

To my surprise, Mr Webb himself came out to meet us.

'I imagine you're delighted not to have had to climb all those stairs in this heat,' he beamed, gazing proudly past us at the elevator. 'Florence is so full of old buildings, we're one of the very few with a lift. It makes all the difference, I believe, particularly to you ladies.'

I bit back the remark that I could have climbed the stairs in half the time it had taken us to arrive, and not felt quite so queasy either.

Inside his office, Mr Webb sat down at a desk which

seemed far too high for his diminutive stature. If it wasn't for that strip of black moustache, he'd resemble nothing so much as a schoolboy waiting for lessons to start.

'Now that we're here, it's hard to explain *why*,' James began. It was something I'd been asking him ever since he met me from the tram with the news that he'd made an appointment for us with William's lawyer. *What for?* Mr Webb wasn't about to share private information. He hardly knew us. What possible reason could there be for our presence in that office, save for nosiness? James had replied that it had been clear Mr Webb wanted to say something to me that last time we met, and that as I was practically William's spokeswoman now that he was so unwell, it was reasonable that I drop in to introduce myself properly. And anyway, why on earth would the lawyer have agreed to see us if he didn't think we had any business being there?

Still I was far from convinced. What if Mr Webb reported back to Evelyn that we'd been here?

'The fact is that my mother here has been companion to Mr North for the last three months and feels she has a duty of care—'

'I am worried about Mr North's health and safety,' I said, determined to speak for myself. 'He has been growing weaker at a rate that leaves his doctors flummoxed.'

I stopped short of confessing that I no longer administered Dr Pearson's medicine, which had caused William so much consternation on the morning of the ball and which seemed to be doing more harm than good.

'I am truly sorry to hear that.' Mr Webb's delicate face wore a grave expression and I got the impression he was genuinely saddened. 'What is it you think I can do for you?'

He addressed himself to me directly this time. I hesitated.

'When we met the other day in the street, it seemed as if you wished to tell me something.'

My words hung in the air and, for a moment, as Mr Webb's expression remained impassive, I thought I had made a tremendous error of judgement.

'I confess I find myself in something of a dilemma,' the lawyer said eventually. 'I am torn between concern for my client and my duty to keep all client information confidential. It is this latter that ensures my lips must stay sealed.' He sewed a line across his lips with an invisible needle.

'I understand,' I said, getting up to go.

'However, perhaps I can introduce you to someone who might be able to speak more freely.'

Mr Webb picked up a fountain pen and scrawled something across a sheet of stiff, yellowish paper. When he pushed it across the desk I saw it was a name, followed by an address here in Florence.

When I reached out to take the paper, the lawyer's hands held on to it, resulting in a momentary tug of war.

'I have a personal *regard* for Mr North.' Through his spectacles, Mr Webb's eyes appeared exaggeratedly round. 'I wouldn't wish him to come to any harm.'

'What an odd thing to say,' said James as we made our way back out to the street. 'What do you think he meant by it?'

'It's probably just a turn of phrase,' I said. But privately I thought the whole thing had been odd – that the lawyer, a busy and important man, had agreed to see us in the first place, that he then had nothing he could tell us, though he had clearly wanted to. I looked at the name written on the card. *Jerome Fielding*. It was familiar, but I couldn't place it.

We arrived outside the address some twenty minutes later, having twice become lost and had to enquire of passers-by. I was feeling hot and bothered, and not at all sure what we were actually hoping to achieve. Only James's look of grim determination kept me from suggesting we abandon the whole mission and sit down for a drink outside the nearest café.

Piazza dei Peruzzi, No. 6, was a four-storey stone building facing on to a narrow square, with an arched wooden doorway and tall, ochre-painted shuttered windows.

'But who exactly is this Jerome Fielding?' James asked yet again as we stood outside, looking up.

The apartment we were looking for turned out to be on the third floor, no lift this time, so we trudged up the curving staircase, our footsteps echoing on the stone. Outside apartment 3b, we exchanged a glance, and I could tell that James was thinking, as I was, about the absurdity of the situation, that we were about to knock on the door of a perfect stranger without any idea what we would say when he opened it.

But our knock, when we eventually summoned the nerve, went unanswered.

'Another dead end,' said James.

We were about to descend the staircase again when the door of 3a swung open, revealing an elderly man, hunched over and smiling broadly, as if we were visitors he'd been expecting.

'*Si*, Mr Fielding. Of course,' he replied in English when we showed him the name and address, and repeated, '*Dove?*' with much hand-gesturing. 'But he is right now having dinner.'

The old man raised his eyebrow, as if we might share his

astonishment at the eccentrically early hour his neighbour had seen fit to dine.

My shoulders sagged. A wasted trip, then. The elderly man seemed devastated to have disappointed me, his large, bloodshot eyes growing watery. Then his craggy face lit up.

'But the restaurant is only two streets away from here. You can find your friend and eat together.'

We thanked him and hurried away. It was only when we were approaching the unassuming trattoria where the man had assured us Jerome Fielding dined each evening that we remembered we had no idea who we were looking for. No description, nothing.

It being such an uncivilized hour by Italian standards, there were only three tables occupied, all of them, it appeared, by English diners. At one, two women in their fifties, over-dressed for such a modest establishment in silk and pearls, ate their soup in silence while reading their Baedekers. At a table in the middle of the restaurant, a tired-looking young couple tried to keep the peace between their warring off-spring. 'Leave him *alone*, Hugo,' the woman said, in the bone-weary tone of someone who has repeated a certain phrase so often it has ceased to have meaning. And there, right at the back, sat the man who had to be Jerome Field-ing. As if he felt us looking, he glanced over, and my brain gave a jolt of recognition at the sight of that high domed forehead, the thinning hair.

'Mr Fielding? My name is Constance Bowen.'

Jerome Fielding, arrested in the act of delicately filleting a grilled trout, looked alarmed.

'Perhaps you remember me,' I said. 'I'm Mr North's com-panion up at Castello di Roccia Nera. I was there when you and your friend came to view the collection, and when you brought a letter the next day.'

Now we had him.

'Yes, of course. Please, join me, won't you?'

We told him that we had run into Mr North's solicitor – a small white lie to make our presence here less inexplicable – and when he'd heard about Mr North's declining health, he'd suggested we come here.

Jerome Fielding frowned and chewed, frowned and chewed.

'I'm not sure,' he said, when his mouth was finally clear, 'how I can help you.'

'Perhaps you might tell us a little of how you came to Castello di Roccia Nera?' I said, desperate now that this faintest of hopes seemed to be fading. 'Your visit caused something of a stir. Apparently, Mr North isn't in the habit of inviting strangers to admire his art.'

'That's because we weren't *admiring* it, as you say, Mrs Bowen. Well, not merely admiring it. We were *assessing* it.'

'Assessing? Why?'

Fielding took a long sip of his wine. Judging from the open bottle sweating in an ice bucket, this was not his first glass.

'Look here. Are you sure Webb told you to talk to me? What's all this to you, anyway?'

I glanced at James. Part of me wondered, just as Jerome Fielding did, exactly what I was doing here, betraying my employers – my *friends* – by digging around in their business. But there was that tightness in my chest still, a sense of something bad stalking the castle corridors. I remembered William's agitation the morning of the ball, how he seemed to be fading in front of my eyes.

'The truth is, Mr Fielding, Mr North's health is

deteriorating rapidly. Yet I believe there are things he would like to explain to me, if he were only able to think and talk clearly. Any light you can shed . . .'

Jerome Fielding relayed a forkful of trout to his mouth. For a large man, he had quite feminine mannerisms and, as he ate, he dabbed periodically at the corner of his mouth with a starched napkin. I could see he was struggling with something internally.

'I should say that my son and I are here completely independently of the Manettis,' I added, feeling, as I spoke, the loaded weight of the words.

Our companion sat back in his seat, his gaze flicking between us.

'I'm going to trust you, Mrs Bowen. Because you're an Englishwoman and you remind me of my own mother and because, frankly, I'm damned sick of hanging around Florence, waiting.'

'But what are you waiting for?' I could sense James's impatience and sent him a silent message not to push things. I got the feeling Jerome Fielding's good will could swing either way, depending on the wind – or the strength of the wine.

'As you know, my colleague Doug Ayre and I are from the University of Cambridge. We did indeed meet Mr North at his gallery in London, but the invitation to Italy didn't come until around four months ago, when Mr Webb contacted us out of the blue to inform us that Mr North intended to update his will and make us a bequest. He used to attend the university, you see. I think, from all accounts, that was one of the happiest times of his life.'

The cogs began to slide into gear in my head.

'He was bequeathing you the art collection?'

Jerome Fielding nodded, the light bouncing off the sheen on his high forehead.

'And the castle.'

My head shot up. Surely that had to be a mistake? The castle had belonged to Cecily Chisholm, who had in turn inherited it from her first husband. I knew from casual remarks Evelyn had made that she believed it would be hers eventually. William didn't think much of Roberto, I knew, but he wouldn't make a will leaving Evelyn nothing, leaving Nora homeless. 'But Mrs Manetti—'

'—will be well provided for. I don't know the details, obviously, but I believe there's a house in Wiltshire – lovely county, Wiltshire – and a very decent cash allowance. Between you and me' – he leaned forward so I got a waft of garlic and wine – 'I think Mr North just wanted to keep the castle and the collection out of blackshirt hands.'

He sounded triumphant, and I remembered how his eyes had followed Evelyn hungrily around the room. Men's wounded pride. How small it made them.

'Four months ago. So that would have been shortly after William's haemorrhage?'

'Exactly. Nothing like a brush with mortality to prompt a chap to get his affairs in order. He asked us to come out to Italy to take a look at the place and decide whether we could accept the bequest – you understand, there's a responsibility which comes with such a generous gift. One must commit to paying for the upkeep and the security, all the running repairs. Of course, in reality, it was just a formality. Some of the works in Mr North's collection are of immeasurable importance. Doug and I were agog with excitement, I don't mind telling you. The idea was for the university to establish an educational centre here at the castle – the William North Foundation – offering fellowships to classical scholars, perhaps part-funded by opening up the collection to the public for a small fee, so that they could spend time writing and researching in the library and the archives. Mr North was all in favour.'

'So you accepted the bequest?' James asked.

'What do you think? I came up to the castle the very next day with a letter for Mr North, confirming our grateful acceptance of his generous gift. Meanwhile, Mr Webb said he would get the paperwork drawn up for the new will, and then we were to pay another visit, this time accompanied by the insurers. Only then Mr North's health took a turn for the worse, and we've been hanging around here ever since, hoping the old chap would perk up so we could get on with things.

'I missed my wife's birthday, and she wasn't too happy about it, I can tell you. And now here you are, telling me he might never recover. Which is a terrible loss, obviously. Such a great man. *Et cetera*. But what a tragedy for the university, and for us too!'

James walked me to the tram terminal at the Duomo. It was that time of day when molten gold coated the surfaces of the city – the piazzas and rooftops, the leaves and the hats and the upturned faces – but James was too tightly coiled to notice.

'What I wouldn't have given to see Evelyn and Roberto's faces when they discovered they were being evicted from the castle,' he said glumly. 'It's rotten luck William North hasn't been able to keep that appointment with Mr Webb. Now they will most likely never know. People like them get away with everything.'

33

I SLEPT POORLY AFTER returning from Florence, the strains of a violin once again haunting my dreams, and by the morning there was a pressure throbbing against my eyeballs. Roberto had already gone to the city to do whatever it was he did, and though Evelyn tried to insist I join her for breakfast I made an excuse and stayed with William in the pergola in the courtyard garden, where Massimo had set him up on a steamer chair surrounded by pillows. 'But I'm all alone,' Evelyn protested, sounding more childish than her own daughter.

William seemed content to watch the sky through the green canopy of the vines and listen to Nora reading to him from a book about King Arthur, with Rupert North's name in the flyleaf in heartbreakingly childish writing. All around us the stone walls of the castle with their coverings of roses and honeysuckle and ivy were alive with the sound of insects. It should have been soothing, but instead the incessant buzzing only amplified the disquiet of my own thoughts, and when a column of ants crossed the stone path in front of me all I could think of was Philip Wheeler's insistent, clawing hands.

I'd left my spectacles in my bedroom and went upstairs to

fetch them, treading softly so that Evelyn wouldn't hear me from the dining room and make another attempt to cajole me into eating with her.

At the top of the stairs, I stopped at a noise just above me. Just my luck that Evelyn would be right there, sitting in the armchair in the reading nook, desperate for company. But when I emerged silently on to the upper landing, it wasn't Evelyn there but Alina, on her hands and knees in front of one of the wooden wall panels, which had swung open, as if on a hinge. Drawing closer, I was intrigued to see that the panel had been concealing a cupboard, recessed into the wall, and that something inside this cupboard was commanding Alina's complete attention. She reached her hands inside, just at the very moment I got near enough to see what was hidden there.

'Is that a gramophone?'

Alina's whole body, still painfully thin apart from the small bulge of her stomach, jumped at the sound of my voice.

'Constance. You startled me.'

Her face flushed the colour of dried blood.

After so many broken nights, I was used to feeling as if my brain was out of step with my surroundings, but this was so strange I was scrambling to make sense of it.

'I found it when I was cleaning here this morning,' she whispered. 'Nora likes to sit here and draw, and she spilled some ink and didn't want Roberto to find out.' She gestured to the wall, where, sure enough, there was evidence of a faint spray of black ink. A cleaning cloth lay discarded on the floor nearby.

'And I leaned against here . . .' She closed the wooden panel and then put both palms flat against the wood. To my astonishment, the whole thing swung open, revealing the hidden cupboard set into the wall where once an alcove might have been. '. . . And found *that*,' she finished, gesturing to the large object that had been concealed inside.

I dropped to my knees and reached inside to lift the lid of the gramophone, which was a compact, wind-up model in a wooden travelling box. Inside, a record was already in place. I wound the lever on the front of the machine, ignoring Alina's look of wide-eyed panic. When the music started, I found I wasn't surprised to hear what it was.

'Tchaikovsky concerto,' I said, when the mechanism had slowed enough for me to read the label. 'For violin.'

Immediately I was convinced the music I'd been hearing in the night, the ghostly strings that seared through my sleep until I believed they were coming from the walls themselves, had in fact come from this hidden gramophone.

But who would have done such a thing? The fact was, the secret cupboard was at the top of the staircase, where anyone could have access to it. Family. Guests. *Staff.* I thought about how I'd found Alina reaching into the wall. How guilty she'd looked.

But if the question of who was perplexing, it was nothing to the question that rang around my head like the clapper of a bell.

Why? Why? Why?

Hours later, I was still feeling shaken as I picked up the bowl Alina had left out on the sideboard for William's supper. Because of his swallowing problems he was restricted now to liquified food, soups or pulverized vegetables. It was the kind of food you'd give to a baby but, even so, he rarely managed more than a couple of mouthfuls.

I arranged the bowl on a tray, together with a spoon and a glass of water that I poured out from a jug, angling my body so that William wouldn't see how I needed to steady my right hand with my left on the handle.

As I crossed the room, I was so focused on willing my hands to stay clamped firmly to the lip of the tray that I failed to check on Solomon's position and tripped over his huge front paws where he lay by William's feet. I managed to grab hold of the tray, but the bowl slid off and dropped to the floor, spilling its contents, and before I could stop him, Solomon had wolfed the lot.

'Damn it!'

I sank to the floor with my head in my hands. Was everything I did doomed to failure?

I had always been someone who saw, not the clouds, but the crack of light between them. But here in this place with this man who was not getting better, I was enveloped by a wave of hopelessness. I was alone in a strange country and things were happening that I could neither understand nor control, and I had no idea who I could trust. James was right. I should stop deluding myself that I could protect William and pack up now to return to England with my son.

I became aware, through my misery, of a warmth on the back of my neck. When I looked around, I saw to my enormous surprise that William, for whom all movement now involved Herculean efforts, had reached out to lay his hand on my skin. Knowing how much the gesture would have cost him, something shifted and crumbled inside me, and I grabbed hold of his hand in both of mine and pressed the palm flat against my cheek.

34

THAT NIGHT I dreamed someone was chasing me up Black Rock Hill. I woke up with my pulse racing to a commotion, a woman shouting downstairs in the castle. Throwing open the shutters to a pastel-coloured dawn sky, I wrapped my shawl tightly around me and ran out of the door.

As I made my way along the corridor, I recognized the woman shouting as Alina, and she was soon joined by a male voice I assumed was Massimo's. I was gripped by a fear that something had happened to William. What else would have Alina, normally so self-contained, crying out like that? At the bottom of the stairs I saw Alina and Massimo leaning over a long, dark shape laid out on the ground.

As I drew near, Alina turned around. 'Constance, I'm so sorry to wake you. It was a shock, that's all.' She stepped aside, and now I saw it was not William lying there on the floor, but Solomon.

I closed my eyes, swaying, and Alina, misunderstanding, put her arm around me.

'It is upsetting, I understand. But he is still alive. Just.'

I felt ashamed then, of the pure, unadulterated relief that had shot through me when I realized William was not dead.

Poor Solomon. The enormous black dog was lying on his side, a puddle of vomit beneath his great, square head and a white foam around his lips. Only the slight raising and falling of his stomach indicated he was still breathing.

'He has eaten something bad,' Alina remarked. Her husband said something in Italian, and she nodded. 'I don't understand. He never leaves Mr North's side. There is more vomit in the corridor. He must have been suffering like this all night. Massimo will go to the kitchen to look for charcoal.'

That's when I remembered the bowl of food I'd dropped on the floor of William's sitting room. Could it have been that? I felt faint at the thought. Anything that could bring down Solomon, who stood as tall as my chest, could have done far worse to a man in William's condition, even in the minimal quantities that were all William could manage.

I dropped to my knees and buried my head in the dog's neck.

'I'm sorry,' I whispered.

Getting to my feet, I locked eyes with Alina.

'I think it might have been Mr North's food,' I said, only now remembering that it was Alina herself who had left it there for him. 'I dropped it on the floor.'

'That's not possible,' she said coolly. 'I watched that food being prepared. We all ate the same.'

Back in my room I sank down on to my bed and tried to rearrange my thoughts.

Perhaps Solomon had eaten something else? Except, as Alina said, he never left William's side. But if it was the food, why had the rest of us not been affected? William's meals were only a mashed-up version of our own. I was now convinced beyond doubt that something was very badly wrong in the castle. The hidden gramophone, the humiliating episode of the tiara. All of it was leading somewhere. But though my mind scrabbled to make the connections, I could not – or would not – join up the dots to see the bigger picture.

By the time I got downstairs again Alina and Massimo had somehow managed to drag Solomon outside to the courtyard garden, where he lay panting in the shade, Alina crouched down next to him.

'I think he will be all right. The charcoal will clear out his system.'

All through that long day, I pushed my concerns over what had happened to the back of my mind as I tried to calm a dangerously agitated William, shuttling between him and Solomon, reporting back on the dog's progress. Only at tea-time when Solomon finally came lumbering back inside to resume his usual position at William's feet, did the tension in the room lift. But with the easing came the return of my fear.

I was reading to William from a collection of comic stories by P. G. Wodehouse. In recent days, we had come to an unspoken agreement to avoid anything too downbeat or tense and stick to books that were gentle or amusing. Now I read story after story, hardly stopping to take a breath in case an unwelcome thought should nudge its way in.

I tried not to look at Solomon, because every time I did I was reminded of his head lying in a pool of vomit and of the bowl of food he had so greedily lapped up from the floor. Then I would look at William and imagine him eating from that same bowl and the room would grow hot and airless until I forced myself once again to concentrate on the pages of the book.

By the time I went up to my room, claiming a headache

to get out of going to dinner, my head really was throbbing. Once inside, without distractions, there was no respite. Something Solomon had eaten made him ill. As far as anyone could tell, the only thing he'd eaten out of the ordinary was William's spilled dinner. And since William's food was ostensibly the same food we'd all eaten, only pulverized to a semi-liquid form, it followed that something must have been added to bring about such a reaction.

I thought back over the past weeks since William had begun ailing again. The litany of symptoms that flummoxed Dr Pearson. The bouts of stomach cramps and nausea that came and went seemingly without reason, the headaches and dizziness and episodes of confusion.

But when I tried to follow that train of thought to its conclusion I always came up against the solid brick wall of who could possibly be capable of such a monstrous thing. I made a mental list of people who might have had the opportunity. Alina was the one who brought the food in. I hadn't forgotten how I'd come across her on the upstairs landing, reaching into the hidden cupboard towards the gramophone concealed there. Then I remembered how Renata had been grumbling because Evelyn was getting more involved in the kitchen. And now I was thinking about Renata herself. Hadn't William more or less bought her from the Wheelers? How much resentment might that have fostered? What if she was still in communication with her former employers? There was no love lost between William and the couple he'd helped to bankrupt.

Alongside this train of thought ran another on a parallel track in which all of the strange things that had happened to me here were coupled together like separate carriages. There was the humiliating episode with the tiara and Evelyn's apparent misdirection, but no sooner had I thought of that than I remembered seeing Alina coming out of my room through the window of the Manettis' corridor on the afternoon of the ball. The crying in the night must have been someone who lived in the castle, surely, but then what explained the phantom figure I'd chased through the corridors, that glimpse of white nightdress disappearing around corners? Other memories came to me – Klara Fletcher's face when her peacock fan was found in my bag, that sense of things being moved around in my room, my conviction down by the stream of being observed and followed. That damn violin.

Just as it seemed like all the separate spiralling thoughts must come exploding out of me like a Catherine wheel, there came a knock at the door.

When I opened it, Alina was standing there, her eyes huge and wild.

I took a step back.

'Constance, we have to talk. I can't stop thinking about Solomon. Can I come in?'

She tried to push past me, but I held my ground.

For a second or two we stared at each other.

Then Evelyn's voice sounded from the end of the corridor, making us both start. 'Is that you, Alina? What on earth are you doing up here? Massimo's been looking everywhere for you.'

Alina froze, then she turned to me again.

'Come with me, Constance. It's dangerous here. I keep thinking about what you said about the food Solomon ate. I think you're right.'

She put her hand on my arm and I shrugged it off as if it had burned me.

'*Alina. Massimo is waiting to leave.*' Evelyn's voice was louder now as she approached.

'Please, Constance, come.'

Confusion churned in my gut, alongside the conviction that I couldn't trust anyone.

'You'd better go,' I said, stepping back.

Alina gave me one last, intense look, whether of fear or anger I couldn't tell, and then she was gone and I was back in my room, locking my door with fumbling fingers.

There was no possibility of sleep that night. Instead, I lay awake hour after hour, listening to the castle breathe and sigh around me.

I found myself coming back again and again to the night I'd heard the child crying softly outside my room and given chase to the ghostly figure in the old-fashioned nightgown. I'd tried to put the darkroom out of my mind since then – those terrible photographs of Evelyn – but now I forced myself back there, recalling how I'd followed the apparition inside. Hadn't there been something else in there that had snagged my attention? Something besides those pictures of Evelyn?

I thought back to how I'd burst in and seen the shallow trays on the worktop, the framed photographs on the wall.

I sat bolt upright as something occurred to me. Surely I must be mistaken?

I lay back down, but the thought would not leave me alone. I knew that as soon as the household started stirring again it would be impossible to check whether what I believed I'd remembered was real or yet another figment of my sleep-deprived imagination. The darkroom was next to the kitchen at the back of the house. There were always people in and out. If I wanted to set my mind to rest, I would have to go now.

I forced myself up. The clicking as I turned the key in the lock sounded deafening in the stillness of the night and I stopped, rigid, listening to see if anyone would come. When I finally set off down the corridor, the shadow cast by the lamp followed me along the stone walls, matching me step for step.

At the top of the main staircase I glanced towards the wood panelling, picturing the gramophone hidden inside and remembering how the violin concerto had felt as if the bow were being drawn across my nerves. I wasn't crazy. Someone had deliberately been trying to scare me. A red-hot splinter of rage propelled me downstairs.

The darkroom door was closed, as always, and there was a moment when I convinced myself it would be locked, but when I turned the handle the door creaked open just as if it had been waiting for me.

Inside, I made my way past the counter with its shallow trays of developer and fixer and went straight to the framed photographs on the back wall. Ignoring the rally scene, with its tiny dictator, dwarfed by his own flags, I stopped by the second image. Holding up my lamp as close as I could, I stared at the picture, and the group of shiny, pinafore-clad girls stared back. They'd been arranged in a very general age order with the youngest, a chubby-cheeked child with white-blonde hair, in the front. But it was the back row, where the older girls stood, that captured my attention. This row consisted of three girls of around fifteen or sixteen. Two were complete strangers, but the third, the one in the middle with long fair hair tied with a dark ribbon, was definitely, now I looked at it closely, Olivia Averell.

The photograph itself was innocuous. An attractive group portrait in pleasant surroundings. Probably a school, I surmised. But it was the strangeness of it. That Roberto should have known Olivia when she was such a young woman, and yet I'd never heard of the connection. I cast my mind back to when he'd first introduced me. He'd said she came from New York, and I knew he'd spent time in America with his mother, but he hadn't mentioned they'd met there.

All this time I was steeling myself to look again at the photographs of Evelyn. Not because I wanted to see them again. Far from it. But because I couldn't help feeling they had something to do with whatever was happening here.

But when I searched the line strung out over the counter I saw they had been replaced by a series of photographs taken after the earthquake. Piles of rubble. Cracks in stone walls. Even a picture of the shattered remains of the gargoyle that had so nearly landed on me, part of its mouth still intact, lips pulled back, teeth bared.

I started rifling through the piles of photographic prints that littered the room. When these yielded nothing, I went to the filing cabinets. By now I knew I had already well and truly crossed the line from investigation into trespass, so I hardly hesitated before pulling open the drawers and leafing through the contents. More landscapes and city streets, more portraits of people I didn't know.

Only the bottom drawer refused to open. I tugged it three times, hoping it might just have been stuck, but I finally had to accept it was locked. I cast around the room, searching for a place where a key might be hidden. Then I remembered the gold chain Roberto wore around his neck, with its little gold key. Hope gave way to desperation. I knew that both William and I could be in danger, and I needed answers fast. And at this very instant the only place I could think of looking for them was in that drawer.

For a wild moment I thought about going upstairs and turning left into the Manettis' wing, creeping into Roberto and Evelyn's bedroom while they slept in their four-poster bed. The chain was delicate. One little tug could be all it took.

Then I remembered how, after Walter died, leaving his desk drawer locked and no key to be found, James had managed to open it, using two paperclips. 'A trick I learned at school,' he'd said proudly, standing up and brushing his trousers down. 'It's easy once you know how.'

I didn't have paperclips, but I managed to bend one of my hairpins into a right angle, with a loop on one end that could be used as a handle, as I'd seen James do. A second hairpin was straightened out then bent back in two, leaving a very narrow loop at one end. James had explained the general principle, which was that this second pin went in first to create the tension needed to turn the lock, while the other one opened it up. When James had done it, the drawer had popped open straight away, but I didn't really know what I was doing and my palms were slippery, my hair now half up and half down, falling into my eyes. I rattled the pins, just as I'd watched James do. Nothing. Somewhere upstairs, a pipe creaked, and I stopped still, the fingers that held the pins trembling.

I withdrew the pins then reinserted them. Once. Twice.

By the fourth attempt I'd given up hope of success but kept going anyway, because giving up meant facing up to not having any other plan of action. I dug the first pin into the bottom, then slid the second over the top, reaching it right to the back then bringing it out slowly, then turned the bottom one. *Click.*

I sat with the pins in my hand, paralysed both by fear that someone might have heard and disbelief that it had worked. Then, quickly, I threw the ruined hairpins on to the top of the cabinet and yanked open the drawer, drawing in my breath sharply when I saw, on the very top of a tall stack of photographs, the pictures of Evelyn, as shocking now as the first time I'd seen them. I held up my lamp so that I could scrutinize her eyes, which were wide open, trying to read her expression. But it was impossible. Steeling myself, I picked slowly through the pile, looking for something – *anything* – that might shed some light on the things that had been happening in the castle. There were five pictures of Evelyn in that series, all obviously taken during the same photographic session on what I now knew to be the counterpane of her bed. Naked. Bound. Gagged.

I felt queasy, like a voyeur. Yet the need to understand what was happening here was stronger than my instinct to look away. Beneath the pictures I'd already seen were others in the same vein, some taken in a different bedroom, a couple even outside in the woods. I'd assumed the whole pile would be of Evelyn, so it was an unpleasant surprise to come across other photographs further down of different models, some similarly tied up, others merely posing naked. All of the other sitters were young. Some seemed very young indeed.

And one of the youngest of all was Olivia Averell.

For a moment I thought I might actually vomit, and stood, swaying, with my eyes shut. Then I straightened up, carefully placing the photograph on the counter where the developing trays were. In the light of my lamp, I saw that this Olivia was at most fifteen years old. She wore her hair long, with the front section held back by a ribbon. Her body was that of a woman, and yet her face wore the soft, unfinished look of a child. She was smiling shyly at the camera and her expression was one of extreme embarrassment mixed with something else which I couldn't quite put my finger on, until I realized it reminded me of how Nora looked at Evelyn sometimes when she was trying hard to please her.

A wave of pity engulfed me and I thrust the photograph guiltily back into the stack. I had no appetite to see more, but still I forced myself to flick through the remainder. Near the bottom, I made another very surprising discovery. Five more photographs of subjects who were naked and in two cases also bound.

Only these were all men.

Back in my room, I locked the door and sank down on to the bed with my head in my hands. I had never thought myself a prude, but the contents of that drawer had shocked me to the marrow of my bones. The youth of the sitters – one of the young men had looked even younger than Olivia Averell. The expression on the American heiress's face.

That charming, attentive Roberto might have taken those photographs, standing behind his camera, instructing his sitters to move this way and that, seemed beyond comprehension.

I tried to piece it all together in my head.

Was there something, perhaps, between Roberto and Olivia? A love affair started when they were both living in New York? I thought of the bashful but hopeful expression on her face in the photograph. It wasn't the look of someone in love, but rather in the grip of a schoolgirl crush. Certainly, the times I'd seen them together she had seemed ill at ease. I remembered the first time I'd met her at the de Havillands' garden party, when she had emerged, flustered, from the pergola where she and Roberto had been ensconced. What if he had persuaded her to sit for the picture when she was an infatuated young girl and now held it over her? A photograph like that released into society could do untold damage to a young woman's reputation and marriage prospects. What might she agree to do to stop that happening? Slip an antique fan into her neighbour's bag at dinner? Dress up in an old-fashioned nightdress and run through the castle corridors? I'd assumed it was a child ahead of me that night, but perhaps my imagination had filled in the gaps, the legend of the girl in the wall uppermost in my mind.

If Roberto was blackmailing Olivia, what was to say he wasn't doing the same to Evelyn? She was certainly more robust than Olivia, but, even so, those photographs would destroy her if made public. She'd be powerless to refuse him. I thought about all the little things that had happened, the medicine vials being swapped around, misdirecting me to Alice de Havilland's room to pick up the tiara. Had she gone along with those cruel ruses under duress?

But the question of why still eluded me. That there had been a campaign to make me feel as if I were losing my mind and to discredit me publicly was now becoming clear to me. And though it was a relief to know it was not all in my head, any feelings of vindication were swamped by the knowledge that someone was deliberately targeting me in this way. For what possible reason?

When that thread broke off there, I seized on a new one. William. Solomon's dramatic illness after eating William's food and William's perplexing and unexpected decline might conceivably be a coincidence, yet everything in me was telling me there was something sinister happening here, that someone was tampering with William's food to make him ill. I thought about Jerome Fielding hanging around, waiting for William to make good on his promise of a bequest, and Mr Webb coming to the house for an appointment William was too ill to keep. I remembered Evelyn taking Jerome Fielding's letter from me, assuring me she would give it straight to William.

What if Roberto had found out that William intended to change his will? The promise of a house in Wiltshire would mean nothing to him. It was here in Florence that he wanted to make his mark, to prove himself a man to be reckoned with. Then there were his gambling debts to be paid, his lifestyle to support. And the blow to his patriotic pride should the castle fall into the ownership of a British university.

And yet, this was Roberto, not some monster. I had known him to be petulant and childish at times, with the occasional cruel word to Evelyn, but he was also funny and charming, the way he could fix his whole attention on you as if it mattered to him how you were, as if *you* mattered to him.

Then I thought about how he'd insisted on Nora's nose being straightened and the things he'd said to Evelyn about Nora being too plain to be Evelyn's child, and Evelyn being too old to get pregnant. I thought about the photographs in the drawer downstairs.

All through the rest of that sleepless night I wrestled with my thoughts, trying to find the connection between the two threads. If Roberto was, with Evelyn's enforced help, slowly poisoning William so that Evelyn would inherit the castle and the collection, he must be hoping that William's decline would be attributed to his earlier illness and no further enquiries made. But equally he must know that if an autopsy were carried out and traces of poison found, he and Evelyn would come under suspicion, particularly once it became public that William had intended to change his will – which it no doubt would if the university tried to press its claim. Unless . . . unless . . .

. . . unless another, more obvious, suspect was found.

As soon as the grey dawn revealed itself through the slits in the wooden shutters I dressed and stole out of my room, closing the door silently behind me.

Downstairs at the back of the main hallway, near the alcove where Philip Wheeler had tried to force himself on me on the night of the ball, the telephone rested on an elegant carved wood table. As I picked up the heavy brass-edged receiver from its cradle, there was a loud *ding* and I held my breath, listening for the sound of footsteps on the stairs, my stomach hard with fear. When none were forthcoming, I turned the dial for the operator, giving the name of James's *pensione*, as I had done previously, but because I was talking so quietly, it took three attempts before I made myself understood, by which time my hands were so slippery with sweat I could hardly hold the handpiece.

I'd waited until the earliest time I felt it was permissible to telephone the *pensione*, but still the proprietor's voice was thick with sleep. When I asked for James she launched into a speech in Italian that I didn't understand. In desperation I interrupted her, *James Bowen, per favore*, and there must have been something in my voice because finally she broke off and I heard a door creak, followed by the distant sound of her shouting up the stairs. My nerves stretched like elastic and, just as I thought they must surely snap, there came James's voice on the line and I felt myself slump with relief.

When I tried to whisper it came out as a croak.

'I can hardly hear you,' James kept saying. 'Speak up.'

I managed to convey to him some of what had been churning through my mind this long, sleepless night, pressing upon him my suspicion that William was in danger and that I was being set up to take the blame.

'There's no time to explain everything. Please come quickly. And bring the—'

The line went dead as a hand reached over my shoulder to depress the cradle where the receiver rested, disconnecting the call. In place of James's reassuring voice, there was now only a dead void and my own breath echoing back to me as I turned slowly around.

35

I HAD BEEN EXPECTING Roberto. He was quite often up early, leaving the castle in his black uniform, the heels of his long leather boots clicking on the stone floor. My relief, when I found myself instead face to face with Evelyn, her delicate features ethereally pale in the dawn light, was overwhelming.

'What on earth has come over you, Constance? Telling James such rotten things about us. After everything we've done to help you?'

Her voice was choked. There was a split second when I entertained the idea of denying everything. Instead, I decided the truth was the better option.

'It's all right, Evelyn. I know about Roberto's photographs and the things he's made you do. I know you feel like you don't have a choice. He's depraved, but it is not your fault.'

'I don't know what—'

'Let me help you. Please.' I took her hands in mine, feeling how fragile they were, and was surprised to find myself engulfed by a wave of protectiveness towards her. People made such terrible mistakes in the name of love.

Evelyn, who was wearing her silk belted kimono, looked startled. She hesitated, and my nerves twisted as I saw her

300

glance at the telephone. Robbery, trespass, attempted murder, even. If she called the police, it would be my word against hers.

But when she spoke it was in an urgent whisper.

'Come with me, quickly. Roberto will be down any moment. He knows you have been talking to people in town. He knows you suspect him.'

'But how——?'

'Florence is a small place, Connie, and Roberto's family reach is large.'

'I'll go to my room. James will be here shortly. He'll bring the police.'

'Not likely. There's a big rally in the city centre. All the regular *polizia* will be there, as well as the blackshirts. Anyway, you're not safe in your room. It's the first place he'd look. Quick, follow me.'

She beckoned me up the stairs, but I hesitated at the bottom. I knew Roberto hadn't left yet. If he got up now, we would bump straight into each other.

'Quick, Connie. There isn't much time.'

I'd never seen this side of Evelyn. Sober. Determined. I had to trust her. What choice did I have?

We reached the upper landing, where Alina had found the gramophone hidden in the wall cavity, and for a terrible moment I thought Evelyn would lead me through the doorway towards their bedroom where Roberto presumably lay sleeping. Instead, she crossed to the back and the low doorway where the narrow spiral stairs led up to the roof of the castle.

'Roberto will never go up there,' she whispered. 'He is frightened of enclosed spaces.'

'Aren't you coming?'

'If I don't go back, he will suspect something. Don't worry,

Connie. Roberto wouldn't miss the rally for the world. He loves the chance to march up and down, being admired. You know how he is. You'll be safe up there until he leaves.' She turned away, then back again. 'You know he's not a bad person. He just doesn't always know where or how to stop.'

My heart was hammering, my breathing made ragged by fear and by the effort of climbing all those stairs, so that by the time I emerged on to the roof, blinking into the daylight, I felt as if my lungs were about to burst.

I leaned against the battlements, all the strength draining from me, feeling suddenly faint, despite the gentleness of the early-morning sun.

I don't know how long I stayed up there on the castle roof, looking out across the countryside to where the golden city floated in a soft haze, but as the heat gradually built I became uncomfortably aware of the lack of shade. Peering down over the parapet, I could see where the earthquake had caused cracks to form in the castle walls like snakes that slithered across the stone.

The sun climbed in the sky and the hillsides and valleys stirred into life around me. Two birds flew on to the parapet and stared at me, heads on sides, as if wondering what I was doing all the way up here. I saw a pony and trap passing in the road far below and heard the sound of a car's engine far away.

Now I heard voices, and footsteps on gravel. *James!* My chest lifted as I crouched down to peer over the battlement, but when I saw the dark heads of Alina and Massimo coming through the iron gates I was thrown into indecision. Though I was almost sure now that Alina had nothing to do with what had been going on, still some vestige of doubt remained. The image of her on her hands and knees in front of the hidden cupboard, reaching in towards the gramophone, proved hard to shift. But as they crossed the courtyard towards the main entrance I changed my mind. Of course I could trust Alina. She was my friend. I stood up, ready to call down to them, but as I opened my mouth there came a new voice.

Roberto.

He was standing at the front door, addressing them in Italian. I flung myself back down on to the ground, the blood rushing around my ears. I heard him laugh. *Perhaps he was leaving?*

But there was no car door slamming. No turning of the engine. Instead, when I dared peep back over the top, I saw the three of them disappearing into the house, directly underneath where I stood.

The sun was now burning the skin on my cheeks and across my forehead. I sat in the one corner of the turret that had a sliver of shadow and put my hot face in my hands, lack of sleep combining with the heat to bring on a state of near delirium where sounds and smells blurred together and the only thing that existed was the sun and the time passing.

A noise jolted me out of my trancelike state. A door clanging down below. And now, unmistakably, footsteps on the stairs. I clambered to my feet. I hadn't heard Roberto leave the house. Could it be him, coming to find me? Or perhaps James had arrived without me noticing. He would be trying to be unobtrusive, wouldn't he? Perhaps he'd slipped in through the kitchen? Hope and fear battled it out inside me as the footsteps grew louder. I glanced around, as if a hiding place might magically appear from nowhere. Then the door to the staircase burst open.

Evelyn looked more flustered than I could ever recall seeing her. High spots of colour in her tightly stretched cheeks.

'Oh, thank God. I thought you were Roberto.' I struggled to recapture my breath. 'What's happening? Has he left yet?'

Evelyn didn't speak. Unsmiling and stern as she was now, she looked suddenly every bit her age. I stared at her in confusion, waiting for her to explain. Even when I heard more footsteps behind her, my mind struggled to catch up with my senses, horrified realization dawning at the exact moment Roberto himself emerged on to the roof.

'You know I can't stand those steps.' His voice was querulous, his skin clammy. 'It's like the walls are trying to crush me to death.'

He looked at me and sighed, as if it was all my fault.

My eyes flicked between husband and wife, trying to force my thoughts to understand.

'Evelyn,' I tried again. 'You don't have to do what he wants. I'll protect you. I'll destroy the photographs.'

Roberto let out a bark of laughter. 'Do what *I* want? That's very funny. Surely you must know by now who rules the roost around here?'

I looked from one to the other, not comprehending.

'But the photographs . . .'

Now, finally, Evelyn spoke.

'Oh, Connie, you are a funny old thing. *I* suggested that Roberto take those pictures. I know what he likes. I know *who* he likes. That's what happens in a marriage. You give him what he wants so he doesn't go elsewhere.'

Belatedly, I understood. Things sliding into place in my mind.

'And is that why you were so set on the will staying as it is? To keep Roberto from looking elsewhere?'

Evelyn looked at me as if I were a small, particularly obtuse, child.

'Partly. But not entirely. I'm surprised I have to tell you these things, Connie. The inheritance – the castle, the collection – is my insurance policy to guard against what the future might bring. I won't always be pretty, but I'm going to make damn sure I'll always be rich.'

All this time Roberto was standing with his hands on his knees and his head bent, his dark curls falling forward over his face, as if he couldn't bring himself to look at me.

'James will be here any moment,' I said, my voice rising. 'He'll bring the police.'

'They'd never believe him. Everyone knows Roberto and his family around here. They're practically royalty. Anyway, I've told you, they'll all be occupied at the rally. And the streets are closed so that the trams will be late running. James will have to walk if he wants to get here, and really, it's all just a bit too late, don't you think? Uncle Bill is almost past the point of no return. In fact, it would be a kindness for someone to put him out of his misery. He's had his time. You didn't know him, Connie, when he was in his prime, galloping around these hills on his black horse. He'd have hated living like this. He's so weak now, a pillow popped over his face for just a moment . . . He'd thank us for it, if he could speak.'

'You're crazy, Evelyn. The authorities will know right away.'

Evelyn scrunched up her nose.

'Oh, I don't think so, do you? He has been declining for so long, who is going to question it? And if they do insist on doing an autopsy and find traces of anything . . . *unusual* . . .

in his system, who do you think they're going to blame? His loving niece, or the strange companion who came out of nowhere and saw phantoms and heard noises in the night and mixed up his medicines and proved, very sadly, to be of such a nervous disposition? There are so many witnesses, after all.'

I shook my head, uncomprehending. 'Unusual? What do you mean?'

Evelyn smiled. 'Let's just say it's eye-opening what you can find growing quite openly around here, once you know what to look for.'

'You're talking about *murder*, Evelyn?' The word sounded preposterous spoken out loud.

She tutted, the smile gone. 'Don't be melodramatic, Connie. It's just hastening something that would have happened anyway. And besides, I'm the injured party here. I was devoted to Uncle Bill, and how has he repaid me? By disinheriting me from a fortune that wasn't even his to start with. This castle belonged to my Aunt Cecily. That means I have more of a right to it than he does!'

I turned to appeal to Roberto.

'Surely you're not going to just go along with this?'

He grimaced.

'To be very frank, I'd rather not, Constance. I have no appetite for this kind of thing. But Evelyn is so impossible when she has her mind set on something. And she has some *things* of mine that could do untold damage to my standing in the party. I know you know what I'm talking about. I could tell you've been in my darkroom. That was private, you know. You had no right.'

Instantly the images of the naked young men – boys, really – flashed across my mind.

'James is on his way, Roberto. You still have a chance to do the right thing.'

'Or what?'

'Or—'

'What is your precious James going to do to me, Constance?' Roberto was grinning in a way I didn't like. 'Will he try to kill me, I wonder . . . or kiss me?'

I stared at him. *Had he completely lost his mind?* But something dark was snaking through the veins and arteries in my feet and ankles, working its way northwards.

'What do you mean? What are you saying?'

'Oh, come on, Constance. Surely you've noticed the way he stares at me the whole time, like I'm a glass of water and he's just crawled through a desert on his knees?'

'No, no. You've got it wrong. It's Evelyn he was looking at. I had to warn him about it.'

Evelyn laughed.

'Oh, Connie, you're too much. Your son no more has eyes for me as for that chimney stack over there.'

'That's not true. It's a wicked thing to say. I'd know. I'm his mother.'

But it was like someone rubbing a fogged-up window with their sleeve, things becoming clear that had previously been blurry and impossible to define.

'Has he ever brought a woman home?' Evelyn wanted to know. 'I can see from your face that he hasn't.'

'You're both mad!' I shouted. 'And you won't get away with what you're doing. I'll tell everyone. I'll make them believe me.'

'You see, that's the problem,' said Evelyn. 'That's why things have become so *unpleasant*. It was never the plan for you to get hurt. We're not monsters. We *liked* you. You were just an insurance policy in case too many questions were asked. But now you've gone poking around . . . well, you've really left us no choice, have you?'

She was looking at me as if waiting for my agreement. Then she turned to Roberto.

'Come on, darling one. Let's get this over with.'

He threw up his hands and, darting nervous looks at me, shook his head.

'That's too much, Evelyn. We never discussed this.'

'Yes, well, we didn't know, did we? But this works, don't you see? It fits the pattern. The poor unstable English-woman, finally driven to the brink.'

I was looking from one to the other, waiting for their meaning to become clear.

Evelyn took a step towards me. Then stopped and looked over at Roberto again.

'Well, come on then. I can't do it alone. She's twice my size.'

And now, too late, I realized what she intended, why she'd insisted I come up here to this spot from which there were only two ways down.

'I just don't see why I have to be involved,' said Roberto.

'Do you want to be penniless? To live out a life in rural Wiltshire, taking photographs of sheep?'

Before I knew what was happening Evelyn had grabbed one arm and Roberto, after an apologetic glance, had hold of the other. Now I was struggling, kicking out, shouting for Alina. 'I really wish it didn't have to be this way,' said Roberto, looking away so he wouldn't have to see my face, while, from Evelyn's stoical expression, she might just as well have been wrestling with a small child who didn't want to get dressed.

The battlements were low and within seconds I was leaning backwards over them so that the stone stump where once the gargoyle monkey had been was in my line of sight.

Panic bubbled up inside me, together with an engulfing sadness that I wouldn't get to say goodbye to the people I loved. As my feet lifted from the ground I closed my eyes tight so that Millie and James's faces would be the last things I saw.

'Ow!' There was a cry and a sudden loosening of the grip on one of my arms as I staggered, astonished to feel solid stone through the soles of my shoes.

I opened my eyes. Roberto, white-faced, was on his knees, twisting to grapple with something behind him, while Nora stood a few feet away, pale and unmoving as a statue, one arm outstretched and red spatters on her clothes.

'What have you done?' screeched Evelyn, rushing to crouch next to Roberto, whose contortions had shifted him around, revealing the hilt of William's dagger sticking out of his thigh.

'She stabbed me,' gasped Roberto. 'The little *bitch* stabbed me.'

'You were hurting Mrs Bowen,' said Nora, finding her voice finally.

'What do I do?' asked Evelyn, and I realized that she was talking to me, her eyes turned in entreaty. 'Do I pull it out? Help me, for god's sake.'

I didn't reply. Instead, I made my way towards Nora, and, putting my arm around her shoulders, steered her through the open doorway.

'You're not leaving, Connie?' Evelyn's voice followed us down the narrow staircase, echoing off the stone walls.

'You wouldn't leave me like this, surely?'

36

One week later

WILLIAM'S RECOVERY ASTONISHED everyone. Without the steady drip drip drip of poison into his system, his resilience and sheer bloody-mindedness steadily set about righting the damage Evelyn and Roberto had done. Dr Pearson brought in a nurse to oversee his convalescence, a cheerful, rotund woman from Eastbourne who'd come out to Florence to care for a dying English lord and had never gone home, finding her services much in demand among the elderly Anglo-American community.

The police doctor who'd come from Rome to take blood and stool samples had found traces of three different substances that could cause 'grave harm' to the human body, but he guessed there might have been even more. In the drawstring pouches Evelyn carried everywhere, to touch up her lipstick and perfume, there were crumbs of organic matter that were later identified as the remains of a species of wild mushroom called the Amanita pantherina, which grew plentifully in the woods around, known to cause ill effects in humans such as sickness, confusion and hallucinations.

Renata had recounted to the police how, latterly, Evelyn had begun hovering in the kitchen when William's food was being prepared. Privately, I wondered if I might also have ingested some, remembering my confused thoughts and how I'd struggled to separate what was real from what was not.

In one of the nature books in William's library I'd read about other, deadlier mushrooms in the Amanita family: the death cap and the destroying angel, both of which could be found locally. Alina was convinced Evelyn had made a mistake in giving her uncle the less lethal variety, but I preferred to believe there was some small, still decent part of her that wanted to give him a fighting chance.

We would never know. By the time James arrived, alone, the police occupied with the rally as Evelyn had predicted, Evelyn and Roberto had disappeared. A trail of blood led to their bathroom, where the dagger had been discarded, and then out to where their car had been parked. I'd been in the kitchen, hurriedly filling in Alina and Massimo on what had happened, when we heard the slam of a car door and Massimo ran outside just in time to see the spare wheel attached to the rear of Roberto's green car disappearing through the gates. The couple fled first across the border to Marseilles and were now thought to be on a ship heading for New York and the protection of Roberto's wealthy mother. Before departure they'd sent telegrams to Roberto's Italian family and the authorities protesting their innocence.

The *squadristi* of which Roberto had so recently been a part flexed their considerable muscle to protect their own. Even after William was well enough to describe waking up one time to see Evelyn switching his medicines – the time he'd lashed out when I tried to give him his daily dose – the police chief dealing with the case decided his account was not to be trusted. He had been in the grip of a substance that brought on hallucinations, they insisted. Nora's testimony of what she'd witnessed up on the castle roof was similarly dismissed as the imaginings of a lonely, impressionable child who had formed an unnatural attachment to an adult who showed her kindness. And Alina was a servant and so bound to echo whatever her employer – William North – said.

In vain I described the photographs I'd seen. As Roberto had got rid of all physical evidence – the bottom drawer of the filing cabinet left hanging open and empty – there was simply no proof. The same thing went for the poisoning of Solomon and the stone gargoyle that had almost crushed me, which I was now convinced had been Roberto or Evelyn's doing. The other things – William falling from the sofa when I was so sure I'd left his stick within reach, things being moved in my room, footsteps behind me on the hillside – would also remain a suspicion in my mind, rather than a fact.

No charges were brought, no moves made to bring Roberto and Evelyn back from exile. On the other hand, neither did the police make any attempt to accuse me of wrongdoing, as the Manettis had demanded in their telegrams.

I apologized to Alina. In the clear light of day, I couldn't believe I'd ever doubted her account of how she stumbled upon the hidden gramophone while cleaning. She was magnanimous and generous, though she still looked pale and I knew she must be worrying about her future. William had already been in touch with Jerome Fielding to discuss transferring the castle and the collection to the university while he was still alive, so that he could oversee the establishment of the trust. Despite my sympathy for Alina and Massimo, I could understand why he was doing it. After everything that had happened we all needed a fresh start.

Eight days after Evelyn and Roberto's flight, James and I sat in the courtyard garden under the sagging pergola vine.

He'd been such a calm, reassuring presence over the last week, and I'd deliberately pushed the things Roberto had said about him to the back of my mind, drawing comfort instead from being in his company. Only at night, in the privacy of my room, did I allow myself to go over the allegations Roberto and Evelyn had made about James, searching in vain for a different explanation. After the initial flat denial – *they were trying to hurt me, that's all* – snatches of memory had come back to me from the past. James's form master at school alluding to some 'silliness' between James and one of the other boys, and Walter asking if he meant fighting and him saying, 'Not exactly,' with a strange look. James growing upset when Walter referred to Oscar Wilde as 'that degenerate' after he found Millie reading *The Picture of Dorian Gray*. There had been no courtships over the years, no covert looks when we passed a pretty girl in the street.

At first, I shut down these thoughts as they arose. Only after a day or two had passed did the shock wear off enough for me to probe my own response, as one might prod a sore tooth, in search of whatever lay beneath the hard shell of my denial, and I discovered something quite surprising. It wasn't the thing itself I found abhorrent – the idea of two men enjoying love in the same way as a man and a woman – but rather it was the implication for James. For my son, whom I loved so very much. A choice between a life of loneliness or one of criminality. And for me, no grandchildren. The hardship of the future that lay ahead of him shredded my heart.

'Mr Tucker will be wondering if you're still alive,' I said now.

This was James's boss at the accountancy firm, a lugubrious man with a pipe permanently clamped between his lips, so that the one time I'd met him my hair had stunk of tobacco for days afterwards.

James was quiet, his expression unreadable in the dappled shadow of the green leaves overhead.

'Actually, I have left my job.' He darted a nervous glance at me and then instantly looked away. 'I was always unhappy there but I think I had fallen into a kind of trance, doing the same things every day, convincing myself everyone else also led lives that were one compromise after another. Then when you said you were coming here to Italy, it plunged me into a state of near terror because if you could change your life like that, it meant that not everyone had to settle for a life to be endured rather than enjoyed. I think that's why I was so against the whole notion. Because if my mother could break free like that, then there was nothing to stop me doing the same. And that frightened the life out of me.

'Then, once your letters started arriving with your descriptions of the landscape and the light and Florence itself, I couldn't think about anything else. I asked to take two weeks' annual leave and Mr Tucker told me it wasn't convenient, and, well, I'm afraid I handed in my resignation.'

'Oh my.'

I was astonished. The James I thought I knew didn't make such impulsive gestures. But then it was becoming very clear that the James I thought I knew didn't really exist. Instead, here was this young man, with his shy smile and all his layers and secrets. Still, I was worried for him. So many young men were unemployed now, the cost of the war weighing heavy on the economy. It was only just over a year since the General Strike, workers coming out in support of better pay for the miners, no trains or buses, no newspapers on the streets. Was it foolish of him to give up a steady, dependable job so many would be glad of? On the other hand, change was so hard to come by. Shouldn't he be allowed to seize his chance of adventure, just as I had?

'What will you do now?' I asked him.

He shrugged.

'I rather think I should like to travel more. Not here. Not with that man in charge, marching the country into extremism. Perhaps Paris. I could teach English. But first I will escort you and Nora home.'

Though Evelyn had declared herself in one of her telegrams to be *heartbroken* at being *torn apart* from her *darling daughter*, the stark fact of the matter was that she had deserted her. Subsequently, Nora's father had been tracked down to a farmhouse on the edge of Dartmoor, where he was living in a communal arrangement with a group of misfits – mostly other former soldiers – who lived off the land without running water or luxuries of any kind. To my secret relief, the local solicitor who had been dispatched to talk to him reported that he had grown quite agitated at the suggestion that Nora might live with him. Instead, the decision had been reached that she spend the summer at the house in Sussex, where Evelyn's parents lived with her brother and his wife and children, before starting boarding school nearby. At William's expense.

In the absence of anyone else, I had agreed to accompany her to England. I didn't want to leave William and Florence, but it had become too dangerous for me to stay in Italy, with Roberto and Evelyn still trying to smear my name. Roberto's family were well connected in the area, and anti-British sentiment building all the time. Nora, James and I would be setting off the next day. I had grown very fond of the child by this point and privately worried how she would get on in a girls' school, which could be a cruel place for those who stood out. Even now she was finally freed from the contraption on her nose, Dr Pearson having been prevailed upon to remove it the very day after Evelyn and Roberto's rushed departure, she was unusual-looking and she had no experience of trying to fit in.

It was too early to see what long-term effects might result from such a traumatic and public rejection by her mother. I hoped that the fact they had never been close, despite Nora's best efforts, might mitigate against permanent emotional scarring, but she would need a lot of bolstering up. For the time being and despite all she had done and witnessed, Nora had chosen to believe that Roberto had had a 'funny turn', as she put it, and that he and Evelyn had gone away to recuperate. I felt uneasy about going along with the deception, but the alternative, telling a little girl that her mother had chosen her husband over her child, was unimaginable. Sooner or later she would have to face the truth, but not yet.

Little steps.

Meanwhile, she was excited about the prospect of finally making friends, and I wouldn't be so far away for weekend visits and holidays.

William, of course, was in no state to look after a child, despite the rapidity of his recovery. Besides, even if he had been in perfect health, it was clear Nora was in need of more company than the castle could supply.

'I expect you will miss this place,' said James now, looking around at the mellow sunlight pooling on the lawn and, beyond it, the castle wall, crowning golden near the top. 'And its inhabitants,' he added.

'Of course.' I bent my face to inspect the splinter of wood my fingernail was worrying at on the arm of my chair.

'As long as you aren't hoping—'

'I'm not hoping for anything.'

We glared at each other for a moment, and it was James who softened first.

'You are an impossible woman,' he said, a smile twitching around his mouth.

For a moment we sat in silence, taking in the sounds of the garden – the incessant buzz of the insects in the honeysuckle that clambered up the castle walls, the call of the wood pigeons, Renata singing to herself in the kitchen.

'You know,' I told him, 'I am so very glad that you're my son.'

Before he returned to spend a final night at his *pensione*, James and I went in to see William, who'd insisted on being brought downstairs in defiance of the nurse and Dr Pearson, who would have preferred him to be confined to his bedroom while they supervised his recovery. I'd hardly seen him at all over the preceding days, when there were so many questions to be answered and investigations carried out, and he was still shockingly thin, his wrists protruding long and bony from the sleeves of his robe. But there was colour in his gaunt cheeks now that he was free of Evelyn and Roberto's ministrations, and the spark was back in his eyes. The doctor had warned there might be liver or kidney damage as a result of the fungus Evelyn had added to his food, but so far, thankfully, there seemed little evidence of that.

'Next time we will try to make your stay more eventful,' William said slowly.

James's mouth fell open in surprise, until he realized it was a joke.

'At least Mother has finally agreed to leave,' James said. 'I kept telling her it wouldn't be safe for her to stay here, surrounded by Roberto's Fascisti pals. But she is nothing if not stubborn.'

'Agreed.'

There was a look that passed between them then that was not quite amicable, but not far off.

After James had left, William and I sat in his sitting room, separated by a shaft of slanted sunlight in which dust motes danced. Kathleen, the cheerful nurse, bustled around, plumping pillows and humming something remarkably tuneless until William snapped.

'Enough, woman.'

Kathleen raised her eyebrows at me over his head.

'Someone's feeling better,' she remarked tartly as she left the room.

'I think I preferred you when you were at death's door,' I told him, after the door had closed behind her.

William let out a laugh that turned almost immediately into a cough.

'I should let you rest.' But as I got up to go, he started shaking his head.

'Stay. Please.'

In all the time I'd been in Italy I couldn't remember William North ever saying 'please'. I sat back down heavily.

William seemed agitated. He glanced at me, and then away again and then back, as if he was working himself up to speak. I wondered if I should go to call Kathleen back, if perhaps he might be suffering a relapse.

'Shall I—?' I began, at the exact same moment he began to speak, so that we both stopped, abruptly. My instinct was to paper over the ensuing awkwardness with mindless chatter, but for once I stopped myself.

'I wish you weren't going.'

William looked fixedly ahead as he spoke in his still-laborious speech, so it took a moment for his words to properly sink in.

'I am sure you and Kathleen will manage just fine without me.'

He didn't smile, and I wished I hadn't spoken so flippantly, but my heart was racing.

'The thing is . . . I think I need you.'

It was what I had, in my wildest, most foolish dreams, imagined I wanted him to say. And yet hearing the words said out loud, it felt all wrong. For all his miracle recovery, William was still an invalid, and I was the woman who'd cared for him during his weakest moments. I was in love – I acknowledged that finally to myself – but I wasn't a fool. I knew how easy it would be for him to confuse gratitude with something more.

'You will be fine,' I told him. 'Now that the danger is

passed you will be back to your old life before you know it. Back to the dinner parties and the fawning ladies.'

'I don't want my old life. I want you.'

This last was said so fiercely and sternly he might as well have been telling me he never wished to see me again. There was a pressure building up in my chest and my temples were throbbing.

'You think you want me or need me because of what has happened, but when you are quite recovered you'll see that it is only relief talking, and misplaced appreciation.'

I didn't look at him as I spoke, in case my own secret, selfish desires were written all over my face. From the corner of my eye I noticed him again becoming flustered, his hands clenching, his breath fast and uneven.

'Don't tell me what—' But whatever William was about to say next was lost to a fit of coughing that brought Kathleen bustling back into the room.

'Someone has overdone it, I see.'

I could only imagine what effect the nurse's iron-clad jollity would have on William, who hated to be interrupted at the best of times. For myself, I was seized by a feeling of absolute dejection. The moment I had hardly dared dream of had come and, rather than seizing on it with both hands, I had pushed it away.

I wanted him to want me, but not as a nursemaid or a rescuer but as a woman. I wanted to inspire in him not gratitude but love and, yes, lust. Why not? It wasn't too late for me. I had faced down ghosts and poisoners and doubters and finger-pointers, and Philip Wheeler with his wet lips and probing tongue. I had proved my worth.

But knowing that I was doing what was best for us both

didn't stop me feeling, as I left Kathleen to tend to her querulous patient, as if a hole had opened up inside my heart big enough to drive a fist through.

The day of our departure was one of those damp, grubby days you occasionally get in Florence in summer where the sun can't burn through the haze that turns the whole world grey. I was selfishly glad not to be leaving when Tuscany was in her finest clothes, making the wrench that much sharper.

Nora, dressed in a pale pink pinafore and clutching Matilda tight to her chest, was fidgety with excitement. Now that her face was clear of metal straps, she looked younger than ever and so full of anticipation my heart contracted.

Despite Evelyn's many faults, her selfishness and her casual cruelty, I chose to believe she had tried to love her daughter. While Roberto had wanted Nora's nose straightened to make her more of an asset to him, I chose to believe Evelyn had hoped that if Nora could be made to look less like her father, the man who'd come home from the war and taken his fear and his shame out on his wife, then whatever was missing in her feelings for her daughter would be magically restored.

'Will they like me, do you think? My cousins?' Nora had asked the same thing an untold number of times since arrangements had been finalized for her to spend the summer in Sussex with Evelyn's parents and her brother and his children, and each time I'd reassured her that of course they would, because they were family, though I was privately far from confident.

In September she'd be starting school, and I told her she'd be an exotic novelty, because who else in the school could claim to have lived in a castle in Italy? I knew little girls could be unkind, but I hoped Nora's eccentricity might yet prove an advantage rather than a curse. And if it wasn't, I was determined to be on hand to reassure her that she was perfectly fine just as she was. Better than fine. And that sometimes you had to wait to find your place in the world.

Alina was driving us to the station, where we would meet James. She waited at the bottom of the stairs, her stomach now unmistakably rounded under her skirt and her expression grim.

'I will come back to see you,' I said as I passed her, stopping to press her hand. 'And you must come to stay with me.'

But we both knew how impossible such a thing would be.

William was in the *salone* waiting for us. Solomon, now fully restored to health, sat by his side with his ears pricked, as if he was aware how much danger his master had been in and was now alert to any new threat. Nora knelt on the floor and threw her arms around the neck of the dog she'd once been so nervous of. 'I will miss you,' she cried into his sleek black fur. Then, she got to her feet and threw her arms around William too. 'And you, Uncle Bill. I wish you were coming too. Will you be all right here by yourself?'

'He's not by himself. He has Kathleen and Alina and Massimo.'

'And Solomon,' added Nora. 'And when Mummy and Roberto come back, you will have them too.'

William and I exchanged uneasy glances but said nothing to contradict her.

From outside came the sound of wheels on gravel. Alina bringing the car around to the front, I guessed. Nora, too excited to settle, ran out to check that all her bags had been safely transferred to the car boot, leaving William and me alone. It was my chance, perhaps my only chance, to say what was uppermost in my mind and heart. Otherwise, I knew I'd carry my regret with me, always.

'I need to explain,' I said hurriedly. 'My response last night. It was not through want of—'

'William! You *darling* man!' Louise Power stood framed in the doorway, clutching an armful of dusky pink roses. There was a single rose in her black hair and her lips glistened matching pink. She was like a perfectly composed painting, standing there with the muted light reflecting on her face, and the gloom of the hallway behind so she shone in vibrant, glowing relief.

'The gossip that has been flying around town, darling. You just wouldn't believe. You know what this place is like. Kick one and they all limp. Of course, I pay it no heed, but as soon as I heard Evelyn and Roberto were . . . away . . . I came *running* to help.'

Now she looked at me, as if only just noticing I was there.

'Ah, Mrs . . . Buchanan, isn't it? I hear from Nora that you are heading home now. I don't blame you a bit. We are an exhausting bunch out here in Italy, always some drama going on. No wonder you'll be wanting to get back to your nice, safe life back in England. But have no fear, you are leaving him in excellent hands. I'm here to take over all caring duties until dear William is back to his usual, objectionable self.'

By now she'd crossed the room to stand behind William, and when she said the word 'objectionable' she laughed and rested her hands on his shoulders.

What could I do but take my leave, there and then, in

front of Louise Power's calculating gaze and William's own, that was harder to read but no less intense?

'Don't go,' I thought he said, but his voice was so muffled it might have been anything.

'He's saying goodbye,' declared Louise Power. 'And I'm sure he'd want to thank you too, for all your loyal service.'

We gazed at each other, William and I, across that high-ceilinged room, with the portrait of the bearded man looking down from the wall, his face still frozen into its tortured expression and the damp, grey Tuscan heat pressing through the window.

'Goodbye then.' My own voice was tinny and brittle, rattling off the stone walls, which may or may not have housed the bones of a young girl who knew too much, and I thought about all the ways women are made silent or silence themselves for fear of saying the wrong thing.

The words I couldn't speak were hot coals burning my mouth as I turned and walked away. Out through the double doors and across the vast entrance hall, emerging beneath the bared teeth of the surviving monkey gargoyle, into the hot, overcast day.

'Are you ready, Constance?' Alina had her head on the side, appraising. 'Are you sure there is nothing you have left behind?'

She was giving me a last chance, I realized.

'You've left Great-uncle Bill behind,' Nora said matter-of-factly. 'You should fetch him with us. You're his companion. You belong with him.'

Startled, I glanced into the window of the *salone* and caught Louise Power's eye. She lifted her hand and then bent over William, so that her long black hair curtained his face.

'No. Nothing,' I told Alina.

We climbed into the car, with Nora bouncing around in the back, too excited to sit still, and as we drove out through the iron gates the engine backfired, the sound echoing off the facade of the castle like sniper fire.

'Don't be sad,' said Nora, leaning forward to take my hand. 'We carry the things we love with us.'

It was what I'd been telling her for the past few days, whenever she'd seemed worried about leaving everything she knew behind here in Italy.

'When did you get so wise?' I asked, trying to smile.

The car plunged beneath the thick canopy of trees as we twisted and turned down the steep, narrow, wood-lined road, and when we finally emerged the sun had broken through a gap in the cloud, setting the hillside briefly and gloriously ablaze.

We carry the things we love with us, I repeated to myself, wiping away the tear that was trickling down my cheek. Meanwhile, Alina turned the car on to the straight road that led towards Florence and the train station and, eventually, home.

37

'Her name is Jemima and she's frightfully clever and she wears spectacles like an owl, and I think I should like to have some spectacles just like hers.'

Nora was helping herself to another slice of jam roly-poly and custard.

'This is awfully good, Mrs Hancock,' she called out.

'I should think so,' came the reply from the kitchen, but I could tell my twice-weekly housekeeper was pleased.

It was the third visit Nora had made to my house in Pinner from her boarding school, and I was trying not to show how delighted I was to hear she'd finally made a friend. After returning from Italy she'd spent most of the summer with Evelyn's stuffy brother in Sussex, who'd reported himself to be 'unnerved' both by her self-sufficiency and her refusal to engage in conversation involving her mother. Though she'd only been at boarding school a matter of weeks, she'd been struggling to fit in. But now, this wondrous Jemima had befriended her, and I sent her a wordless message of thanks.

After lunch we sat at the dining table and played cards while Mrs Hancock polished the wooden furniture in the front parlour.

There came the sound of an engine on the road outside.

'A taxi cab 'as just pulled up,' reported Mrs Hancock loftily.

Mrs Hancock disapproved of most motor cars, but most particularly of taxi cabs. '*What's wrong with the bus, I should like to know?*'

Suddenly there came a loud squawk. ' 'Eavens above, there's an 'orse coming out.'

Nora dropped her cards and ran to the front window.

'Solomon!' she cried. 'Mrs Bowen, Solomon is here.'

I joined her at the window, my legs suddenly turned to jelly. And there, emerging from the black cab, filled out and handsome with only his cane giving away his recent debilitation, was William.

By now, Nora had flown out of the front door and had her face buried in Solomon's neck. I followed her in a daze and stood in the doorway, my eyes meeting William North's over the top of her head. I'd forgotten the blueness of them, jewel-bright in the dove-grey autumn day.

'I thought I'd call in,' he said, and his voice was slow and deliberate but also strong and unfamiliar.

'Of course. It's wonderful to see you looking so well.'

And he did look almost rude with health, his skin browned from a summer under the Italian sun, contrasting with the silver strands in his closely cut beard.

We had had very little direct communication over the past three months. The thought of Louise Power opening my letters and reading them aloud in her mocking voice meant I'd restricted myself to the odd postcard, and he in turn had been equally unforthcoming. I'd relied on Alina for updates to his progress, but I knew the pregnancy was taking up all her reserves of energy, so I'd kept my letters to a minimum. The upshot was that while I'd known he was recovering well, it shocked me to see how changed he was.

Mrs Hancock could hardly hide her curiosity at our unexpected visitor and found excuses to remain in the front parlour, where we sat stiffly on the rarely used furniture while Nora told William all about Jemima and the spectacles and her new teachers. 'And where is Matilda?' asked William, casting around for the rancid old doll.

Nora fixed him with a very severe look.

'I'm *nine* now, Great-uncle Bill. Dolls are for little children.'

I happened to know that Matilda was packed away in a pocket in Nora's case, but I held my counsel.

We lapsed into a silence, broken only by the rhythmic swishing of Mrs Hancock's duster. The room still stank of furniture polish and the pungent smell, combined with the strangeness of the situation, caused a pressure to build up in my head until I felt as if I would explode if I had to stay there a moment longer.

'Shall we go into the garden? I expect Solomon needs to stretch his legs.'

William looked at me with gratitude.

'I'll come,' said Nora, jumping up.

To my surprise, Mrs Hancock got heavily to her feet and held out her hand to the child. 'Why don't you an' me go to the kitchen to make Mr North something tasty for his tea, since he's come all this way?'

Nora looked doubtful, but she was nothing if not obedient and she took the outstretched hand. I was flabbergasted. In the fifteen years Mrs Hancock had been coming to the house, she'd rarely evinced much interest in my life and had viewed my sojourn in Italy with the utmost suspicion. People were almost always more complex than one gave them credit for, I'd come to understand.

Stepping out through the French doors in the back room, the throbbing in my head instantly lifted. It was a typical early October day, overcast but relatively mild, and the leaves on the silver birch at the end of the garden were still thick on the branches in their newly adopted shades of yellow and orange. Frank Lawson next door was mowing his lawn with his new motorized mower, and I was glad of the background noise. The smell of petrol mixed with newly cut grass wafted over the hedge on the gentle breeze.

'How are you getting on with your plans for the William North Foundation?' I asked him as we strolled slowly around the perimeter of the garden.

'Very well. In fact, it has quite given me a new lease of life. And the castle too. It's a building that needs people and energy and ideas and creativity. Otherwise, it festers.'

'Alina and Massimo will be sorry to leave.'

He stopped in surprise.

'Didn't Alina tell you? I've asked them to move into Evelyn's old wing with their children. Massimo will be the on-site caretaker and Alina is going to oversee the archives. She always was wasted as a housekeeper.'

'Oh, that's wonderful.' My eyes were misted with pleasure. 'A place of their own. But who will look after the children? Please don't tell me Massimo's mother is also moving in.'

William laughed. 'No, one of Massimo's younger sisters is coming. She is delighted for the chance to get away from home, it seems.'

We resumed walking. Now that William wasn't needing to lean so heavily on his cane, he was at least three inches taller than me, making me feel, for once in my life, almost dainty by comparison.

'And you?' I asked, darting him a sideways look. 'Will you be staying in the castle too?'

He shook his head.

'There is too much history there for me. Rupert and Cecily. Evelyn and everything that happened.'

'Any news on that front?'

I hoped he couldn't hear the wobble in my voice that betrayed how heavily that scene on the castle roof still weighed on me, how at least once a week I still dreamed I was back there, being hoisted over the battlement, looking down on the gravel of the forecourt far below, and woke up with my breath ragged and my face wet with tears.

William shook his head again. He'd had his hair cut, I saw, and it made him appear more youthful-looking.

'They seem to have gone to ground. Roberto's mother blamed Evelyn for dragging her son into a scandal and threw the two of them out without a cent. I can't imagine he'll stay with her now there's no money coming his way, and Evelyn knows no one out there in the States.

'You know, at first I wanted them to be brought back to Italy and made to face justice. But I've come to believe they are already being punished. Exiled over there without money or social status and only each other for company.'

'And you, William? Where will you go?'

'I don't know. Perhaps my apartment in Paris. Isn't that where your son is now?'

'James?' I laughed. 'He'd love nothing more than to be in

Paris, but instead he has ended up at a school in Lyon. Still, he is enjoying himself. He loves the freedom of being somewhere new, I think. Would you consider returning to New York?'

'I don't think so. I wouldn't relish being on the same continent as Roberto and Evelyn.'

'Florence, then. You could get a place in town near your friends. Near Mrs Power, perhaps.'

I didn't dare look at him. The spectre of the woman Evelyn had dubbed the Black Widow had haunted my thoughts ever since I'd looked back through the castle window and caught sight of her leaning over the back of William's chair, her hair shielding his face from view.

'Oh, I don't think so. Louise Power is well on her way to snaring her fourth husband, by all accounts. She met him in Rome after I made it very clear I hadn't the slightest interest in being the next Mr Power. And anyway, I don't know if I want to be so far away from here.'

'Because of Nora?'

'Not only Nora.'

By now we had reached the end of the garden, where the branches of a weeping willow brushed the grass. William reached for my hand and gently led me around to the far side of the tree, shielded from the house. I felt light-headed and strange, as if the day had taken on the quality of a dream.

'I've missed you horribly, Constance.' Now he was standing in front of me, holding both my hands in his, and I hoped he couldn't tell how very much I was trembling. 'There hasn't been a day when I haven't thought about coming to find you, but I wanted to be whole again, not an invalid you felt sorry for. I'm still not quite there, but you know that patience is not my strongest point.'

I tried to turn away, overcome with feelings that seemed too hot and too raw to unpick, but William held my hands fast, forcing me to finally meet his eyes. I felt myself dissolving, the centre of me turning liquid and warm.

'This is who I am, William,' I burst out. 'This house in Pinner, this quiet life, this too-large body, these lines around my eyes, this grey in my hair. "Old and fat." You remember?'

'The man who said those words – that *idiot* – isn't who I am any more. I was eaten up with bitterness at the blows life had dealt me. The man I am now, this man right here, who can't tear his eyes from you, thinks you the loveliest woman in all the world.

'I would gladly give up Paris and Italy and New York and move to Pinner if it meant I could be with you.'

I made a face.

'Let's not be too hasty.'

'Thank god for that.'

We both laughed, and then stopped abruptly, gazing at each other in a moment that seemed to encompass the world – the sparrows twittering in the branches above us, the weak October sun pushing its way valiantly through the clouds, Frank Lawson clearing his throat in the garden next door. The blood was roaring in my ears, rushing around my body, filling me up until I felt I was drowning in it. Then William stepped forward and put his arms around me, and all the uncertainty fell away, leaving only a sense of things fitting together, of being exactly as they should be.

'Now I should very much like to kiss you,' he murmured into my ear. 'And after that I would very much like to marry you.'

His lips grazed my cheek before finding my mouth. I

breathed in the smell of him – leather and musk and a lingering scent of pine and olive-wood smoke that took me directly back to Italy. What began as a brush of warmth on my lips soon became something more urgent, and my body responded even before my mind caught up with what was happening as he held me crushed against him, our bodies one single pulsating mass of nerve-endings and skin and sinew and bone and desire. He broke off to gaze at me. 'I love you,' he said, his eyes scanning my face as if it were the most beautiful painting he'd ever seen. This time it was me who pulled him in for a kiss, my lips finding his hungrily, as if unable to bear one second more separation. Still I felt as if I were in a dream, and only Solomon's large, wet nose pushing in between the two of us to separate us finally convinced me it was real.

'Mrs Bowen! Great-uncle Bill! Where are you? Come quick. I've made delicious fish-paste sandwiches.'

William grimaced, and I jabbed him playfully in the ribs. He caught the ends of my fingers and drew them to his lips before taking my hand in his and squeezing it tight as if he'd never let it go.

'We're coming, Nora,' I called, as we smiled at each other, dazed, and my voice sounded like someone else's, clear and light, with laughter burbling under the surface of it.

'We're coming, dear.'

Epilogue

Florence, spring 1946

A s I STAND at the window of the *salone*, my back deliberately turned to the devastation the retreating soldiers
left in their wake, I feel warm breath on my neck and have the
sense of something solid and comforting behind me, and I
lean back so that William can wrap his arms around me.

'I'm so happy to see you,' he murmurs into my ear.
Although he has only been in Florence a week longer than
me, any absence feels like years at our age, where every extra
day together is a gift.

'But the castle, William . . .'

'It's not as bad as it looks, my dear. Superficial damage,
that's all. And all the artworks are safe.'

The William North Foundation, of which William is
still patron, took his advice and had all the paintings pack-
aged into crates and hidden in various cavities in the castle's
stone walls. Perhaps the little violin-playing girl of the
legend was looking out for them, because none was ever
discovered.

That evening we have dinner with Alina and her middle

son, Lorenzo, who spent much of the war stationed on a remote Greek island. We are waited on by her beautiful daughter Pia, who besieges us with questions about how she can get to Hollywood to become a film star until Alina says, 'One thing at a time, Pia. Let's first reclaim our home, and then perhaps we can capture America.'

We are sitting at the dining-room table, which has been carved with names and little messages in German and Italian and initials inside crudely drawn hearts. Alina says she will have it sanded down, but William tells her to leave it. 'It's an artwork in its own right,' he says. 'One day it'll be worth a fortune.' He still insists he's retired from that side of things – the galleries, the paintings, the thrill of a find or a negotiation – but I know better. He is relishing the prospect of helping restore the castle to its former glory.

Alina looks older. The war was not easy for her, or for anyone with strong ties to the British or Americans. But we don't talk about the past or about the losses – Massimo to a heart attack in 1938, her older son Bruno to an Allied bomb in northern France.

Instead, we look to the future. I talk about little Gracie, Nora's surprise war baby, courtesy of an American GI who died when his ship home was torpedoed, without ever knowing he was to be a father. Nora has already resumed her law degree, determined to specialize in this new field of human rights. There is no changing her mind once she decides on a thing, and Lord knows we will need people like her in this changed post-war world.

'How is James? And his friend Pierre?' Alina glances at Lorenzo as she speaks. He has inherited his grandparents' conservative views.

'James will be joining Pierre back in Paris soon,' I tell her. 'I've so enjoyed having him around.'

Sometimes I feel guilty to have found so much pleasure in the midst of this terrible war. We holed up with Nora at William's lovely country cottage in Wiltshire, the same one he originally intended leaving to Evelyn. James arrived at the eleventh hour, before Paris fell, and took a post teaching French in a local school, exempt from conscription by virtue of his age and the fact that schoolteachers were on the reserve occupations list. Disappointed at once again 'missing out' on service, he nevertheless found huge rewards in being in front of a class, and in the letters that arrived from Pierre nearly every day. Seeing him finally happy lifted a boulder I hadn't even realized I was carrying until it was gone.

Then there was Gracie. The indescribable joy of a new baby in the house. And of sharing that joy with William. 'Don't misunderstand, I loved every minute of our lives before,' I say to Alina, wanting her to know just how little I take for granted – the travelling, seeing New York and Paris and Rome, all the fascinating people. 'But there's something special about being home.'

Only once do we mention the Manettis. Evelyn has been dead many years now, of course, taking her own life in a motel in a not very nice part of Miami after being dumped by the latest in a long line of unsuitable young boyfriends, but Alina tells me Roberto is finally home after three arduous years spent as a POW in the Soviet Union. 'You would not know him,' she says. 'The war has broken him. His hair is completely white.'

We go to bed early. I'm tired after the long journey, even though William arranged for me to have a lift the whole way with Jerome Fielding, who is helping with the restitution of the collection. And though William would never admit it, I can see how much this trip has already cost him physically. When he's overdone things, his weakened left leg slows him down.

We sleep in Evelyn and Roberto's old room, which is the only one where the bed hasn't been either looted or burned for firewood.

We fit around each other in the old familiar way, my head in the crook of his arm, my arm across his chest.

'I had a strange moment earlier,' I say into the skin of his shoulder. 'I started thinking about everything that happened to me here in this place, and I found myself asking myself what I did, how much of what happened was because of me. But then, talking to Alina earlier, I wondered if I should be asking the opposite – why didn't I do more? Not just back then in 1927, but ever since. Look at how much Alina lost in the war, while I sailed through it with my family all around me. What have I actually *done*?'

William shifts position so that he is raised on his elbow, looking at me.

'What have you done? You've given me the happiest years of my life. You've been a mother to an unloved little girl who grew up strong and ambitious because of you. You've supported your son and never once asked him to be anything other than what he is, no matter how troubled his life has been.

'You're brave and you're extraordinary and I love you more with each day.'

Later, when William is asleep and my cheek rises and falls with the steady movement of his chest, I lie awake and think about what he said. He is right, I think, that there are ways of being human that have nothing to do with our place or standing in the world, about the things we do or don't do, but are about our relationships with the people around us and the things we give them by being ourselves and allowing them to be the same.

But we don't only exist in relation to others. I think of Millie speeding down a hill on her bicycle with her legs straight out and her hair flying behind her, and of William lost in a painting. I think of Charles Lindbergh's solo flight. So many hours, just him and the endless sky.

And yes, I think of myself, on a train heading into the unknown, watching the unfamiliar scenery of France and Italy unfurl itself through the window like the reel of a movie where I don't know the end or the characters or even the story. It is enough merely to be in it at that precise moment.

The moment is enough.

Author's Note

Florence – described by Mark Twain as the City of Dreams – is generally agreed to be a place of such perfection that taking liberties with it feels like an act of wanton desecration. So please forgive the following instances of artistic licence:

While Settignano and Fiesole are both real places, situated on neighbouring hillsides to the north-east of the city, Black Rock Hill, which I conveniently placed between the two of them, doesn't actually exist – neither the castle, nor the rock itself, with its dark legend.

Similarly, while Florence has indeed been at the epicentre of earthquakes in the past – most notably in May 1895 – my book is set in 1927, which was mercifully earthquake-free.

Conjuring up the sights and smells and atmosphere of 1920s Tuscany while locked down in 2020 London was made infinitely easier by immersing myself in other people's books. If you're interested in reading more about Italy during this era, I recommend *A Castle in Tuscany* by Sarah Benjamin, *A Tuscan Childhood* by Kinta Beevor, *Fenny* by Lettice Cooper and *Enchanted April* by Elizabeth Von

Arnim. *Lady Chatterley's Villa* by Richard Owen was also very useful in providing insight into a well-known English writer who may or may not have inspired one of the characters in this book.

Acknowledgements

It's a very strange experience to write a novel set in a beautiful foreign city while in the depths of lockdown, confined to home, not able to travel on a local bus, much less a plane. What a time we all had. I'd like to extend belated thanks to all those who got us through, particularly the health workers and the teachers and the supermarket staff and the scientists. You are absolute stars.

Another star is Louise Power, who lent her name to a character in this book, courtesy of her sister Barbara Enticknap, all in aid of raising money for CLIC Sargent, the charity that supports young people with cancer. Louise, your surname was a gift for a writer, and I want to wish you a very special and happy Big Birthday!

On a more personal note, I want to thank Felicity Blunt, to whom this book is dedicated, who absolutely changed my life back in 2010 when she agreed to be my agent. And her ace assistant Rosie Pierce, and Sarah Harvey and all the other folk at Curtis Brown. Also Deborah Schneider, who never gives up on bringing my books to a US readership.

At Transworld, thanks, as always, to Jane Lawson, the most supportive editor a writer could wish for. And to

Alison Barrow – publicist, philosopher and pal. Also to Hayley Barnes, Kate Samano, Sarah Day, Louis Patel and Richard Ogle and everyone else who works so hard on getting my books in the best possible shape and then bringing them to the attention of as many people as possible.

I was frankly terrified when I first joined the North London Writers, because they're all insanely clever and I thought I was bound to be unmasked as not a *real* writer at all, but their feedback has been immeasurably helpful in stopping me heading down blind alleys and taking the plot in directions it really ought not to go, as well as invaluable suggestions such as 'If you give him a boner, it'll show his human side,' so a heartfelt grateful shout-out goes to Anna Mazzola, Marianne Levy, Neil Blackmore, Emma Flint, Adi Bloom and Karol Griffiths.

All my writer friends deserve a mention here, for getting me through this last bizarre year, but I'll single out Amanda Jennings and Lisa Jewell – that gorgeous lunch by the canal was the first time I dared believe we might be getting back to some semblance of normal life. Props also to Marnie Riches, Colin Scott, the Prime Writers and the Killer Women. Can't wait to see all of you in real life in the very near future. We have an awful lot of catching up to do.

Thanks also to my non-writer friends. Like so many people, my friendship group suffered some shattering losses during the pandemic. Special thanks to the Aunties, without whom this last year would have been so much harder to navigate.

Thanks to my sister, Sara, who has had to shoulder so much more than her fair share of family responsibilities. And to Michael, Otis, Jake, Billie – and Phoebe – if I had to spend the best part of a year locked down with one group of people, I'm very glad it was you.

Finally, to everyone who has bought one of my books over the past few years, or borrowed one from the library, as ever, I'm more grateful than I can say.

A DANGEROUS CROSSING
Rachel Rhys

England, September 1939
Lily Shepherd boards a cruise liner for a new life in Australia and is immediately plunged into a world of cocktails, jazz and glamorous friends. But as the sun beats down, poisonous secrets begin to surface. Suddenly Lily finds herself trapped in a ship with nowhere to go . . .

Australia, six weeks later
As the cruise liner docks, a beautiful young woman is escorted on to dry land in handcuffs. Two passengers are dead, war is declared, and Lily Shepherd's life is changed forever.

What has she done?

'An exquisite story of love, murder, adventure and dark secrets' LISA JEWELL

'Gripping and ripe with danger' *Sunday Express*

'An utter treat . . . a glorious mix of proper old-school glamour and a plot full of class war, politics and sexual tension . . . A masterful storyteller' VERONICA HENRY